The
People
We Keep

Center Point
Large Print

**This Large Print Book carries the
Seal of Approval of N.A.V.H.**

The People We Keep

Allison Larkin

CENTER POINT LARGE PRINT
THORNDIKE, MAINE

This Center Point Large Print edition
is published in the year 2021 by arrangement with
Gallery Books, a division of Simon & Schuster, Inc.

The text of this Large Print edition is unabridged.
In other aspects, this book may vary
from the original edition.
Printed in the United States of America
on permanent paper.
Set in 16-point Times New Roman type.

ISBN: 978-1-63808-113-5

The Library of Congress has cataloged this record under
Library of Congress Control Number: 2021942939

For me, because I needed to write this.

For you, if any part of this book helps
you feel a little more understood.

For my family of friends,
who have jump-started my heart
and kept it running.

I love you.

But I know that someday,
someday, I'll offer up
a song I was made to play . . .

—Chris Pureka, *Compass Rose*

The
People
We Keep

— Part One —

— Chapter 1 —

November 1994
Little River, NY

I'm standing at the end of my driveway in the dark, watching Mrs. Varnick's trailer, waiting for her lights to go out, getting really pissed off. I've been watching for at least a week and her lights went out at eight thirty every other night. She must have picked up a clear signal on reruns of *Lawrence Welk* or *Hee Haw* with her rabbit ears, because it's a quarter to nine and she's still plopped in her BarcaLounger in the living room with the TV flickering and every light in the house blazing like she owns the damn electric company.

I decide I'll wait until nine and then go for it, because she's deafer than Mozart or Beethoven or whoever the deaf one is, and she probably has the TV cranked up anyway. But it's freezing, my legs are bare under my skirt, and doing my little *so fucking cold* jig isn't getting my blood pumping anymore. So I tell myself Mrs. Varnick must have fallen asleep in her chair. The woman eats dinner at four in the afternoon. She's got to be snoring away, dreaming about Lawrence and his powder blue tuxedo shirts by now.

Grabbing my guitar, I move in, walking soft, keeping low. The car isn't locked, but she wasn't kind enough to leave the keys.

I squeeze my *Ren & Stimpy* keychain flashlight between my teeth to keep it lit and aimed at the spot my instructions refer to as the "ignition tumbler." I don't know why they couldn't just say "place where the key goes." Thank goodness I read through the instructions in the library when I copied them. I had to look up most of the terms. So I take my dad's screwdriver and shove it between the metal *ignition tumbler* and the plastic of whatever the place underneath it is called. I can't get the tumbler part to come out and I have to keep prying at it around the edges the way you open up a paint can, all the while looking up to check on Mrs. Varnick every few seconds.

Finally, it pops. I shove the screwdriver into what I assume is the ignition switch, hold my breath, and turn. The car hiccups. I let it go. If I can't make this work, I'm screwed. I promised myself I wouldn't get into wire stripping and removing dashboard panels. It's all too complicated and I have to be able to put the car back like nothing happened. I wiggle the screwdriver. Try again. This time the engine turns and the car starts. Headlights off, I back out of Mrs. Varnick's driveway, watching her living room window carefully. She doesn't move.

• • •

By the time I pull into the parking lot of the Blue Moon Cafe, it's a quarter to ten, and everything started at nine. I run in, guitar case banging against my leg. The tarnished brass clips and peeling bumper stickers snag the top layer of my skirt. Some guy in a leather vest is on stage singing that song about cats in cradles. His voice is nasal. When he breathes, you can hear his saliva.

The place is packed. I stand in the back and look around, trying to figure out what I'm supposed to do—do I get up on stage after that guy is done?—when this girl wearing a knit cap and fingerless gloves hands me a clipboard.

"Sign up here." She gives me a pen. Her eyelashes are so pale they're almost white. "We're supposed to cut the list off at nine thirty, but you're close enough," she says, sighing like she's bored with absolutely everything. "Bring it to me when you're done." She points to where she'll be in the corner of the room.

There are twelve names on the list already, first five crossed out. I lean against the wall so I can balance the board on my knee. The pen barely writes, and it takes forever to fill out *April, Little River* in the name and hometown boxes, scribbling over each letter to carve an indent into the paper. I don't put my last name, even though everyone before me has. *Sawicki* doesn't

15

have that show biz ring. All the other performers are from Buffalo or Hamburg or East Aurora. I should've at least said I was from Cattaraugus, someplace big enough to have its own post office. If the pen worked, I'd scribble over my line and start again.

I don't have titles for my songs. I try to think of something to call them, but as I'm staring out at the room, running through the lyrics to the first one in my head, I notice that there are a lot of people. Maybe fifty. My legs are wobbly. I want to sit down. I write *untitled* in both of the song spaces and check a box that says *original,* leaving the box for *cover* empty.

When I walk over to give the board back, my stomach flops like a tadpole drowning in air, making me wish I hadn't eaten so many Pop-Tarts for dinner. The eyelash girl is perched on a stool, hunched over a paperback she's holding very close to her face. It's so dark I don't know how she can even see the words. She must be one of those people who can read no matter what's going on, because I stand next to her and hold the sign-up sheet out for a whole minute before she realizes I'm there.

"Thanks," she says, dropping the book in her lap without marking her place. She takes the clipboard back. I hope she doesn't notice the way my hands shake. "Have a seat. It'll be a while." She looks out at the audience—little cafe tables, four chairs around each one. There's like eight tables out there and every chair is filled. I figure I'll just sit on the floor against the wall, but Eyelash Girl stands up on the middle rung of her stool. "There," she points to a table up front, "there's a seat right there." She nods at me, waving her finger toward the chair. She expects me to take that seat and I can't think of an excuse.

I weave my way around the tables, knocking my guitar case against knees and chair backs, whispering *sorrys* as I go. Cat's Cradle guy finishes. Everyone applauds politely. He takes a breath we all can hear and says, "Here's a little ditty I think you guys know." His first few strums are sour but familiar.

I try to make eye contact with the guy sitting next to the empty chair. He's too busy talking to the other people at the table to notice me, so I tap the chair leg with my boot. Nothing. I put my guitar case down and fumble with one of the clips, catching his glance in the corner of my eye. But when I look up, he's back to talking, so I have to sit down and lean over to tap him on the shoulder to ask if it's okay if I sit. I feel like an ass, since I'm already sitting, but he says, "No problem," and offers his hand. "Jim."

"April," I say, meeting his grip firmly, the way my father taught me—a good "seal the deal" shake. I pull away to position the guitar between my legs so no one can take it. Right before the

17

chorus I realize the guy on stage is trying to play *Free Bird*. When I look up to check Jim's reaction to the acoustic crucifixion of Lynyrd Skynyrd, he's already turned around, busy talking to the woman sitting next to him. His hair is a brown horseshoe with wiry strands spread across the shiny skin in the middle of his head. The remaining total comes together in a long skinny ponytail wrapped in a plain rubber band at the base of his neck. The woman he's talking to has grey hair like steel wool, braided and not even fastened at the ends, left to unravel over time. She looks like Mother Nature, and the man on the other side of her could be King Neptune with his long white beard and tattered navy cap. They must have come here together and I'm cutting in on their party of three.

I wish, just a little bit, I'd come with someone. I told Matty I had to study for math. I don't want him to see me play until I'm sure I'm not going to get up there and choke.

"I'll help you study," he said, giving me the toothy grin that usually gets him everything he wants.

"We never study when we study," I told him. "I'm totally failing."

His eyes flashed with hurt when I sent him away, but I couldn't stop thinking about what his face would look like if I got on stage and my voice croaked and my fingers wouldn't move.

18

I wish I'd brought my dad, but he's always with Irene and the boy now. It's his guitar anyway. "Your inheritance," he said when he handed it to me on my sixteenth birthday. "Music is in your blood, Ape." I know really he forgot it was my birthday, but I took it just the same. I should have told him about this. Made him drive me. When it's my turn to go on stage he could whistle with his fingers in his mouth like he used to at my elementary school plays. But I'm sure the boy is busy wetting the bed or picking his nose and Dad and Irene have to be there to watch.

People applaud again. That guy walks off stage. I clap because he's leaving, and I wonder if that's why everyone else is clapping too.

Jim turns to me and says, "This is Wisteria and her life partner Efrem." He leans toward Mother Nature and King Neptune and says, "April," pointing at me. They wave and I wave back. Wisteria's cheeks dimple like crab apples when she smiles, and Efrem's eyes are crinkly and kind.

Before anyone can say anything else, this skinny scarecrow man in a worn out brown fedora gets on stage and reads off the clipboard. His voice is low and whispery. "Next up, Luke Barstoldt from Cheektowaga is here to sing *Sweet Baby James*, by James Taylor, and *Teach Your Children*, by Crosby, Stills and Nash, or was that when they were Crosby, Stills, Nash, and

Young, I can never remember." He shifts around awkwardly, holding his hands out at his sides like a bad stand-up comedian. "Geez, isn't anyone playing originals?" He looks at the audience like he's waiting for a response, but everyone is dead silent. "Well, in any case, let's give it up for Luke."

I am proud while we all applaud, because I wrote both the songs I'm going to play—one about losing my virginity to Matty, and the other about my father and Irene and the boy— but Luke Barstoldt quickly snuffs out my smug when he starts playing and it sounds like James Taylor himself has blessed the audience with his presence. He has long skeleton hands and his fingers move fast even though everything else about him is slow and soulful.

Wisteria and Efrem are next. They argue with the scarecrow man about their song choice. Scarecrow says because of its length, *Canadian Railroad Trilogy* should count as both their songs, but they say they should get to play two separate songs. I think they're all joking, but Efrem gets red-faced. He covers the microphone with his hand and mutters something to Scarecrow. Scarecrow concedes, throwing his arms in the air and walking off stage without introducing them.

Efrem plays ukulele and Wisteria bangs a tambourine against her round butt. She's a shrill soprano, but his voice is gravel. They sing into the same mic even though there are two on stage. He's a half beat behind her on the lyrics.

"These guys are here every week," Jim says, resting his arm on the back of my chair, "and they never get any better."

I smile and hunch forward, so my back doesn't touch his arm. "When are you up?" I ask.

"Oh, I'm not playing. I mean, I do play, but not here."

I don't know if I'm supposed to ask more or let it go. I let it go. It's freezing. I pump my hands, trying to trick feeling back into my fingers. "Cold in here."

"Yeah," Jim says. "Here's the trick." He raises his hand. Eyelash Girl must have looked up from her book at just the right time. She comes over with a small pad of paper and a pen, ready to take an order.

"I'm fine," I say, because I only have a handful of coins I swiped from the ashtray in Mrs. Varnick's car.

Jim doesn't hear me. "Could we have a hot water for her, and a refresh on mine," he asks.

Eyelash Girl gives him a dirty look and clears his mug.

"This will help," he says. "Hold it or drink it. Either way. And they can't charge you for hot water."

When Eyelash Girl comes back with our mugs, I make a point of saying thank you as sweetly as

I can. She gives me a dirty look too, and I decide I will leave her all of Mrs. Varnick's change as an apology.

I cup my hands around the mug and hold it up to my face, breathing the steam into my lungs, like cigarette smoke, only clean.

"Better?" Jim raises his mug in my direction.

"Much. Thanks."

"No prob. You gotta learn the ropes. And if you know the ropes, it's your job to teach them."

Wisteria and Efrem finish their songs and come back to the table, flustered and blushing. Jim stands when they sit, applauding loudly. "That's the stuff, man," he says, and mimes tipping a hat in their direction. When he sits, he crosses his leg over his knee and rests his arm on the back of my chair again. I don't think he's hitting on me. I think he's just less into personal space than I am.

A girl about my age climbs on stage. To get away from Jim's arm, I rest my elbows on my knees like I'm going to pay super close attention. Scarecrow says, "Next up, Marion Strong singing two of her own songs. Her first is *South* . . . followed by *North*." He laughs one big open-mouthed haw. "No, seriously, folks, her second song is *Awakening*. Ladies and germs, the lovely Marion."

Lovely is a stretch. She looks like she didn't even try. Stretched out sweater, baggy jeans, dirty work boots. It's one thing to go for that whole *don't give a shit* appearance when you do, but she looks like she really doesn't give a shit.

Marion strums once and twists the knobs on her guitar. "Alright," she says into the mic in a soft voice. She strums again. "Alright. That sounds good." Her face cares. Her face looks like she gives a shit now. She takes a deep breath, closes her eyes halfway. "Alright, here we go."

She doesn't just strum out some opening chords. Her song has an intro. It's complex fingerpicking, not just a running head start on the lyrics. Her hands move furiously up and down the neck of the guitar, and I feel like I'm watching something that's a little too private. Then she closes her eyes and opens her mouth and her voice is bigger than the rest of her. It's clear and arched and she's telling this story about a lover who won't steer his ship south for the winter. She says she's done. She's going to go where it's warm, but where's he gonna dock his boat when his sail gets caked with ice and the sea is frigid and choppy? "How will you feel when you're cold and alone up north when everyone's south?" she asks, and I want to answer, because I can picture him huddled by an oil lamp in the cabin of an old damp ship, a single tear running down his face. I can see he's miserable without her and I want to tell her that. There's metaphor or simile or some term I would know if I paid attention in English. It's full and beautiful and her guitar sounds like rough and rolling waves. I can't stop watching her. She ends the song with hard, rhythmic strums, holding the guitar out in front of her like she's presenting the final reverberations to us as a gift. I strain to keep them in my ears until there's nothing left to hear.

Her next song is even better. Loud and angry. She pulls sounds from those strings that I didn't think were possible, like she's playing two guitars or three. I can't keep track of her fingers to figure out how she does it. But even if I could—I mean, it's not like I know enough about playing to pick it up from watching someone else.

I want to hear it all, every word, every note, but I get stuck in my head. I can't stop thinking about how I have to get on that stage and my songs don't have similes or metaphors or fancy finger-picking. I can't stop picturing myself forgetting how to hold my guitar, opening my mouth to squawk like a ragged old crow.

All of a sudden, everyone's clapping. Some people are even standing to applaud for Marion Strong. I clap hard and my palms sting. Marion bows her head slightly and smiles, her moon face ruddy and shining and gorgeous.

The scarecrow guy gets up on stage. I tap Jim's shoulder. "Watch my guitar?"

He nods.

I weave through the seats and tables, trying not to look at the people. I don't want to think about all those eyes watching me, or worse, not watching me. All those eyes looking at their neighbor, widening to say, *Who does this chick think she is?*

In the bathroom mirror, I stare at my own eyes. I look at them until they sting because I don't let myself blink and it smells like someone smoked a clove in here not too long ago. When I finally do blink, my eyelashes get wet. I rip a piece of paper towel from the roll on the sink, fold the corner and brush it under my lower lashes to dry them before my mascara runs. I sort through my bag, find my eyeliner and focus everything on lining my eyes with a thin black line. I pretend I'm an ant, following the curve of my lashes, the way we learned to do line drawings in art class. Slow. Millimeters at a time, until I don't hear the crowd and I don't hear the music. I just hear my breath. In and out. So warm it fogs the mirror. I smudge the lines with a twisted piece of paper towel. By the time I'm done my body is loose and warm, my head floating on my neck.

I go out and take my seat, trying hard to cling to the calm. My index finger has a smudge of eyeliner on the nail. I fixate on the smudge until the next singer is done, and the next one too, and Scarecrow Man is on stage again.

"Now we have two untitled originals from April."

My heart squeezes tight like a fist. I flip

my guitar case on its back and undo the latches.

The scarecrow shuffles papers on the clipboard. "Just April? Looks like we have a Madonna on our hands."

Everyone laughs, but I pretend they aren't real. They are eyeless. They are bowling pins. Giant black bowling pins in chairs, wearing hats and beaded necklaces, hand-woven shawls. They can't see me, and I can't hear them.

I climb on stage and sit on the stool. I don't know what to do with the microphone. Scarecrow must sense that, because he's almost back to his seat, but he returns to pull the mic closer and angle it at my mouth. "Thanks," I say, and it echoes through the room, bouncing off the bowling pins.

My first strum sounds wrong and I realize my fingers are not where they should be. I strum again, pretend to fiddle with the tuning. "Okay," I say into the mic once my fingers are firmly in their starting position.

I strum three times, close my eyes and start to sing:

Your eyes tell me what we're gonna do,
And it's not like I haven't thought it too,
And it's not like it's wrong.
No, it's not like that.
So I close my eyes, and you take my hand.
We're both in the right place,

And it seems like the right time . . .
The right time.

I keep my eyelids shut tight and hear my voice coming back to me from the corners of the room. Bowling pins wearing wire-rimmed glasses, the black lines around my eyes, the change from Mrs. Varnick's car, hot water in a cup. I think of all these things and I see myself on stage, like I'm up in the rafters watching.

When I'm done, there's applause and it's loud, and the audience is full of people again. People who like me. It's not polite. It's real and it just keeps going. I wait and wait. I adjust my guitar on my lap and the applause dies to a few random claps.

For the next song, I am brave. I sing about my father. I sing, "Don't forget you made me. Don't forget you made me the way I am." And I look right at people in the audience. Right in their eyes, like I wrote the song about them. A guy with dreadlocks, King Neptune, the scarecrow. I sing to Marion Strong and the girl with the white eyelashes. I finish the song looking right into Jim's eyes. When it's over, he stands to clap. A few other people stand too, and the applause is the loudest sound I've ever heard.

They're still clapping when I get back to my seat. Someone in the far corner whistles. I sit, but I'm also hovering above myself, and smiling so

27

big that my whole body is a grin and my head is warm and fuzzy like the first time Matty kissed me.

Scarecrow gets up on stage and says "Th-th-that's all folks," like he's Porky Pig.

I rest my guitar in its case, latch each of the clips slowly. I don't want to leave. I don't want it to be over. I want to climb on stage again to play more songs and keep them clapping. I don't want to go back to an empty motorhome and my stupid math book.

Everyone collects themselves, pulling on hats and scarves, big sweaters and secondhand coats. People walk past me on their way to the door. A few smile or say, "Good job." A guy in a tunic gives me a thumbs up.

I dig my mittens and scarf from my bag.

"I'll walk you out," Jim says, like that's what I was waiting for.

"Thanks."

"Pretty girl. Dark parking lot. You got to." He shakes his head. It's fatherly. But that's how everyone else is too. Fatherly. Brotherly. I can't picture King Neptune jumping from behind a truck to rape and pillage.

Jim pulls my chair out of the way as I stand. I walk in front of him until we get outside. The James Taylor guy shouts, "Night, Jimmy!"

"Night!" Jim shouts back, then, "Hack," under his breath like a cough.

"I thought he was good," I say, letting my feet drag on the parking lot gravel.

"They're all hacks. You and that Marion girl. You're the only ones who have any chance of making it. And maybe not even Marion." He says it like it's fact, not opinion.

"She's better than me," I say, and I know it's true, but I'm high. My head is spinning. Making it. I have a chance of making it. I have more of a chance than Marion. I don't even know what *it* is, and I don't think Jim is the one who gets to hand it down, but I want it. The air is crisp. My breath makes clouds.

"She's—don't get me wrong, she's good. But you're the real deal. You're the whole package. That's what it's about. Everyone buys into the package."

He takes a pack of Marlboros from his pocket and smacks them against his palm until one sticks out. He holds the pack to his lips and pulls the cigarette with his teeth. "Want one?" he says from the side of his mouth.

I shake my head.

"Good girl." He cups his hand to his face. Lights up. Puffs. "Save those pipes," he says into the smoke.

"Will do," I say. "Thanks."

"Where's your car?"

"Over there." I gesture vaguely. "I'll be fine now. Nice to meet you, Jim." I shake his hand,

and sprint to Mrs. Varnick's car so he won't follow. The risk of attack is low. The risk of Jim noticing the loose ignition switch is high.

I get the car going again and drive home singing my songs to myself over and over, hearing the applause like it's filling the car. The drive home isn't long enough. The exact sound of that clapping starts to slip from my head when I turn down our street.

I park the car in the tire ruts in Mrs. Varnick's driveway, push the ignition tumbler back in until it pops, and toss the screwdriver in my bag. I walk slowly to the motorhome, memorizing the way it feels to tread the path: the give of the pine needles, the dense winding roots. I am hardwiring my memory, because for the first time it doesn't feel like this will be the rest of my life.

The motorhome shifts under my weight when I climb inside. I turn on the TV, curl up in the driver's seat, and fall asleep to black and white static.

The next day, I fail my math test. I can't even answer most of the questions.

— Chapter 2 —

This test was your chance to prove yourself," Mrs. Hunter says, shaking her head at me with fake concern. Her weather-girl hair barely moves. She hands over my paper, marked with red like it has the chicken pox.

I should have held on to my test until the end of class so I could escape before she started grading. But I turned it in early with the smart kids, because there were song lyrics flashing in my head and I had to scribble them in my notebook before I forgot.

"I did prove myself," I say.

"Ape-rul!" She crosses her arms over her chest, pursing her perfectly lined lips. She was a beauty queen before she was a teacher. I wonder what her talent was.

"I proved I can't do math," I say, dropping the test in the trash can by her desk. I stop in the doorway to wave goodbye. Elbow, elbow, wrist, wrist, and a big smile like I have Vaseline smeared across my teeth.

"April Sawicki!" she yells after me as I walk away.

I don't see any point in going to the rest of my classes. I've failed so many math tests already this semester that unless I get perfect scores for the rest of the year, I'll be stuck in summer school not understanding algebra all over again. And it's not like I'm doing much better in English or science.

I grab my black and whites from my locker, change in the bathroom, and head to Margo's. When I get there, the diner's empty, except for Margo, who's perched at the counter, her pink high heels kicked off, bare feet twisted around the bottom rung of the stool. Her toenail polish matches her shoes exactly.

She's filling saltshakers and watching The Weather Channel on the little TV over the counter. "Florida's getting a lot of rain," she says, shaking her head when she sees me. "Bad for the oranges. They get watery."

"What's the forecast here?"

"I missed that part." She pinches spilled salt from the counter, tosses it over her shoulder for luck. "It'll roll around again in a minute."

"Sure," I say, grinning. Margo can tell you what the weather is anywhere else, but she never catches the local report.

"Aren't you supposed to be at school, young lady?" She screws the top on a shaker and slides the ones she's finished down the counter to me.

"Failed math. No point." I grab four shakers in each hand and walk around, placing them on tables.

"I'm harboring a fugitive," she says, waving her hands in mock horror. "The truant officer is going to have a field day."

"They don't have those anymore, I don't think." I finish placing the shakers and sit on the stool next to hers.

"Did you at least give it your best shot?"

"Not really." I twist my promise ring around my finger and avoid making eye contact.

"Well, not everyone's cut out for school, you know? I didn't graduate and look at me. I did just fine for myself." Margo finishes salt and moves on to pepper. "This isn't because of that Matty Spencer, is it?"

"Naw."

She raises her eyebrow, scrunches up the corner of her mouth. She's being polite calling Matty by name. Usually, she calls him Golden Boy, and she doesn't mean it in a nice way. "That kid could charm the pants off a snake," she told me once, and I wondered what it made me. But that's the thing about Matty. No one else knows him like I do.

I tell her the truth to change the subject. "You know that guitar I got for my birthday?"

"Yeah." She turns her head away from the shakers as she pours, so the pepper dust won't make her sneeze.

"I played at the Blue Moon last night."

"Oh, girlie!"

"Just open mic."

"How'd you do?" she says, holding her fist to her mouth, then, "You did great," before I even answer. "I know you did."

"I did okay."

"Well, where was my engraved invitation? Your dad go?"

"No." I balance shaker lids in a pile while I'm waiting for her to finish the next pepper. She's pouting like a little kid. "You're busy," I say, "I didn't want to bother you." Partly I feel bad I didn't invite her and partly I'm just embarrassed for her. The pouting isn't as cute as she thinks it is. She would have stuck out like a sore thumb in that crowd. They were all odd ducks, but Margo, she's a different kind.

"Well, that's not a bother; that's exciting." Pepper spills. She uses her hand to corral it to the end of the counter and sweeps it into the shaker. Only a little ends up on the floor. "Hey, wait. How'd you get all the way out to the Blue Moon?"

I smile. "You don't want to know."

"What are you doing to me?" She swats my shoulder with the towel she keeps tucked in her apron and gets up to go behind the counter. "You know I don't have money for bail just lying around."

"I'll save for my own bail. I have to go to summer school anyway, may as well be for good reason. Can I pull extra shifts? Keep me out of trouble," I say, batting my eyelashes at her. I don't tell her Matty and I talked about saving for a wedding. She'll get too excited about dresses and flowers or launch into another lecture about Matty and how sixteen isn't old enough to be making the kinds of decisions that aren't easily undone, and either way, she'll forget I ever asked about the extra shifts.

"Hon, things are tight." She looks me over and sighs. "Let me see what I can do. I'll crunch numbers and check the schedule."

"You don't have to pay me overtime or even full on the extra shifts. It'll be like undertime. Or I'll just go for tips like I used to."

She shakes her head. "I double you up on Lorraine, she'll get pissy with me. There's not enough tables to have two girls on at the same time." She looks me right in the eyes. Margo can read my face better than anyone. "Let me think on it," she says.

Margo dated my dad in high school and then they tried to date again after my mom left us. That was back when we lived over the Wash 'n Fold on Ames Street, before we got the motorhome. The whole apartment smelled like soapsuds.

When they went on dates, Margo would pick up my dad so she could see me too. She'd braid my hair or help me dress my dolls while he rounded up his wallet, shoes, and keys and checked the score on his radio one last time.

Margo always wore bright pink lipstick. Her red hair was all sprayed up like a helmet of big round bubbles, even though the other women in town were wearing their hair down and getting it feathered. She was thick around the middle, but she always wore miniskirts. When I asked my fourth grade teacher how long a paper had to be, she said, "Like a skirt. Long enough to cover the subject, but short enough to keep it interesting." Margo's skirts were always interesting. They covered everything, but just barely. And when she moved, you couldn't help but watch, just in case they didn't. She knew it too.

"You gotta maximize your potential," she told me once, flexing her foot before slipping it back into her impossibly high pink pump. "I don't got a bitty waist, but I've got killer gams. Play up what you got, toots. That's the secret."

I don't know how long she and my dad tried to date. All I remember is that one day she took me to the lunch counter out at the Wal-Mart in Harristown instead of just eating at her place or making fluffernutters at our apartment. She wore shiny blue cream eye shadow. In the car on the way over, she even let me dig the little plastic tub out of her purse and smear some across my eyelids so we'd match. We had soft pretzels with big white flakes of salt; hot dogs with mustard, ketchup, and relish; and cherry slushies.

"What I want you to remember, girl, is that I'm not breaking up with you," she said, looking me straight in the eyes. "You and me, we're still good. Okay? You remember that."

I tore pieces off my pretzel and shoved them in my mouth, washing them down with slushie without hardly chewing, until I got brain freeze and my eyes teared.

"It's nothing to cry over, honey." She spit on her napkin and wiped my cheeks hard. "Your father's a good man, April. He always means to be a good man. He just . . . he gets in the way of himself, you know?"

I didn't know, but I nodded.

"None of this is about you. No one in their right mind would leave you." Her eyes got wide after she said it, and she put her hand over her mouth. "I mean . . . I mean . . . Now, sweetie, you haven't even touched that hot dog yet."

I ate it all. Every last bit, like it was my job, to show Margo how perfect I could be when I tried. I didn't want to give her any reason to break up with me too.

I threw up in her car on the way home. Right on my white tennis sneakers, and she wasn't even mad. Chunks of pretzel and hot dog, all bright cherry red.

"I can get a new floor mat," she said, patting

my leg. "You aimed good. Except for your shoes."

Later, my father put my sneaks in the bathtub and hosed them down with the showerhead. Even after he washed them, they had pink splatter stains and smelled like sour milk. "We'll leave them on the fire escape when you aren't wearing them," he said. He never said anything about Margo or the breakup.

After that, on Sundays, when my dad went to his card game, Margo would give her secret knock on the door and we'd go downstairs to do her laundry together. I loved folding her clothes: polyester leopard-print leggings and zebra-striped tunics, dresses with big Hawaiian flowers and shoulder pads. Lace slips and nightgowns. And some of the underpants didn't have a back, just a string. I couldn't quite figure out what was supposed to go where, but they were all silky and bright. One pair had a tiny rhinestone heart.

I wipe down menus and ketchup bottles until eleven thirty, when Ida Winton lumbers in and takes her table in the corner.

"Why aren't you in school?" she asks, groaning as she slides into the booth, which means her knee is acting up again. Which means we might get rain.

"I learned it all," I say.

She opens the menu and smacks her tongue

against her teeth. "What do I want?" she asks herself in a baby voice.

I wait for her to finish looking at the menu like she doesn't always get the same thing. If she's in for lunch, it's a meatloaf sandwich with American cheese and mayo, no lettuce, no tomato, with a side of cheese fries and gravy. If she's in for dinner, it's mac and cheese with a side of cheese fries and gravy.

"April, you know what I want?"

"What?" I put my hand on my hip, make my eyes big, and say it like I'm talking to a little kid, but she doesn't notice.

"I think I'll have a meatloaf sandwich, but here's what I want: Mayo and cheese. American. No lettuce. No tomato, or anything like that." She wrinkles her face and shivers. As she hands me her menu she says, "Oh, and what the heck, I'll have a side of cheese fries."

"Okay," I say, and take a step like I'm leaving.

"Wait! Can I get gravy for those?"

"Sure thing."

"Aren't you gonna write it down?"

"All up here," I say, tapping my forehead with the pen.

Margo works the kitchen until Dale gets in at noon. She's slicing tomatoes.

"Order up! Ida special!" I mark an order slip *I.S.* and clip it to the clothesline over the cutting board.

"Gross," Margo says. She slides a salad toward me and tops it with three tomato slices. "Mrs. Ivory any minute now. Make sure she takes her pill first."

Sure enough, when I get to the dining room, Mrs. Ivory is sitting at the end of the counter, handbag on her lap like someone might steal it. I deliver her salad with a bottle of ketchup instead of dressing and a glass of water. "Take your pill," I say, watching until she does.

After my dad bought the land and we moved out to the motorhome, I didn't get to do laundry with Margo anymore. "Stop in and see me after school sometimes," she said on our last Sunday night at the Wash 'n Fold. So I did, every day after school, because I didn't like going back to the empty motorhome. I ordered pudding or creamed corn, or whatever I'd rounded up enough change to get. When Margo had something that wasn't moving, she'd wink at me and say, "Beets are on special today, sweetie. For you, thirteen cents." If it was slow, she'd tell me the special came with dessert. And whatever the special was, I ate it, even if I didn't like it, just so I wouldn't hurt Margo's feelings. I'd spread my books out on the back table and try to do my homework, but mostly I just watched people.

Sometimes my dad would pick me up on his way home from a job. He'd sit in the car and honk until I came out because he refused to set foot in the diner. Most days, though, I'd stay and help Margo close up. Then she'd drive me home.

If my dad wasn't back yet, she'd idle in the driveway and shake her head. "Oh, I hate to leave you here," she'd murmur, clucking her tongue. "No place for a girl to live."

"It's our clubhouse," I'd say, repeating what my dad told me when I complained about the motorhome. "Not many kids get to live in a club-house."

"I'd take you at my place if I could, you know," she'd say, sighing. "But what can I do?"

I never knew how to answer.

Closing up with Margo all the time, I learned the ropes of things. I knew where she kept the extra ketchup and the hot sauce, and it was no problem for me to get them for customers if Margo was busy. And if customers needed something else when I brought them their condiments, I'd take the order in my school notebook, tear off the page, and bring it to the kitchen.

"I can't hire you, kiddo," Margo said. I was only eleven. "I'd have CPS and the DOL all over my ass for child labor. But if you take orders and people leave you tips, I mean, what am I gonna do about it? You're not on my payroll, right?" She winked at me and put an apron on the counter. "I'm not giving this to you, but if you take it, I'll pretend I didn't see nothing."

When I was fourteen, she took me to get my work permit and we made it official. She even bought me a new apron—white, with a big daisy on the bib. "I'm proud of you, kiddo," she said, her eyes shining.

"I didn't do anything. I just got older."

"Ain't that the truth? That's what we're all doing, right, girlie?" She put her arm around my shoulder and squeezed me until I was smushed against her boob. "Tst. Just got older!" When she laughed, I could feel her whole body shake against mine.

I didn't know if I was supposed to hug back or say something or what. Except for Margo, no one ever hugged me.

Dale comes in, so Margo works the dining room with me, but she lets me keep all the tips. We finish the lunch shift, do refills and wipe downs, count out the drawer, and play Old Maid at the counter until my real shift starts.

"I don't get why you're failing math," Margo says, pulling a card from my hand. "Not once have you made a mistake with the drawer. Not even when you were little." She puts a pair of kings down.

"It's not the same math," I say. "It's like if train A is running at x speed and train B is running at y, which one will get there first."

"Is one of them an express?" Margo cringes as I pull a card from her hand.

"Yeah, they don't tell you that." I put down threes.

"Then how you supposed to do the problem?"

"That's what I'm saying!" I angle my hand so she can take another card.

"They should teach you useful stuff, like how to fight with the power company when your bill is wrong. You want to know when a train comes in, you read the schedule."

I know what she's saying doesn't add up to a hundred percent, but I like that she's siding with me just the same.

Margo gets stuck with the odd queen.

"Old Maid," I shout, slapping my last pair on the counter.

"Well, you don't have to go calling me names, Miss April," she says, scooping up the cards to deal another round.

Ida comes back at four thirty for dinner. "How was school today, April?" she asks, following our usual script.

"I didn't— I saw you at lunch."

Ida blinks at me, panicked.

"It was fine, Ida," I say. "School was fine." I go to put her order in before she can say anything else.

• • •

Margo drives me home after we close up. "Alone again?" she asks when she pulls in the driveway. Icy rain smacks the windshield.

"He's been over with Irene and the boy for a couple months straight now."

"I don't know what he's thinking leaving a young girl by herself all the time." She sighs. "You know I'd take you at my place if I could."

I want to ask her why she can't, but I don't want to make her feel worse.

She shuts the engine but leaves the radio on. It's Bon Jovi. "Well, I've got good news and bad," she says, "which you want first?"

"Bad," I say.

"Bad news is, I crunched numbers and I still can't figure how to give you extra shifts. You can come an hour early to the ones you already have, and I'll give you first dibs if anyone calls in sick, but I can't afford it otherwise, honey."

She's looking right in my eyes and I know she can tell I'm disappointed. I make myself smile, and say, "Hit me with the good news," praying that coming in an hour early wasn't it.

"The good news is I called Gary, over at Gary's Tap Room. He wants you to play on Friday nights. I told him you were the best thing since sliced biscuits." She pats my arm and her bracelets jangle.

"You haven't even heard me play."

44

"I know." She tips her head back and laughs. I love it when she cracks herself up. "I know! I know! I put on my good sweet voice and told Gary you were our own little Joni."

"I don't think I sound anything like Joni Mitchell," I say, feeling heat rise in my cheeks.

"Oh, Gary's deaf in one ear anyway, hon. It don't matter one bit what you sound like."

Margo's been seeing Gary. She thinks I don't know, but Matty and I were three rows behind them at the movies a few weeks back. They made out like teenagers the whole time.

"I only have three songs," I say.

"Then you better write more!" She kisses me on the cheek, and I get out of the car. She waits for me to unlock the door to the motorhome, like I couldn't just climb in through the boarded up window at the back if I lost my key.

I shut the door behind me, leaning against it so the lock latches. Turn on the TV for noise and light and grab my dad's buck knife from under the sink, because I feel safer when I can see it. I sit down with my guitar and try to write for a while, but I come up empty.

When I brush my teeth for bed, I see a big pink lipstick smudge on my cheek in the bathroom mirror. I don't wash it off.

— Chapter 3 —

I sleep in till eleven a.m. and then work the antenna on the TV until I get a soap in clear enough to watch. There's static and I can't always tell who's who, but the chatter lets me pretend I'm not alone. The mean lady, the one my mom always loved, just had brain surgery and it made her remember she has a twin sister named Sandra. Everyone's shocked, forming a search party. Her ex-husband just said, "Searching for Sandra is asking for double trouble." I can't understand how my mom used to watch this stuff. Like really watch it, not just have it on for noise.

I set out a pencil, my math notebook, a can of diet pop, and grab my guitar. I need to write at least three more songs by Friday. At least.

Strumming through the chords I know, I flip-flop the order until it starts to sound like a song—E, C, D, G, back to E—before I move on to lyrics. I'm trying to come up with rhymes for *lies—surmise, prize, tries, french fries*—when I hear a twig snap outside. I want to pass it off as TV static, but then I'm sure I hear footsteps.

I grab my dad's buck knife and inch toward the door, trying to keep the motorhome from shifting. If whoever it is didn't hear my guitar, maybe they don't know I'm here, and that has to give me a better chance.

Those footsteps get closer. The blinds are closed and I don't know if I can peek out without being seen. The door is locked, but the handle moves a little as someone tries to turn it. I hear the scrape of metal on metal, maybe a lock pick. I use the point of the knife to part the blinds and see bright blue eyes shaded by brows like fat fuzzy caterpillars. It's my father.

"You're supposed to be at school," he says as I open the door.

"You're supposed to be at work," I say, stepping aside to let him in.

He eyes the knife. "What the hell you doing with that thing?"

"What the hell you doing leaving your kid to fend for herself in the wild?"

He laughs. "Ape, it's not even close to wild. And I told you, Irene will let you crash on her couch if you babysit for her kid." He wriggles out of his jacket, sits at the kitchen booth and pulls my notebook over. "Skies," he says studying it. "That would be my vote." He scribbles *skies* on my list and pushes the notebook back to where it was. "See you've got the old guitar out."

"Yeah, I've got *my* guitar out," I say, picking it up by the neck with my free hand. "I got a gig."

"A gig?"

"Yeah. Friday night at Gary's. You should

come." Then I add, "If you can get away from Irene and the boy," so he knows Irene isn't welcome, although I'm guessing he figures anyway at this point.

"I'll see what I can do."

"Yeah, well it's probably going to be a regular thing and all."

"I think you can put the knife down, Ape," he says, and I realize I must look crazy, standing there, guitar in one hand, dirty buck knife in the other. I set the knife back under the kitchen sink but don't let go of the guitar.

"Coffee?" my dad asks.

"We're out." I sit down without offering him anything else.

"I'll bring some by next time." He pulls a cigarette from his shirt pocket and slides to the end of the booth to light it on the stove.

"What are you doing here?" I ask.

"Why aren't you at school?" He takes a long drag and looks around for an ashtray. I down the last swig from my pop can and slide it across the table. "Thanks," he says, dropping ash in the can. A wisp of smoke curls from the hole.

"Why aren't you on a job?"

"You first."

"I quit," I say, staring him down. I'm not apologizing.

"Me too," he says, staring back. He takes another drag and blows smoke out his nose.

When I was a kid, he'd do that and tell me he was a dragon. I thought it was hysterical. "Laid off. Faust doesn't need as many men in winter. Decided to keep the young guys. Says he don't want a heart attack on his hands." He holds his cigarette in his mouth, leans back and cracks his knuckles. He looks thinner than he used to. His cheeks are hollow. I thought a good woman was supposed to fatten a man up, but I'm pretty sure the only thing Irene is good at is convincing my dad she's a good woman. "Sucks to get old, you know what?"

"Interesting," I say. "I'll avoid it at all costs."

He shoots a finger gun at me and clicks out the side of his mouth. "She's a quick one, I tell you." He says it like he's talking to God, or an imaginary friend.

"So why you here? School tell you I quit?" I lay the guitar in my lap and make chord formations with my fingers, but don't strum.

"Naw, didn't tell Irene about work yet. We're supposed to buy the kid some Nintendo thing for Christmas. She's gonna be pissed now." Ash falls on his shirt; he brushes it off before it burns through.

Last Christmas, Irene and my dad gave me a card with five scratch-off tickets tucked in the envelope. I won three bucks on one, but I couldn't even get the money because I'm not old enough. The card had *Merry Christmas to you and yours* printed inside. I made my own card for them out of a folded up piece of loose leaf. It said *Merry Christmas* on the front, and on the inside, *Up yours and yours.* I drew every letter alternately in green and red crayon. Irene went in the kitchen after I gave it to her at Christmas dinner. She stayed in there a long time and when she came back, her mascara was runny and she smelled like Peachtree, so the card was a success.

"You've just been hanging out here when I'm gone?" I ask. I don't like the idea of him in my space.

"Here or the duck blind. Depends on the weather." He picks at a callus on the side of his finger until the skin comes off. He just leaves it on the table, this little round piece of skin.

"How long?"

"Week or so."

"And you didn't ever wait for me to get home or leave a note?"

"Come on, Ape. I already got Irene on my case."

"Whatever. You got to go now. I'm writing for my gig."

"It's *my* motorhome." He gets up and walks into the bedroom at the back and slides the accordion door shut.

I use a piece of notebook paper to pick up his callus and throw it in the garbage.

. . .

My dad won the motorhome from Molly Walker in a poker game. It wasn't even high stakes.

On the outside, Molly seemed pretty damn close to perfect. She was in church every Sunday and sewed costumes for all the pageants and school plays. On Christmas she'd drive the three hours to Syracuse to volunteer at a soup kitchen. She had sweatshirts for every holiday, even Arbor Day, and put a coordinated flag on her front porch too. And she won first place in the Fourth of July bake-off every year (except for an unfortunate experiment with crepes three years back). Molly tried so hard to be perfect, but she wasn't, and everyone knew it. All that other stuff—the sewing, the volunteer work—was a cover up, like penance to make up for the fact that she would bet on anything. Margo always said Molly would bet on which way the toilet water would swish down or how long it would take for the stoplight to change. She'd bet on Little League games, how many fish her husband, Hank, would catch on his next fishing trip, or which of the Newton kids would crack their head open skateboarding. She had bets of every size going all over town, and then there were the poker games. If Molly could round up a full table, they'd go through a whole weekend, and by Sunday night everyone would be propped on their fists, looking like hell, hopped up on coffee boiled down to syrup. At the end of those games there was a massive rearranging of who owned what and who wasn't talking to who. Sometimes property lines changed.

Molly almost always ended up on top, until the losing streak. It started with a bet on the Gary's Tap Room bowling team, which seemed like a slam dunk, but Gary spent the day before in Buffalo gorging himself on Chinese food. His fingers swelled so bad they got stuck in the bowling ball and his team tanked the tournament. After that, Molly couldn't seem to get anything right.

The problem was, losing didn't slow her down any. She'd stop for a few days or a week, but then she'd start up again, and lose just as bad. And since it's impossible to hide anything in Little River, everyone knew about it.

One time, Margo had a two-for-one coupon and brought us a whole bag of name-brand cheese puffs and they were the best thing I'd ever tasted. My dad and I ate a few handfuls, and then he went out on a job. I put the bag away on top of the fridge, closed up with a twist tie, but I just kept thinking about those cheese puffs. I couldn't pay attention to the TV. I didn't even want to leaf through Margo's hand-me-down catalogs. All I could do was think about those cheese puffs. I went back again and again. At first I closed the bag up after every handful, but then I just gave up and went whole hog. I ate until the bag was empty and the roof of my mouth had strings of skin peeling off. I even turned the bag upside down and poured every last bit of cheese powder in my mouth. I think that's the way Molly Walker felt about gambling. When she wasn't doing it, she just couldn't think about anything else. And when she was all out of every other last thing to gamble, she bet the motorhome.

Most of the men in town wouldn't play with her anymore, either out of pity for poor Hank Walker or because they didn't like to gamble with a woman to begin with. My dad didn't have any problem gambling with a woman and he flat out didn't like Hank Walker, so he and Molly sat at our kitchen table playing five-card until it was so late it was morning again. Molly bet Hank's tackle box. Dad bet his wrench set. Molly bet her winter coat and said she'd cut it down for me too. Dad bet his snow tires. Molly bet tuna casseroles every Friday for six months. Dad bet shoveling her roof all winter. Molly bet something in a low voice that made Dad blush. Dad bet his next paycheck. Molly bet the motorhome and called it a see and raise. Dad said since it didn't even have a motor it was just a see and since it was so late he wanted to call it, and that's how we got the motorhome.

Hank left Molly the next day. Took his tackle box before Dad could claim it. Dad got the idea that we could live in this motorless motorhome while he built a real house. "I just need to get us a spread of land," he kept saying. I pictured someone taking a knife and spreading land out in front of us like peanut butter on a slice of bread.

The spread he finally found was at the dead end of a dirt road at the very edge of town. He bought it from Mrs. Varnick when her husband died. It was cheap for a reason. Seven acres without a good spot to build a house. There were outcroppings of bedrock and no easy place to lay pipes. Pine trees everywhere. It took my dad a year to clear brush and boulders and dig a well, two more to get a foundation in, but then he met Irene and the boy and stopped caring about making sure we got "our piece of the pie." The foundation filled in like a swimming pool, drawing swarms of mosquitoes and a humongous snapping turtle. Then my dad stopped coming home altogether.

I try to write for almost an hour, but the only good rhyme for lies *is* skies, and I don't want to give my dad the satisfaction. I hear him snoring from the bedroom, this *honk-sheeeee* noise that sounds like a cartoon. His Carhartt work jacket is wadded up in the booth and I know his truck keys and wallet will be in the inside pocket. I put his jacket on and decide to go stock up on groceries.

He's parked all the way at the end of the driveway. Truck turned to the road, backed in to ensure an easy escape. He's always acted guilty like that, even when you can't point to anything specific he's done wrong.

Since it's his gas, I drive out to the Big M in Harristown instead of shopping at the Nice N Easy in Little River. I change all the presets on his radio. Irene has him listening to Christian rock and Evangelical talk show crap. He used to like The Doors. He listened to Floyd. He used to say Bob Dylan was God.

There's three hundred bucks in his wallet. Cash. He doesn't trust banks. I start out thinking I'll spend it all, but then I feel bad and rein it in to a hundred. It's not all he has. There's probably a stash in a hole cut in the mattress or taped under one of Irene's dusty-pink La-Z-Boys. It could even be in the truck somewhere, so Irene won't come across it while she's cleaning. It's not like he doesn't owe me, but there won't be any more coming in for a while. So I take four twenties and two tens and shove them in the back pocket of my jeans as I walk across the Big M parking lot. Inside, I grab a cart and hit the aisles. Family sizes and name brands on everything. No more store brand toaster cakes and dented tuna cans for me. I spend five minutes debating the merits of yellow American cheese singles versus white ones before I decide to buy both and do a taste test. I buy Pop-Tarts in five different flavors and Coke in glass bottles that look like they came from the fifties. I get three bags of cheese puffs like the ones Margo got us that time—the ones that are more crunchy than they are puffy. I buy cold medicine, ibuprofen, and tampons, and stock up on soap and toilet paper so I don't have to steal from school. I walk around for over an hour filling up the cart, counting on my fingers and rounding up to make sure I don't go over a hundred. I don't want to pull out my dad's wallet at the store. And I don't want to have to put anything back. Not today.

In line at the checkout, this woman behind me with frosted mom hair and a big coupon wallet watches me unload my cart onto the conveyor belt. "Sweetheart, I think you missed a few food groups," she says, like she thinks I'm dumb enough to hear it as suggestion instead of criticism.

"It's for a party," I say.

When the checker rings everything up and it only comes to ninety-three dollars, I pick out two Mars bars, a bag of M&M's, and four packs of Juicy Fruit from the rack next to me. Mrs. Coupon Wallet shakes her head. "Take the change off her bill," I say to the checker, while Coupon Wallet is busy loading her six gallons of milk onto the belt. It's only a dollar and change, but I'm sure it's enough to throw her off her game.

It's two thirty now, so on my way back I swing

by to see Matty. He's walking. Halfway home. Just turned onto Woodland Road, Bills cap pulled low over his perfect face. I drive real slow next to him. He picks up speed, doesn't look over. I wonder if he realizes it's my dad's truck. Maybe he thinks his evening will be made busy with a shotgun and a preacher. Maybe he doesn't know whose truck it is and thinks I might be some kind of pervy serial killer. I keep his pace for all of Woodland, but when we turn onto Edgar, I get a good glimpse and he looks panicked and I feel bad. I roll down the window and yell, "Hey, butthead!"

He turns around. His face is blank and kind of white, but then he realizes who it is and smiles that big Matty smile that's just about him and me.

"Why does you driving this big truck make me nervous?" he says, climbing in the passenger side when I slow down enough for him to get in. He kisses me on the lips, his head blocking my view. It doesn't matter. I know these roads.

"I am an excellent driver," I say.

"Okay, Rain Man."

"Okay nothing. I know what I'm doing."

"I'll say." He smacks his hand on my thigh. It stings the slightest bit. He uses the potholes as an excuse to bump his hand up higher and higher and I use them as an excuse to slide my leg toward him, so eventually, his hand is right there and he's rubbing his finger up and down the seam of my jeans right where the legs meet and there's that thick part, all the seams coming together, and he's making me crazy and I want to close my eyes but I'm driving. He's acting like he doesn't know. Pretending like the bumps in the road just led his hand there and he has no idea what it's doing to me. He's humming and looking out the window, but there's that great big smile across his face. By the time we pull into his driveway, he's got my jeans unbuttoned.

We make out in the truck for a while even though his mom is at work, his dad is on a job out in Olean, and his little sister has Girl Scout cookies to sell or something. It's more fun this way. His bedroom is getting old. And it's not like anyone will see. His nearest neighbor is a quarter mile away, and there's so many pine trees.

I still have my dad's jacket on, but my jeans are hanging over the seat. Matty unbuttons his pants, grinning. Even when we kiss I can feel his movie star smile. His grandfather was a poster boy for the U.S. Army Air Forces during World War II, and with his strong brow and noble chin, Matty looks like he could have been the one painted in the clouds holding a rocket bomb. His smile feels like sun breaking through.

"Do you have something?" I ask, determined to keep my wits about me.

"In my room." He takes his pants off and climbs on top of me. It's flopping around in his boxer shorts, like it's spring loaded. We're in our underwear, but I feel him trying to push the right things together.

"Go get it."

"April!"

"Go."

"Come on." He sits up, but he's still on me. Things are still aligned. He runs both hands through his hair.

"You come on." We've been through this almost as many times as we've done it.

"I'm trying to," he says, his voice so strained it's more grunt than words.

"Matty."

"I'm not cheating on you." He holds his hand up, flat palmed. His pale brown eyes look golden in the afternoon light. "Scout's honor. You won't catch anything."

"Pregnancy is an awful disease," I say, trying to wriggle out from under him so we don't have an accident. He's trigger happy.

"Do you know how hard it is to get pregnant? Seriously. I'm being serious. My cousin Lindsey has been trying for years."

"She's like fifty."

"That has nothing to do with it," he says through his teeth.

"I think it does. There was an *Oprah*."

"Would it be so bad?" It's new, him trying different angles like this. Usually he flat-out begs and gives up easy. "We already know we're getting married. Right? And you already dropped out of school." He's talking fast, like he does when he's trying to scam his mom into a later curfew or a new skateboard. "It probably wouldn't happen anyway, but everyone says it feels so different, like so much better. For both of us. Not just me. It'll blow your mind, April."

"It'll blow your mind, April," I say, making my voice crack like his. I laugh and I enjoy it when he looks wounded, like I broke his new Tonka truck. I put a pin in his plan. I love that I'm the only person who doesn't cave just because he's beautiful.

He's a little less excited, but he still hasn't budged. I think he believes he can pout his way to victory. "You have a choice," I say, mimicking his mom and how she gets all calm and reserved when he tries to pull a scam. "You can either go inside and get a condom, or you can go inside and do your homework while I go home. Either way. The choice is yours, Matthew John."

"Mark Conrad says Tonya lets him do it without a condom all the time, and she hasn't gotten knocked up."

"Well," I say, "you're not Mark Conrad, and if Mark Conrad jumped off a—"

"Mood killer." He sighs so hard it makes my belly shake. "Pretending to be my mom is not hot."

I snap the band of his boxer shorts. "Then you're going to do homework?"

"I'll be back," he mumbles. He doesn't make eye contact when he pulls his pants on and gets his keys out of his backpack. He walks funny going up to the house.

When he comes back, it's over pretty fast, so I don't think I killed the mood all that much.

What I don't get about sex is why the actual doing it part isn't as great as all the stuff leading up to it. I always want to do it, but then, after, I wish we could go back to the moment right before, when it feels like I'll go out of my mind if we don't. It's like an itch you have to scratch, but then it turns out the itch felt better than the scratching, and it fools me every time.

I turn the key in the ignition enough to get the radio to play without starting the engine, and rest my head in Matty's armpit. We share one of my glass-bottled Cokes. He talks about the job he's going to get when he graduates in spring, and how Mark Conrad says the factory is paying three bucks over minimum now. He's calculated how much we could pay for a trailer and beer money, and if he went hunting with his Uncle Barry, we could have deer meat in our deep freeze and save a ton. I stop listening when he starts in on the awesome venison burgers his Aunt Gloria makes and how she could teach me.

Bob Dylan is playing on one of the presets. It's

Lay, Lady, Lay, and I laugh because it just seems too appropriate. Matty says, "No really, it's like the best burger I've ever had, and it's like free from nature." When Bob gets to the part where he sings about not waiting for your life to start, just having cake and eating it now, I know what he means is pretty much the exact opposite, but I start to feel like I'm a million years older than Matty and maybe even from another planet. I start to feel like Matty is the opposite of cake.

We're stuck in our own stale breath and it's fogging up the windows. "I have to go," I say, sitting up, grabbing my jeans.

Matty tries to pull me back into his armpit.

I twist away. "No, really." I kind of shout it. "My dad doesn't know I have the truck. I have to go." I pull my jeans on and lean back to do the button and the zipper. My shirt rides up. There's a wet spot on the seat.

"Oh, okay," Matty says, giving me that broken Tonka truck look again.

I rub at the wet spot with my hand behind my back, trying to pretend like my panic is about my dad getting mad and not the life Matty is spreading out ahead of us. "My dad just—he got laid off and he's all pissy and Irene doesn't know . . ." The clock says it's 4:23, and pretending I'm panicking about my dad starts to make me actually panic about my dad. He probably isn't sleeping anymore.

Matty says, "See you tomorrow," but then he tries to stretch it out by kissing me more. He moans gently, like he thinks he can work me into going at it again.

I rub my hand down his leg until I get to his knee, then I reach over and hand him his backpack. "I gotta go."

He's walking funny again. I stay to make sure he didn't lock his keys in the house when he went to get the condom. As soon as he opens the door, I honk twice and drive away like my tail's on fire, kicking up a trail of dust. Rocks hit the underside of the truck like a barrage of bullets from one of those boring war movies my dad used to watch on Sunday afternoons before Irene made him spend the day at church.

Matty left the condom on the floor mat, full and floppy like a jellyfish. I don't notice it until I'm at the end of Woodland. This isn't exactly a busy road. I know I won't get caught, so I open the car door at the stop sign and drop it, praying it will get driven over and dusted up before anyone can see what it is. It leaked on the mat. I search my dad's pockets for a tissue or a napkin, even a handkerchief, but I don't find one. I do find a small box in his inside breast pocket—black velvet with a rounded top. The hinges creak when I pull it open. The ring inside has a diamond so big I start to wonder if my dad has any stashed money left anywhere. It's real too. I scratch it against the window and it leaves a thin etched line. I put the ring box in the left pocket, where he keeps his wallet, as a warning, so he'll know I know about it. I flip the mat over and wipe it on the carpet underneath. When I flip it the right way again, it looks even cleaner than it was to start.

There are three lights in town and I hit all of them red. Then I get stuck behind Mrs. Ivory, who can't drive any faster than fifteen miles an hour and probably shouldn't drive at all. Turns out she's going to visit my neighbor, Mrs. Varnick, and I'm stuck behind her the whole way home. By the time I pull in the driveway, the clock says 4:57, and before I can even throw it in park, my dad is standing on the steps of the motorhome, holding my guitar by the neck like prize game.

"God damn it, April!" he screams when I get out of the car. "Where the fuck were you?"

"Shopping," I say, and start unloading my groceries from the back of his truck into a pile on the ground. I don't look at him. I tighten my jaw and ignore his temper tantrum with a fake smile the way my mom used to. "A growing girl's gotta eat."

"I told Irene I was getting out early today. At three thirty," he says.

I smile again and keep unloading. Don't say anything. Don't apologize. The Coke bottles clink against each other when I set that bag

64

down. Otherwise it's quiet and I can feel it in the air, the way he's about to explode, like how the teakettle gets extra still just before it boils. The metal steps of the motorhome rattle. Even though I'm not looking, I know he's starting to shake and I'm sure he's holding the neck of my guitar hard enough to make his knuckles turn white.

"God damn, April!" he screams, and then there's an awful crack. Just one. Loud and sharp and it stays in my ears even after it's done and I know I will hear it for days.

"There, I took something that's yours. How do you feel about that, April? How do you feel about that?" he says.

I palm the ring box and drop it in the bag with the cheese puffs as I carry it over to my pile. It's the last bag. The cheese puffs crunch when I set it down. I take his jacket off and drape it on the front seat of his truck.

"Fine," I say, and toss him his keys.

— Chapter 4 —

I don't have jack shit to do, so I pace the motorhome singing *Should I Stay or Should I Go*. The singing starts so low it's only in my head, but once I get going I'm loud and bouncing around and the whole motorhome shakes.

Since I swiped the ring from my dad a few days ago, I've been expecting him to come back for it. The suspense is making me crazy. Anytime I hear a noise—Mrs. Varnick closing her car door, or a tree branch falling, or buckshot—I jump out of my skin and my heart starts up fast like someone hit it with jumper cables. We learned about fight or flight in science class. It's like your instinct to deal with a situation. I'm not sure what my instinct would be if my dad came for the ring. It's not even a fair trade. His ring is still in existence. My guitar is a pile of broken wood. I had to cancel my gig at Gary's Tap Room, but I'm guessing my dad isn't sitting around thinking that I'm the one who got wronged.

There's a hole in the carpet on the floor, right by the sink. I kick the edges while I dance, making it a little bigger every time I pass. No extra shifts at the diner, and Matty is grounded because of the other day when one of his neighbors saw us going at it in his driveway. Plus, his parents don't want him hanging out with a high school dropout.

"Do do do do do do trouble! Da da da da da da double!" I shout more than I sing. I just need noise. I'm doing this move where I shake my butt and then jump and spin around when I see a car through the slats in the blinds. It's Mrs. Ivory's big beige Mercury. Sometimes she gets confused when she's visiting Mrs. Varnick and ends up in our driveway instead. The thing that really gets me is that Mrs. Varnick lives in a double wide. I live in a motorhome. It's easy to tell the difference.

I go outside and knock on the car window. "Shove over," I yell. "I'll drive." It's a stone's throw to Mrs. Varnick's, but last time Mrs. Ivory almost hit like four trees on the way.

I peek in the window, but it's not Mrs. Ivory. It's Irene, sitting in the driver's seat with her seat belt off, clutching a plastic baggie of what looks like dirt. "I thought you were Mrs. Ivory," I say, backing away.

Irene opens the door. "I was just giving her a ride."

Irene has come to claim her ring. My dad must have told her he was going to propose and now she's here and she's pissed. I want to turn tail and run, but I don't even have real shoes on. Irene's not like a marathon runner or anything, but I'm sure she could catch up with a kid running in flip-flops. I start toward the motorhome to barricade myself inside. But then Irene gets out of the car and spills the baggie of dirt on the ground.

"Shit," she says.

I've never heard her curse. She looks like she might cry. I hadn't noticed it before, but Irene kind of looks like my mom. At least like the one picture I have of my mom. That's probably what my dad sees in Irene. I think about telling her this, but I don't want to deal with her crying in my driveway. I'm not in the mood.

"It's okay to spill dirt in the dirt," I say, crossing my arms over my chest. "It's not like it can get any dirtier than dirt." I wish I could make myself shut up, but the words keep tumbling. "I mean, it's already dirt, right? There's nothing—"

"It was coffee," she says, walking up to the motorhome like the fact that I'm talking to her means she's invited. "Your dad said you ran out."

I walk in front of her and up the steps. I don't slam the door in her face, but I figure if I don't talk to her she'll realize she's not wanted.

"Could we make some tea?" Irene says, climbing in with her head down low, like she's not sure the ceiling will accommodate her five-foot-two frame. "I was hoping we could sit down and have a talk." She looks around, lingering on the dirty laundry piled on the passenger's seat, my muddy boots on the floor, the pile of guitar pieces on the table, and I can feel her judging all of it. "Because you and me"—she eyes me like

I'm dirty boots—"we've never really had a talk, you know?"

I hate the way she says "a talk." Like it's a cookie or a pet or a new pair of shoes, something more than words falling out of our mouths.

I sit at the table and pull my feet up on the seat, flip-flops and all. In Irene's apartment, you have to take your shoes off before you get past the welcome mat.

"You and me," Irene says, "we haven't exactly gotten off to the best start."

I picture the words coming out of her mouth like hard pieces of plastic. Like those magnets kids have sometimes so they can spell words on the fridge. *Cat. Mom. Dog. Dad.* I picture Irene's words collected in a basket that she hands to me. There's our talk, right there. All jumbled up until it makes no sense.

She pokes around, peeks in cupboards until she finds the teapot. I watch her when her back is turned. Her waist is really tiny, but her black dress pants sag at the butt and don't do her any favors. She'd look better in a skirt.

When she glances back at me, I stare at my feet. Margo painted my toenails over the summer and there's a sliver of pink left at the tips.

"Do you think you could say something?" Irene asks. "I mean, this is hard, April." Her eyeliner is melty, pooled in the corners of her eyes. She doesn't usually wear this much makeup. Her sweater looks new. I wonder if she came from something, or if she got all dressed up just to see me. "I'm talking to you and you're acting like I'm not even here."

I want to say *Wishful thinking,* but her hands are shaking and it's making me nervous. I'm not sure what her angle is—why she hasn't asked about the ring yet. "Use the water in the jug." I say, holding my leg up just above the bench, using my toes to make my flip-flop flop against my foot. "The stuff from the tap looks like piss."

"Okay." She lifts the lid off the teapot, looks in the hole, and sniffs. She pours a tiny bit of water from the jug into the pot, swishes it around, and dumps it in the sink. Satisfied, she fills the pot and plays with the burner until she gets it to light. I don't tell her there's no tea. I'll save that for after the whistle blows.

She looks at me, but when I make eye contact, she pulls a strand of hair in front of her eyes to check for split ends. When I look away, I can feel her watching me again.

"Your dad didn't mean it," she says, sitting across from me, pointing to the pile of splinters that used to be my guitar.

I collected all the pieces after he left. Every bit I could find. I mean, it's not like I could glue them back into a guitar and have it work. I know that. I know. I just didn't have the heart to throw them away.

70

"He doesn't mean a lot of things, but that doesn't put anything back together," I blurt out before I remember that I'm trying not to talk to her.

Irene doesn't say anything. She just stares at me like she's measuring up everything about me to see if it's good enough to even get close to her perfect self and her perfect son and her perfect church-going life. I was bored before, so I braided my hair into like eight or nine braids and I probably look like an idiot. Plus, I'm wearing my dad's old plaid flannel, cinched at the waist with one of his cracked leather belts, and a pair of leopard-spotted leggings Margo gave me after she shrunk them in the wash. I wish I could excuse myself and change into something that doesn't make me feel like a freak show, but I don't want Irene to get it wrong and think I even care what she thinks.

I remember Irene from before she had anything to do with my dad. She was in high school when I was in elementary. She had the lead in *West Side Story* and danced on the stage in these red ballet slippers and after I saw it I used to twirl around and pretend I was her. Colored my sneakers with red magic marker and everything. She was beautiful and her parents were so proud they brought roses in that shiny plastic wrapping and her father ran up to the stage to give them to her when she took her bow. I don't think it was too long after they found out she was pregnant with the boy and kicked her out of the house.

"Why are you driving Mrs. Ivory's car?" I ask, pulling the rubber bands from my hair like I'm just fidgeting.

"Your dad bought it for me." She looks kind of young when she says it, like a kid who just got a pony. It doesn't occur to her that I can't get my dad to buy me groceries voluntarily.

"You could sail to France in that thing," I say, picking at the cracked inlay on my guitar neck.

"I know, right?" she says, giggling like we are girlfriends. "It's three times the size of the Datsun." She smooths hair behind her ear. "Duncan Ivory doesn't want his mom driving anymore. He sold it to us cheap because I promised to take Mrs. Ivory to her appointments."

The teapot whistles. Irene gets up, turns off the heat, takes the pot from the burner. "I had to drop her off at Mrs. Varnick's, so I decided I'd come see you."

"Lucky me," I say.

I know she heard me, but she pretends she didn't. She opens the cabinet where we keep plates, closes it, opens the next one and takes out two mugs. They're also Margo hand-me-downs, chipped and cracked from too much use at the diner. Irene rinses them with the jug water, touches the chips with her finger like it might repair them. She starts fishing around in drawers. I'm pretty sure this isn't about the ring. I don't think she could keep a poker face this long.

"Oh! You know, I think we're out of tea," I say like the thought just occurred to me. I try not to smile, but I feel my mouth going there anyway.

I watch her shoulders creep to her neck. She slams the drawer closed. "Damnit, April! I'm trying. I am trying here." She sits across from me in the booth and drops her head in her hands. "I don't know what I did to you," she whispers, poking at the splinters of my guitar like she's playing pick-up sticks. Move one sliver without the others collapsing. "I love your father. How does that hurt you? I don't get it."

"Because you're an idiot," I say.

"Not fair, April." Her voice breaks. I can see tears well up. "Not fair!"

"Is it fair that you took him? That you take all of it? I get crap and you get a new car? What's fair about that, Irene?" I get up and walk out, slamming the door behind me. I pace in the driveway, walk around the car and kick the tires, feeling the sting in my toes.

Irene comes out. She's standing on the steps, just like my dad when he smashed my guitar, but she's crying, mascara running down her cheeks like dirty slug trails. "I just wanted us to get along. I thought—I just thought since I'm pregnant with your little brother or sister you might decide you give a shit. You might try to be my family too."

The jumper cables hit my heart again. "Yeah, that's what my dad needs. Another kid." I stand between her and the car so she can't get away yet. "Fucking brilliant! Especially since he does such a good job taking care of the one he already has. Smart, Irene. Good one."

"April," she says softly, and I think she's going to say something else, but she crumbles, shoulders shaking. I can see her tears fall to the ground, raining on the coffee. A part of me wants to tell her that she was so beautiful I wanted to be her. A part of me wants to say *Yes, I'll be your family, because I don't have one either.* But I can't. I don't work that way.

"He's with you because you look like her," I say, picturing myself smacking her basket of plastic letters, scattering our talk everywhere. "My mom. You look like her." I walk off into the woods and wait by the flooded house foundation, kicking at the thin film of ice with the edge of my flip-flops until I hear her drive off in Mrs. Ivory's car.

After Irene leaves, I go back to the motorhome and dig around under the mattress until I find the ring. The box doesn't look so new. It's not just that it's covered with pocket lint. I didn't notice before, but if you look close, some of the velvet

74

is rubbed off the top. I open it, take the ring out, and slide it on my finger, stacked on top of the promise ring Matty gave me. It's a little loose, but it almost fits.

The diamond is big like a tooth, and glows like there's a light inside of it. Round, but not quite perfect, with a tiny black dot in the center where the bottom is cut off, where it doesn't come to a point. It's a miner's cut. The words are just there in my brain. I know it's a miner's cut and then I realize that I know this ring. I remember twisting it around on her finger while she held me in her lap. I remember this ring and her hair falling, so long over her shoulders, I had to brush it out of my face. Her hair had sun streaks of gold and copper and the ring was platinum. Everything sparkled. I take it off my finger and read the tiny letters of the inscription.

When my father was twenty or so, he played guitar at a coffeehouse in Syracuse if he was between carpentry jobs. He'd play for a free meal and whatever people would put in his tip jar. "You can't be proud when people will feed you," he'd say. They both told me the story when they were together. They each had their own part, like it was a play, but he'd never tell any of it after she left, so I don't remember everything. I wish I did.

The people at the coffeehouse liked him and he always got a good crowd. He didn't write much, so it was mostly covers, but he played the covers other people didn't. James Taylor was huge, but he never played *Fire and Rain*. He'd do the obscure stuff, so people thought he wrote the songs himself because they'd never heard them—Ella, Nat, Fats Waller. Maybe some Dylan B-sides.

He'd been playing all night when my mom walked in with a group of friends. They were talking and laughing and he couldn't stop watching her from the makeshift stage. She wore a short red dress with tall brown boots and when she smiled it was big and the room got brighter and he felt like the world was a better place.

She would chime in, back when they were happy; she would say that she walked in with a group of friends to get coffee. After that they were supposed to meet some boys somebody knew. They were talking, not paying attention to the music, but then my mother heard my father singing *Autumn Leaves*. She'd never heard the song before.

"He sang my name," she'd say, and wink at him. "So, I started watching to figure out if I knew him. I didn't, but by the end of the song I decided I wanted to." She would sing the whole song when she told the story—the tale of a left behind lover who remembers his love when the leaves change color and fall from the trees. Her voice was thin, but pretty.

So that's how they met, because of some stupid song. But he lived in Little River and she lived in Syracuse and her parents expected her to marry a doctor or a lawyer or an astronaut. "What did I want with a husband who was always jumping around on the moon?" she'd say.

He didn't have a lot of money, so one night when he missed her so much he couldn't stand it anymore, he drove up to Buffalo to ask his grandfather for his grandmother's ring. He had it engraved with a line from their song the very next day and drove all the way to Syracuse in the middle of a snowstorm to ask her to marry him, right in front of her father. And when she said yes, but her father said absolutely not, she said that Jesus was a carpenter and that was good enough for her. So they had a little wedding that no one on her side came to and *Autumn Leaves* was their first dance.

Part of the problem with wedding songs is that people don't listen to the words enough. With my parents, it was like the song decided it. They never had a fighting chance.

I roll the ring around in my hands. If I turn it the right way, all I can read of the lyrics is *When Autumn leaves*.

— Chapter 5 —

We should just go," I say to Matty. We're hanging out in his uncle's deer blind since I'm not allowed at his house anymore and I try to avoid him ever spending time at the motorhome.

"Go where?" he says, blowing into his hands. The blind was a better place to hang in the summer.

"Does it matter?" I jump around to stay warm. "Anywhere. Not here."

"What's so bad about here?" He pulls a sloppy hand-rolled cigarette from behind his ear and lights it, coughing. This smoking thing is new. He picked it up from Mark Conrad and now he thinks he's a badass. I don't smoke, but his parents will blame me when they find out. They blame me for everything. His mother stopped liking me after mine left. As if me and my dad had a disease her family could catch.

"What's so *great* about here?" I say. "We're dying on the vine, Matty. There's a whole world out there."

"What's got into you, Ape?" He makes a fish mouth when he exhales. Mark Conrad can blow smoke rings, but Matty's come out like sad little clouds.

I fan the smoke from my face. "Don't call me Ape."

"It's just getting good, you know? I'm almost done with school. We're almost there."

"I won't be done with school."

"It's not like it matters. You'll get a new guitar. You can play at Gary's until we get married." He picks a piece of tobacco off his tongue and looks at it. "Not like I want my wife playing in a bar, right?" He starts to laugh, but it turns into a cough. "After that, you can stay with the kids and I'll bring home the venison."

The deer hunting obsession is getting way worse. I'm guessing Mark Conrad does that too.

"What if I still want to play at Gary's when we're married?" I say, twisting my promise ring around my finger with my thumb.

"Ape—" I give him a look and he quickly adds "—rul. That's not what married girls do."

"So what, am I supposed to join bible study and make potluck in my crockpot?"

"Potluck isn't something you make," he says, shaking his head like he's old and wise and I'm so foolish. "You make jello or stew." He stubs his cigarette out on the bench and slides to the floor. "Come here." He spreads his legs out. I sit between them and he wraps his arms around me. "It's gonna be good." Cold seeps through my jeans. Matty kisses my ear. Whispers like he's trying to get a baby to stop crying, "You'll love it. I promise."

I want that to be true. It would be so much easier. But I'll never belong the way Matty does. I only fit with him because we've been this way forever, from when our moms used to drink tea at his house every day. He doesn't see me how everyone else does. He doesn't notice that none of his friends ever talk to me. And because he's Matty, because everyone wants him to like them, they don't say what they really think. They just pretend I'm not there. It's not something a few years and some jello will change.

Matty laces his fingers through mine. My hands have been in my pockets; his feel like ice. "Trust me, Ape. We're good here."

When I get home, my dad is parked in front of the motorhome, sitting on the hood of his truck. I see him from the end of the driveway before he sees me, smoke and hot breath swirling. My head says turn tail and run, like a warning light flashing over and over again, but the walk back from the deer blind was long and it's like twenty out. My feet hurt because my boots are too small, and I just don't have the energy to play these damn games with him anymore. So I tell myself I'm only shaking from the cold. I hold my head high and try to walk past like he doesn't exist. He jumps down and grabs my arm.

"What'd you say to Irene?" His fingers dig into my armpit, even through Margo's old down jacket.

I look him right in the eyes and give him my blank face, like I'm dead. I'm a corpse. Corpses can't talk.

He pulls my arm up. I can barely keep my feet on the ground, "What did you do to her?"

My hand is pulsing. I give him a big, sick smile. "I told her you're Father of the Year," I say. "That's one lucky kid you got on the way. Congratulations." My nose smarts and I know the tears are coming. I fight them. Close my eyes and imagine I'm running, feet pounding on pine needles in time with my heart, air stinging my lungs until I can barely breathe.

He pushes me away. "You show her respect," he says.

"Like you do?" I open my eyes and back out of his swinging range. "Telling her you still have a job? Getting her knocked up when you're broke? Blowing money you don't have on a car?" I shake my head and smile, trying so hard not to cry. "You're a shining example, Dad. I'm sure your new kid will look up to you."

"Maybe this one won't be such a little shit." He throws his cigarette down, stomps it out, and opens the door to his truck.

"What? Going already?" I laugh and it sounds like it's coming from another person. Something's come unlatched. I can't stop. "Why don't you come in for some tea, Dad? We'll have a talk."

"Irene's boy's got a band recital," he says, staring me down. "I want to be there."

"I told her she looks like Mom," I say, getting closer. "But Mom was prettier. And she had the good sense to leave you."

I see his hand coming like it's slow. Tobacco stains on the tips of his fingers and every line in his palm. All I can see is that hand—it eclipses the sun—but I can't make myself move out of the way. I'm a corpse again. Corpses can't move.

— Chapter 6 —

I pack everything. I don't know where I'm going and I don't know how I'm getting there, but anything that could be useful gets thrown in a garbage bag—three cans of baked beans, two and a half boxes of Pop-Tarts, the last Coke, toothpaste, flashlights, fuel cans for a camping cookstove that came with the motorhome and doesn't even work. I need supplies. Reinforcements. Survival tools. I wish the damn motorhome had a freaking motor and I could just drive it away.

When one bag is full, I tie the end on itself and throw it up front. Before I even get to the bedroom, I can barely see out the windshield. I didn't know we had this much stuff.

The world is ending, or at least I'm done with it. I keep thinking I need a plan, but so far, this is it: shove everything in bags.

In the bedroom, I take the lumpy pillows; all the clothes in the closet, even the ones that aren't mine; and the pilled pink blanket with fraying satin trim.

Do I need sheets? I do need sheets. You can use them for things like escaping from windows or pulling a person out of a ditch. I picture myself hanging by my hands off a bent sapling, bare feet dangling over a ravine with a river raging below.

I wish I had someone to come with me, pull me out if I get stuck. *Tie the sheet around your waist, April, before you get too close to the edge,* I tell myself. *Tie the other end to a tree. There's the plan. No falling in ditches without a lifeline. You can't afford to.* I wad up the sheets and the mattress pad and jam them in the bag.

I take my mom's ring out from under the mattress and shove it in my pocket. The box digs into my thigh, but that's good. I know it's there.

I get down on my knees and reach my arm under the mattress until it's all the way under, the side of my face pressed against the edge. I feel for the photo and pull it out. It's rippled and crumpled and there's a stain across my mother's face where I had to pick off a soup noodle after I saved it from the trash. It's her wedding day and her dress is simple.

I tuck the picture in the corner of the bathroom mirror and study our faces, doing my best to ignore the swollen red marks on my cheek. I look like her, and I wonder what it is that's different between the way Irene looks like her and the way I do. What makes it okay in Irene but not me? Maybe it's the nose or something about the way my mother and I have the same dark eyelashes and a dimple in our chins when we smile.

This picture lady, in her white veil and bright blue eye shadow, plays my mother in every memory. When I think of her now, where she could be, what she might be doing, she's still wearing her wedding dress and her face always has that perfect grin.

I slip her photo between the pages of my favorite book—the one she liked to read me about Max and all those wild things—and shove it in with the blankets. It's the last bag. I tie it closed and throw it on top of the pile. I still don't know what I'm doing. I pace until I do. A plan works its way into my head a step at a time and then it's all there.

I open the last bag again, tear a page from the book, and sit down to write.

I walk past the elementary school on my way. My dad's truck is on the grass even though there are still empty parking spaces. Mrs. Varnick's car is in a handicapped spot but doesn't have a sticker. Her grandson plays the violin and he sucks. Matty's sister plays the recorder. I don't know what Gary's son plays, but I see his Harley. I wonder if Margo rode on the back. Those concerts take forever. Long and painful. Squeaking reeds and kids chewing on drumsticks when they aren't hitting cymbals off beat.

It's a five-minute trek from the school to Irene's apartment. The front of the building is lit up nice like it's an architectural gem, even though the paint is peeling and someone spray-painted

WWJD in yellow on the front step. I sneak around the back of the building to stay in the shadows, and get a splinter climbing the rickety wood fire escape. The sliver is thick and grey, stuck right in my palm. When I yank it out, the blood forms a tiny red pearl. I wipe it on my jeans.

It's easy to get in. Irene leaves the window in the boy's room open just a crack. He's got croup or asthma or something like that and always needs fresh air. Waste of heat, if you ask me.

His room is painted dark blue and he has a red bunk bed with yellow stars all over it. I bet my dad built that bed for the boy. His blankets look so much warmer than mine. I take his sheet, just in case, wrapping it around my arm to keep it from trailing.

There's a Tupperware container of leftover Hamburger Helper in the fridge like it's just waiting to be my road trip food. I take that, one of Irene's forks from her good silverware set, and a half-eaten package of Chips Ahoy! for dessert.

By the door, hanging from a wooden rack painted with the words *Bless Our Happy Home,* is a row of keys. The boy's house key hangs from a blue and yellow lanyard, next to the one for the mailbox on a paper clip, which is next to Irene's praying angel keychain. I use the boy's key to pry open the angel's ring and circle Mrs. Ivory's car key around until it slides off.

I turn the knob on the front door to lock behind

me so maybe it'll take them a while to figure out anything even happened. I'm careful to close the door slowly, but the click of the latch sounds like a gunshot in my head. Everything is always louder when you're trying to be quiet. I spin a story about Irene asking me to take her car to pick up the boy and babysit for him after the concert so she and my dad can go out, but no one stops me on my way across the parking lot.

Mrs. Ivory's car is backed into a space at the far end of the lot. My dad has Irene trained for his constant getaway plan. The car is spotless. Cleaner than Mrs. Ivory ever kept it. Vacuumed and dusted in all the cracks and crevices. There isn't even any gunk in the indents of the steering wheel. The mirrors have the same streak-free shine as every surface in Irene's apartment, and the floor mats are brand new. Irene's got this angel air freshener strung from the rearview. It matches her keychain, and smells like the bathroom at Margo's Diner. I pull it off and hang it like a Christmas ornament on the hedge that outlines the lot.

Irene's legs are shorter than mine, but when I fumble for the lever to move the seat backward, the trunk opens instead. I go out to close it, but grab Irene's emergency kit first, turn it over and look inside, so if anyone's watching they'll think I meant to open the trunk.

Back in the car, I survey the parking lot. It

looks clear. I find the right lever, but the seat still won't move, so I jerk my body forward. The seat gives and I get smushed against the steering wheel. I yank the lever and push back until it feels about right. I mess with the mirrors because I know you're supposed to, but I don't know where they're supposed to be.

Cars start much easier when you have the key. First try, no problem, and I'm out of the parking lot and down the road like nothing is wrong or out of the ordinary. I take the long way so I don't have to drive past the school and risk catching my dad outside for a smoke. And even though Mrs. Varnick is at the recital, I turn the headlights off when I drive past her house. Just in case.

First order of business is to yank garbage bags from the front of the motorhome and throw them out the door. Then I work on shoving them in the car. When I cram a bunch of bags into the trunk with my foot, something crunches loud in a way it's not supposed to.

I can't fit everything and I don't have time to sort it, so I pull the bags from the trunk, ripping them open to make sure I keep the important stuff: my book with the picture of my mom tucked inside, clothes, empty guitar case, blankets, food, cassettes, rhyming dictionary. I wad up sheets and blankets and stuff them behind the driver's seat. Clothes go behind the passenger's seat. The ring goes in the glove compartment. Food up front for easy access. Everything else gets left behind, scattered on the ground. I take a quick pass through the motorhome, pee one more time. Then I leave, pulling the door hard until it clicks shut. Hide my key under the mat. I don't want it anymore.

When I back down the driveway, I run over a plate or a cereal bowl. Something fragile. I feel it snap under the weight of the car.

The lights are on at Matty's house, but no one's home. I watch for a minute from outside to be sure. His mom leaves the kitchen light on all the time so it looks like they're home, because she never locks the door. I let myself in, sprint through the living room like lightning, and tiptoe up the creaky steps to Matty's bedroom.

I lie on his bed one last time and look at the glow-in-the-dark solar system stickers on his ceiling. The lights are on, but I can still see the stars because I know they're there, pale yellow against off-white. We stuck them up together, standing on his bed, mattress jiggling under our feet. At first we tried to do constellations, but we only got as far as Orion before we gave up and started plastering stars and planets everywhere. We bonked heads and Matty fell backward, pretending it knocked him out. When I leaned over to see if he was okay, he pulled me down too. That was the first time he kissed me.

I curl the blanket over my body and breathe in Matty. I start to feel like I could stay in this bed. I could wait here for him and get married and learn how to make venison burgers and kiss his mom's ass until she likes me. I roll up the other side of the blanket into a cocoon. I could go to church and make potluck or bring potluck or whatever the hell you do with potluck. I could return the car. I could finish high school. I could be that person, the one who stays. The one who makes good on things. But then I think about inertia. That whole body at rest thing. I think about how wives don't play guitar in bars and double dating with Mark Conrad for all eternity. Matty coming home with a six-pack every night, covered in factory grease. I think about Molly Walker and all those holiday sweatshirts. If I stay, I will always be a body at rest. And I can't even make regular hamburgers.

I get up and root around, pull Matty's favorite sweater from the pile of clothes on the closet floor. His navy blue cotton roll neck. Thick and warm, and it smells like he does when he's just gotten out of the shower. I pull it on and lean over the bed to kiss his pillow. Like the kiss will be there waiting for him when he gets home, and he'll know it's there. I leave the note I wrote him on top of the kiss, the pearl promise ring he gave me tucked in the folded paper. My eyes sting. I pinch myself hard on the fleshy part under my thumb, like my mom used to do when she was crying and wanted to hide it.

Matty's house looks smaller when I back down the driveway. Smaller and sad. All lit up; warm and inviting and no one home to enjoy it.

By the time I get to the highway, I'm flat out sobbing. I get myself together and wipe my face on my sleeve, but then I realize it's really Matty's sleeve and start all over. I wish I'd left him more, but I just couldn't write it. All the note says is: *Matty, I have to go. I'm sorry. Love Always, April.* I wrote it on the last page of *Where the Wild Things Are.* That's the part where Max finally comes back home and the food his mom made is waiting for him, because even though he was acting like a horrible kid she still loves him enough to make him dinner.

I've never driven on the interstate, only the back roads that snake around Little River. My knuckles go white and my palms sweat every time a truck passes, but it seems like the fastest way to get distance. Irene was nice enough to leave me with a little more than half a tank of gas, but by the time I get to the Waterloo exit, I'm three hours in and running low. I don't know where the next rest stop is, so I exit, pay the toll with coins Irene left perfectly organized in the change compartment, and find a gas station.

I have a hundred and seventy-eight dollars

saved up from work. Tip money and the little extra Margo started throwing me on top of my shift. When I pull out the wad of ones and fives to pay for gas, I realize I didn't say goodbye to Margo. I call from the pay phone outside, sure she's staying at Gary's and I'll get the machine. But then she picks up and says hello, and she knows it's me even though I don't say anything back.

"Oh, girlie," she says, her voice blurred and watery. "What did you do?"

— Chapter 7 —

Ithaca, NY

I decide to spend the night in the parking lot of the Wilson Farms gas station just off the interstate, so I can get going and get gone as soon as I wake up. I park around back, out of sight, but cops keep pulling in. There's a clear view of the cars when they enter the parking lot, but then they drive toward the front of the building and I can't see them anymore. Three in an hour and I can't get to sleep. I know they wouldn't notice me unless they were looking, and they probably aren't looking yet. They're most likely stopping for donuts or coffee or cigarettes, but every time a car door slams I jump three feet out of my skin and can't settle down until way after they leave.

Cop car number four pulls in and enough is enough. If I'm not going to sleep, I may as well move. It's safer anyhow.

On the way back toward the interstate, there's a sign that says ITHACA and that it's forty-one miles from here. I'm not looking forward to getting back on I-90, and don't know where I'm going other than away, so Ithaca is as good a destination as any.

A few months back Gary drove down to Ithaca

to meet with some guys starting a brewery. He loved the beer. Came back with as many kegs as he could fit in his truck, but he sat at the counter at Margo's Diner and complained about Ithaca through his whole dinner. Soup, salad, meatloaf, coffee, and lemon meringue pie, mouth full and everything. He couldn't stop talking about how much Ithaca pissed him off.

"Freaking dirty hippies," he said to Margo when she brought him extra gravy. "From the looks of them, there isn't a shower in the whole damn city."

"Amazing anything gets done," he said when I cleared his dessert plate, wiping his hands on his jeans even though he had an unused napkin right there on the counter. "They're all wacked out on weed and oh, *Peace, dude-man.*" He flashed me a finger vee and an exaggerated goofy grin, curling his bottom lip under to look like he had buckteeth. "And the cops ride around on bicycles with flashing lights on their asses." He laughed hard and his face turned red. He was always too intense. "I guess if you want to rob a bank, do it in Ithaca."

So I feel like the sign for Ithaca is fate or something close to it. I don't have plans to rob a bank, but I did steal a car, and I'm pretty sure I can get away from a cop on a bike if I need to. Plus, if Gary hates Ithaca, I'm thinking I'll like it.

I follow the sign and make the turn. I was too nervous to pass anyone on the interstate, so I got stuck behind this truck going fifty for what seemed like forever. The road to Ithaca is full of curves and I can't see too far ahead because it's dark. I'm still only going fifty, but it feels fast. And since I have a destination, I'm not as antsy.

On the phone, Margo said that Dad and Irene hadn't quite put two and two together yet. Dad stopped by the motorhome after the boy's recital to make me apologize to Irene. He was so freaked when he found it trashed that he actually went inside the diner to ask Margo if she knew where I was, even though it's been seven years since the breakup and they hadn't said two polite words to each other that whole time.

When I called, Margo promised she'd talk to him. Tell him that he needed to let me go. That the car should be mine anyway and I've been taking care of myself for practically forever and sixteen and a half is almost eighteen and I just needed out and he owes me. She promised, and Margo doesn't make promises lightly. "I may be a lot of things," she told me once, when I asked her if I really looked okay in the homecoming dress I found at the rummage sale, "but I'm nothing if I'm not honest, girlie. I just don't see the point of telling it any way other than how it is."

• • •

I didn't think forty-one miles would be all that long, but following the twisting road makes me tired. I watch the miles tick by on the dashboard like it'll tell me something, but I didn't think to look when I started, so all I know is that I'm five miles farther than I was the last time I looked. My eyelids are heavy. I want to let them drop. Rest my eyes for a second. I give in once and instantly feel like they're glued shut. When I finally get them open, I'm all the way on the other side of the double yellow line. I yank the car back and almost go off the road. I have no problem keeping my eyes wide after that.

A sign says it's five miles to Ithaca, and then a few minutes later there's a campground. I'm too tired and broke to look for another option. I pull over at a hut by the entrance, but it's closed up and the lights are off. There's a sign on the door. I can't see what it says. When I get out to look, someone yells "Hey!" and I practically jump out of my boots.

In the moonlight, I can see a tall figure crossing the main road. "Too late for check-in," he says. His voice is deep and rough. I picture tobacco-stained sandpaper hands. The green glow of his watch shines suddenly, but not bright enough to see him any clearer. "Past midnight."

Behind him, there's a small cabin, lit up and

96

warm. I hadn't noticed it when I pulled in. I wonder if he was sleeping. Maybe those lights weren't on before.

"Sorry." My voice is thin. "Is there someplace else I can go?"

"This is the last campground open," he says, getting closer. I can see the outline of his face now. Long beard, furry hat. He turns to look behind him and I catch his profile—beak of a nose. "And we close for the season on Thursday."

"Please, is there any place I can go?"

"Ah, stay here." He yawns, belting out an arching sigh, stretching his arms in the air. "Bathrooms are open. Showers are coin-op. Any campsite. No one's here anyway. We can settle up tomorrow." He turns and walks toward the cabin without fanfare.

"Thank you!" I yell after him.

"Sleep tight," he yells back.

By the time I get in the car, the lights across the road have gone dark and I can only see the edges of the cabin because I know it's there.

I park at a site across from the bathroom. I'm feeling ambitious. Light a fire, craft a tent of some sort from the blankets I have. I keep the headlights on and search for sticks to toss in the fire ring, but in the shrubs there's a pair of eyes, reflecting green. My blood stops running. I tell myself it's just a raccoon or a possum. I try to stay calm. But twigs snap behind me. I scramble back to the car. Lock the doors and sit in the driver's seat very still, trying to watch the windshield and the rearview mirror at the same time, waiting for whatever was out there to get me. Nothing happens. Nothing at all. I yawn so hard it feels like my face could split in two. My eyes tear.

There's too much shit in the car for me to sleep on the back seat, so I crank the driver's seat down as far as I can, pull some sheets and blankets out, and try to get comfortable. I leave the headlights on until I'm almost asleep, fading in and out. My eyes jerk open a few times when I think I hear someone talking. I don't let myself imagine psycho killers with hook hands. It's raccoon chatter. It's just raccoon chatter, I know it.

When I do sleep, I dream about Matty. I'm hanging off a cliff. No rope, no sheets. I forgot my lifeline. He's reaching for me. My hand can't meet his. My fingers slip through soil, dirt falling in my face. I wake up screaming, body jolting against the seat like I'm landing hard.

After that, I can't fall back to sleep. I play a game with myself counting out the minutes, then turning the car on to see what time it actually is.

When I check the clock at 5:32, I'm seven minutes short. I turn the car off, start counting again, but next thing I know I'm waking up and it's bright and the windows are frosted inside and out. When I check the time, it's 8:30. I stumble from the car, bundled in blankets and sheets.

The campsite is dirty, littered with gum wrappers and burnt scraps of foil. There's a half-melted plastic produce container in the rusty fire ring. I walk to the end of the campsite to look down the path and there's the lake: about as blue as blue gets, banks lined with willow trees. Out a ways from shore, a layer of mist hangs above the water, thick enough to disappear in.

It's disorienting to see a lake where you didn't know there was one. I feel that strange false aftershock, like when a car accident almost happens, as if I could have walked into the water in the dark without noticing the cold lapping at my legs.

I cross the dirt road to the bathroom. My toes ache from being jammed in my boots all night. I was convinced something might give me reason to get out of the car and run. It's weird, the places your brain can go when you can't see what's around you. In the light, there's nothing scary about this campground. It's dirty and run down, but everything looks harmless.

The bathroom building smells like a swamp. There's no heat and it's not even closed off from outside. A screen just below the ceiling spans the length of each wall. My breath is thick in the air, like the cloud it forms could start to snow. I drop two quarters in the coin box for the shower and undress, hoping that by the time I'm ready to hop in, the water will be warm. Pipes whine and thump. The water is the color of rust and shoots from the showerhead in hard, progressively longer spurts. I stick my hand in to test for heat and it's like being pierced by a billion frozen pins. It takes a buck fifty in quarters to get the water to lukewarm. I jump in and lather up as fast as possible. My body is covered in goose bumps that don't go away even when the water turns all the way to burning hot. As soon as I get some good suds going in my hair, the water shuts off completely. Soap in my eyes and I can't find any more quarters in the change pile on the wooden bench. I throw in two dimes and a nickel, praying it will work, but I lose them to the shower gods. My teeth chatter. I sob. I worry the water will freeze in icicles on my body, so I wrap myself in the sheet and rinse my hair in the bathroom sink while I wait to run out of tears.

After I settle up with the park ranger for last night, I'm left with a hundred and fifty-eight dollars. If I know anything about money, it's that it runs out fast. To save gas, I walk to town from the campground. It takes a long time on sore feet, but I don't have anything else to do and I can't exactly go blowing money on sightseeing.

The houses on the way are old. Some of them have porches that sag, peeling paint, loose shingles, bedsheets or flags for curtains. But some are freshly painted with fancy wood trim that looks like bicycle spokes.

There's a dog on the porch of a house with a Grateful Dead flag in the front window. He isn't leashed. He looks like a pit bull and I start walking faster. I think about crossing the street, but I don't want him to chase me. I walk an even pace, pretending I'm calm. He barely raises his head to watch me.

The center of town is called Ithaca Commons and it's blocked off so it's just for people, not cars. The stores are painted bright colors like a village out of a movie. Like it might not be real.

I'm not sure what I'm looking for. Something cheap to eat, maybe a place to get warm for a while so I can plan my next move. There's a brick building that has DAIRY painted on the outside even though it's a bakery. I buy a donut and a cup of coffee from a lady with long white braids and take a seat at a wobbly table by the window.

The people who walk by just look different. They're wearing a lot of clothes. Layers and layers. Thick hand-knit hats with flaps that cover their ears, or they have hair like they just got out of bed. Corduroy pants cut up the seam and turned into bellbottoms with bright patchwork pieces. There's a man in a long skirt walking around like he's nothing out of the ordinary. I've never seen anything like it. *Freaking dirty hippies,* I think, smiling as I try to picture Gary walking around The Commons wearing a flowing skirt and his Harley jacket.

I eat my donut slow, breaking off teeny tiny pieces, chewing them down to mush before I swallow. After I drink half my coffee, I go back to the cream and sugar table and load the cup with cream so it'll last longer. I eat every last crumb of donut and wait for the final drop of coffee to roll down the seam of the paper cup into my mouth.

"Want a warm up to go?" the lady with the braids asks as I stand up and collect myself. "On the house." She holds the coffeepot above the counter.

"Thanks." I walk over with my cup. She takes it from me and pours until it's full.

"Cold for November," she says. "Stay warm, sweetie."

"You too," I say, taking the cup back from her carefully. I throw some more change in her tip cup. Now I'm down to a hundred and fifty-five dollars, but even when you don't have much, you always have to tip. Margo says there's no excuse.

I walk down one side of The Commons and up the other, looking in windows. There's a store-front full of shirts and bumper stickers that say things like ITHACA IS GORGES, MY KID BEAT UP YOUR HONOR STUDENT, and I NEED A MAN LIKE A 🐟 NEEDS A 🚲 . Another shop seems to sell nothing but silver rings and weird pipes made out of glass. There's a used bookstore and a place that sells old clothes—like Mrs. Ivory would wear—for a dollar a pound. There are bead curtains and cracked CDs hanging all over the place and one of the stores has the caterpillar from *Alice in Wonderland* painted on the glass. I wonder if this is what it feels like to go to Europe. It's a far cry from Little River.

I walk past a coffee shop that's dark inside even though it's open. Lit candles in glass cups line shelves on the walls. It looks like a cave. There's a HELP WANTED sign in the window.

— Chapter 8 —

U m, a girl here wants to help us," this blond guy yells toward the back room.

Everyone in Cafe Decadence looks at me. I stare at my boots, let my hair fall in my face. Long hair is like carrying a hiding place with you everywhere you go.

"Carly will be out in a sec," the guy tells me. His voice is low and dopey like a cartoon character. His hair has streaks that are almost white. No one is that sun-kissed in upstate New York in November. He looks like he should be someplace warm. California, Florida, Barbados. He should be surfing. He hasn't been in winter long enough to fade.

"Thanks," I say, but he's already taking an order. A woman in a lime green dress coat asks for something called a "half-caff soy mocha," and the blond guy knows what she's talking about.

I move to the side and try my best to look like I belong. There's a bulletin board on the wall covered with neon flyers. Voice lessons, dog walkers, tutors, auditions, roommate, new play, babysitter, anarchist book club—fringes of phone numbers cut at the bottom. There's even a personal ad, handwritten and photocopied. It says: *You want me. Your body knows. Heart will follow. NSWM. Agnostic. Bi. Let's explore your wildest fantasies and silliest whims. Must be open to anything; like Depeche Mode.* The picture is a naked man sitting the wrong way on a chair so the chair back covers his privates. He has chicken legs. He's wearing a black bowler hat; his eyes are rimmed with liner and there's a fat black tear drawn on his cheek. He's sticking out his tongue. It's long and pointy. One of the phone numbers is torn off. I don't know what *agnostic* means, but it sounds like some kind of weird sex thing. I can't imagine the person who not only looked at that picture and wanted to do agnostic things to this guy, but also had the courage to pull off the phone number in the middle of the coffee shop with everyone watching.

"Here about the job?"

I jump back, hoping what I was looking at isn't obvious. A short, skinny girl with spiky black and purple hair smiles at me. She has a ring in her nose, right in the middle like a bull, and holes in her earlobes filled with what look like tiny black tire rims.

"Yeah," I say, straightening up. "April."

I offer her my hand, and she shakes it. Her grip is weak, palm icy and damp.

"Carly. You done this before?" Her voice sounds scratchy, like she has a bad cold.

"Um, I waited tables for like five years." I try to look in her eyes, but it's impossible. There's too much else to look at. Tattooed blue wisps, like the tips of tentacles, creep from her shirt collar, reaching up the left side of her neck. "After school and stuff."

"Any experience as a barista?"

I shake my head. I don't even know what a barista is. "I'm quick to the uptake," I tell her. It's what Margo always said when she bragged about me to other people.

Carly sighs. "I was hoping for someone with experience." Her eye shadow matches the streaks in her hair. She looks back at the line of people. She's already done with me.

I will myself not to cry. Not to think about icy pin needle showers forever and ever.

"Thanks anyway," I say, head down, hair falling. Hoping to get to the door before I lose it.

"Hey, wait," Carly says. "Going home for Thanksgiving?"

"No."

"Well, there you go. You're hired." She laughs and it's this weird little cackle that reminds me of stepping on dry leaves. "Everyone and their roommate will be out of town that whole fucking week. If you can work through break, I'll train you myself."

"Thank you," I say, trying not to smile too wide.

"Can you start tomorrow?"

"Sure."

"Come in after the morning rush. Ten thirty. Half pay for training. Once I don't have to hold your hand, it's five fifty an hour, shift meals, and your cut of the tip jar at the end of the week. Okay?"

I nod.

Carly hands me a piece of paper. "Fill this out and give it to Bodie when you're done," she says, pointing to the blond guy.

"Thank you."

"Ten thirty," she says, and walks into the back room without saying goodbye.

I can't fill out half the form. I don't have an address. I don't have a phone. I don't even know which street the campground is on. I write my name, and then, under work experience, I write *Waitress, Margo's Diner, Little River, NY, 1990–94*. It's the only thing about me that's still true.

— Chapter 9 —

There are two more nights before the campground closes. I think maybe I should pull a few numbers from the roommate ads on the bulletin board, but who's going to take in some girl with nothing but a car full of crap and a dwindling wad of crumpled dollar bills to her name?

I wander around town looking in store windows, hoping an answer will come to me. Just outside The Commons there's a tall brick building that reminds me of my high school and would seem just as menacing, except there's a guitar store on the first floor with a big shiny window to show off the beautiful curves of rows of guitars hanging on the walls.

I'm not used to seeing stores for just one specific thing you wouldn't starve without. Even the auto parts store in Little River sells livestock feed and canned goods too. It feels like I'm starving without a guitar. If I still had mine, I wouldn't notice the cold in the campground and I wouldn't feel hungry right now. I could play until my fingers throbbed and then walk around with fresh indents in my calluses to help me remember that the world can disappear and I can float in sound and breath and nothing else has to matter.

There's a twelve-string acoustic hanging front and center in the window. The finish looks silky, not shiny like mine was, and I can tell even through the glass that it would feel nice to hold. Set into the neck are pearly bits carved into flowers and leaves and a squawking bird. A white paper price tag hangs from one of the tuning pegs, spinning in an air current, not easy to see. I don't know how much a guitar costs, but I know I don't have guitar money. My dad bought the one he gave me when he was seventeen. When I was a kid, before it was mine, every time he lifted that guitar from the case, he'd strum it and smile. "That's why you spring for the big guns, Ape. That's why." He saved summer construction job money for two years to buy it. I step closer to the window, tip my head, squint hard, and manage to see *$1,849* handwritten in pencil before the tag spins away again. If I added up all the money I've made in my whole life, I don't think it would be eighteen hundred and forty-nine dollars.

A man with a bushy black beard walks up to the guitar and waves at me through the window. "Come in! Come in!" His voice is booming, even though it's muffled by the glass.

I turn away, pretend I haven't seen him. Walk fast, head down, as if just looking was a crime. Like my need for that guitar could ooze through my skin and melt the sidewalk. I rub my thumb and ring finger together to feel the callus that will wear away soon. When it's gone, there won't be anything about me that's special anymore.

My face hurts from the cold. I press my palm to my nose to warm it, but my hands are freezing too. I walk to Woolworth's and order a pretzel and a cup of hot water at the lunch counter so I can thaw out before I walk back to the campground. I eat the pretzel slowly, taking tiny bites, chewing carefully. It reminds me of Margo. I lick my thumb and use it to pick up the big white chunks of salt left on the paper plate. After I get every last one, I pick a quarter from the change on the counter, leave the rest for tip.

I call from the pay phone outside. She picks up on the first ring.

"Margo's Diner, today's special is chili con carne."

I don't make a sound.

"Where are you?" she asks.

"Can't say."

"Hon, you can trust me."

"You can't feel bad about not telling people what you don't know anyway," I say, because I've seen the toll it takes on her when she can't tell the truth about important things.

"You're safe? Ten fingers, ten toes? Not sleeping on the street?"

"I'm fine." There's a row of chewed up gum along the top of the phone. The wads are different sizes, but they're lined up perfectly. Pink, white, green, yellow, blue. I wonder who put them there—if it was one person or a group effort.

Margo sighs like there's air leaking from her tires. "You're making me prematurely grey, girlie," she says.

I don't know how Margo would ever know if she does go grey. She's been dyeing her hair Cinnamon Red Hot for as long as I've known her. But I still feel bad. I can picture the worry crease she gets between her eyebrows before one of her sick headaches sets in.

"Did you talk to him?" I ask.

"Haven't worn him down all the way yet." She sighs. "He says if you bring the car back by the weekend he won't file a report. Bought you a little time, at least."

"You know I won't be back by the weekend."

"Gary's gonna talk to him. Thinks it's a man-to-man thing. Gary's pulling for you too, you know. Says if he had a daughter he wouldn't give her reason to run off in the first place."

"Thanks."

"Saw that Matty Spencer. He made me promise if I talked to you I would say to call."

My heart beats crazy when I think about Matty. I don't say anything.

"He's walking around like someone pumped his puppy full of buckshot," Margo says, clucking her tongue. She starts to say something, but stops and takes a deep breath instead. "You won't call him, will you?"

"Don't think so." My nose stings. The phone crackles and a voice tells me to deposit ten cents to keep talking. I only have a few pennies in my pocket.

"I have to go," I say. "No change."

Margo says, "You call me. Promise you—" before the connection drops.

I keep the phone to my ear for a little while longer and pretend she's still on the line telling me about the new beer Gary is serving, or how someone accidentally put a tomato on Ida Winton's sandwich and she freaked out again right in the middle of the diner.

There's a phone book on a shelf under the booth. I hang up and check for Sawicki, just in case. Find an Alice, a Paul, and a D. Sawick, but no Autumn. I look up her maiden name, but it's Johnson. There are like seventy million A. Johnsons, and again no Autumn. This is just one phone book in one city. There are millions of phone books and she could be anywhere. She could be married again with a new name, maybe even a new daughter, and it occurs to me that I'll probably never see her again. Good thing I don't want to anyway.

On the walk back to the campground, I count out of state license plates to pass the time. Two from Pennsylvania. One from Michigan.

Vermont. Texas. New Mexico. Massachusetts. Ithaca College stickers in back windows. I wonder what it would be like to have your mom and dad pack up your car and send you off to college, ship you packages of cookies through the mail. Ask about your grades and threaten to pull your allowance for making C's. That actually happens to real people. To these people. It isn't only something you see on TV. These kids aren't looking for their moms in a phone book.

I pass a driveway with a kit car under a carport, covered in a tarp—the way Gary stored his for winter—and all of a sudden, I realize how I can buy time with Mrs. Ivory's car.

— Chapter 10 —

I walk around the campground looking for left-over wood to build a fire. I'm all alone and even though I know people just moved on into winter, it feels like the end of the world or a bomb went off and everyone knew to take cover except me.

The things people leave behind are strange. There's an assortment of forgettable junk: hair clips, condom wrappers, bottle caps, crushed soda cans. But then there are accidentals, things that had people saying "Oh shit!" when they were halfway home. Or maybe they were just missing something, left with a vague idea they'd find it eventually under that pile of mail or in the junk drawer. Eyeglasses, a cheap charm bracelet with greening silver charms (coffee cup, teddy bear, airplane, shooting star, four-leaf clover), a set of keys looped on a soggy rabbit's foot, a screwdriver with *R.S.* carved into the sweat-stained wood handle. I wonder if any of the owners were happy to lose their stuff, wallowing in the freedom of leaving it behind, a chance to get glasses that don't have brown plastic frames.

I find more than enough firewood. At one site, someone left half a bundle when they cleared out. I try to use the cigarette lighter from the car to light it, but the wood sizzles and won't catch. I eat the rest of the cookies from Irene's apartment and sit in my car, wrapped in sheets like a mummy to stay warm, waiting for dark.

The sun is at the horizon when my eyes get heavy, and then when I wake up, it's the darkest dark I've ever seen and my hands are so cold I can barely move my fingers. I feel like the cold has seeped into my bones and will never go away.

Margo went through this phase where she believed in visualizing what you want. She had a series of cassette tapes that talked about holding pictures in your mind until they become reality. I try to think warm, picturing a hot sun melting away icicles that are stuck in my bones like pushpins, the melted water dripping into a warm bath, steam opening my pores. I try hard. It's clear in my mind, but the cold won't let go.

I fumble around for my flashlight and pull every warm piece of clothing I can from the back seat. Then I head out with R.S.'s screwdriver in my bag, bundled in so many layers I can barely bend my arms at the elbows.

At ten thirty in Little River, things are dying down. Gary's Tap Room is the one place still open and even the crowd there will start to grumble about getting home. Only hardcore loyals stay until midnight, when Gary closes.

Ithaca is alive. People on porches smoking. Music leaks from open doors. Bob Marley,

Grateful Dead, and that Chili Pepper band Matty's cousin from New York City taped for him off the radio, all swirl together, making a big stew of sound. I have to walk right past the kit car house. I can't follow through with my plan until everyone goes to bed, so I wander up one street, down the next, looking in lit up living rooms from the sidewalk like I'm window-shopping for people.

There's a girl perfectly framed in one window, holding a red plastic cup and spinning around. Her long hair flares like a skirt. There's just enough light from the flickering porch lamp that I can see a guy out there smoking, staring at her through the glass as if she's magic. She has no idea he's watching her. She throws one arm into the air and spins faster, finally collapsing on a couch in front of the window. The smoking guy moves away like he doesn't want to get caught.

In another window, kids crowd around a ping-pong table bouncing a ball into plastic cups. No one has any paddles. I watch until my teeth chatter, then I get moving so I don't freeze.

Three houses down, the porch is packed with people and as I walk past, a shirtless guy yells, "Hey, you!"

I look back.

"Yeah, you!" His hairless chest is splotchy red from the cold. "I know you. Girl from lit class! I know you."

"I don't think . . ." I struggle for words. I felt invisible and it seems wrong that he can see me.

He jumps over the porch railing and stands really close to me. He has a round face and cheeks that are too chubby for the rest of him. A mane of shaggy hair like a lion. "Margaret, right?"

"April," I say.

"Yeah, yeah, April. April," Lion Boy says like he's stuck on the word. "April. April from lit class." He stares hard and I worry he might kiss me. "Have a beer!" He pushes his cup into my hand.

His buddy jumps down next to him. Bare-chested too, shirt tied around his head like a turban. "Who'd you give your beer to, man?"

"Dude! This is April from lit class," Lion Boy tells him, pointing at me like his friend wouldn't know who he was talking about otherwise.

"Girls like their own beers," the turban guy says with a smirk that gives him dimples. "Get April from lit class her own beer. She doesn't want your cooties."

"April," Lion Boy says, grabbing my arm, "I'll get you your own beer."

I know this is stupid and I don't even like beer, but I'm cold and hungry and lonely and they think I belong, so I let Lion Boy lead me into the house. I don't want to be one of those girls who ends up duct taped to a chair in someone's basement like in the articles Margo clips for me. She always says she worries no one taught me to be wary of people in the right way, but I don't think Lion Boy and his friends count. They're not even adults.

It's warm inside. Stuffy from too many people breathing in too small a space, but I don't care. I have hope of being able to feel my face again. There are broken hockey sticks mounted on the walls, crisscrossed like those swords you see over a fireplace in movies about British people. The couch is covered in NHL bedsheets, and someone is burning incense that smells like dirty feet.

Lion Boy lets go of my arm and I follow him to the kitchen. He pumps the keg and fumbles for a cup. While he's pouring, I survey. Most of the people in the living room are guys, big ones with dopey drunk beer faces who spit when they talk. There's a group of five girls in the corner looking around, giggling like they are among gods. Another one wears a short jean skirt and a shirt that shows her whole belly. She tries to wrap herself around a guy who is too busy cheering on an arm wrestling match across the room to pay her much notice. Other than those girls, it's what Margo would call a sausage party, but they all seem harmless enough.

"Here, April from lit class," Lion Boy says, thrusting a beer into my hand. It's green-tinged and sloshes over the sides of the cup onto my boots. "Oh god! I spilled on you! I spilled on you, April! I'm sorry." He pulls a grimy towel from the fridge handle, bending to wipe my boots.

"No prob," I say, thinking I should shed a few shirts and try to fit in. Lion Boy is too drunk to notice, but the girls in the corner are eyeing me like they think I smell bad.

I wriggle out of two layers of flannel, tie them around my waist, and lean against the wall so I can keep a good eye on the kitchen and the living room. I am trying my best to look like I don't give a crap about anything.

When Lion Boy is done with the towel, he loops it back over the fridge handle and pours another beer. He rests his arm behind me on the wall and leans in. His breath smells sharp.

"Why is it green?" I ask, taking a sip of beer to keep Lion Boy from getting too close. It tastes like what my father would describe as "stale piss water," although, who's going around drinking piss water to compare?

"Huh?" Lion Boy says, eyes half-closed.

"The beer? It's green?"

His face lights up. "It's a Seuss party."

I raise one eyebrow, which is better than saying anything in most situations.

"You know," he says, "like Dr. Seuss? *Green Eggs and Ham*?" He pats his head. "Wait!" He hands me his beer and runs to the living room.

119

Fishing under coats on the couch, he finds a tall red and white striped fuzzy hat and pulls it on his head. The girls in the corner laugh.

"Yeah? Yeah? Like it?" he says, taking a minute to bob to the music, a song about ants marching around, before he struts back to the kitchen. "Green beer and ham! Aw, yeah." He grins, nodding like he approves of himself.

I smile because I feel like I'm supposed to. I wonder why we always thought kids who went to college were magically cool.

"So, you're all like grunge and shit, huh?" he says, leaning into me again. He's still not wearing a shirt and his armpits don't smell great. He's like radiating heat.

"Sure," I say, nursing my beer.

That's the end of our conversation for a good ten minutes. He stands and bobs to the music, fighting to keep his eyelids from slamming shut, the stupid hat still nesting in his curls. I watch the girls in the living room. I don't understand the way they act like these boys are another species. They're just boys. They aren't worth all the giggling and lip gloss.

I ask to use the bathroom. Lion Boy breathes in hard through his nose and opens his eyes wide like he's waking up.

"Okay, so you go up the stairs and then you make a—" He holds his hands up, trying to figure out which is right and which is left. "I'll show you." He grabs my hand, threading his sweaty fingers between mine, and leads me across the living room. We walk up creaky, crooked steps. It's the second door on the left.

I close the door behind me and have to push hard to get it to stay shut. There are porno mags on the back of the toilet and a hair clog in the bathtub drain so big it looks like it could grow legs and run away if it wanted to. I pee hovering as far above the seat as possible and wash my hands with hot, hot water. I wish I could run every part of me under hot water. I'm still not thawed.

When I open the door, the room across the hall is open. There's a black light and someone painted a drippy skull and crossbones on the wall with Tide so it glows. Lion Boy sits on the bed strumming an electric guitar that isn't plugged in. Thin metal chords sound vaguely like *November Rain*.

"You play?" I say.

"Yeah, you?"

"A little."

He's wearing a shirt now. A white one with a face on it that looks kind of like one of the statues from Easter Island. The stupid Seuss hat is on the bed next to him. He hands the guitar over. "Play something," he says. Suddenly he doesn't seem like such a lame-ass bonehead. He plugs the guitar into a small amp and turns the volume down.

I've never played an electric. The strings are thicker and feel like they will leave my fingers bruised, but I don't mind. I play the song I wrote about my dad, the angry one, and I almost cry, but I don't. I bite my cheek and strum hard like it's just part of the song, until I can pull it together and sing again. I don't care that Lion Boy is watching; it feels like being me to play this guitar. I finish the song and he asks me to play another one. I play *Lay Lady Lay*.

"Did you write that too?" he asks when I'm done.

"Dylan did," I say, laughing.

"Does he go here?"

"He's in our lit class," I say, because I don't know how to explain Dylan to someone who doesn't know.

Lion Boy slides his fingers under my hair and kisses me. I don't even know his name. His mouth tastes like sour beer and something burnt, but it's actually kind of nice to be kissed. He grabs the guitar from me and lays it in its case. We lie on his bed and kiss for ages. It takes him forever to work through all my layers of clothes. It's hot and sweaty and my skin sticks to his. He falls asleep before we really do anything. We're just lying there in our underwear groping each other and he drifts off, lips still pursed, arm over my waist. He snores a little, wrinkles his nose a few times. He looks so peaceful. I don't think I've ever felt that peaceful in my life.

When I'm sure he's not going to wake up, I lift his arm and sneak out from under it. I throw clothes on and sprint to the bathroom. On the way, I peek down the stairs. Everyone is gone except for the girl in the belly shirt and her boyfriend. He's holding his hand to his forehead. She's crying hard.

I decide I can probably get away with a shower. I wad up like twenty sheets of toilet paper to remove the hair from the drain. I make the water so hot that my skin feels like it'll burn up and peel off. Use someone's Head & Shoulders and wash the bar of soap hard before sudsing up my body. When I'm done, I realize that touching any towel in the bathroom will interfere with my clean state, so I use one of my flannel shirts instead. I poke around and find a hair dryer under the sink. Use my fingers as a brush and do the best I can to untangle all the knots and blow my hair out straight, so it won't look messy in the morning.

Lion Boy is snoring away when I get back to his room. I layer on the rest of my clothes, leaving my wet shirt hanging over his desk chair. There are two rolls of quarters on his desk. I take one, telling myself it's fair payment for the shirt. His guitar is just lying there in its case, shiny and clean. Can't be more than a few years old, so there's no great history. But you can't do that.

You don't take someone else's guitar. It's like a code.

When I walk downstairs, the fighting couple is gone. I dig my screwdriver out of my bag so I won't have to fumble for it in the dark, snake it up my shirtsleeve, and slip out the door.

— Chapter 11 —

The screws on the license plate are rusty. I can't see well, but I smell the breakdown of old metal and feel rust in the way they turn. It makes me think of pulling nails from scrap wood with my dad, back when he had illusions of building us that house. He'd yell at me if I bent the nails too much so they broke before they came out of the boards. And I remember that he didn't yell at me when I stepped on one. It went right through the sole of my old ripped sneakers into the middle of my foot. It hurt so bad I stopped feeling the pain. I tried to hide it, because I thought he'd be mad and scream something like *Damn it, Ape! We'll never get this house finished if you don't stop fucking around!* But the blood soaked through my sneaker and it was impossible to hide. My dad turned white when he noticed. We couldn't get my shoe off because the nail was still stuck in my foot and neither of us could stomach the pull, so he scooped me up in his arms and we went to the ER.

When he carried me in through the automatic doors, everyone in the waiting room looked at us, and I felt more important than I ever have otherwise. The tetanus shot hurt like hell, but my dad held my hand, and the nurse gave me apple juice and way more tissues than I actually needed. That night, my dad tucked me in and checked my bandage, smoothed my hair, and played Cat Stevens songs on his guitar until I fell asleep.

I hum *Wild World* under my breath while I work the second screw. When I get to the chorus, I whisper the words to myself because they're the only lyrics I remember. My hands are raw. R.S.'s screwdriver sucks ass. The metal part is bent at a funny angle and the handle is full of splinters.

I get the third screw out, but the plate sticks in place. When I rest the screw on the ground, the plate swings down and splits my knuckles open. My whole hand throbs, but I keep going like it didn't even happen. I can't stop now, and I need both hands to get the last screw to turn. By the time I'm done with the front license plate and move to the back one, my fingers are sticky.

I take off a flannel, use it to wrap my hand, and work the screws on the back plate hard to get the job done fast. I'm careful to use my good hand to pull the car cover down as far as it will go, so no one will notice what I've done.

When I walk back to the campground with the icy plates stuck under my shirt, I have a lump in my throat that feels like it could kill me. For once, I wish I could cry, but it's just not happening. The pain in my hand is so far beyond tears.

I do the best I can to clean the wound in the campground bathroom, ripping strips from the boy's sheets for bandages. Then I get back to work before my fingers can stiffen, swapping the plates on my car. I hide the old ones with the spare tire in the trunk and vow that I'll put everything right again as soon as I can.

Chapter 12

When I wake up, there's a note on my windshield. A blue half sheet of paper stuck under the wiper right in front of my face, reminding me that I have to leave tomorrow. It freaks me out to no end that the campground guy came over and put it there while I was sleeping. I didn't wake up and he didn't think to knock on the window or announce himself or cough or anything. I wonder if he watched me sleep. I wonder if he got something out of watching me sleep. Like those businessmen Matty told me about who buy dirty underwear, or the agnostic guy on the flyer at Cafe Decadence. I suppose if you have a thing for watching people sleep, working at a campground is a good place to get your rocks off. To each his own, as Margo would say. And I don't guess anyone ever got hurt from someone just watching them.

I walk to the bathroom, relieved I don't have to get in that awful shower, but when I catch myself in the mirror, I scare the shit out of me. Blood, streaked down my cheek, wiped along my jaw. I must have slept on my hand. I bled through the sheet strips. I do the best I can to clean my face with freezing sink water and realize that I can't exactly go serving people at a coffee shop with a horror movie bloody stump.

Back in the car, I wriggle into my cleanest flannel, pull Margo's hand-me-down leopard-print leggings on under my long skirt for extra warmth, and gather my hair into the most professional ponytail I can manage with one hand. I wrap a new strip of sheet around my knuckles and walk into town, even though it's only eight a.m. and I don't have to be at work until ten thirty.

I stop at the pharmacy, buy a bottle of peroxide and a roll of gauze, and take care of my hand in the employee bathroom. Then I go to a funny little shop that sells bulky sweaters and blow eight bucks on fingerless gloves to hide the bandage. They smell like incense even after I've left the store. I wonder if anything in Ithaca just smells like normal, or dryer sheets, or nothing.

Even if they pay me today and have hours for me tomorrow, which isn't likely, there's no way I'm going to be able to find a place to live by tomorrow night. But I can't think of other options, so I go to work and hope for an opportunity to present itself.

There's a long line at the cafe when I get there. I walk up to the counter and Carly stares at me with narrowed eyes, like she's considering telling me I need to wait my turn.

"April," I say. "You hired me."

"Right, right." She nods. "Come on back." She points at a customer, a guy with a brown corduroy cap like old fashioned newspaper boys wore. "You're up." She takes his travel mug and starts making his order immediately, leaving me to figure out how to get behind the counter on my own.

There's a plank door thingy where the counter meets the wall, like at Gary's bar. You're supposed to lift it to pass, but this one is piled high with coffee mugs, so I duck under, as low as I can, staying hunched a little longer than I need to because I have visions of sending the mugs flying.

I clear it, stand, and play with a loose thread on my glove while Carly makes the coffee machine hiss and spit.

"You're short on details," Carly says, and I can't tell if she's talking to the customer.

"Me?" I ask.

She nods. "No address, no phone."

"I'm new," I say. "I don't have everything figured out yet."

"Let me know when you do." She gives me a hard stare like my math teacher would when I told her I did my homework, but my dad spilled his beer all over it.

Carly is wearing a blood-red velvet beret, a navy nylon dress like something Mary Tyler

Moore would wear, torn fishnets, and combat boots. The points of her blue inked tendrils peek out from the high neckline of her dress. I wonder what they are. Moonbeams? Snakes? Octopus arms?

She shouts, "Half-caff hazelnut cap," and hands the travel mug back to the newsboy man. "You know how to use a cash register?" she asks. It takes me a sec again to realize she's asking me and not him.

I nod.

"It's two seventy-five," she says. "Ring him up."

I don't understand how that cup of coffee could possibly cost two dollars more than a regular cup of coffee, but no one else seems to think it's a problem. The customer hands me a five, and I thank the gods of new jobs or coffee or whatever, that this register is the same as Margo's.

"Do me a favor," Carly says. She's already on the next order. "Take those mugs to the kitchen, and while you're there, stick your head outside to tell Bodie his break is over. Tell him I said to stop smoking up and get his ass in here."

I duck under the plank and grab as many spent coffee cups as I can. There are piles of dirty dishes by the sink, so I put them wherever I find space.

Outside, the blond guy who was behind the counter yesterday is leaning against the wall, balanced on one foot, smoking a small squat cigarette. He's not wearing a jacket and he doesn't look cold. He's sunshine. His blond stubble catches the light and makes it look like his face is glowing.

"You're that girl who wants to help," he says, taking a deep drag, holding his breath before he lets it out. The smoke smells like a dead skunk and reminds me of Lion Boy. My face flushes.

"Bodie?" I say.

"Yeah." He sighs. "Let me guess. Carly wants me to get my ass in there."

"Pretty much."

"April," he says, smiling so wide that his eyes turn to slits like a cat. "That's your name, right?"

"Yeah."

He takes another drag. "April showers bring May flowers, but what do Mayflowers bring?"

"Huh?"

"Pilgrims, man." His top lip all but disappears when he smiles. "Pilgrims." He stubs his cigarette on the bottom of his shoe, pats me on the back, and says, "Let's go before Carly's head like totally explodes."

I take my first break at one. Carly sends me to the kitchen to tell Bodie what I want for lunch and says I can eat up front if I promise to be chatty with the customers, because that's what

132

they're going for. Everybody knows your name and whatnot.

Bodie makes me a turkey sandwich, snacking on potato chips as he piles them on my plate.

"Onward, Pilgrim," he says, handing me the sandwich. He leads with his chin when he smiles and even though he's got this perfectly chiseled face, he still manages to look dopey.

I carry my plate and a plain cup of coffee to a table in the corner. The sandwich has green mushy stuff on it, and Bodie made it, so I'm skeptical, but it's actually really good. Maybe it's just because I'm so hungry for real food, or maybe it's that guys make better sandwiches because they aren't dainty about it.

I'm so focused on chewing, on the taste of food, I don't even look out the window. I'm just eating.

"This seat taken?"

I jump. My knees hit the table and I spill my coffee. It's the guy with the newsboy cap from this morning. He has a bowl of soup in one hand and his coffee mug in the other.

"I'm sorry," he says. "I didn't mean to scare you." He puts his bowl down, pulls a napkin from the table stand and wipes up my coffee. "I'll get you a refill."

"It's fine," I say. "I'm too wired anyway."

"Okay if I sit?"

I want to tell him that I'd rather he didn't

because I'm having an intimate moment with my sandwich, but I remember what Carly said about being chatty, so I say, "Fine by me," in as friendly a voice as I can muster.

"Adam Jergens," he says, offering his hand.

I wipe my fingers on my skirt and shake. "April." There's no need to get into last names.

"First day, huh?" Adam says, plunging a spoon into his soup. He holds it to his mouth, making tiny waves as he blows.

"Yep." I'm not trying to be rude, I just can't think of anything to say to him. He's not a student. He's old. Like maybe thirty. I feel like I'm in over my head talking to Bodie and Carly, so this is just too much. He's not old like Margo, where it's easier to talk to her because she's old. He's like that in-between old, where I'm sure he thinks he was just my age not long ago.

"Are you a townie or a student? I haven't seen you around before." He eats another spoonful of soup without blowing on it. No slurping whatsoever.

"Neither. Just got here," I say, wishing I could figure out how to speak full sentences again.

"It's a hard place to leave," Adam says. "I came for school. Tried moving back to Boston after I finished undergrad, but the world doesn't seem as right anyplace else."

"It's nice here." I take a huge bite of my sandwich.

"Where you staying?"

I hold my finger up while I chew, but the bread is dense and crusty and the wait for words gets ridiculous. "Here and there," I say finally, even though I still have food in my mouth. Margo would totally yell at me.

He laughs. "You're into specifics."

"Campground," I blurt out, despite the fact that I meant to keep that information classified.

"Brave girl! You must be freezing."

"I do okay," I say.

"I'm sure you do," he says, smiling. His teeth are too small, so it looks like he has too many of them. He's not much bigger than me. His cheeks are round and flushed and he has a little button nose. His hat is probably covering a receding hairline and his eyes have the faint start of the kind of crinkles Margo calls crow's toes. I had this book about Santa Claus as a kid, and Adam looks like one of his elves, the one who wasn't good at making toys and had mismatched shoes.

"Well, I tell you what," Adam says, "they know me here. They'll vouch for me. I'm safe." He digs his wallet out of his back pocket and fiddles through some business cards until he finds the one he's looking for. He pulls a pen from his shirt pocket, writes a number on the back. "You get too cold at the campground, you call me."

I want to jump at the chance to take another warm shower and sleep on a couch in an actual building with actual heat, but something about Adam saying he's safe makes me worry he's not. My dad always says anytime someone offers you something you have to figure out what's in it for them. I don't think Adam could be in it for whatever free coffee I could pass his way, so it's exactly the kind of situation Margo would warn me about.

Adam holds the card out, but I don't take it, so he kinda shakes it—the way you jog a fishing lure—until I do.

"Why would you . . ."

"I know what it's like to be your age," Adam says. "I wouldn't go back if you paid me."

I tuck the card in the band of my skirt without looking at it. Mumble, "Thanks," to be polite, but set in my head that his place is not an option.

I think about dropping hints to Bodie that I need a couch to crash on. Maybe just asking if he knows someone who needs a roommate or where there's a cheap hotel or rooms for rent. Not coming right out and saying "Can I stay with you?" because that would be needy and gross, but giving him the opportunity to offer. Except every time I get close to Bodie to start a conversation, he nods or winks, or gives me that chin-first smile, and I clam up. I practice what I should say in my head while I wipe down tables, settling on: *So, I need a place to crash for a few days while I find new digs. Any idea where to look?* I get to the point where I'm pretty sure when I say it out loud, I can make it sound like something I just thought of. But by the time I work up the right resolve and Carly sends me to the kitchen with dirty dishes, Bodie is gone.

Some guy with curly red hair, a backwards baseball cap, and total pizza face is hacking at a head of iceberg lettuce with a cleaver, yelling "Ha!" with every slice, dumping the remains into a bin on the sandwich prep station.

I don't introduce myself, and he doesn't bother looking up. I put the dishes on the counter and walk out. As the door closes behind me, I hear the sharp smack of the cleaver against the cutting board again, and he yells, "Take that, motherfucka!"

— Chapter 13 —

K nowing I could be warm on a couch at Adam's place makes it that much colder at the campground. In elementary school they taught us about stranger danger, but what if hypothermia is a possibility, and the stranger has a warm place to stay?

I start my car and let it run with the heat full blast until it's so warm I can hardly breathe. Then I turn it off and sleep until I wake up shivering again.

That business card in my bag, tucked in the inside pocket so it won't get lost—the thought of it makes my teeth itch. At least if I was duct taped to a chair in Adam's basement I'd be warmer than I am now. I think about calling from the pay phone by the bathrooms. Instead, I start the car again. Soon as the air turns warm, I put my hands in front of the vent. Hold them there until I feel like they might burn.

When I wake up, the campground man, with his flappy hat and ruddy beard, is watching me through a clear spot the sun melted in the ice on the windshield. My heart jolts. I reach over to make sure the door is locked. The guy taps the window, his finger cracked and yellowed. With his other hand, he slaps a piece of paper on the glass, writing side down, so I can read what it says: *Car out 9 AM.*

His eyes are the exact same grey-blue as the sky behind him.

I nod.

He crumples the paper, jams it in the pocket of his jeans as he walks away.

It's too cold to even think about using that shower. I run to the bathroom to pee, brush my hair and teeth, and change my bandage. The cut across my knuckles is starting to scab, but it's still pretty grisly. At least it's not red and puffy. According to Margo, when she used to check my scraped-up knees, that's the sign of infection you have to watch for. She knows all that stuff because her mother was a nurse.

I don't have anything to pack up from the campground, because I've slept in my car the whole time, but it's strange to just go. I feel like I should take something or leave something. Like this was my first home away from the motorhome and there should be a gesture about that. I choose a stone from the fire ring. It's smooth and grey, charred on one side. It smells like a campfire, and I wish I'd made one while I was here. I drop the stone in the well of the car door and drive away.

About a mile from downtown, I park my car on a side street, outside a house with a rainbow flag hanging from the front porch. I scoped it out the day before and all the parking spaces close to downtown are pay ones, or else there's a time limit. But here it's free, I just have to move to the other side of the street before morning.

Sometimes I get words stuck in my head, circling until they sort themselves out and play in my mind like a song. On the walk into work, I think, *Where you gonna stay, where you gonna stay, where you gonna stay whereyougonnastay,* over and over in time with my footsteps. I try not to think it, but the second I stop fighting to keep the words from my brain, they sneak back.

I like working and I'm good at it. I love the order of everything—that there's a stack of coffee cups right next to the machines, and a bin for silverware, and a station just for sugar and cream. It's not the same as Margo's Diner, but it's familiar. As long as I'm foaming milk or running dishes, I can forget the workday will end. And I'm proud when Carly looks at me in the middle of the afternoon rush and says, "I don't know what I'd do without you." It's only my second day.

Adam doesn't come in even though he said he was a regular. I wonder if he isn't—if they don't actually know him at Decadence and he's not safe. I wonder if he's mad I didn't call. Insulted

I'd rather sleep at the campground. I wonder if he even remembers he gave me his number.

My shift is done at three, but the girl who was supposed to take over for me calls at 2:45 to say she has a psych exam and can't come.

"Rich bitch," Carly mumbles. "Some people only work because Mommy and Daddy don't send enough beer money." She looks at me. Presses her hands together like she's praying and says, "Please, April, can you stay?"

Of course, I say yes. Warmth, another shift meal, as much coffee as I can drink, and a bathroom. The excuse to stay is even better than the extra money.

The sun is low in the sky when Adam shows up. He's with a woman. Her hair is bouncy and shiny. She doesn't look like she has any makeup on her face except for bright red lipstick that turns her mouth into a Valentine. She's very tall and wears a black coat that buttons all the way up to her neck and goes almost to her feet. It hugs her waist and she's impossibly skinny, like you can't believe her stomach and intestines and all the other stuff that makes a person could actually fit in the tiny space of her. And I can't quite figure out why, but I'm jealous. I guess I wanted Adam to be a lonely guy who was waiting for me to call, but here he is with this woman who looks like an old fashioned movie star. He wasn't waiting on me last night.

They stand away from the counter. He leans in to talk to her. She looks at the menu on the wall and puts her hand on his arm as she tells him something. I can't hear what they say, because Carly is blasting this CD that sounds like a dead cat wailing. The woman takes off her coat and sits at the table in the window, the one where Adam and I sat yesterday.

Adam comes up to the register. "Braved the campground?" he asks, and I wish he wouldn't say it so loud because I don't want Carly to find out. Luckily, Carly is in her own little world, hunched over the counter as she works out the schedule for next week, nodding her head to the music like she agrees with it completely. Adam orders a black coffee, handing over his travel mug, and then a skim latte. I make the latte with two percent.

I try not to watch them, but I can't help it. When Adam brings the movie star woman her coffee she flashes him a megawatt smile and takes the mug with both hands like the latte is a precious gift. Their fingers touch. He likes that. I can tell. He sits at the table. They pull notebooks from their bags, pointing to each other's pages with their pens, scribbling and comparing. Eventually they lose interest in their work, chatting and laughing until the sky outside is solid dark and people start ordering food again.

Some guy orders the sandwich special and

I have to run to the kitchen to give the Lettuce Murderer the slip. We still haven't said two words to each other. I should probably introduce myself, but he's washing dishes and I want to watch Adam and that lady, so I just yell, "Order up!" hit the bell, and get myself out front as fast as I can. "I'll call your name when it's ready," I say to the guy who placed the order, and then I look over at the table and she's gone. Adam is sitting alone, his notebook open again. At first I think maybe she's just in the bathroom, but her coat is gone too.

Carly goes out back to smoke. I grab a pot of coffee and duck under the counter to give Adam a refill, like I've seen Carly do with the guys who drink drip.

"Thanks, kiddo," Adam says, and I hate him for calling me kiddo.

"Hot date?" I ask, like a new nerve has suddenly sprouted in my body.

Adam gives me a total *as if* look. The way my face would be if someone asked me the same thing about Bodie. It scares me that you can get to be an adult and still feel that way.

"Anna's a client," Adam says. "I'm working on a design for her."

I nod. Am I supposed to ask for what? Am I supposed to already know? I never read his business card. I knew if I let myself look at it, I'd call.

My wrist hurts, but I can't switch hands because the other one is all cut up. I rest the coffeepot on the very edge of the table. I don't think it will burn the wood, but I don't want to risk setting it down completely.

"Should I put clean sheets on the futon?" Adam asks, and I think I wanted him to ask that. I think that's why I haven't spent my day in a scramble about where I'll stay tonight, but now that he's asked, my stomach feels twisted and turned around, and I can't believe I haven't made any actual plans.

"I'm fine at the campground," I tell him.

"No, you're not. It closed today."

It freaks me out that he knows, like maybe he was checking up on me. He must see it on my face that I'm freaked, because he says, "Tom Bilford's in my euchre league," and points to his head. I don't know if it's what he means, but I immediately think of the guy with the earflaps hat, smacking that note against my windshield this morning.

"Euchre's for church ladies and old drunks," I say automatically. It's what my dad would say anytime someone suggested playing euchre instead of five card. I think I should apologize, but Adam looks amused.

"I'm too young to be an old drunk," he says, laughing. "So I guess I need change for the collection plate."

144

"Sounds about right." I fight a smile. I wonder if Tom Bilford told Adam about me. I wonder if Adam asked. I pick up the coffeepot. "I should get back to it," I say, pointing to the counter.

"You didn't answer." Adam's eyes are still sparkly from laughing.

"Wouldn't you like to know," I say, because I can't decide, not because I'm trying to be mysterious.

"Will she or won't she?" Adam says. "I'll be waiting by the phone with bated breath."

"Keeps life interesting." I put the coffeepot on the burner and go into the kitchen like I have something to do in there, when really I just need to get away so I can think.

The kitchen is empty. I swipe a slice of bread from the sandwich station, hoping it will soak up the excess coffee in my stomach so I can figure out if that churning feeling is telling me something about Adam or it's my own fault. As I'm shoving bread in my mouth, I get the kind of tingle on the back of my scalp that comes from being watched. I look up and realize the Lettuce Murderer is standing against the wall next to the fridge. I don't understand how I could miss an entire person with flaming red hair, except that he's very still. I freeze midchew. He looks at me, puts a finger to his lips. And then, with lightning speed, he lunges, smacking the prep counter with his bare hand, so hard it echoes. He looks at his palm, shows me the black smudge. "Spider," he says.

"Yeah," I say, and try to swallow the gluey wad of white bread in my mouth. It hurts all the way down.

When Carly comes back from her smoke break her hair is messy and she looks like she just woke up from the kind of thick nap where you drool all over the pillow. She hums to herself and it's either a totally different song from the one playing on the sound system or she's tone deaf. It's hard to tell with the shit music she listens to. Most of it doesn't even sound like music, just noise and screaming.

She wipes down the espresso machine and checks the paper roll on the register.

"April, May, June," she says, smiling at me when she looks up. "July, August, September." She reaches over and pushes hair from my face. She's a little shorter than me, so she rocks up on her toes to tuck the strand behind my ear.

I don't really know how I'm supposed to react, but since she's being so friendly, I ask her about Adam. "What's he all about?" I say, using words I heard from a girl chatting with her friend at a table by the counter this morning. "I told him, point-blank," the girl said, "that is not what I'm all about."

"Adam? He's a townie," Carly says, waving

her hand with a flick of her wrist. She stares at me and sighs. It's a long stare and I'm not sure what it means, but it doesn't make me feel better about Adam.

"Can you work all day tomorrow?" she asks.

"Uh huh," I say, looking past her, out the window. The dark seems so much darker than it did yesterday. I wonder if maybe I should ask Carly if she knows a place I could stay. I try to think of the right words. Maybe I could ask her to let me sleep on her couch. Maybe that would be the easiest thing. Just one night. More time to think and another day of earning money. If I had a couch and she asked, I would say yes, so it's not the craziest thing.

"Don't you ever have class?" Carly asks.

"I'm not in school," I say.

She scrunches her eyebrows so they almost meet. "I thought you went to IC."

I shake my head and it feels like the wad of white bread is still stuck in my throat.

"Huh," she says. "Huh."

I worry I've done something wrong even though I never said I was in school. I worry she'll ask more questions, but she stares into my eyes and says, "I'm going to get a sandwich," as if she's making a major confession. She turns on the toe of her boot and stomps to the kitchen like she's about to conquer food.

I wipe the counter and decide to call Adam

after work. But Adam doesn't leave. He's sipping coffee that's probably gone cold, hunched over his notebook, scribbling. I catch his eye too many times when I look over, even when I try not to, and I feel like a deer being watched from the blind. This is the kind of thing Margo warned me about. Someone paying too much attention. But I don't know how you're supposed to meet people, how you're supposed to tell if someone likes you in a normal, friendly way.

Adam has his shirtsleeves rolled to his elbows. His forearms are more muscular than I would've expected. He's not big, but he's probably strong.

When the kitchen closes, the red-headed kid leaves. Before the door swings shut, I hear the frantic howl of a pack of boys out on The Commons, and that lightning-storm feeling takes over my stomach again and won't go away.

At ten p.m. the only people left are Adam, a table of students working on a project, and a guy in the corner reading Stephen King. Carly turns the front door sign to CLOSED, but none of them seem to notice.

I count the drawer because Carly says her brain feels like it's full of pipe cleaner fuzz. "Not the wires, just the fuzz. Green and yellow, mostly." Her smile tells me she's being strange on purpose. This is her humor and I think I get it. Maybe.

Now that she thinks I lied about school I am too scared to make my problem her problem. I need my job too much to risk asking about her couch. But I remember one time some truckers at Margo's talked about boondocking at Wal-Mart instead of paying for a hotel and you're allowed to sleep in those parking lots. I decide on the way out, I'll ask Carly where the nearest Wal-Mart is. She doesn't have to know why I'm asking. People don't think about Wal-Marts that way. She'll probably assume I'm out of toothpaste or toilet paper, because she probably thinks I'm a normal enough person with a normal enough place to sleep.

Carly dumps the rest of the drip coffee and unplugs the espresso maker while I band up bills and slip them in the bank bag.

"Alright, guys," Carly shouts to the remaining customers, "you don't have to go home, but *I* don't want you."

I run to the kitchen while they pack up to leave, so I don't have to talk to Adam.

It's warm in the kitchen. I wish there was a way to store that warmth inside me. It will be cold in that Wal-Mart parking lot and I will be alone in that car and instead of raccoons there will be truckers.

I hear Carly saying goodbye to customers and then she comes back to the kitchen. We put our coats on.

"Whoo, today felt twice as long," she says, winding her scarf around her neck as we walk to the front door.

All the words I need to ask are right there in my brain, ready. But Adam is waiting outside.

"Cold tonight," he says as Carly locks the door. He blows clouds into the air. I want him to go away. In the shadow of the doorway his face is hidden and I can't remember what his eyes look like.

"Yeah, you're not kidding," Carly says, shoving her bare hands in her pockets. "Where are you parked?"

"Oh, I walked," Adam says, even though I'm sure Carly was talking to me.

"That way." I point toward State Street, but with a vague gesture, so I won't give Adam too much information.

"Well, I'm over there," she says, jogging in place. "See you!" Before I can ask about her couch or Wal-Mart, she's bounding away like she can outrun the weather.

I'm left with Adam and he ruined my chance and I shouldn't go home with him. You don't go home with men you don't know. I am certain Margo would say that. I don't want to ask him where Wal-Mart is, because if he knows about boondocking, he'll know where to find me, and maybe asking will insult him. Margo would also say you have to watch out about making men mad.

"My place is up the hill." Adam points in the opposite direction of my car.

"Have a good night," I say, trying to keep my words friendly.

"Do you want—"

"I've got it figured out. Have a good night." I run away at the same pace Carly did, so hopefully it looks like I'm running because of the weather, not because I'm trying to escape.

— Chapter 14 —

There's a party four houses down from where I parked. I don't have the energy to walk over and see if it's a place where I could spend time. All the people who came into the coffee shop left words in my head and I just want quiet.

The streetlight flickers. We don't even have streetlights in Little River. When it's dark, it's just dark, and if you need light, you bring your own. I get in my car and don't start the engine.

I'm not sure where to drive. I could go to the gas station and ask about Wal-Mart, but it feels like so much effort for something that might not be better. I know how to get back to the campground, and from there, if I follow the road north along the lake, eventually I'll find the sign for the highway. Maybe I could stay at the motorhome again for a few days before anyone noticed. I miss the company of my tiny TV and knowing what the land around me looks like even when it's dark. I recognize the men who stumble home after Gary's closes. I know their children. I understand who's dangerous and how to hide from them, mostly. I don't know these boys shouting at the party, and the streetlights make me feel like a doll in a display case.

I think about hiding on the back seat, covering

myself with sheets and clothes so no one can see me. Once, in the woods behind the motorhome, I turned over a rotting log and there was a tree frog underneath trying to hibernate for winter, his body curled up and tense like he was in a trance. When I tried to put the log back, I worried I might have squished him against the frozen ground or left him too exposed. I wasn't sure he could snap out of it to move himself. I feel stuck in my brain that way.

The party is getting louder. It's not like the party at Lion Boy's house; there's an edge to the sound. Tears drip into the collar of my coat. I know it's bad to be wet when it's cold. I try to picture the times I fell asleep in a booth at Margo's Diner, pretend the angry noise outside is chatter and kitchen sounds and Margo telling stories. Outside, someone walks between my car and the streetlight. I keep my head down and wait for the light to shine on my face again, but it doesn't. When I look up, Adam is there, hand raised like he was about to knock on my windshield.

Something isn't right about how he's found me, but seeing a face I recognize makes the blood flow back to my fingers. I wipe my cheeks, turn the key in the ignition.

"Are you alright?" he asks as I roll down the passenger window.

"Why are you following me?"

"I was hungry." He holds up a plastic bag with a box in it. "Calzone. You want half?"

"No." I can smell the calzone, greasy and warm. I want him to take it away before I cave.

"You sure?" He smiles. "You've got to be cold."

"I'm fine." I want him to leave, except once he does, I will have sent away the one person in the world who knows where I am.

"Come to my place." His cheeks are chapped from the cold.

I have thought long and hard about what he would get from this arrangement, and there's only one thing I can figure out. "No, thank you," I say, sweetly as I can.

"Park in front of my house at least," he says. "So I know you're safe."

I point at him, at how he found me. "How do I know *you're* safe?"

"I'm not stalking you. I was worried."

"You don't even know me!"

Adam bends, hands on knees, so he can look at me better. He's different from Matty, like he's grown into his body. His stubble isn't spotted and sparse. "Please. I'll sleep better." He shifts a little and the streetlight shines over his shoulder into my eyes, turning him into just the shape of a person.

"I live right up the hill," he says. "It's a nice street. Quiet."

I look through the windshield at the pack of boys collecting outside the party house. One of them is shoving another one; the rest are laughing but it looks like the wind could change direction way too fast.

"Fine," I say, but when Adam reaches for the door handle, I flinch. I don't mean to. It just happens.

"Okay." Adam backs away. "It's on Hudson Street. Third white house on the left. You know Hudson?"

I shake my head.

"So if you make a U-turn here and then—" He looks away. A car drives by and the swish of tires on the wet road drowns out the rest of his words. I don't want to hear them anyway. My brain can't hold the information. I'm just too tired. I am so tired. I hope the streetlights are dim enough that he can't see the tears welling up in my eyes.

Adam stops giving me directions. "Okay," he whispers, like he's saying it to himself. He leans toward the window, careful not to rest his hands on my car. "Here's what we'll do. I'll walk home and you drive slow behind me. There aren't many people on the roads right now, and it isn't far, so it'll be fine. Okay?"

"I'm sorry."

"Don't be sorry." He gives me a smile and waves his arm like *Let's go.*

I start the car, do a U-turn, keep pace with him as he walks on the sidewalk.

He has a slight hitch in his giddyup, as Margo would say. Heavier on his left foot than his right. His shoulders slope forward; the back of his neck is bare. No scarf. He walks quick, swinging his bag of takeout, looking over to check on me again and again.

When we start to climb the hill, he can't walk as fast and it's almost impossible to drive slow enough. He waves as I pass, pointing to the left I'm supposed to take. When I see him in my rear-view mirror, he's completely caught up in making sure I go the right way. It is so much more effort than I'm used to anyone giving me and I start to think that maybe it's fine. Maybe all of it is fine. Not everyone is as squirrelly as my father. Margo was always nice to me for the sake of being nice, so it is a possible thing.

At the stop sign, I lean across and push the passenger door open. Adam runs over. Gets in, his weight shifting the balance of the car. He smells like dryer sheets.

"You don't travel light," he says, eyeing the jumble of blankets and clothes and garbage bags in the back seat.

I don't know how to explain myself.

"Hey." Adam touches my arm with the tips of his fingers, light, and I don't flinch. "You don't have to tell me. I won't ask. I've been there too."

I nod, wondering where it is he thinks I've been.

He pulls his hand away and looks out the window, but I feel the imprint of his fingers still.

On the radio, a low voice says, "Hey, this is Tommy Flash, I'm kicking it live here on ICB. I'd like to send this next one by Pearl Jam out to all my boys in the West Tower."

Adam laughs. "College station."

I've learned since I got here that the town is in a valley with schools on both the bordering hills, but "College" always means Ithaca College. When people are talking about the other one, they say Cornell, and I think that's on the other hill, not the one we're heading up.

We make the turn on Hudson and Adam points to a big white Victorian with a row of black metal mailboxes by the front door. There's an open parking space out front. He shows me where to make a U-turn. We are quiet as I drive back to the spot. We listen to the song. It's about a girl telling someone not to call her their daughter.

I park.

Adam opens the car door. "I'm asking one more time," he says.

My fingers are cold enough to hurt. I have to pee already and there's no bathroom I know how to find. I get out of the car. Leave my stuff, keep the key clenched in my fist. Adam doesn't make a big deal about it, which makes it easier to follow him to the front door.

There's water rushing. A river or a creek. I feel the water in the air, but I can't see it, even when I strain my eyes to look into the dark behind the house. I can go in and use the bathroom and then tell him I want to sleep in my car. I don't have to stay. He won't make me stay, I'm pretty sure.

He lives on the top floor. The stairs squeak when we climb them. There are other doors. Other people. Someone baked cookies. Someone's listening to reggae.

The lock makes a loud click when he turns the key. He flicks a switch and the apartment is flooded with light. The walls are bright white and the ceiling is high, slanted at weird angles. He has the kind of old metal radiators that make the heat smell like melting crayons. There's a big desk with a tilted top. A black footlocker for the coffee table. Bookshelves built into the walls filled with books and CDs. The futon is clean and white. The hardwood floor has a rug in the middle that's woven in bright colors. No one in Little River lives in a place like this. It's not cluttered with things that were useful once and might be useful again. Nothing is old or worn out that doesn't look that way on purpose.

Adam kicks off his boots at the mat and I do the same, feeling strange about losing that level of protection. Now I will have to stop for my boots

158

when I leave. Bend over to put them back on or grab them as I flee and try not to slip running downstairs in my socks.

"Can I use the—"

"Oh, yeah." Adam points to the hallway. "The bathroom is right there."

The bathroom door is open. To the left there's a kitchen, enough street light coming through the window that I can see the stove and a small table. But on the other side of the bathroom, there's a door and it's closed. I can't tell if it's the bedroom or a closet and I start to worry that the futon is where Adam sleeps. I close myself in the bathroom, turn the lock until it latches, and try to run through everything Adam said to me about staying at his place. I thought he talked about making up the futon like it was something extra he would do. But I've never been in an apartment like this before. Maybe I don't understand how he lives. Maybe he doesn't bother folding it down for just one person.

After I flush, I wash my hands the best I can around the bandage and pull my fingerless gloves back on. Margo would never have let me work in knit gloves. They're already pilling and full of crumbs and coffee dust that won't shake out all the way. My fingers feel stiff. I know I should wash the cut and change the bandage, but I left all that stuff in the car.

"Okay, do me a favor," Adam says when I get

back from the bathroom. He's pulling the futon away from the wall. "Grab over there."

I don't know how to say I'm leaving.

He pushes the top of the futon forward and picks up the edge of the bench at the same time. My arms are shorter and my hand hurts, but I reach as far as I possibly can to make it work, because he asked me to. The frame unlatches and the futon flattens. I feel the stretch in my muscles even after I've let go.

Adam climbs on the futon and opens a cupboard under the bookshelves behind it, pulling out sheets and a blanket and three pillows. The blanket is fluffy and the sheets are crisp. Three pillows. But he wanted my help with the futon, so it's probably not something he does every night.

I stare at my boots by the door, think through the motions it will take to slip my feet in and run.

"You know, you can take your gloves off," Adam says, and I go so quickly from being worried about leaving to worrying that he's noticed how gross my gloves are—that he might not want me in his bed, on his clean sheets.

I stare at the pillows and think about the dark outside. I don't want to be anywhere. The blanket looks warm. "I cut my hand," I say, like it's some kind of apology. "At the campground. Firewood."

Adam climbs off the futon. "Give it," he says, curling his fingers at me.

I place my hand in his.

He peels my glove away. Winces when he sees dried blood on the bandage, but he unwraps it without hesitation. Leads me to the bathroom, runs water in the sink until it's warm and guides my hand into the stream. "Just let it rinse for a sec," he says, raising his eyebrows, eyes sad, like he's sorry I'm hurt.

My cut is sort of puffy and the water stings, but when I flex my fingers, I feel like the ice I've been carrying in my bones starts to melt.

Adam opens the medicine cabinet, lines up iodine and bandages and medical tape along the side of the sink. He smells like soap and night air and a little bit like Matty, like they use the same shampoo, or maybe that's just what men smell like when you get close enough.

He pats my hand dry with a cotton ball, squirts iodine over the cut, making yellow-brown splash marks in the sink. He has a small hoop in his left ear. I'm not sure how I missed it before. It's silver, twisted like a rope, tarnished in a way that looks cool.

"Does it hurt?" he asks.

"It's fine." My voice sounds so small. I try to keep my hands steady, but my knees start shaking, like the movement has to go somewhere.

Adam pats my hand dry again with a new cotton ball, then wraps it with careful turns of the bandage roll and just the right amount of tape. "Good as new."

All the blood in my body rushes to my cheeks. Our eyes meet and there's this funny flash in my brain. He has very nice green eyes.

He turns away to rinse out the sink.

The floor is tiled with all these tiny tiles. Black and white octagons, and the grout between them is grey, but I don't think it's mold or dirt. I think it's supposed to be that color, since everything else is so clean. Being here is better than another cold night. Maybe all of this is fine even if that closed door is a closet.

"Thank you," I say.

Adam puts the iodine in the medicine cabinet. "You hungry?" he asks. Looks over at me. Our eyes meet again.

I touch his cheek with my good hand, press my lips to his and feel the heat of him all the way to my toes.

He opens his mouth. I open mine, inch my tongue toward his, but he's pulling away.

"No. Don't—" He takes a step back like he thinks I'll kiss him again if he doesn't make extra space between us. "That's not—" He shakes his head.

My throat cramps so hard I can barely breathe. I push past him, out the bathroom door to the living room to grab my boots.

"Hey," Adam calls, following. "Don't go. You don't have to—that's not . . ." He stares at me, eyes wide. "Just wait. Wait, okay?"

He goes into the kitchen. I stand by the door, holding my boots. I don't know what I'm waiting for and the curiosity keeps me from leaving even though I'm burning all over from how embarrassed I am.

Adam comes back with his calzone split onto two plates. "Will you stay?"

I shake my head. Step into a boot. I don't know what I thought he'd get from the kitchen that would make this okay. I can't even look at his face. I slip my other foot in its boot, don't bother tying laces.

"Please?" he says. "I'm going to go in my room to eat and sleep and you can have this whole place to yourself."

He pushes a plate at me and even though the cheese is cold and congealed now, it smells amazing. I am too hungry to refuse.

He says good night and that I can come get him if I need anything, like it's settled that I'll stay and eat and sleep on that futon by myself. Then he goes into his bedroom and shuts the door.

I eat fast, standing away from the futon so I won't spill on anything but myself. Then I kick my boots off but leave all my clothes on. I don't make the bed, just throw down the sheet and lie on top of it. Pull the blanket over me and try to take up as little space as I can, like sleeping on half the futon will be half the burden. I thought I understood and I don't and I have that math class feeling in my chest. The tightness pulls in on me and my insides might pop like a balloon in a vise. In my head, I kiss him over and over. His lips are chapped, but mostly soft. That horrified look on his face. My thoughts are too bright and loud for me to fall asleep. But I'm warm. At least I am warm, and my hand feels a little bit better.

When the sky is just beginning to turn blue, I fold the blankets and sheets, stack the pillows next to them. I don't think I can push the futon back into a couch myself. I worry it will make noise if I try, so I leave it. Tiptoe into the kitchen to place my plate in the sink, then I sneak out the door, carrying my boots down the stairs so my footsteps won't make noise.

I drive to The Commons, park one street over from yesterday. Maybe today I'll get up the nerve to ask Carly about her couch. Today is also the day we get paid and divvy up the tip jar and I don't know how much money it will be, but maybe it's enough. Maybe one of those Xeroxed posters with the fringed edge will have a phone number I can call, a room I can rent for cheap. Or maybe I'll buy a map and drive away to find someplace new, where I haven't humiliated myself yet.

I sit on a bench across from Decadence and wait for it to open. The clouds break apart and a beam of sun shines through. I close my eyes and pretend I can absorb the light like a sunflower.

When I open my eyes again, Adam is walking toward me. I want to get up and walk away, but he sees me see him, so there's no exit that isn't awkward.

"Hey," he calls, with a bend in his voice like he's worried. "You didn't have to leave. I was going to make pancakes."

In the sunlight, I can see the freckles on his nose. The chapped skin on his lips that I felt with my own. He looks kind. Normal. And I feel terrible for all the things I thought he could be.

I pick at a bubble of paint on the bench. "I didn't want to bother you."

"Did you sleep okay?" he asks, like he actually wants the answer. I don't think anyone in my entire life has ever been so wound up about whether I slept through the night.

"Yeah." When my answer makes him smile, I smile without even meaning to, like I'm a mirror.

"What happened—it's not—that's not why I invited you—"

"It's fine," I say, replaying the part from last night when he stepped away because he didn't trust me to stop kissing him. I watch a gull swoop in to grab an old french fry from the ground. "It's fine."

"I was homeless once. And no one noticed me. So I'm trying . . . I'm trying to notice you.

165

But maybe I'm not . . ." He takes a deep breath. "Maybe I'm not doing it right."

My nose stings. I hate that he called me homeless, like I'm already stuck this way. I'm tipping on the edge of tears and I wish Carly would come and open the door to Decadence so I'd have a reason to walk away.

"How old are you?" Adam asks.

"Nineteen." I don't let it snag my voice, so it comes out like truth. Eighteen is too convenient and I know I can't pass for twenty-one. I look young for sixteen when I don't try hard enough.

Adam studies my face like he's testing this number—stretching to see if it breaks. "You working all day?"

"Till six."

He reaches in his pocket, pulls out a key. "In case you want to shower on your lunch break, okay? You can have the place to yourself."

"You don't have to—"

"I wasn't trying—" He looks like he's about to cry, "I wasn't trying to use you, okay? I wish someone had helped me. That's all it is." His eyes are so green.

I take the key from him. Loop the ring around my finger, squeeze it tight in my palm.

"There's towels in the linen closet. Poke around as much as you want. Whatever you need, okay?" Adam pats my shoulder, quick and awkward.

"I'll stop by on my way home, and we'll—we'll see, if you want to stay again, okay?"

I nod. I am not going to fall apart over this. I won't let him hear my voice break. But when he walks away, the words grow in my chest. "Thank you," I yell.

He looks back and waves. His reusable coffee cup is hooked on his messenger bag. I wonder where he's getting his coffee this morning.

— Chapter 15 —

It's hard to pay attention at work knowing there's a hot shower waiting for me at lunch. It's not even just about the shower. I feel like it's been so long since I was completely alone. Even at the campground there was always the possibility of people. I don't know exactly what it is I want to do that's so different from what I'd do if someone could see me, it's just the idea that I can breathe all the way out, that maybe for a moment I don't have to be ready for someone else to appear.

I'm so distracted I need to ask most of our customers for their orders twice. I accidentally shortchange one of the regulars and have to run outside to give him the missing five when I realize. Luckily Carly is at class and Bodie does stuff like this all the time, so he doesn't see my mistakes as mistakes. But I hate to think of the Bodie catastrophes I'm not catching while I'm causing my own.

At lunch, I ask Bodie to make my sandwich to go. I walk up the hill to Adam's house because walking to my car would take almost as long.

The downstairs door is open. I feel weird going right on in, worried someone will stop me, but no one's around. When I climb the stairs, it smells like someone's baking frozen pizza on the second floor.

As soon as I get inside Adam's apartment, I lock the door behind me, kick off my boots, and slide around in my socks to look at things. The futon is back to being a couch, but the blankets and sheets and pillows are still stacked at the end, like maybe he's planning for me to sleep here again.

He has two black canvas chairs like movie directors have. The coasters on the footlocker are slices of a skinny birch tree. Behind the futon, the bookshelf built into the wall is filled with books that are actually his, not from the library. I stand on the futon so I can see them. A red cloth-covered dictionary with gold letters on the binding. Matching rust-colored books called *Encyclopedia of Architecture*. A yellow one about how the pyramids in Egypt were built. A bunch of paperback mysteries. Then there's all the CDs. Simon & Garfunkel, Eric Clapton, and Jane's Addiction. Miles Davis and Chet Baker. David Bowie and a bunch of movie soundtracks. He likes U2, but I can't hold it against him, because he has three Bob Dylans and they're good ones. *Highway 61 Revisited*, *The Freewheelin' Bob Dylan*, and *Blood on the Tracks*, which is my favorite. When we lived over the Wash 'n Fold, my dad had that one on 8-track and I listened to it with my cheek pressed against the speaker so I could feel the harmonica in my teeth.

I haven't heard that album since my dad dropped the 8-track player down the stairs while we were moving out. So many of those songs never get played on the radio and I miss the way they feel in my brain. Adam's stereo is next to his desk, and I don't think he'd mind. I don't think he'd mind at all, so I take the CD from the bookshelf. The disc in the player is a band called Red House Painters. I swap in Dylan, lie on my back on the floor and listen to *If You See Her, Say Hello*, because that song is the one I missed the most. Adam's rug is rough and the fibers are scratchy in a way that feels good on my back. Listening to Bob Dylan's voice swell through the lyrics is like drinking cool water when your mouth feels like it's stuffed with cotton.

I sing along. Super quiet, in case Adam's neighbors can hear, but my voice still echoes. I can't sing it straight. My voice is too low to sing it up high and too high to sing it where Dylan does, so I sing around him, swooping between his notes the way I always used to, my own song for his song. I miss my guitar. I never even learned how to play this one and I wish I could. Tears slide from the sides of my eyes, dripping in my hair. I want to keep listening, all the way through

Shelter from the Storm to *Buckets of Rain*, but the longer I lie here, the harder it will be to move. I put Red House Painters back in the CD player and Bob Dylan back on the shelf.

There's a photo in a frame on the bookcase. Adam and a group of guys, and they look young, like college young. They're holding beers and smiling, leaning against each other. Adam looks happy, but not as much as the other guys, and it makes me like him more. I wonder if it was taken before or after he was homeless. I wonder if there's an after for me. If I have a chance to have my own place with high ceilings and shelves full of music someday.

I don't have to poke in the linen closet, because Adam left a towel and washcloth for me on the sink. I am alone, alone, alone and the water is hot. His soap smells like peppermint and makes my skin tingle and when I'm done, I feel like a dirty window that's been washed until it squeaks. He left the bandages out for me too. I can't find a hair dryer, so I get dressed and eat my sandwich in the living room with one of the director's chairs pulled up to the wall so I can hang my hair over the radiator. I want to listen to more of *Blood on the Tracks*, but I worry I might fall apart. So I play Red House Painters and I like it. The lead singer's voice sounds echoey and slow and it matches the sadness that runs under Adam's smile in that picture.

When I'm done eating, I have to run the whole way back to Decadence to make it in time, but I am warm and clean and fed and happy.

— Chapter 16 —

Adam comes into Decadence at a quarter to six. I'm standing on a chair, trying to unscrew the side panel of the espresso machine, because Bodie somehow dropped a penny in the seam and then conveniently disappeared into the kitchen. Kelsye, the girl whose shift is after mine, is in early, so she takes Adam's order. I give him a quick wave, but I'm so scared of losing the screws or dropping the panel that I can't manage a good look to see if he's happy to see me. By the time I get the penny and put everything together again, Adam is sitting at his usual table by the window, but his back is to me.

I go into the kitchen to sign out. Bodie is hunched over the stove, spooning something into a bowl. "Here," I say, throwing the penny at him when he turns. He catches it. Slips it in his pocket like this whole thing was about him getting his money back.

"Here," he says, and hands me a soup bowl full of mac and cheese, toasted bread crumbs sprinkled across the top. "Something I'm trying out."

"Smells good," I say, and he beams.

"The secret is mustard."

I wince.

He says, "Trust me."

"Okay," I say.

"If you like it, tell Carly?" Bodie grinds pepper over my bowl. "I want her to make it a special."

"Sure," I say, and the way he looks in my eyes makes me think we could be having a moment. But then he says, "Is Kelsye here?" and the turn in his voice is so obvious.

"She's busy," I tell him, and take my mac and cheese out front so I don't have to talk about Kelsye anymore.

Adam is reading, newspaper folded to the exact column so he can hold it with one hand and eat his sandwich with the other. He doesn't look up when I get closer.

I felt so sure about the plan. I didn't ask Carly or Bodie. I didn't look for slips of paper on the bulletin board.

"Can I sit here?" I ask, and wonder if he can hear my heartbeat.

Adam looks up, staring for a minute before he grins. "Of course."

I pull his key from the waistband of my skirt and slip it across the table. "Thank you," I say, and I want to say more, but I don't have the right words.

"Everything work okay for you?" Adam asks. I nod and he smiles. I wait for him to offer for me to stay again, but he just says, "Good!"

174

I can't make myself ask. It's already a lot that he's done for me.

Adam eyes my dinner. "I didn't know they had mac and cheese!"

"It's a Bodie experiment," I say. "Want some?"

I dump a spoonful on the side of Adam's sandwich plate and we try it together, like it's a dare. The mac is warm and gooey and the cheese makes strings. It tastes a million times better than the stuff that comes in a box.

"Bodie's that blond guy, right?" Adam says.

"Yeah."

"I don't know why I expected it to be bad."

I laugh. "I know. Me too."

"It's awesome."

"You can have more if you want." I push my bowl toward him.

"I don't want to take your food."

"It's fine," I say. "Really." I'm eager to give him something. Anything.

"You eat it," he says, smiling.

He tells me about the article he's reading on a new museum in Barcelona. How interesting he thinks it must be to design a space to show off art you haven't even seen.

I don't want him to know that I'm not exactly sure where Barcelona is, if it's in Italy or Spain, or it's like Luxembourg. Maybe Barcelona is *in* Barcelona, and maybe if I'm nineteen I should know that. So I focus on what he said about the building. "You mean like someday paintings that haven't even been painted yet will hang there?"

Adam nods. "I wonder what it's like to make a landmark." He tells me he's an architect, but not that kind of architect.

Then he asks what I was doing to the espresso machine before, so I tell him about Bodie and the penny and he laughs. I feel like our whole conversation is some kind of secret test and his laugh means I passed.

After dinner, I take our plates into the kitchen, and Adam is waiting when I get back. He holds the door for me on the way out. He nods, I nod, and we walk to my car together.

"Why were you homeless?" I ask.

"I got in a fight with my father," he says.

"Yeah, me too." I don't want to talk about my father, so I don't ask questions about his. And maybe he doesn't want to talk about his father, because he doesn't ask about mine. But it's not uncomfortable to walk together, my footsteps filling the beats between his, and I don't flinch when he gets in my car.

Adam throws his bag on one of the black canvas chairs and says, "What can I get you?"

"What do you have?" I ask, giving him a big smile, trying hard to act like I'm completely comfortable standing here in his living room.

"Water, milk, Coke?" he says.

"Coke," I say.

He goes into the kitchen and comes back with a can of Coke and a bottle of beer.

"There's beer too," he says, plopping down on the futon. "If you want one." He rests the can of Coke on one of the birch coasters and uses a bent metal corner of the footlocker to open his bottle with a quick pound of his fist.

I crack the can open, slurping the foam so it doesn't drip on his futon, and say, "I'm good with Coke, thanks." I can't afford a buzz. I know enough about men to know the good ones don't ever want to be alone with a sixteen-year-old girl. And I'm pretty sure Adam is one of the good ones. I can't afford to say something that will give me away. I already messed up with him once.

"So you're an architect?" I ask. He moved on from it quickly in the cafe, like he was self-conscious. Like how I'd feel if someone asked me to sing in the middle of just being normal. "You actually make buildings?"

"Well, in theory," Adam says. "I'm getting my PhD now. And I'm not supposed to be working outside of teaching, but that woman I met with at Decadence? Anna. She's converting a barn, and has ideas she doesn't know how to implement, so I'm helping her draw up plans. She's my first client."

Everyone I knew in Little River worked on their own houses, turned barns into garages and garages to extra bedrooms, but they didn't ever seem to have much of a plan.

"Is it hard to design a building when you've never built one?" I ask.

Adam seems surprised by my question. "I'm about to find out, I guess."

He kicks off his boots and lines them up, side by side, heels against the trunk. He's careful about everything—how he touches my arm or leans closer to show me a sketch from his notebook—like he understands that I might be scared and doesn't want to add to it. I've never been around someone who didn't have at least a little bit of reckless bubbling under their skin, but he doesn't.

We talk for hours. I don't understand a lot of what he's telling me about his doctorate program at Cornell, the classes he's teaching and something or someone called a TA, but he doesn't seem to expect me to. And eventually he starts talking about ordinary things.

He's twenty-seven. He's from a place called Needham. He used to smoke, but only cloves. He quit when his favorite professor died of lung cancer in August, but when he's working he still reaches for cigarettes that aren't there. Now his ashtray holds loose change.

It feels like we're playing house on an old

fashioned TV show where the couple comes home and talks about their day. I never thought people actually did that. My dad, when he did come home, used to sit and smoke and be all stuck in his head like he wasn't even there.

Adam's voice is soft, but it fills the room. There's more space than furniture, so every word echoes just a little. My extremities are thawed. The dark is outside. I wish this was actually what life was like, even though it's just this simple little thing. Two people sitting on a couch.

Adam clears his throat and looks at the ceiling. "Another Coke?" he asks.

"Sure," I say.

And then we're back on the couch with his beer and my Coke and talking like we're old friends or new friends, or I don't know what. Like he's forgotten how I almost kissed him last night.

He wants to get a dog and maybe a kayak. He wants to have a kid someday. His girlfriend left him last year. He doesn't say why. I want to know, but I don't think I should ask. I tell him I left someone. I tell him that sometimes, it's only about the person leaving. Sometimes, the person being left did nothing to deserve it.

It's after midnight, I'm sure. My voice is hoarse and scratchy. I don't think I've talked so much to anyone ever. I don't tell him about my dad or the motorhome, but I tell him about stealing

Mrs. Varnick's car, even though I don't say why. He laughs big and I can see all his tiny teeth. I make it sound like something that happened ages and ages ago. When I was just a kid pulling a prank. I tell him about Ida and her orders and he tells me about how he tended bar to pay for college. We swap stories about weird customers and crazy cooks.

The conversation lulls for a second and I yawn too big to stifle it.

Adam taps my leg. "Alright, up," he says.

I stand. He pulls the futon away from the wall and I help him lay it flat again. We hold opposite corners and fluff the sheet up in the air like it's a parachute. We don't talk, as if the process of making the bed is a solemn occasion. I feel the weight and the strangeness of it low in my belly.

When we're done, Adam says, "Are those enough pillows?" like an apology, like he's supposed to know how many pillows I like. "Were they enough?"

"Yeah." I stare at his lips, at the stubble along his jaw. This time the bed is made and I know where he sleeps and that he's not expecting anything from me. But no one has ever talked to me the way he does, with all the little details of a life that's not like mine. Everyone I knew before—they were people who were around my whole life. We lived from the same angle. But

Adam is interesting and he thinks I'm interesting too, and he's seen so much more of everything than I have.

"Well, okay," he says, and I think he gets what I can't make myself say. But then he turns off the light and starts to walk into the hallway.

I don't want this to end. I grab at his hand. Just a quick pull.

And then his lips are on mine and his body is on mine and the sheets on the bed we made are quickly crumpled. He kisses my collarbone, the palm of my hand, smooth skin on the insides of my wrists, places no one's thought to kiss before, and he's not in any kind of hurry about it.

He touches me softly, gently. It starts out feeling like that longing I had with Matty that always ended up in a bunch of nothing, but Adam touching me feels so much bigger than what it is and gives way to this flood of warmth, like a dam breaking, that makes me gasp and grab hold of the pillow. I run my hand down his belly. His body jerks when I get close. He breathes through his nose and it tickles my cheek. He's small and soft under the blankets. He finds my hand with his and pulls it away. We kiss more before he gets up and goes into the bathroom for a while. I'm not sure what's happened or happening. Is he getting a condom? Is he going to the bathroom? He runs the faucet the whole time. When he comes back he gets in bed behind me and wraps me in his arms. "You're so warm," he says in a sleepy voice. Brushes my hair out of my face with his sweaty palm. "Sleep tight."

— Chapter 17 —

I wake up before Adam does. His arm is draped over my side, sticking to my skin, and he's breathing stale beer breath into my neck. The sun streams through the windows. We've kicked the blankets off and I'm only in my underwear. I want to cover myself, but I don't want to wake him. His fingers are pressed against my belly and I wonder if they'll leave pink prints behind. His hand is smooth and his fingernails are clean.

I've never spent the night with anyone before. Matty had a curfew. I'm worried Adam might be upset to see me when he wakes up, and it will be like when I thought he wanted to kiss me and he didn't, but so much worse. Or maybe he'll be mad that we didn't have sex. I can't just grab my boots and run down the stairs if I want to leave. My clothes are lost somewhere in the tangled sheets.

Slowly, carefully, I twist around under the weight of Adam's arm. His hat is on the pillow next to him. His hair isn't sparse like I expected. It's thick and wiry and sticks up in every direction. I try to reach across him to pull the blanket over us to cover myself, but he stirs and opens his eyes. I hold my breath. He smiles when he sees me, a clear, happy smile that stops the scramble in my head.

"Mmmm." He stiffens his body into a stretch. He rubs his hand up and down my side, kisses my cheek and pulls me close to him. My bare chest against his, our legs warm and sweaty.

"I swear," he whispers into my ear, "I wasn't expecting *that*." And I know he means it, that if I hadn't grabbed his hand, he would have gone to bed and left me alone in the living room to wait out the buzz from the four Cokes I drank.

I don't know what to say, so I kiss his cheek back, but he turns his head to kiss me for real. I feel him through his boxer shorts, getting hard against my thigh, but he pulls away.

"Morning breath," he says, grabbing his wadded T-shirt from the floor. "I'll be right back." He goes into the bathroom and closes the door. The faucet runs again.

I pull a corner of blanket over myself, try to tuck it around me in a way that's flattering. I don't want him looking at me too much in the bright morning. With his chest hair and full stubble, he looks so much older than Matty and I worry there are ways that my body could give me away. When I turned twelve, Margo bought me a training bra and gave me warnings about getting my period and growing hair in weird places, but maybe there are other ways I'm sup- posed to change past what's already happened and I don't even know. Adam would, because he lived with a girl who was probably his own age. I look around the room like maybe there are clues about her, but of course there aren't. She's been gone for a while, and it's not like he'd have a naked picture of her hanging on the wall so I could see what a woman is supposed to look like.

When Adam finally opens the bathroom door, he doesn't come back to me. I hear cabinets open and close, water pouring and then the burbling sound of a coffee maker.

I am not sure what to do with myself. I yell, "Are you making coffee so you can go get coffee?"

"Busted!" Adam shouts. "I need fuel for my walk to the coffee shop."

"Me too." I find his long sleeve flannel wadded on the floor and wear it, like women do on TV. Like I've done this before and it's no big deal.

"You sleep okay?" he calls.

"Yeah," I say, walking into the kitchen, bare feet on the cold floor. My legs feel so naked. I'm worried he doesn't want me, that I'm doing something wrong and that's why he didn't come back to bed, why he doesn't want me to touch him. I'm worried it means I won't be welcome for long, that maybe I'm not even welcome now, but then he brushes my hair out of my face and says, "God, you're gorgeous." He gives me the kind of kiss that makes me grab the counter to steady myself because I'm not sure which end is up.

Adam holds my good hand while we walk to the coffee shop together. And we're clean and smell like peppermint soap, and I'm wearing one of his sweaters with the sleeves rolled up, because we're going to wash all my clothes in the laundry room in the basement of his building tonight and fold them while we watch *Seinfeld* and order calzones from the place down the street, and I know it's stupid, but it means everything to me to have plans further ahead than the next twenty minutes.

When we get to The Commons, Adam drops my hand and says, "Here. Take my key again." He's blushing. "You know, in case you need to stop in at your lunch break, or you go home before I do."

I know he's saying *home* like it's nothing, just the place he lives, so I try not to be that girl, the kind who takes the most stupid little word and lets it turn her inside out.

"Thanks," I say quickly.

He brushes his lips against my cheek. "I'll let you go in first, so they don't think we're together."

My blood stops short in my veins. I'm sure I

don't look like I'm playing it cool this time, because he kisses me on the mouth and says, "Just so it's easier on you at work. And so I can watch you walk away."

— Chapter 18 —

Pilgrim! How goes it?" Bodie says in his lazy lilt when I walk in. He's taking orders up front, and the line is almost out the door. He has a pencil behind his ear and chews on a red coffee stirrer like it's a piece of hay. "Do you know how to total when there's more than one item?" he asks, while I duck under the counter.

I reach from behind him and hit the add button. "Now put the next one in," I say.

"Thanks, P." Bodie gives me that great big grin that makes his eyes all but disappear. "Carly called. She'll be in late. Problem with the espresso delivery."

The way he says it makes me think maybe it's some kind of code, but what he could be saying between the lines is lost on me.

"What did you do if you didn't know how to add up items?" I ask.

"I just did each one as a separate transaction," Bodie says, moving his coffee stirrer to the other side of his mouth. He scoops espresso into the little metal basket, tamps it down slowly, carefully, like it's the only thing he has to do all morning.

It drives me crazy. "I got this." I grab the tamper out of his hand. "You take orders and I'll get them done," I say, even though I still have to look at the board to see what goes in which drink. I throw my weight into tamping the coffee and screw the basket into the machine, but by the time I finish the drink, Bodie is too busy chatting up some cute hippie girl in a chunky sweater to have an order for me. "Next up?" I ask.

The girl smiles. "Oh, I don't know what I want yet." She steps back like she's just now going to look at the board and think about her order.

"I'll come back to you," I say, pointing to the person behind her, who looks relieved. Hippie girl and Bodie move to the side, continuing with whatever the hell they're talking about, and I go into full gear.

Carly comes in a few minutes later with a sack of coffee slung over her shoulder, walking bowlegged because it's so heavy. Bodie doesn't even look up or offer to help. I've got the line down to three people now, if you don't count the hippie girl, and I don't. The last person in line is Adam. He smiles at me whenever we make eye contact.

Carly dumps the sack on the counter with a loud thump. "You are a saint," she says, hugging me dramatically when she gets to my side of the counter. It makes me blush like when Margo hugs me. "I was dreading what I'd walk into, leaving Bodie in charge. He's lucky he's cute, huh?" She rolls her eyes. "Bodie! Kitchen!"

Bodie pats the hand of the hippie girl, takes the pencil from behind his ear, and writes something on a napkin that he hands to her. And as ridiculous as Bodie is and as much as it's nice to have Adam smiling at me while he waits for his coffee, I still wish just a little bit that whatever Bodie was writing he was writing for me.

"Alright, alright," Bodie says, walking past us.

Carly takes one of the dish towels and snaps it at his ass. "Could you be any more blond?" she says as he walks through the door to the kitchen.

"Don't hate me because I'm beautiful!" Bodie screeches, the door swinging shut behind him.

— Chapter 19 —

We don't have sex, Adam and me. There could be a big difference in the way you have sex with a teenage boy in the back of his mom's station wagon and the way you have sex with a man who you live with. Maybe I'm supposed to seduce him. Maybe I'm supposed to drive to the mall when my shift is over and buy lacy things to wear to meet him at the door when he comes home. But I don't go to the mall after my shift. I go back to Adam's place, and I wear Margo's old leopard leggings and one of Adam's sweatshirts, and drink a Coke and watch *Ren & Stimpy* until he gets home. And then we order pizza and play Rook until we can't stop yawning.

Adam never asked me to move in exactly. He just kept offering me spaces for my things. My clothes are hanging in his closet, which was half-empty anyway, like the girl before me left that space and Adam never even thought of spreading his clothes out to the other side. My toothbrush lives in the cup on the edge of the bathroom sink with his. A few of the mugs from Margo's Diner are in the cabinet with his nice mugs and he uses them like he doesn't even mind the chipped rims. I wish I had someone to ask if this is how it happens. It's the kind of thing I'd ask Margo if I could.

I didn't even know my dad knew Irene before he stopped coming home. So I certainly don't know if she asked him to stay or he just stopped leaving. Matty and I were going to get married before we got a place together, and even though, deep down, I didn't want to marry Matty, at least there was some kind of order to that plan. With Adam, I feel like there's something I'm missing and I don't even know where to find it.

Sometimes, when Adam has a couple beers, we fool around on the futon in the living room that's always folded up like a couch now. I sleep with him in his bed. But we don't have sex ever, and we don't do much more in bed than kiss good night.

Once Matty and I started messing around, all he ever wanted to do was have sex. Sometimes I wasn't sure if he heard a word I said, but it's like he was addicted to me and that mattered more than the kids who teased him about his weirdo girlfriend or his mom picking at him to find someone better. It mattered more than when I bruised his ego with a joke or turned him down when I didn't want his grabby hands on my body. I knew I had this power over him, and I liked it.

Adam hears every word I say, but he has to be drunk to want me and even then, he can always stop. The fooling around part with Adam is better than sex was with Matty, but I worry it means that this isn't going to last, and I want it to. More than just because I want a place to stay, but because I like being with Adam. I like talking to him. I like the way we have patterns, that things are the same most of the time.

At night, when Adam turns the light off, we confess things to each other. Stupid stuff, mostly. Adam says he's afraid of clowns. I tell him about the way starlings flocked in bare tree branches in the winter in Little River, so many that they looked like leaves, and when they up and flew away all at once, it would make me scared for reasons I don't know how to say. I tell him like it was years ago. Not weeks.

We lie there, staring at the ceiling, looking for shapes in cracks we can just barely see in the street light that leaks through the blinds. Sides touching, holding hands, like Matty and I used to when we watched clouds as kids.

Adam tells me that he slept with a blankie until he was twelve. I say that I used to sing Whitney Houston into a pencil at the top of my lungs. He cops to liking Air Supply. I tell him about the pink puke sneakers I had from the time I threw up in Margo's car. I don't tell him why I puked, just that my dad didn't see the need to buy me new shoes. But even that feels like I'm saying a little too much, because I have to be so careful about the whens.

There's a part of me that wants Adam to know everything, like if I told him, my life could start from that moment and nothing before would count. It wouldn't even leave a stain. But if he knew everything, he wouldn't like me anymore. He couldn't. The catch in all of it is that if he knew and didn't care, he couldn't be the Adam I want him to be. Either way I'd lose him.

Eventually his grip on my hand gets softer. "What are you thinking about?" he asks in his slow, sleepy voice. He likes to talk until the very last moment before he falls asleep.

"A tree frog," I say. "What are you thinking about?"

"Donuts," he says, and then he's done for the day, breathing softly through his mouth.

In the dim light, I watch Adam drift away, the vee between his eyebrows softening until it disappears, and I wonder what it must be like to be one of those people who sleep soundly and wake up rested.

They say you spend like half your life asleep, but I think I've been awake for most of it. I wonder if I'll ever stop waking up at the slightest little noise, thinking it could be my mom sneaking back home to take me with her. I wonder if sleeping is something I could ever learn to do.

— Chapter 20 —

I call Margo on Sundays at two o'clock from the pay phone outside of Woolworth's. It's my deal with her. She says someone needs to keep track of me. She says I can call collect, but I don't. I take a roll of dimes with me. Last time I called, we used up the whole roll and I couldn't stop shivering for hours afterward.

I don't want to use the phone at Adam's or at work. I don't think anyone is tracking the call. It's not like I'm someone important, like in those movies where a kid goes missing and men in black suits with fancy equipment swoop in and take over the family room to wait for phone calls and ransom notes. I'm pretty sure if I hadn't taken Irene's car or trashed the motorhome, my dad wouldn't have even noticed or cared that I left. And I don't only sort of believe that in a feeling sorry for myself way. I know it's the truth and I think it's better to call a spade a spade. But I use the pay phone just in case, so there's no chance anyone in Little River could ever find out about Adam. And I don't mention him to Margo. I just tell her I have a room in a boardinghouse, even though I'm not sure if boardinghouses are a real thing that still exist. I ended up confessing I was in Ithaca, but I tell her that I'm probably going to switch to a better place soon, so there's no point in giving her my address. I think she knows I'm telling tales but worries if she pushes too hard, I won't call again.

"Oh, thank god, girlie," she says when she picks up the phone. "I thought you might not call."

"I said I would. I always do."

"I know." Her voice sounds worn. "But I always worry."

"Well, knock it off," I tell her, trying to laugh. "You'll give yourself wrinkles."

I wait for Margo to laugh and tell me I'm too much or say that when God made me he made a mistake and gave me too many funny bones. She doesn't.

She sighs. "Gary finally talked to your father. He says as long as you've found a place to live and you're working and he doesn't have to support you anymore, he can't see any point in making you bring the car back and you may as well keep it."

I feel like someone just knocked all the wind out of me. I grab on to the side of the phone booth with my bare hand. The metal is freezing cold, but I'm worried I'll fall over if I let go, like maybe my knees have forgotten how to be knees. The relief about the car, about not having to go back, that freedom isn't as sweet as I thought it would be. "So, I guess he figures I'd cost him an old Mercury's worth of groceries between now and when I turn eighteen."

"I thought this is what you wanted," Margo says.

"It is." There's a new piece of gum on top of the phone. It's neon yellow. It's still wet. I wonder what flavor it was. "But you know."

"I do. I know, sweets."

The phone clicks and the recording tells me to add more change.

"I should go," I say, even though I still have a ton of dimes.

"April," she says. She almost never says my name.

"What?"

"Your dad got hurt."

"I'm not even sure he has feelings," I say.

"They let him out of the hospital this morning."

I drop a dime in to get the recording to shut up. "What do you mean?"

"Gary, when he went to talk to your dad, he took a couple friends and some of them had opinions about things."

"Me?"

"You, Irene Bartkowski, a few other things. Gary didn't realize there was bad blood there. But Chuck, you know, he's Gary's bartender, he was friends with Joe Bartkowski. He has opinions about why Joe left."

"So he hurt my dad?"

"Gary says things just escalated. Fast. But he got in the middle and took your dad to the ER. It's a few broken ribs."

"And he's okay?"

"Right as rain, safe as houses," she says. "Gary drove him home. Ribs hurt, but they'll heal. And knowing your dad, he's happy for the pain pills."

"Bonus." I want to pull the gum off the top of the phone. I want it gone. I have to concentrate hard on not touching it. It's like this urge.

"I didn't want to hide the truth from you, but I don't want you to worry. It's men being stupid. You know how they are."

"Yeah," I say. "I do."

"Next Sunday," she says.

"Next Sunday."

"Stay safe, sweetie pie."

"Margo," I say.

"Yeah."

"Love you."

"Oh, girlie, you know I love you too."

The recording kicks in again asking for more change. I let the phone disconnect.

I go into Woolworth's and use the rest of my dimes to buy a card for my dad. I grab the first one that says *Get Well*. It has a picture of a mouse in a hospital gown that's open in the back so everyone can see his tail. I don't know what to write, so I just sign my name. I think about addressing it to Margo, because I know she'd understand and do something so the postmark is unreadable, but then I decide to send it right to my father. He paid for his freedom with a Mercury Sable. He's not coming to look for me. I buy a stamp from customer service and stick the card in the blue mailbox outside the store.

Later, when Adam falls asleep, I sneak out of the apartment, walk to the house with the kit car in the driveway, and return the license plates. Adam wakes up when I climb back into bed.

"You smell like cold," he says in his foggy sleep voice, and cuddles up to me.

"Cold isn't a smell," I whisper, kissing his forehead. "You're sleeping."

He doesn't say anything else. His breathing goes back to loud and metered. Under the covers, I find his feet to warm mine.

— Chapter 21 —

One of the spoiled college bitches Carly is always complaining about actually shows up for her shift in the afternoon. So I get to leave at what normal time would be if the other people who worked at the cafe made a habit of showing up for their shifts. It's weird. I've been picking up everyone's slack since I got here, so when I get to actually leave at the end of only one shift, I feel like I'm playing hooky. There's suddenly this part of the day I haven't seen in a very long time. There are infinite possibilities. The air feels different.

I walk back to Adam's apartment. The college kids who rent the places downstairs must be at class or sleeping. It is so quiet. I decide I'll sit in the sunlight and put my feet up and read. Maybe if I work my way through Adam's books I'll have things to talk about that are far from who I used to be.

I get myself a Coke from the fridge and stand on the couch in my socks to look at Adam's books. But instead of choosing one, I stare at the picture of Adam from college, really look at the other guys this time. I wonder where they ended up, because since I've been here, none of them have called. Adam hasn't done more than go to euchre with a few other townies. And even though he smiles at me all the time, it's a few degrees faded from his smile in the picture, and you can tell he wasn't quite happy then. I wonder if maybe all you do is meet people and lose them and your smile fades the further you go because you have to carry the space they leave. Maybe it all just turns into old pictures on a bookshelf, engraved rings, memories of sticking stars to a ceiling, and maybe the space gets bigger and heavier every year.

I use the phone number Adam left on the fridge and call him at his office.

"Yo," he says when he picks up.

"Um, it's me," I say. "April."

"I know," he says. "Caller ID. I don't usually say 'yo' when I pick up my phone."

"I'm home early," I tell him. "Just thought I'd let you know." It reminds me of when I lived over the Wash 'n Fold and I had to call my dad after I got home and locked the door behind me. That was when he worked at the electric company, before he got fired. When he had a work number I could call.

"Hey, I'm just grading papers," Adam says. "I can work on them later. Want me to come home? We can go do something. See the falls, maybe."

I say, "Yes, I'd like you to come home," and the words don't feel as strange to me as I'd expect.

Adam picks me up and says we're going to Tackonick Falls, but when we get there somehow Tackonick is actually the way Taughannock is pronounced.

I like the way Adam looks when he's driving— his hat pulled back further than usual, a few curls peeking out around his forehead, the scratched wire-rimmed glasses he only wears in the car sit slightly crooked on his nose. I like the way he focuses on the road completely, as if I'm precious cargo and he's being very, very careful.

He parks and we walk on a crushed stone path along a creek. I hear the rush of water from the falls long before we see it. The creek is close to dry and the water that's left is almost completely frozen. When we get closer to the falls the boulders in the creekbed are glazed with ice, thick and white like frozen milk. None of it looks real. The cliffs are so high and it's hard to tell what's frozen and what's moving water. I blink and think maybe when I open my eyes I'll just be looking at a plain old creek in plain old woods, but the falls are still there, like someone painted a huge picture and left it for us. My eyelashes are heavy with snowy droplets, and everything looks blurry and bright and misty. My teeth chatter.

"It's too soon, isn't it?" Adam says as he wraps me in his arms. Somehow he's still so very warm. I hug him back. "But . . ." He wipes mist off my cheek. "I think I'm falling in love with you."

He kisses me before I can say anything, which is good, because I don't know what I should say.

We stop at Wegmans just outside of town and buy food for dinner. Not the quick kind of dinners we usually have. Adam buys tiny round steaks that get wrapped up in paper at the meat counter, asparagus, big fat egg noodles, and real garlic, not the chopped stuff in the jar Dale used at Margo's.

Adam stops at the liquor store on the way home and leaves the car running for me while he goes in to buy a bottle of wine. And I'm nervous because I know something is different about this, but I'll never be different enough to not have lied to him.

Adam sets me up in the living room with the TV remote and a glass of wine and the bottle just in case. He tells me I get to be a lady of leisure while he makes dinner. I flip channels for a while, but TV chatter is a reminder of my old life. It makes me feel like a bag of coffee spilled in the dirt and I realize I'd rather listen to the rhythm of Adam chopping things in the kitchen, the clink of pots and pans, and the sound of water boiling. I drink my wine and pour some more and think about how these are the sounds of what a home is supposed to be. This is what most people grow up to. I lie on the futon with my hair falling over the side to the floor and watch the way the light changes as the sun sets, and the smell of garlic gets warmer and fuller, and I think of it all like a song, with words I can't quite hear yet. I hold my hands like I have a guitar and pretend I'm strumming to try to focus the words in my head. Something about deception, something about perception, and something about home and love boiling in the kitchen and light turning to dark on the ceiling.

"What are you doing?" Adam says.

I jump to my feet, my imaginary guitar falling to the floor.

"There's something you don't know about me," I say, and instantly I wish I could catch all those words and push them back in my mouth like they never happened.

"That you've had too much wine?" Adam says, kissing me on the forehead.

I steady myself on the arm of the futon. "It's that . . . it's that . . . I'm, I-I play guitar."

"Air guitar?"

"Real guitar," I say. "I don't have one anymore. But I did play. And it's just, it's important. It's the most important, and you didn't even know."

"Well, thank you for telling me." Adam smiles in the way that makes his eyes crinkle.

"Thank you for being somebody I could tell," I say, and my eyes well up.

"Hey, hey," Adam says, wrapping his arms around me. "It's okay. Someday you'll tell me all of it."

"I'm sorry."

"We all have our weepy wine nights," he says. "It's what makes us human."

"I thought it was opposable thumbs," I say. It's the one thing I remember from science class. I like the word *opposable*.

"That too," he says. "Thumbs and the ability to get weepy out of nowhere when we have too much wine. Those are the two things that make us human."

After dinner, when we lie in bed together, I help Adam form chords with his fingers. We sing Air Supply songs to the ceiling and strum our imaginary guitars until our voices get sleepy and hoarse.

— Chapter 22 —

In my head all morning, I celebrate my one-
month anniversary of being at Adam's place.
While I'm taking orders and making espressos,
there are lyrics about home and the sound of
coffeepots gurgling and beers in the fridge (that
I finally have the courage to take) swimming in
my mind, trying to put themselves together. Four
whole weeks, and it's almost Christmas, and I've
bought him a present—a record player I found
at a thrift store, some Dylan records, a best of
Simon & Garfunkel, and an Air Supply LP—and
tonight after I'm done with work, we're going
to get an actual Christmas tree of our very own
and decorate it with strings of popcorn and make
stars out of egg cartons and glitter, because Adam
can't believe I've never made an egg carton star.

I didn't tell him that I've never had a Christmas
tree. Margo always invited me over when she
decorated hers: a vintage aluminum one with
pink lights, and feather ornaments that all came
from the same set and match perfectly. I tell him
about Margo's tree like it was really mine. Like I
belonged at her place.

And I certainly don't tell him about the first
time I walked in the door of my dad's new place
with Irene and there was a Christmas tree right

there in the middle of the living room with lights and ugly ornaments the boy made and a star way up top, so close to the ceiling that my dad was the only one who could have hung it there. When I saw the tree, I could see the whole situation of it in my mind—them singing and decorating, being warm and family and all that crap. It's not like I wanted to spend an afternoon listening to Irene coo about the boy hanging painted pinecones all over the tree while a Buck Owens Christmas album played on repeat in the background. It's just that I couldn't help but remember all the times my dad told me we couldn't have a tree because it was a waste of money or a waste of trees or there was no point in giving a fuck anyway.

So when we're eating breakfast before work and Adam says we should go get a tree, I just smile and say, "Sounds great," and tell him I'll pick up some cider on the way home. Because it sounds like a normal thing to do, and the eggnog Margo always had when we decorated her tree used to sit in my stomach like a brick for hours.

Later, Adam comes into the cafe and has lunch with me over at the corner table, pretending we're just friends, like always, because it's easier. I'm used to hiding the things I really want anyway.

"So," Adam says, "I'd like to spend Christmas with you. If you want to."

We spent Thanksgiving together, but mostly we

ignored that it was Thanksgiving, because it was all new and awkward. I worked at Decadence that morning and brought home turkey sandwiches and we watched a couple movies on TV. But even though it's not like I had anywhere else to go for Christmas, this feels official. With plans and a tree and making a fuss.

"Yeah," I say, staring into my bowl of beef barley soup, making work of picking out all the carrots. "I mean, we're already getting a tree."

I actually like carrots, but building a pile of them on the side of my coffee saucer is easier than having to look in Adam's eyes. I could scare him with how much I want. Everything good could slip away, like when I used to try to bring sand home from the playground in my tightly closed fist.

Around four o'clock, Adam's client, Anna, comes in by herself. I'm replacing the register tape, so I say, "I'll be right with you."

Anna sighs like having to wait is the biggest inconvenience of her entire life. And, of course, because everyone else who changes the tape smashes the roll of paper in without paying attention, the slot you have to feed the paper through is beat up and bent and the process kind of reminds me of the open heart surgery Matty and I watched on TV after his dad put up the satellite dish. My first three tries fail and I have to go get scissors to cut the paper to a point and try again.

Bodie comes out for a refill on his hot chocolate. His fingers are black, which means he's been in the kitchen sketching instead of washing dishes. When he sees Anna, he tucks the red stirrer straw he's always chewing behind his ear, leans on the counter so he's totally in her face, and says, "Can I help you?" in this completely gross fake-manly voice.

"Half-caff skim latte with sugar-free vanilla, please," she says.

Bodie stares at her perfectly painted Valentine mouth and bites his bottom lip. "Large?"

"Small."

He wipes his charcoal fingers on his jeans and makes her a medium, looking over to smile at her more than he's watching what he's doing. I worry he'll burn himself again, like he did last week when some girl with blond dreadlocks and big boobs whispered her order in his ear like it was a secret only he could know.

When Bodie hands Anna her drink, he makes sure their fingers touch and says, "Two twenty-five" which is what a small costs.

She hands him a five, but I'm still working on the register tape. I've almost got it, but some of the paper is bunched on one side, so I have to use a knife to finish jamming it through.

"Oh, keep the change," she says, like it's no big deal to pay more than twice what she's been charged. All I have left to do is close the register lid, so she wouldn't have to wait more than two seconds.

"Thanks," Bodie says. He grabs a pencil from under the counter. "Hey, do you think I could give you a call some—" but she's already out the door.

I almost feel bad for him, but then he says, "Pilgrim, can you make me a hot chocolate? You make them better than me," like I'm supposed to swoon. Like he still believes in the power of his charm, even after he got shut down.

When I make his hot chocolate, I kind of hate myself.

On the way home, when I stop at the drugstore to buy a tube of dark red lipstick, I hate myself a little bit more. But when I get home, put the lipstick on, and study my reflection in the bathroom mirror, I love the way my lips look like a Valentine and I can't stop staring.

After I get the lipstick perfect, I pull my hair back in one big twisty braid that falls over my shoulder, because Adam told me once that it looks pretty that way. And it does. I don't look like the old April anymore. I look like maybe I could really fit here. Like this is the place where my life gets to start, and maybe I'm ready for it.

I hear Adam's footsteps on the stairs and my heart bangs around in my chest in a good way.

"Lucy, I'm ho-ome," Adam calls as he opens the door.

I stand my lipstick tube up on the shelf Adam cleared for me in the medicine cabinet and run out to meet him.

"Hey," he says, hugging my waist. He spins me around and kisses my neck. "Ready to get a tree?"

"Yeah." I kiss him back, and my lips leave a big red smudge on his face. He doesn't wipe it off.

Adam drives us out of the city through wide-open farmland where the sky looks big and the land is just arching out in front of us. He turns down a dirt road lined with short, fat pine trees and parks in front of a rickety white farmhouse.

"Stay here," he says, "I'll be right back."

He leaves the car running for me so the heat's still on, sprints up the porch steps.

A tall, skinny guy with curly hair down his back comes around from the side of the house, an axe slung over his shoulder. He's wearing a green elf hat.

"Hey, man!" I can hear Adam say. The guy puts his arm around Adam and they hug, bumping shoulders and shaking hands at the same time. Adam slaps some cash into the guy's hand, and the guy passes his axe to Adam. They walk to the far end of the porch and the guy points to the field of trees on the side of the house. Adam nods. They shake hands again.

Adam gets back in the car, resting the axe carefully on the back seat. "Okay. Billy says the trees on the far end of the lot are the best."

"I like his hat," I say.

Adam laughs. He drives us further down the bumpy dirt road until we can't see the farmhouse anymore and it's just me and him and this miniature forest, like we're in a fairy tale. It's starting to snow, even though there are hardly any clouds. We walk around, holding hands, looking at trees from every angle as if we're making the most important of decisions.

When my teeth start to chatter, Adam takes his hat off and drops it on my head. "You can wait in the car if you want," he says.

"No, I'm fine."

He kisses me, and then we decide that the tree we're kissing in front of should be our tree, even though it's a little sparse on one side.

"Are you sure?" Adam says.

I nod. "It's part of our history now."

Adam walks to the car and comes back with the axe. It's that time of night just before it gets dark when the light is orange, and everything looks brighter, and seeing him chopping at our Christmas tree, looking golden, his breath forming clouds, makes me wish I took pictures or painted or had some way of keeping all of this in my mind exactly as it is so I'll never forget.

When we get home, Adam cuts the rope on the car and we haul the tree up the stairs together. It's heavy and we're clumsy and the needles scratch my hands, but it smells like a whole entire forest right in our stairwell. We get to the top of the stairs and then realize we should have unlocked the door to the apartment first. Adam put the keys back in his pocket after he unlocked the downstairs door.

"You got it for a sec?" Adam asks.

"Sure," I say. He lets go to dig for the keys. The tree is too heavy. My hands slip and it slides down the stairs until the trunk hits the wall with a thud.

"Shit," I say.

Adam laughs. He opens the door to the apartment and then runs down the stairs to grab the tree, carrying it back up all by himself like it's not even heavy.

"I dented the wall." I point to the trunk-shaped gash. "I'm so sorry."

"Hey," Adam says, "it's part of our history."

We don't have a stand, so we put the tree in a bucket of rocks and Adam moves it around the living room looking for the perfect spot.

"A little to the right," I tell him, and he scoots

the tree, shuffling his feet along the floor. "No, left." He shuffles back. "No. Maybe if you turn it just a little and then move it to the right?"

"Are you seeing how long you can get me to move this tree around the living room?" Adam asks, grinning.

"Yes." I run away from him and jump on the futon like it's base and I'm safe as long as I'm touching it.

Adam puts the tree down and charges at me, laughing. He picks me up by the waist and swings me around. "What am I gonna do with you, huh?" he says.

"Love me?" I say. We haven't said the L-word since he said he thought he *might* love me the other day at the falls. We've avoided it. But then I just blurt it out, what I want most, like those are the only words that make sense.

"I already do," he says, and puts me down. He takes his hat off my head and looks at me. "I love you, April. I completely and totally love you."

"I love you too," I say, and they are the biggest words I've ever said.

Adam scoops me up in his arms and carries me into the bedroom, and when he lays me down on the bed and kisses me, it's totally different from all the other times we've kissed. He grabs my hair in his hands, and there's an urgent feeling between us that hasn't been there before.

This time when he goes into the bathroom,

he doesn't run the water, and he doesn't stay in there. He comes back with a condom. And when we do it, it's better than everything that led up to it. It feels like more than sex. Like I finally get it—all of it—understand what the fuss is about. It's about him holding me tightly, my skin pressed against his skin and the way he kisses my neck, how he whispers, "I love you, April," over and over again, and it all turns into something big and powerful and so much more than just two little people in a bed.

"This," Adam says, when it's over, "is the most right I've ever felt." His cheeks are damp against mine, and I think it's just sweat, but then he sniffles and it sounds like he's crying.

"What?" I ask, without knowing what I'm really asking. I don't know the right question or if there even is a question. But I know it's the most right I've ever felt too, and I don't want to cry. I want him to be happy with me.

"Can I tell you something?" he says.

"Yes."

"When I was fourteen, I slept with my stepmother."

"Oh."

"I mean, she made me. And then she held it over my head that it happened. That she could tell my dad at any moment and he would send me away. So I didn't tell him and I couldn't stop her. But then he found out. He caught us."

"Is that when you were homeless?" I ask.

I can feel Adam nod his head.

"I slept in the park or hid in the library. He didn't even care until a cop caught me sleeping on a bus bench and brought me home. Then he sent me to live with my grandparents and told them it was because he wanted me in that school district." There's a super-long silence, but I can tell Adam isn't waiting for me to say something, he's trying to find his words. "My dad didn't even leave her. Like I was the fault. I was the problem. Even though I was fourteen. He's still married to her, I think. I don't know for sure, but he didn't leave her when it happened."

"What about your mom?" I ask.

"She's an alcoholic. I guess my dad felt like it was easier to pay her alimony so she could sit in her condo and drink herself to death. You know, instead of getting her help or caring."

I hug him tight like somehow it could fix things.

"In college once," he says, "I told one of my friends. We were up late drinking and I couldn't get it out of my head, what happened, so I told him, because maybe it would make me feel better for someone to know. But he was all, 'Dude! Older chicks!' like it was something I'd chosen to do. It was the worst feeling, to have my friend not get that it wasn't a good thing, that I was just a kid. So I never told anyone else."

216

I squeeze him tighter.

"That's why I took so long to—for us to—"

I kiss him so he doesn't have to say it. "It's okay. It's nice that we waited."

"I think I'm conditioned to feel like if I have sex, something bad is going to happen. Like it's just wrong no matter what. Scars only fade to a certain point, you know?"

I think about the nail mark in my foot and how you can barely see it, but it's still there and always will be.

"Then, with you, all of a sudden, it just felt right," he says. "It feels like being with you is the best thing I can do."

I wipe his cheeks and kiss them and kiss his nose and smooth his hair off his forehead, because I don't know what to say. I don't want him to hurt anymore.

"Millie, my ex," Adam says, "she left because she needed more. She said I was weird about sex. Closed off to her. I just—It never stopped feeling wrong. And I couldn't tell her. I couldn't make myself say the words, you know?"

I nod, because I can't say any words. I will never be able to tell him how old I am. There's no point we'll come to where he's so in love and happy that it won't matter. There isn't a far-off day when I'm really nineteen and this will be a funny story. He won't ever see what we just did as being any better than what his stepmom made him do, even though he's given me things I didn't know enough to want before.

"I don't blame Millie for leaving." His face looks a little funny when he says it, a softness in his eyes, and I think maybe he does blame her some, even though he doesn't want to. "Now, with you, I realize that it's better she left. She needed someone who could be honest with her about who they are, and I couldn't be. Not with her. With you—it's like you accept me and I don't even have to ask you to. I don't have to defend myself. Millie always came out of the gate with something that was wrong with me. You can't be yourself in defense mode. You know?"

And I wish I didn't know. I wish I didn't have anything to defend. So here's what I decide: Nothing before this matters. It all starts now so I can give Adam everything.

I wake up to Adam leaning on his elbow, watching me sleep, and it makes me smile. I'm all of a sudden a person who gets to be loved so much that even when I'm sleeping someone is interested in me. He brushes the hair out of my face and says, "Hey there," and gives me a kiss I feel all the way to my toes. The fact that we have to get up and go to work seems cruel.

We do pre-coffee coffee, get dressed, and shuffle out of the apartment. It feels like everything is fake, but in a good way. Like better than real. Happily ever after and kind of like a dream and then I get to work and Adam stands in line for his post-coffee coffee and I'm behind the counter and I feel this longing for him. I want everyone else to fade to black so it can just be me and Adam in his apartment and that's all there is in the world.

When Adam gets his coffee and has to leave, I miss him. Like actually feel that tug in my chest, even though I know I'll see him tonight. It's Wednesday, so we're ordering pizza from The Nines and watching *90210*. I love the way we have different days for different things. But even knowing what I'm looking forward to doesn't stop the tightness in my chest when I watch him walk out the door.

— Chapter 23 —

I remember Mark Conrad telling Matty how to chalk his license. I didn't listen too carefully, because it was Mark Conrad, and he always had plans for ways to get booze, or get into a night-club in Buffalo, or score weed from some guy who knows some guy who knows his cousin, but none of it ever actually happened. Mark always wussed out and blamed it on circumstance, like his cousin was scared straight, or they don't sell the right colored pencils to chalk a license in Little River, or that nightclub was lame anyway. But I remember the basics of what he said—how you had to have white, black, and red colored pencils, and use a twisted-up piece of paper towel to blend things. Thankfully, since I'm only trying to be nineteen, I don't have to worry about the UNDER 21 label on my license. For that, Mark claimed to have some cut and splice trick with special tape and melting the outside plastic, but I doubt it was something he'd actually tried.

When Bodie is outside smoking, I call out, "Break!" to Carly, swipe Bodie's leather pencil case from the messenger bag he leaves on a hook in the kitchen, and run upstairs to the storage room.

The light sucks. I have to lean over a box of

coffee stirrers to work on a shelf by the window and it puts me at this weird angle where it's hard to keep my hand steady. But I don't have to change much—just shape the eight in 1978 to a five on the birthday and issued dates, white out the J for junior license, and then I'm nineteen. When I start working on it, the stuff about the blending and the paper towel makes sense. I focus really small, the way I do when I'm putting on eyeliner, thinking about where I want the pencil to go, and then my hand just does it, one tiny speck at a time. I feel so lucky that as sloppy as Bodie is, he's kind of anal about his art supplies. All his pencils are perfectly sharpened.

Bodie is in the kitchen when I get back. I'm not expecting him to be. He usually takes the world's longest smoke breaks. He sees me holding his pencil case.

Sometimes my brain thinks faster than I even know it can, because I say, "Bodie, you must have dropped this. I found it on the floor under one of the tables."

"Shit, Pilgrim," he says, "you're a lifesaver. That's like my soul right there." And then I feel awful, because the way Bodie feels about his pencils is totally the way I felt about my guitar.

"Favor?" I ask. I can't stop now just because I feel bad.

"Anything," he says, so stupid grateful that I saved his pencils.

"Can you cover for me for like ten minutes? Girl trouble," I say, knowing Bodie is squeamish about those things. He blushes for hours after Carly makes him restock the tampon machine in the bathroom. And as much as it embarrasses me to embarrass him, my desperation makes me brave.

I run to the art supply store, buy a can of something called fixative, spray my license in the alley, and dump the can in the dumpster. Mark Conrad says the fixative is what separates the pros from the amateurs, because it makes it really hard to rub the fake numbers off.

Chapter 24

Carly is in a mood today. She's always in some kind of mood. I've never worked a day with her where the way she was feeling didn't change the air around her one way or another, but this mood is especially bad.

At first I worry it's because I took a really long break to get the fixative, because maybe Bodie didn't cover for me well. But Carly's eyes are lined with super thick black liner and dark shadow. I've pulled that trick before, so I know it's not always a fashion statement so much as a way to cover up dark circles and puffy lids. When I don't let myself get distracted by all that black, I can see how red her eyes are.

"Stop staring," she says, and opens her mouth all slack-jawed and dopey like she's saying I look like that.

She's almost always nice to me. It's been her and me against the spoiled kids. But this is one of those moments that gets me feeling shaky and teary and embarrassed even though it shouldn't. I've handled worse. Why would it matter for Carly to look at me funny? I turn away and distract myself by wiping down the espresso machine, which keeps me busy enough, because I'm the only one who ever bothers to do it.

• • •

After lunch, the phone rings and it's some girl for Carly. She says her name is Rosemary and instead of letting me take a message, she says she'll hold while I get Carly, as if we have one of those fancy phones with a hold button and I won't be balancing the receiver in an empty coffee cup.

I go outside to look for Carly. She's crouched against the wall, perched on the toes of her combat boots, sucking at her cigarette like it's a lifeline, spitting smoke into the air with force. Icicles from the overhang drip on her like rain and that raccoon makeup is streaming down her face. Her tights are ripped. With Carly, you never know if she wanted her tights like that or it happened by accident, but something about her ripped tights makes her look extra sad.

"Phone," I say, trying hard not to stare, pressing my lips together as soon as I get the word out.

Carly holds her cigarette in her teeth and wipes her cheeks with both hands, smearing black all the way to her ears. "Who is it?"

"Rosemary."

"I don't want to talk to her," Carly says, her words garbled by a sob. She tries to stand, but her foot slips and she falls to her knees on the icy gravel.

I run over and wrap my arms around her so immediately that it shocks me. "Okay," I whisper. "It's okay."

She cries into my shoulder. I help her stand. Her knee is scraped up, bloody.

"I'll go get the first aid kit," I say.

"They can't see me like this." She tips her head toward the kitchen door. "It's hard enough."

She looks so small. She's short, but all her bluster and brightness made her seem big. Now she looks like a lost kid.

"I'll be quick and quiet," I say.

"I just want to leave," she says, and her face crumples.

"We can go get my car and I'll drive you home."

I open the door to the kitchen and yell to Bodie that he needs to watch the register until Kelsye comes in for her shift.

"Where's Carly?" he yells back.

"Supplier emergency," I yell, and herd Carly down the alley, hoping that whoever Rosemary is, she's hung up the phone so Bodie won't end up talking to her.

"I'm so stupid," Carly says when we get to the end of the alley. The sobs break through again, even though it looks like every single cell in her body is fighting to hold them back. "I don't even have any place to go." Blood from the scrape on her knee is soaking through her tights; bits of gravel are stuck to her skin.

I keep my copy of Adam's key and my car key tucked in my left boot at all times, just in case.

So I don't even have to go back for my bag. We walk down Aurora Street to avoid the front of the cafe. Carly tries hard to pretend her knee isn't hurting, but I catch her wincing when we cross Green Street and she has to step up on the curb. I grab her hand as we climb the hill on Hudson, because I don't know what else to do, and I think about all the times I wished someone would hold my hand when I felt defeated. I want to ask her what's wrong, but when you feel like that, sometimes having to say it out loud is the worst part.

We get to Adam's and Carly doesn't even look at me weird when I lean against the handrail on the front step to dig the key out of my boot. She's stopped crying, but she keeps wiping her eyes and the smudged makeup makes her look like a cartoon bandit. She stares up at the building.

"You live here?" she says.

"I'm staying with a friend," I say as I open the downstairs door, not knowing if it's okay for her to know. Not knowing if I want her to. Just because she's sad, it doesn't mean I can trust her.

"You know Adam"—she points to her head—"with the hat?"

"Yeah," I say, worried about what she'll say next—what there is to Adam that she knows and I don't.

"I think he lives on Hudson somewhere."

"He does," I say, turning my back as I walk up the stairs.

"Oh," Carly whispers.

I unlock the door to the apartment and hold it open for her.

"It's funny," she says. "I wouldn't have thought . . . But, you know, he's a really nice guy."

"He is," I say.

I show her where Adam keeps the band-aids and iodine. "Do you need help?" I ask, and she makes that dopey face at me, like I'm being ridiculous. But this time it doesn't hurt my feelings, because I know we're on the same side.

I get her a Coke and a hand towel from the linen closet so she can wash her face. And then I pull a pair of my clean pajama pants from a drawer Adam cleared out for me. They're new. Pink flannel with blue cups of steaming coffee all over, like something you'd see the main character on a sitcom wear. And I've been so proud of them since I bought them, but when Carly comes out of the bathroom, I feel silly offering them to her.

"I figured your tights were wet," I say, handing them over.

She looks young without all the makeup on. She takes the pants from me and pops back in the bathroom. When she comes out again she's wearing them, and they look ridiculous under her ripped black dress and silver mesh sweater. Her tights are hanging on the radiator to dry, and her boots are on their sides on the floor.

I don't know how to act or what to say. We plop down on the futon and put our feet on the trunk, taking swigs from our Cokes. I never had girlfriends. Too many people whispered about my dad and his gambling and my mom leaving and the motorhome. If I ever did get invited to some girl's house to play after school, she was never allowed to come to mine, so eventually she got to be better friends with someone else—someone whose mom made cookies and was there when she got home from school, someone who had birthday parties to invite her to. I had Matty, and Margo was my friend too, but that's different. It's not the same as getting to be friends with a girl your own age.

"So, Rosemary," Carly says, "told me she couldn't be with anyone who wasn't out." She reaches over to pick at the cracked leather on the trunk. "It's not like I was particularly *in,* I just wasn't all the way out, you know?"

I nod, but I don't know. I'm not sure if she's talking about a club or a gang or a game that she's not in or out of. But then she looks at me, and I can tell that the way she feels is the way I felt when I left Matty. That it's that kind of loss, and I start to think that Rosemary must be her girlfriend.

There aren't gay people in Little River. I've

never met one, and I never even thought about women having sex with women until just now. Gary would mouth off about the homos who were ruining America, but he was talking about men who sleep with other men, which I know, because I looked it up at the library. I expected homos to be some kind of robber barons or corrupt politicians or evil wizards and it was kind of a disappointment to learn that they were just men who slept with men. I couldn't figure out how that was ruining America, but most of what Gary said never made much sense to me anyway.

I want to say something to Carly, but I don't know what. And as much as I'm not sure how I feel about this girl wearing my pants, crying over a breakup with another girl, I know she hurts and I wish she didn't.

"I get worried I'm going to lose her," Carly says, and her voice wobbles. "So I come out. Like completely out. I tell my parents."

Suddenly she's crying so hard that I feel like I'm going to cry. She can't say words and she's curled up stiff like the sobs are taking everything from her.

"He told me I'm not his daughter," she says finally. "He told me no way he made a dyke like me."

I hold her and I tell her I'm sorry and I tell her she's better than him, because how can I not? And I start to hate Gary. Really hate him, because he's exactly the kind of person who would say something like that to his daughter if he had one.

"She doesn't understand," Carly says. "Rosemary . . . so easy for her with her New York City parents who practically *wanted* her to be gay, because it's like completely and totally in this year. I'm from Allegany. My dad's a teamster. I knew better."

"What did your mom say?" I ask, which is bad of me, because I'm always curious about people's moms and my question is more for me than for her.

"She can't ever disagree with him, you know?" she says, wiping her nose on her sleeve. "She can't ever stick up for me. Not for anything, so why did I think she'd tell him off or tell me she's fine with it, that she loves me, you know?"

"My mom left when I was six," I say. "And my dad's an asshole."

"I'm sorry," she says.

"I'm just telling you so you know that I get it," I say, "that I know how it hurts. Not so you'll feel sorry for me."

She blows her nose into a wad of toilet paper she's shoved in the pocket of my pajama pants.

"I'm not good at crying," she says. "It's either nothing ever, even when I should be crying, or it's like a three-day explosion. I hate it." She takes a deep breath, determined to collect herself, grabs the remote and turns on the television.

We watch a *Spenser: For Hire* rerun and make fun of the puffy-sleeved satin blouses Spenser's psychologist girlfriend wears. Carly grabs my hand and holds it, and you'd think it would be weird, but it's not, because it's not about anything other than the fact that she really needs a friend.

When Adam comes home, we're out on the fire escape so Carly can smoke.

"Hello?" he says as he walks in the bathroom and peeks out the window. It's hard not to jump up and run inside to kiss him, but I don't want to make Carly feel weird, or rub in the fact that I have someone when she just broke up with her someone.

Carly stiffens, like she's been caught.

Adam looks confused, but I can also tell that he gets that she's been crying. "Hi, Carly," he says, trying hard to act like it's normal that she's here so she won't feel uncomfortable. I'm proud of him. "We were going to order pizza from The Nines tonight. Does eggplant work for you?"

"Sure," Carly says, and her back loosens up.

Adam tells Carly she can stay as long as she needs to. I want Adam to myself again, almost as soon as he offers, but it's nice that we can do this for Carly. I finally get to have a friend over. I finally get to be a friend.

We eat pizza and drink beer and watch *90210*, lined up in a row on the couch: Adam, me, and Carly. I almost tell them that it's my first sleepover party, but I think it would be too weird.

Carly sleeps on the futon. She snores. Adam and I lie in bed and giggle every time she gets particularly loud. We have a witness to us now. It's funny the way we just went to bed like that's who we are. We're together and we sleep together and being open about it makes it so much more real. I love it and it terrifies me at the same time, like how I felt when Matty and I climbed to the roof of the high school to watch an eclipse and I stood with my toes at the very edge.

"Looks like you're in the habit of taking in lost girls," I say, poking Adam's shoulder.

"You're the only one who gets to stay forever," he says.

When Adam and I wake up, Carly is still sleeping, so we tiptoe around, trying to avoid the floorboards that are known creakers. Adam makes a full pot of coffee and a huge stack of pancakes, which amazes me, because I didn't even know we had the right ingedients.

"I wanted to make them shaped like something," Adam says, waving the spatula at the pan, "but they all ended up looking like pancakes."

When Carly wakes up and stumbles into the kitchen, with puffy eyes and her black and purple hair sticking out at every angle, Adam offers her pancake-shaped pancakes, and I pour her a cup of coffee.

"You guys pre-caffeinate too?" she says, smiling at us. "You two are cute, you know. It's nice."

Adam cuts orange slices and Carly and I set places at the little card table in the kitchen that Adam and I hardly ever use.

After breakfast, Adam and Carly and me walk to Decadence together. When we hit the brick walkway of The Commons, it strikes me as funny—the three of us, side by side, like we're on our way to Oz and short a lion. And at work, Carly is different. She's chatty. She winks at me when the absurdly picky lady comes in and takes five minutes to get her full order out. She makes me a latte and tells Bodie to watch the register and we take her smoke break together, sitting on milk crates in the alley. She tells me she feels like an idiot, but she really misses Rosemary. She tells me she knows there's no way it will ever work out for them now, but it doesn't change the fact that she's scared to be alone.

"I think maybe everyone is scared to be alone," I tell her. "Maybe when you get down to it, that's why everybody does everything. Maybe all we're doing is trying to be less alone."

"Are you sure you don't smoke up?" Carly says, laughing. She taps the side of my boot with the side of hers.

"I sing," I tell her. "Or I used to. Got to protect the pipes." Then I realize it was a rhetorical question. I'm not good with those. Someone asks me something and I always feel like I should answer one way or another.

"Why don't you sing now?"

"My dad smashed my guitar." I tell her tiny bits of me. Little River, Margo, the diner, the boy. Puzzle pieces, but not too many. Enough that it helps—that it feels like I let some of the steam out.

I'm telling her about Matty and the wife he wanted me to be when Bodie peeks his head out and says, "Can I go to the kitchen now? Psycho chick is back."

"Which one?" Carly says.

I think it's another rhetorical question, but Bodie says, "The one with the nipple ring."

"People have nipple rings?" I blurt out. "Ouch! Why?"

Bodie and Carly laugh.

"That's what you get when you love 'em and leave 'em, Bodes," Carly says, smacking Bodie on the back when she gets up. She stomps out her cigarette and goes inside.

"People pierce lots of things, Pilgrim," Bodie says as I walk past him, and I wonder if he has any rings in strange places. "You'd be surprised. That girl, nutty as a fruitcake, but wow. Crazy, crazy in bed."

When I get behind the register again, Carly is taking an order from some girl who looks like the picture of normal. Shiny brown hair in one of those perfect ponytails without any flyaways, an Ithaca College sweatshirt, and a plain old pair of jeans. Carly raises her eyebrows to me to let me know it's *the* girl. It's so weird, the way that even the most ordinary looking people can hide things.

When the girl leaves, Carly calls Bodie out of the kitchen and makes him swear on a stack of supply catalogs and sign an oath on a napkin to promise that he'll stop being a manwhore. We pin the napkin to the corkboard by the phone, laughing so hard we're crying.

I, Bodie,
will curb my general whoritude
and work to cultivate better taste
in romantic partners and
better common sense overall.

It's also weird, the way you can go from just working someplace to feeling like you really belong.

A few days later, Adam says he knows a guy who has a vacant studio up by the college, and he coaches Carly on how to get out of paying the security deposit. Over pancakes again, because that's like our thing now. This time, Carly brought home a bag of chocolate chips.

"Buddy's tenant failed out of school and left him in the lurch," Adam tells her. "He's already got a security deposit from that guy that he doesn't have to give back; he shouldn't need one from you. If you move in, he won't even miss a month of rent. There aren't enough new students second semester. He's not going to rent it otherwise and he knows it." He scribbles Buddy's number on an old receipt and hands it to Carly. "If he gives you a problem, let me know. I'll call."

As much as part of me wants Adam all to myself again, I feel like grabbing the number away from Carly. Having her stay with us has been like how I always thought having a sister would feel.

I go with Carly when she packs up her stuff. It's this place up by the college. Half a ranch house. Jock boys next door and very un-Carly. I figured she'd live in one of the cool old houses on East State Street or College Avenue, someplace with character.

Rosemary is perched on a chair at the kitchen table. Long flowy skirt, bare feet; she hugs her knees, smoking as she watches us. She's thin with dark hair cut in an angled bob. I've seen her before at the cafe. I thought she was just Carly's roommate. And even then I didn't understand how Carly could stand to live with her. She's exactly the kind of rich bitch Carly is always complaining about. Or maybe she *is* the rich bitch Carly was complaining about. She has this look on her face like she's just too cool to care for any of it.

Rosemary doesn't try to hide that she's watching us. She stares, but she doesn't say anything until we've taken eight trips out to Carly's rusty, orange Pacer, and we're grabbing the last few boxes. Finally she says, "You're not going to introduce me to your girlfriend?"

My face gets hot and I know it's red and I feel so awful, because the last thing Carly needs is me acting like being her girlfriend is some kind of terrible thing. So I rest the box of cassette tapes on a chair and offer my hand to Rosemary to shake. "April," I say. "Nice to meet you."

Rosemary ignores my hand and gives Carly a death stare. "She's perfect for you," she says, and I know it's an insult, even though I'm not sure why.

"Let's go, hon," I say to Carly, picking up the box again. It's funny how two seconds ago I was embarrassed she thought I was Carly's girlfriend and now I'm pissed that she thinks I'm not good enough to be.

When we get in the car, Carly bursts out laughing. " 'Hon'? Really?"

"Too much?" I say.

"You rock," Carly says, and really smiles, not just the smug tight-lipped deal she pretends is a smile.

— Chapter 25 —

Carly said that even though she has her own place, she'd still come by every week for *90210* and pizza, but she calls ten minutes before the show starts to say she can't make it because of a psych paper and we'll have to catch her up next week.

"We ordered a large and everything," I say to Adam when I hang up the phone. I'd even run to the convenience store to pick up a six-pack of Dr Pepper, because Carly likes that more than Coke.

"It's fine," Adam says, handing me a plate with two slices. "I'll bring leftovers for lunch tomorrow."

"She's not going to know what's happening next week," I say. "Even if we explain."

Adam laughs like I told a joke.

When we get settled on the couch he says, "It sucks to be an undergrad. There's so much busywork." And it makes me feel far away from both of them. I barely even did my homework in high school.

The next day, when we're almost through the morning rush, Carly takes a break and has coffee with two guys and a girl at a table in the corner. The girl has a lip ring. One of the guys has bleached white hair with dark roots and skin so pale you can almost see through it. The other one looks like James Dean with black lipstick. They talk in hushed tones that grow into bursts of laughter, then drop to whispers. I can't tell what they're talking about. By the time I finish with one customer, they're being quiet again. When they're loud, I'm taking another order.

After they finish their coffee, they go out for a smoke. Right by the front door, where Carly always tells Bodie he's not allowed to smoke. At first she's just taking drags off James Dean's cigarette, but then the girl with the lip ring offers Carly her own and when James Dean finishes his, he steals Carly's for a few puffs. I wonder if he gets black lipstick all over his cigarettes. I'm not close enough to see.

The pale guy is telling a story and suddenly slaps his palms to his chest and his whole body shakes. He looks like he's exploding and they all laugh so hard they have to lean on each other to catch their breath.

The four of them seem like they belong together. Like they're an advertisement for combat boots or hair gel. I wonder if they found each other because they look like that, or if after they met, James Dean borrowed black lipstick from Carly, Lip Ring convinced Pale Guy he needed peroxide, and who they are now isn't who they would be if they'd never crossed paths.

When her friends finally leave, Carly comes back in and we rotate the stock of flavored coffee on the shelves. I kneel on the counter and she hands me new bags from the cabinet below.

She isn't chatty like she was with her friends. She looks weary, as if she'd rather be wherever they were headed next.

"How much vanilla is left?" she asks.

"Two bags," I say, and I want to crack a joke, but I can't think of anything particularly funny about vanilla. She hands me two bags to tuck behind the old ones.

"How much cherry?"

"Why would anyone want cherry coffee?"

"It's not bad," she says.

"Oh. Three bags," I say. "Did that crazy girl come back today?"

"Which one?"

"Nipple ring?"

"I don't think so." She hands me an extra bag and her bracelets slide toward her elbow. I see a tattoo on her wrist I hadn't noticed before. A thin black line looped into a knot. "Hazelnut?"

"Four," I say.

"Caramel?"

"Three."

She hands me one. "Ugh. The caramel smells so bad."

"I know," I say. "It doesn't smell like caramel."

"It smells like vomit," she says.

It's stupid, but I love that we're agreeing. We might be headed toward a real conversation.

"Mocha?" she asks.

"One."

She hands me the rest. I put them away and jump down from the counter. She yawns and stretches, watching people walk by outside like she hopes someone interesting will show up.

"I think I want to get a tattoo," I say. And really it isn't a thing I thought about, but as soon as I say it, I do want one. A mark to prove I've changed, that I'm not the same sad old April in the motorhome.

Carly perks up. "Nice. What are you going to get?"

"Not sure," I say, feeling the wobble of nerves in my belly.

"There's a place right on The Commons," she says. "They're pretty good." And before I know it, she's arranged for Bodie to cover for us, and for the Lettuce Murderer to come in early to cover for Bodie, so we can take our lunch break together and go to the tattoo shop. It's this spiraling thing where my random thought becomes what I'm actually going to do and it's so exhilarating I forget to be nervous.

Bodie spends the rest of the morning sitting in the kitchen with his tongue sticking out the side of his mouth, sketching on a napkin. We don't know what he's drawing. He won't let us see, and it's hell to get him to fill orders, but when he's done, he gives the napkin to me. "Just an idea," he says. "For your tattoo." It's a white flower with a yellow center and five pointy petals like a star, streams of every color shooting out behind like it's zooming through space. It's beautiful and I can't believe Bodie drew it just for me.

Carly says it won't hurt. Like at all. "It's seriously like not even a big deal, April. You'll be fine. You'll love it." She holds my hand and swings it back and forth as we walk across The Commons to the tattoo store. But when I'm in the chair and I've flashed my chalked ID and signed all the papers, I ask her again, and she says that it *does* hurt, but it's good hurt, like when you have a sore tooth and you can't stop poking at it, which sounds a hell of a lot less appealing than she seems to think it does. At the very last minute, while Carly is squeezing my hand and the needle is buzzing right next to my hip, about to sear Bodie's drawing into my belly forever, I wimp out.

The big, hairy tattoo guy gets crabby. He got the ink and the needles ready and now I'm not even going to pay. It makes me nervous to make him mad, so I blurt out, "Nose ring. I want a nose ring instead," because it's one quick jab instead of a billion little ones.

I choose a tiny fake emerald stud.

"Wicked color," Carly says, nodding her approval. She's not acting like I wimped out, and it makes me feel better.

"Birthstone."

"Diamond is the birthstone for April," she says.

"My birthday is in May," I tell her.

She laughs, squeezing my hand as the needle goes in. "I love it."

Bodie asks to see my tattoo when we get back to Decadence and Carly says, "You wish, Bodie. You wish April would show you where it is."

Bodie touches his finger lightly to my new emerald stud and says, "Maybe I do," before he goes back into the kitchen. And even though I don't want him, even though I'm with Adam and I'm happy that way, the whole thing leaves me blushed and buzzing.

At six, right before Adam gets home, I get so nervous. Maybe he'll be mad that I got a nose ring. What if it's a totally amateur move—this stupid immature thing that's going to make it obvious that I can't possibly be nineteen? Or maybe he'll think I'm a totally different person than he wanted me to be. I stare at my nose in the mirror, like maybe if I look hard enough it will be undone. My nose is red around the stud, so even if I take it out, he'll still see what I did.

When I hear the downstairs door open, I slam the bathroom door shut. I hear Adam's footsteps on the stairs. The door to the apartment opens and closes. I have no choice but to confess.

"I did something stupid," I call from the bathroom.

"April?" he says, like there might be someone else in here yelling to him.

"Yeah."

"Are you okay?"

"Fine. Just stupid."

"What did you do?"

"I don't want to show you."

"I'm sure it's fine."

"It's stupid."

"Did you cut your hair?" He sounds amused.

"No."

"Dye it purple?" He's laughing.

"Uh uh."

"Volunteer for a medical trial?"

"No."

"Get a tattoo of a screaming eagle across your butt?" I hear him snort.

"Adam!"

"Did you eat at that truck stop by the interstate? Because that would be stupid. Those hot dogs look like they've been there since—"

I open the bathroom door.

He stares at me for a second, like he hasn't quite picked out what's different.

"Oh," he says, touching the side of my face. "It's not stupid. It's really hot."

Making love on the bathroom floor is actually a lot sexier than it sounds.

— Chapter 26 —

Adam has finals to grade before winter break, so I'm home by myself a lot after work. It's funny, I spent so much time alone in the motorhome and I was used to it, but now, when I'm alone in Adam's apartment, I can't stand how empty it feels. I tell Carly how I get antsy while we're refilling the milk thermoses during a lull at the cafe. She says, "Let's go out tonight. Cat Skin is playing at The Haunt. You'll love them."

And even though the shit Carly listens to makes me want to puncture my eardrums, I say yes, because the prospect of going out is too hard to pass up. She makes me sign a napkin:

I, April, promise to rock hard.

She pins it up next to Bodie's anti-manwhore proclamation and the stack of other vows we've taken, promising everything from the courteous replacement of register receipt paper to the finding of existential enlightenment on one's own time.

There are no nightclubs in Little River. And it's not like any of us could have gotten away with chalking a license and going to Gary's bar. He knows which kid belongs to which parent and nine times out of ten the parent is already sitting at the bar. Going out in Little River meant the deer blind with flashlights and a nicked six-pack, or hanging out in the gas station parking lot, watching the boys flip their skateboards. I was always just a hanger-on. I came as a package deal with Matty. No one ever invited me out. Margo took me to the movies in Springville sometimes, but that's different.

I tell Carly about how there are no nightclubs in Little River and she gets it. Where she grew up isn't much different. So she tells me to come to her place before and she'll let me borrow some of her clothes. That's even more exciting than going to a club.

This girl in my class, Ashley, had a big sister who would let her borrow clothes all the time and even do her hair and makeup in the schoolyard before the first bell. Heather would hold Ashley's face with one hand to steady it and tell her to suck in her cheeks so she could brush blush in the hollows. I wanted to be Ashley more than I ever wanted anything else.

I walk to Carly's new place, because she said she'd drive me home after. The Haunt is closer to us than to her. She answers the door wearing boots that lace up to her knees, cut-off red plaid pants with ripped tights underneath, and a black T-shirt that says *Nipplehead* across the chest. Her eyes are rimmed with sparkly black and purple eye shadow. When she turns around, the back of her shirt looks like a werewolf clawed her, and the blue creature on her back stares out through the rips in the fabric. I still don't know what it is, but it has a big round eye. Her hair is extra spiky like maybe she cut some chunks out of it, but it looks good. It's very Carly.

"Okay!" she says, bouncing to the closet before I'm even in the door. "Outfit! April! Outfit!"

She might be on something. I'm not good at telling. Maybe she just had too much coffee. She's happy. Like capital *H* Happy. Like capital-everything happy. She's HAPPY, and even if it might be artificially induced, after all the hurt she went through, it's nice to see. She's playing some CD that sounds like nails on a blackboard and a toddler torturing a violin. I'm guessing it's Cat Skin.

Carly sings along, "I ain't, I ain't, I ain't me! You. Ain't. You!" as she pulls clothes from her closet and throws them on the bed. Layers upon layers of black and silver and ripped flannel. There's incense burning and a drippy candle and scarves over the lights so her little apartment looks like a cave. Cozy and artsy and it makes sense. Not like the place we moved her out of.

"Anything you want to wear," Carly shouts.

"Okay," I say, but I've never had free rein of a

closet like this before. I don't even know where to start.

I grab a striped knit shirt and pull it on. It has a low scoop neck and my black bra straps show on my shoulders.

"Try this over it," she says, handing me a grey velvet corset.

I fasten the corset over the shirt and all the fabric bunches up in the wrong places. I hold my arms out to show her, but she's digging in the bottom of her closet.

When she backs out with a pair of black pin-striped pants, she looks at me and laughs. "You have to pull it down." She drapes the pants around her neck like a scarf so she can tug at the bottom of the shirt. She tugs and looks and tugs again and then pulls both sleeves past my wrists.

"Oh, you know what? Hold on!" She runs over to the kitchen area and grabs a pair of scissors from the drawer by the sink. "Thumb holes," she says, and I don't know what she means, but with two quick snips she cuts holes in the sleeves and slips them over my thumbs. "But now I'm not feeling these pants."

"They're okay," I tell her, because I worry if I'm too much of a bother all the good will go away. And this is enough. But Carly has already found a black pleated skirt that's held together with giant safety pins. I slip it on. She scrounges up two pairs of ripped black tights and tells me to wear both of them. When I put my boots on, she pulls the laces out, stuffs them in my purse, and hands me a ball of rough brown twine to re-lace them.

"There," she says when I finish tying my boots. She closes her closet door so I can see myself in the mirror. Somehow the whole outfit works in the way Carly's outfits always work. I don't understand how she can grab random pieces that don't seem to go together and find a way to make them fit. I would have just worn the shirt and maybe those pants and thought I had a whole thing going.

She hands me a lipstick and starts twisting the front pieces of my hair in tiny buns. The lipstick is dark and matte and when I smear it across my lips it makes the rest of my face look very pale.

"It needs something," she says, and grabs a tiny jar of loose black powder and a paintbrush. "Close." She blinks her eyes shut to show me what she means. "Hold still." She steadies my chin and sweeps a thick black line across each eyelid with the brush. It makes me look dangerous. Powerful. I could be a villain or a superhero. The emerald green stud in my nose catches the light and sparkles. I smile at myself in the mirror. I can't even play it cool. It *is* like having a big sister, and it's even better than I thought it would be.

Carly ties the last section of my hair up on

itself and sprays my head with a cloud of hair spray that makes both of us cough. She studies me, swishing her mouth from one side to the other. Finally she steps back and nods. "Good to go." She seems more serious, like whatever was pulling her up has started to wear off. I wonder if it was just adrenaline.

In her car on the way over, she says, "It's the first time I've been out since Rosemary. Since I left Rosemary." She doesn't look at me. Eyes on the road.

"It'll be fun," I tell her. "You'll be fine."

The bouncer tries to smudge the dates on both of our licenses, but the fixative works. He marks Xs on our hands with a black Sharpie before he lets us in. The ink is wet and cold.

"What's this?" I ask Carly, holding up my hand to show her my X, but the music is so loud she can't hear me. The music is so loud I can't even hear *it*. I feel the thumping of bass and shrieks of violin in my body. My ears can't make sense of it. Carly points at her hand and rolls her eyes.

The place is packed, and it doesn't look like there's anywhere for us to go, but Carly grabs my hand, holds it low. She twists and turns her way through the crowd, pulling me behind her. We sneak between people until we get right up to the stage.

I think I see the James Dean guy and the girl with the lip ring at the other end of the stage, but everyone is pushing and dancing and they get swallowed by the crowd.

None of the members of the band look much older than me. I can't stand the way they sound, but I love to watch them. The lead singer is wearing a yellow dress with drippy black paint stripes. She has a tiny round face and a long mess of bright orange hair. She screams, "I ain't, I ain't, I ain't" into the microphone like a little kid throwing a tantrum.

The guy playing the violin has this smirk like he knows he's making painful sounds. When the lead singer screams "You. Ain't. You!" everyone else screams along with her. Even me.

Four songs in, we're still right up at the front of the stage. I've been staring at the guitar player, watching his fingers, trying to figure out which chords he's playing and what effect the array of pedals at his feet have on the sound of his strings. He's wearing a kilt, and by accident, I notice that he isn't wearing anything under his kilt.

When I look up at his face, I realize he's staring back at me. It's weird, us watching each other. I'd been looking at him like he couldn't even see me. When our eyes meet, he smiles, slowly, this creep of movement from the corners of his lips. He's wearing eyeliner. Thick greasy pools of it under his eyes. His hair is long and dark and he has a thick, wide chin with a dimple. They finish the song and start another one. The lead singer screams, "Fuck!" at the top of her lungs about six or seven times in a row and as far as I can tell there aren't any other words to the song. Every time I look at the guitar player, he makes eye contact.

At the end of the song, when he changes picks, he looks me right in the eye, kisses the old one, and throws it at me.

I catch it, which is some kind of miracle, because I'm never that smooth. I slip the pick into my purse. Carly is freaking out. She pulls me through the crowd and into the bathroom to ask how it happened.

"I don't know," I say. "I was watching him play and he just started looking at me."

"Seriously? Don Dickford threw you his pick? He's like notably stoic."

"Do you want it?" I put my bag on the counter by the sink to dig it out.

"No! I couldn't."

"Yes, you can!" I hold it out to her. "Take it. You love them."

She wraps her arms around my neck and kisses my cheek. "I love you! You're like the best friend ever!"

Just as she's pulling away from me to get a better look at the guitar pick, the bathroom door opens, letting in a horrible blast of sound, and Rosemary.

"Oh, am I interrupting something?" Rosemary says like she's bored, pushing her way up to the mirror. She pulls a lipstick from her purse and reapplies it to her already perfectly made up lips.

"Come on, hon," I say to Carly. "Let's go."

As I reach for my bag, Rosemary knocks it off the counter, sending everything in it flying across the disgusting bathroom floor. Lipstick, eyeliner, wallet, the crocheted tampon pouch Margo made me when I got my first period, buck knife, safety pins, chewing gum—Carly and I scramble to pick it all up as if stuff that's been on the bathroom floor of a club will be less revolting if we get to it faster.

"Oops," Rosemary says, even though she clearly did it on purpose. She bends down and pushes the stuff that's near her toward me, scraping my lipstick and the crochet bag into the dirty floor even worse.

"Stop," Carly says through clenched teeth.

"Fine. Whatever." Rosemary stands up. "I was just trying to help." She walks out of the bath-room with a distracted look on her face like she's already forgotten we exist.

— Chapter 27 —

We run from The Haunt, into the cold air. My boots slap the wet pavement hard, making sparks in my shins. Carly runs like someone who knows how. Like maybe she ran track in high school. Her legs are shorter, but each stride takes her further.

She grabs my hand when I start to lag and her palm is damp like mine. We both know Rosemary isn't chasing us, but we need to get away. We need speed so our muscles can work through the itch under our skin.

We run through The Commons, down the alley next to the movie theater, up the spiral of the parking garage, and I swear I feel the concrete move from the force of us.

In Carly's car, we pant and sweat, our bodies fighting against the idea of sitting still. The rush in my veins makes me feel like Carly and I could fly if we wanted to. If we held hands and jumped from the edge of the parking garage, we would probably soar.

"That's why John and Lila didn't wave at me," Carly says, and I think maybe she means James Dean and the lip ring girl. "It's fine to be my friend when Rosemary isn't around, but heaven fucking forbid they choose me."

She stares out the windshield, key in hand, not ready to start the engine. "I can't go home yet." She looks at me. "I'll take you home, if you want to go."

I hear the plea in her voice and I'd stay with her just for that, but I can't go back yet either, to tiptoe into Adam's apartment and lie next to his sleeping self with all this energy unspent. I am mad about Rosemary, but that isn't all of it. I feel like I am actually here. Like someone dropped my mind into my body and it's a shock to the system. I think maybe they were only walking side by side before this and now we are here together, both parts of me.

"No," I say. "I'm not tired."

"Where should we go?" Carly asks.

"I don't know," I say.

We are fogging up the windshield. Carly cranks her window down. I do the same.

"It smells like campfire weather," she says.

It could be the dumbest thing, but I don't think Tom Bilford will care. I don't even know if he lives in that cabin once the campground is closed. I don't think he'll call the cops if he catches us, and at least I'm not a car thief anymore. I am not wanted by the police or my father.

"Worst they'll do is make us leave," Carly says. "Probably."

And I decide not to worry because I want to do it.

We park in a turnout before the entrance and hoof it in. If we get caught, Carly's rusty Pacer plays the part of a breakdown well enough to be our alibi. We plan our excuses in whispers as we walk, like someone might be lurking in the dark, waiting to overhear us. *It was cold. We couldn't find a phone booth. We needed the fire.*

The moon shines so brightly off the water that we can see where we're going. Not a single car drives by. There's no light in the park ranger cabin, and there's no truck out front either. The lake is ours. The night is ours. If there are raccoons in the dark, they won't want a battle. There are two of us. We are full of ourselves, ferocious.

The rhythm of our feet on the pavement—Carly's foot, my foot, Carly's other one, then mine—is just a little off from a song I can't quite gather in my head. I work to stay on beat. Carly notices that I'm noticing and holds her pace steady too. By the time we turn into the campground, we're stomping something complicated. Carly shout-sings "Cecilia!" in her funny gravelly voice. I can't believe she's even heard Simon & Garfunkel, but she knows all the words and we sing it together, keeping time with our feet, laughing when we flub a step. I sing around her crackling, off-key melody, and we sound alright.

We march past my old campsite, moving in further, away from the sightline of the main road and away from Tom Bilford's cabin, in case he comes back. We find a spot by the water, collect left-behind firewood from the sites around it.

"This is really where you stayed?" Carly asks, stacking wood strategically.

"Yeah." I pick at bark on a neatly split log as I wait to hand it to her. "But I wasn't like camping. I just slept in my car."

Carly seems to know how to make a fire and I realize that I could have done this out at the motorhome. I could have dug a pit and drug out some old metal truck bumpers from the trash heap down the road to corral the embers. It wasn't something I needed my dad to do. I didn't have to ask permission. No one was there to tell me no. I read somewhere once about animals caged too long staying put even when someone opens the door. I spent so much time in that motor-home before I realized I could go, and while I was there, I never saw the ways I could make it better.

"Shit," Carly says, and I think it's about the fire, but then she says, "It's been way too cold to sleep in a car."

I hand her another log to stack. If Matty were banished to the woods, I bet his first act would be to make a fire pit. To burn things for light and warmth and just to play with flames.

"If I'd known," Carly says, "I would have— I mean"—she laughs—"Rosemary probably wouldn't have let you stay, but I could have . . . I would have found a place for you."

"It's okay," I tell her, and my eyes are stinging, which is stupid. We can't go back in time so I can stay with one of Carly's weird friends. And anyway, when Carly needed a place to stay, it was with me and Adam. So maybe the only thing that's true is her feelings, but that's still something. "It all just happened the way it happened."

I can feel the lake. I can taste it in the air. The way the water laps at the gravel shore makes sense, like it's part of me. "I feel like this is where I started," I tell Carly. "Like maybe nothing counted before I got here."

"I feel that way about Ithaca too," she says. She pulls her lighter from her jacket. Dumps her pack of cigarettes into her hand. She keeps one out to smoke, stuffs the rest in her pocket. After she lights up, she sets the cardboard carton on fire, tossing it under the tower she's made with our logs.

"You got any paper?" she asks, blowing smoke as she talks. "The leaves are all damp."

I offer her a handful of pocket lint and gum wrappers. "Is it enough?"

"I can make it work," she says, and even though everything around us shines in the moonlight, covered in condensation, I believe that she can.

She balls the lint and throws it under the log tower, where it will catch when the flames start to travel. She's strategic with the gum wrappers, using one after another to keep a flame focused at one small spot.

"Ha ha!" she says, with the first crackle of wood, grinning, like she knew all along it would work. She's different here. Her makeup doesn't shape her face in these shadows. In the moonlight, she's young and strong, and nothing strange. She watches her tower.

"Ha ha!" she says again, when the flames break the surface of another log.

Once the fire is safely raging, we throw damp twigs at it to hear the pop and sizzle. When it gets too warm, we hang our jackets over a tree branch instead of moving further away.

"What was your mom like?" Carly asks.

I think about that wedding dress woman and the tickle of her copper hair on my cheek. "I don't remember enough," I say, because memories of my mom don't always come when I call them. "But she was really pretty and people liked her, and she hated waiting for me."

"What do you mean?" Carly pokes at the fire with a stick, pushing embers toward the center.

"Like she'd take me to the playground, but if

there was no one interesting for her to talk to, she'd want to turn around and go home."

"And she just left?"

"Yeah," I say. I'm not sure if Carly meant for good, or from the playground, but it's true both ways. I remember the shock in my shins from jumping off the swings when I was worried I wouldn't be able to catch up with her.

"If it makes you feel any better, it's not great having a mom who stays when she doesn't want to," Carly says. "It's hard to watch how bad she wants her whole life to be different. How she settles for keeping the peace."

Carly throws another bomb of wet leaves on the fire, and we watch the fury it makes.

"What do you want?" I ask, because I don't know how a person is supposed to piece a life together. I don't want to be my dad or my mom or even Margo. I don't want to be my math teacher, or Matty's mom, or Irene. I know my life can't ever look like the people on TV, but I don't know what there is to want that's available to me.

"Like really want? Like in all of it?" She takes the last drag, tosses her cigarette butt into the fire.

I nod.

"I don't know," Carly says. "I think maybe it's not a thing I want to be or stuff I want to have. It's like—I just don't want to feel wrong, you know?"

"Yeah," I say, and I think I do.

"Rosemary always made me feel . . ." Carly pulls a loose cigarette from her jacket pocket, holds it between her fingers as if she's already been smoking it. "I don't know. She made me feel like she would love me completely if I were just a little bit better than I am." She holds the cigarette with the tips of her fingers and sweeps it at the flames, pulling it back to her mouth fast, puffing furiously to get the light to take. "News flash! This is the best I've got." She looks sad. Disappointed in herself, the way I was every single time I thought I could win my dad back from Irene by memorizing Dylan songs or sewing the loose buttons on his work shirts.

"I like you this way," I say, and the words make me nervous, because they are the most I have and maybe she won't want them. I like her more than anyone I've ever met.

"I don't feel wrong right now," Carly says. "I don't feel wrong with you or Adam." She pokes at the fire again. "Maybe we'll be friends for a really long time." She smiles at me, looks away. "I don't even feel wrong with Bodie." She laughs. "I just feel . . . bossy."

"He needs it," I say.

"He does."

We're sitting too close to the fire. My face feels chapped and hot. "Maybe we can come back and have campfires here," I say. "Like even years and years and years from now." And I try to picture it. This little bit of future that could be mine. A friend and a fire and no one feels wrong. It's the first time I've ever thought of getting older in a real way, where I can picture myself as someone different, not just me right now in a different situation. There's a new person waiting for me to catch up, and maybe she's happy. Maybe she belongs right where she is.

"You know what I want?" Carly says. "I want to jump in that lake."

I look around like someone might be watching.

"It's fine," Carly says. "I swear."

And it's what I want too.

We strip to our underwear. The tentacles on Carly's neck belong to a giant octopus that stretches to the small of her back. In the flicker of firelight, with the movement of her body, he's alive. One of his wavy tentacles is wrapped around her ribcage, under the band of her bra, curling up over her heart.

"It's to remind me," Carly says when she catches me staring. "Don't let it pull you under, you know?"

"Yeah." I study the lines, the way it makes her body into something otherworldly. And maybe I don't know what *it* really is, but I feel like I do.

"Ready?" she asks, and I nod.

We make a mad dash for the lake. When the water hits my ankles it is so cold I want to scream, but I run harder, faster. Carly's wake crashes into mine. We dive in at the same time, plunging into the blackness. I kick my legs and fight to stay under, to feel the cold seep in. To feel every inch of my body. I will be warm again, by the fire, in Carly's car, in Adam's bed. Cold isn't my enemy anymore. I open my eyes and look to the surface. The moon is split to pieces by the water. I hold my breath until I feel like I'll burst.

Carly comes up sputtering moments after I do. We laugh and shout and it echoes across the surface. It doesn't matter if anyone hears us. We are part of this wild.

We dive and surface and dive again, until our teeth chatter, and then we walk from the water like creatures of the deep. Carly has a string of pondweed wrapped around her ankle, a tattoo come to life.

"It likes me," she says, unwinding the weed from her leg. She has rings under her eyes from her makeup and I'm sure I do too. We are becoming raccoons.

We keep the fire going so we can dry off, jumping around in a crazy dance to get our blood flowing. Carly twists the pondweed into a crown and drops it on my head. It smells like mud in early spring. I howl at the moon.

Carly laughs. "If someone saw you," she says, "they'd think you were raised by wolves."

"I wish," I say, and she laughs even harder.

"Me too. Wolves take care of their own."

I place the crown on her head. Her howl is a low, mournful song.

Eventually, we're dry enough for tights, then shirts, then the rest of it. Then the fire fades enough that we need our jackets. Carly kicks dirt at the embers with the side of her boot. I copy her. Soon the glow is completely gone. And then it's us in the moonlight, cold wind against our faces, and the sound of our boots on the road as we walk to the car. Instead of singing, I tell Carly about the motorhome and the spread of land and the house that never happened, and how my dad left me for Irene.

"Do you think," she asks, "you were better off alone in the woods than with the wrong people?"

"I don't know," I say, and then we're quiet. Our footsteps don't sound like *Cecilia* this time.

"I guess," Carly says, "what matters most is that they were the wrong people and we should have had the right ones." She puts her arm around my waist. It makes us both walk slower, but I don't mind.

Carly parks in front of Adam's house. We have the heat cranked. My hair is still damp, and the back of my neck feels like a muggy afternoon in August. I don't want to leave our warm bubble. I don't want our night to end.

"You want to stay?" I ask. I know Adam wouldn't mind.

She shakes her head. "I'm going to crash so hard in my own bed. I'm going to take up the whole damn thing. And then when I wake up, I'm going to eat cereal in my underwear and watch cartoons and laugh with my mouth full."

I picture Carly and her octopus sleeping large and happy.

"The question is," Carly says as I collect my bag from under the seat, "are we tough enough to do this in January?"

I laugh. "I will if you will." My cheeks are dry and hot, my eyelids heavy.

"If there isn't ice," Carly says, "I think we'll have to."

She hugs me before I get out of the car, and waits for me to unlock the front door, flashing her lights before she drives away.

I climb the stairs, avoiding the squeaky spots, and open the door to Adam's apartment, pulling the handle up as I push in to keep it from creaking. I shed my clothes in the bathroom and wrap my hair in a towel so I won't get Adam's pillows wet.

He wakes up when I climb into bed. "You smell like a campfire," he says.

"We had a campfire," I say.

He wraps his arms around me, and he is so

warm, and my eyes are so tired, and when I close them I can still picture the water lapping at the shore, and the way we were wild. Nothing about me feels wrong.

— Chapter 28 —

I have the day off, so I go to Wegmans to get food for Christmas. My ears are still water-logged from the lake and ringing from the concert. It makes everything a little surreal.

There's a list to follow. Adam and I planned meals for the whole weekend over breakfast.

"Sweet potatoes!" I shouted.

"Marshmallows or no marshmallows?" Adam asked.

"Duh," I said, laughing.

Adam wrote *marshmallows* on the list. "How do you feel about cranberry sauce?"

"I could take it or leave it."

"I like the kind that comes out shaped like the can."

"Write it down!"

I grab all of it—every last thing we want. Adam never lets me pay for anything, but I've been saving for our feast. Adam promised Billy he'd help with the Christmas Eve rush at the tree farm, and his plan was to pick up groceries on the way home. I swiped the list from his messenger bag when he was in the shower and when I get home I'll call him at Billy's to say it's already done.

When the groceries are bagged and ready to go and the cashier tells me it will be ninety-seven dollars, I reach into my purse to grab my wallet and it isn't anywhere. I'm calm for like five seconds because my stupid bag is huge and things get lost in there, but then I remember how everything ended up all over the bathroom floor at The Haunt and I start sweating. Like crazy sweating. Like I can't get out of my coat fast enough and everyone is staring at me because instead of paying, I'm tearing my coat off in the middle of the store. And then I think about why everything ended up on the bathroom floor to begin with and I start crying. Big fat tears and my lip is shaking and it's all so embarrassing I can't even handle it.

"I'll be back for it," I say between sobs, looking at my hands, avoiding eye contact with the checker. "I'm so sorry. I'll be back." And I just walk out of the store.

I get in my car, shaking all over like I'm made of rubber bands. My wallet could have been lost in the bathroom. It might have skidded across the floor under one of the stalls, or to the far corner by the sink, under the radiator, or behind the garbage can. But I know that's not what happened. I know where I have to go to get it back.

— Chapter 29 —

I pound on the door to Rosemary's apartment hard with my fist and don't stop even though my hands are freezing and every hit hurts. There's a grey Saab in the driveway, and I'm sure it's hers. I'm sure she's home. I punch at the door like maybe I'll just break it down. She still doesn't answer. I start kicking.

When Rosemary finally answers the door, she sighs hard like this is boring for her, but I see the tremble in her cheek.

"Give back my wallet," I say.

"Wait here." She's wearing a huge grey sweater and goldenrod-colored tights that make her knees look like doorknobs.

I follow her into the kitchen. There are dead roses in a coffee mug on the counter. Dishes piled high in the sink. Carly must have been the one who cleaned.

"I didn't invite you in," Rosemary says.

"I didn't give you my wallet as a present."

Her hands shake as she grabs the wallet off the counter. I snatch it from her and count my money.

"Oh, it's all there," she says. "I don't need your tip jar change."

I turn to leave and I'm almost to the door

when she says, "There is one thing. I mean, I'm curious. What's a child doing running around with a college student? There are laws about that."

"What are you talking about?" I say, trying to keep the shock from my face even though my pulse is pounding so hard she can probably feel it.

"I washed your license. Chalk came right off."

"It was a mistake," I say. "They messed up at the DMV."

"Bullshit." Rosemary isn't shaking anymore. "You're just some random trashy kid and you need to go back to whatever hellhole Little River is and leave us alone." Her eyes meet mine and even though she's trying to be furious I can see her heartbreak. "We would have worked everything out," she says. "Carly wouldn't have left if you didn't push your way in."

"She lost a lot for you," I say. "She needed support." I know I shouldn't speak for Carly, but I feel like if I try maybe Rosemary could change her mind.

"You can't know what she needs. You're a baby." Rosemary gets close and wrinkles her mouth to mock me. It's so ugly. Her breath is hot on my face. "Go home and cry to mommy."

"You don't know anything about me!" I shout, but my words sound so useless.

"I know enough about you," she says, "I'll

go into Decadence. I'll tell everyone Carly is fucking a child."

I can feel my world breaking apart like an old barn in a hurricane. "I'm not sleeping with Carly."

"I'm not stupid," Rosemary says.

I almost blurt out that I have a boyfriend but stop myself just in time. Carly isn't that much older than me and we're friends and that's truth. If any of this leads back to Adam, it means real trouble for sure.

"I only acted like that so Carly could save face," I tell her.

"I saw you two holding hands in The Commons last week. You didn't even see me. In the bathroom at The Haunt. That wasn't for my benefit."

"We're friends." My throat tightens.

"Yeah. I bet you are."

"It's not like that!" I bite the inside of my cheek to keep myself from crying. "Carly is the best friend I've ever had."

"Carly is twenty years old. Why would she want to be your friend? You're a child. You don't know anything."

I feel this weird twist in my mind. Like everything is slow motion and I can see it clearly—how fragile and sheltered and stupid Rosemary is. I wonder what it would feel like to crack her in half like a dried-out twig. "If she doesn't love you," I say, "it's because of you, not me."

Rosemary's face flushes. She's shaking again. "Get the fuck out of my house!"

When my feet hit the front step, she says, "I made a copy of your license. I can call the police any time. What do you think other people will think of your *friendship?*"

She slams the door behind me so hard it sounds like it probably cracked in two.

I don't look back to see if it did. I just leave.

— Chapter 30 —

I can't even remember driving back to Adam's place. I'm just here, in my car outside, shaking. When I get into the apartment, I run to the bathroom and heave up everything I ate for breakfast, retching until there's nothing left. There isn't time to cry. There just isn't.

I throw my clothes into the plastic grocery bags Adam keeps in an empty paper towel roll under the kitchen sink and think about ways to fix things. I could bribe Rosemary. I could tell Carly and she could convince Rosemary. But eventually, it would all lead back to Adam. Eventually, someone would find out and he'd get hurt. And if I tried to stay, I'd always be waiting for it. I'd be sitting around waiting for Adam's life to be completely ruined over something he'd never have done if he'd known. Not in a million years.

I empty my dresser drawers, the ones he cleared out to make room for me, and grab the slippers I bought at House of Shalimar from under the bed. I leave the record player and the records I bought for him by the Christmas tree. I wish I had time to wrap them, wish I was going to be with him on Christmas morning to watch him open them. I sit at the card table in the kitchen and write a note on the back of an envelope. I write that it's because there's something wrong with me and I just need to go and it's killing me and I'll never stop missing him. I sign it: *I love you always, April.*

I want his corduroy barn jacket. The black one with the worn cuffs that he lets me wear all the time. It smells like him and wearing it feels like a hug. When I look in the coat closet, I see a big red bow. It's tied to the neck of a guitar.

I take the guitar. I can't stand to leave it. I can't stand to leave. I go back to the kitchen and place the black velvet box with my mother's ring on top of the note. At the bottom of the page, I write, *I hope this is enough.*

— Chapter 31 —

I try to sneak in the cafe through the alley. Yesterday was payday and I forgot to grab my envelope. I won't be able to cash the check. I always signed them over to Adam and had him do it for me. But I can at least get my share of the tip jar for the week. It's something.

Bodie is in the alley, wearing a Santa hat, smoking.

"Pilgrim," he says in his slow, dazed voice, "you're like a work addict or something. I thought it was your day off." He closes his eyes and smiles like he has a pretty picture in his head.

"Came for my paycheck," I say.

When he hears my voice, he looks at me. "Dude," he says, and I know he can tell I've been crying. I know I'm probably a wreck and a half.

"Can you sneak in and get it?" I ask, and start tearing up again.

"Sure," he says. "Anything for you, Pilgrim." He taps my shoulder with his palm before he walks back inside. I wait, studying the alley. I want to be able to remember everything about it: the smell of wet leaves and soggy cigarette butts, the echo of the water dripping off the fire escape. I wish I could keep it. All of it. I wish I could stay. I pull a wrinkled napkin from my purse and press it to my knee, carving into it with a dying ballpoint pen: *I, April, will miss you.*

"Got it," Bodie says in a loud whisper when he comes back outside. "Figured you didn't want anyone to know, so I snagged it while Carly was helping a customer."

"Thank you." I hand him the napkin, folded in four. "Can you leave this for Carly? On the bulletin board. Maybe like in an hour or so?"

"April," Bodie says, and I think it might be the first time he's called me anything other than Pilgrim. "Are you okay?"

"Sure."

"Why don't I believe you?"

"You're a really good guy," I say, and hug him before I even know what I'm doing.

"Can I help?"

"I wish you could." I squeeze him hard. When I look up, he wipes the tears off my cheeks. I kiss him. I just reach up and touch his face and kiss him. At first, I pretend he's Adam. I pretend I'm saying goodbye the right way. Then I kiss him harder and I know he's Bodie. I hope that it will turn into some kind of amazing kiss where my knees buckle and my heart falls into my stomach. I am hoping for a roller coaster, so maybe it will mean what I had with Adam wasn't something special. But it's just a kiss. After all the times Bodie made me blush and all the times I found excuses to talk to him, it's just a kiss. It's not even a good one.

"I'm sorry," I say, and pull away from him. "I have to go." I run down the alley. I hear him yell, "Hey, Pilgrim!" but I don't look back.

I'm almost to the edge of The Commons when I hear Carly call out to me. I stop. I want to keep going, but it's Carly and I can't.

"April," she says again, out of breath, catching up, and I can tell from the way she's looking at me that she knows I'm leaving. She knows it's time for me to go.

"I can't say why."

"You can tell me," she says, hugging me. "I won't say anything to anyone. Sometimes, you just need someone to know your secret, right? To take the air out of it, you know?"

"If I tell you, you have to live with it," I whisper. "If I leave, I'm the only one who has to."

"I could help you. We could fix whatever it is. Anything."

"If I leave, it won't hurt him as much as if I stay." I start to fall apart. Our hug turns into her holding me up. "Tell him it's all my fault and not his," I say when I get my voice back. "And everything he did, everything he is, is just the best thing I could even picture. Tell him it's not about the person being left. No matter what I do

279

or try or say or pretend, I can't fix what's wrong with me. Tell him that, okay?"

Carly nods. She's crying too. We're a mess, the two of us. And I wish I didn't have to say goodbye to her, because it's so much harder than I thought it would be.

"And you'll be there?" I ask. "When he's sad?"

Carly wipes her cheeks. "I'll make him pancake-shaped pancakes."

"You," I say, and I'm going to tell her that she's my first real honest to goodness friend, she's like my sister. I'm going to tell her how much she's done for me, how much I love her. But I can't say any of it. I can't say it and then walk away, so all I say is "You," and slip Adam's key in her pocket and kiss her cheek and walk away as fast as I can and then faster, until I'm running to my car. The soles of my boots smack the pavement and splash melting ice and salt on my legs. It stings through my tights, and when I get in the car and close the door, everything outside is muffled and I'm stuck with just me and the sobs and my stinging red legs and how it feels like someone just ripped all my skin off.

I start the car and follow the roads out of the city. I just drive. I don't care where. The only place I want to be is Ithaca.

— Part Two —

— Chapter 32 —

March 1997
Brewster, NY

The crowd at Perks is standing room only, but the pickings are slim. I've played here before, perched on this rickety wooden stool, on the platform they cover with worn out rugs, under lights that are way too close to the stage. There are faces I recognize. People who were here last time, who came to see me again.

I make sure I've figured out the balance of the stool and then I test my tunings, clip my capo to the head of my guitar, and tape three extra picks to the mic stand. One of them is my dad's old thick black Gibson pick. It's cracked and I use thins, but I put it there anyway. Because I always have. It used to be one of my rituals—to remind me where I came from, what the first few songs I wrote are supposed to mean—but it's just procedure now.

The stage me is procedure too. Pretend I'm shocked by the crowd. Wide-eyed and *aw shucks* like all my wildest dreams are coming true. Eyes closed, three deep breaths, strum, open eyes. And then I make work of the music, my voice sighing over the audience, fingers strong on the strings.

I don't get the jitters anymore. I miss them. It sucked, in some ways, those moments of shaking and staring at my fingers, wondering if they'd ever be able to connect to my brain again, feeling like I'd lost not just the lyrics to my songs but every word I ever knew. But by the end of those shows, I felt like I could fly. I felt like the whole world was mine and all I had to do was reach for it. Of course, after, when everyone left and the bartender shuttered things up, I'd be in my car, hyped up and alone. Driving until my hands felt heavy on the steering wheel.

Now, that flying feeling is rare, and most of the time I don't bother to chase it. I don't let myself care enough about the audience to get nervous. It's too much work for too little payoff. I get up on stage because my fingers feel right pressing metal to wood, and singing is the only way I hear my own voice because I don't have anyone to talk to. I play and I work the audience like an old habit and they have no idea that I'm pretending they aren't even there. It's private. It's mourning. It's a love song. A map of where I came from and it's just mine, not anyone else's.

I start with *Waiting*. It's a song from my first CD, an EP I recorded in this guy Cole's basement in Red Bank two years ago. When I play the opening chords, a few people applaud because they recognize it. These people in the audience listen to my songs while they live their normal lives, cooking dinner, driving to the grocery store, picking their kids up from football practice or cheerleading. They make my words mean what they need them to mean. To them, this song isn't about Adam. It's about someone they didn't end up with.

Even though I know it's just a fairy tale,
I keep waiting, waiting for you
To rescue me from the pale.
Even though I know it's just a passing
  phase
I keep waiting, waiting for you
To save me from this choking haze.
Even though I'm the one who said
  goodbye, it's true
I keep waiting, waiting, waiting . . .
Waiting for you.

And when I sing, before I close my eyes, I notice that the ones who applauded are singing along. I'll sell them the new CD at least. Maybe a few of the new faces will buy both.

Coffeehouse crowds are better about buying, but I like playing in bars more. Bar people are raucous and fun. They request bizarre songs. They whoop and holler and hold up lighters when you play something they know. Coffeehouse people are too polite. Seas of greying boomers with wire-rimmed glasses and expensive fleece vests, pretending they're still hippies for as long as my set lasts. It's all so self-conscious. They laugh in unison at my mid-set musings, a low, rumbling chuckle. They wait a beat before clapping at the end of a song, like they need a moment to absorb the entire experience. It drives me crazy.

It's not that I don't love playing music. It's just that it's not the freedom it was supposed to be. It comes with its own chains. Leaves me pulled apart and spread too thin. People feel entitled to me. They ask questions they'd never ask another stranger, or even a close friend. They ask how much money I make. Where I sleep. Who my songs are about. What my childhood was like. And they tell me the things they felt when they heard my music. Stories about what they did. How my songs were a soundtrack to their breakup or their sex lives or their morning commute, like that's the only reason I exist. Like none of my music is about me. They leave me holding their memories, as if I'm supposed to know what to do with them.

It's not what people imagine when they dream of being a singer. People don't lay awake at night wistfully envisioning themselves being picked to bones and left in a dark parking lot, trying to coax warmth from a broken car heater. I've played with people who can do it and it feeds them. The kinds of people who play for an audience and it's everything. I'm good, but they're magic. Even though my hands feel right when I'm playing and my voice makes sense when I'm singing, it's not the same thing. What I want the most is much more simple. What I want most is a life that's all mine.

There's a guy in this audience who doesn't quite fit. Younger. More brown than grey. He wasn't here the last time I played. His glasses are retro, black-framed, army issue. He has one of the flyers for the show in his hands. He rolls it tightly and lets it go, over and over through the whole first set.

We are both waiting for the bathroom at the break. There's only one room with *Hommes et Filles* painted in gold script on the door. The door is thin and the knob hangs loosely in its hole. We could look in if we wanted to. The person we are waiting for pees and we can hear. It's uncomfortable.

Flyer Guy smiles at me and squeezes his paper tube. He looks through it like it's a telescope and he wants to see his shoes better. We listen to the woman in the bathroom wash her hands. She coughs before she opens the door. She squeezes past us, giving me a forced smile.

"Go ahead," Flyer Guy says, pointing the paper tube at the bathroom.

"You go," I say. "My seat is safe. You've got competition for yours."

He asks if I'm sure. I hold my ground. It's awkward to stand there, trying not to listen to him go. I look at the black and white photos on the walls. Pretentious and purposely quirky. Nothing like Decadence. Pictures of fruit, dripping with dew and sexuality, posed on a rough wood table like they're having conversations with cruel, comical vegetables. In one picture, I swear a pepper is telling a peach she has a fat ass.

I hear the toilet flush, but he doesn't come out yet. I walk around in little circles and think about the riff for one of my songs. I've carried it with me in my head since Ithaca, unfinished. Something's off about it. Missing words, missing notes. I haven't figured out how to fix it yet. Someday.

Flyer Guy comes out as I'm mid-circle, thinking about the fingerpicking rhythm. I'm moving my fingers like they're on the fret board. I must look a little nutty.

"Lost in thought?" he asks, grinning. Behind his glasses, he has these really nice brown eyes. They're so alive.

"Thinking about a song," I say, feeling my cheeks get hot.

"Like a skier who has to visualize the mountain before he gets off the lift?"

I laugh. "Something like that."

"Good luck with your next set," he says. "Break a leg." I like his smile.

I walk in the bathroom and latch the door behind me. I don't even have to go. I just need a moment to myself so I can catch my breath. I hold my wrists under the water and imagine my fingers turning into icicles, then I turn the water to warm. It's procedure.

I'm almost done with the last song of my second set when Flyer Guy stands up. He weaves his way around the chairs and pulls a pack of cigarettes from his pocket when he reaches the door.

He doesn't come back. I give the crowd a good scan while I'm signing CDs and think maybe I will spring for a motel tonight. Then there he is, in the doorway, smiling at me. I smile back.

He waits as the coffeehouse manager pays me in crumpled ones and fives. I wad up my money and shove it in the inside pocket of my bag.

"Let us know next time you're headed this way," the manager says. "We always get a good crowd for you." And it feels good to hear him say that, to know that Flyer Guy heard it too. I built that crowd from nothing. I had to beg to open for other singers. I played for meals or free coffee. I fought hard for every bit of ground I've covered, and to have a notebook full of places that will book me—it means something.

"Can I buy you a drink?" Flyer Guy asks as I walk toward the door. "There's a bar across the street."

I usually try to grab one of the older guys. Divorced, with a kid who's probably only five or six years younger than I am. The kind of guy who wants me but feels bad about it. I can go home with him and stretch my arms out, say I'm tired and thanks and he'll let me sleep on his couch. Or he'll sleep on the couch and let me sleep in his bed like some kind of penance for his dirty thoughts. I know him. I've met him in more than one town. He's a type. He's easy.

This guy is different. He's probably in his late twenties. He's cute. He knows it. He wants me. I know he does. If I go home with him, I won't crash on his couch. But sometimes, maybe I can just try to be a normal girl and go on a normal date, even if it's only a drink in a bar. Sometimes I can have something that's mine.

So I say, "Yes," and get jitters, actual jitters, so much so that I even stop thinking about how I'll describe them in a song. I just enjoy being a girl out with a guy.

We walk across the street together. He's quiet. His hands shake a little while he fumbles with a cigarette. It's cute, makes me feel shy too.

The place he takes me to is next to the train station. It's dark. Neon and worn out wood. Almost empty. We sit at the bar. He orders Jack on the rocks. I order a Coke. I don't drink with strangers, and my fake ID isn't that great. I only use it when I absolutely have to.

"So, April," he says, when our drinks come, "where are you headed next?"

"New Jersey," I say.

"Uch, Jersey," he says, wincing, and I feel like I have to defend my tour schedule and maybe all of New Jersey.

"Red Bank is great," I tell him. "I play at this place called The Downtown. Good crowd. I have a guy I record with sometimes when I'm there."

"The Downtown what?" he asks.

"Just The Downtown."

"Like who's on first?" he says, grinning. He crinkles his nose and his glasses go crooked. He has big teeth. I like them. I think about how I could paint his smile in a song. I realize I don't even know what to call him.

"You never told me your name," I say. "I'm at a disadvantage."

"Ray." He offers me his hand, and when I go to shake, he puts his other hand over mine, looks in my eyes, and says, "It's really nice to meet you, April."

We talk until last call. I don't want it to end. I don't want to stop feeling like I actually exist in the world. He tells me how he used to be in a band. We talk instruments. He says my guitar is a really good one. The way he says *really* makes me worry that my mother's old ring wasn't enough of a trade and maybe I still owe Adam something.

"I've been thinking about having an electric pickup added," I tell him.

"Thing is, you're better off just getting an acoustic-electric. Don't start cutting into your guitar. You'll kill the soul. I mean, this is what you do for a living, right? You can have more than one guitar, you know?"

"Yeah, I guess. I'm so bad with the gear side of things," I say, pushing my hair out of my face, letting it fall back where it was. "I should probably get my own PA too at some point. I could play in so many more places, and the sound would be consistent."

"Why don't you?"

"It costs. And it's a lot to learn—all the different techie things I'd need to know before I could figure out what to buy."

"You know what? Come home with me." He's shredding his wet bar napkin into tiny pieces. I like that I make him nervous. I like that he has jitters too.

"I don't know," I say, "I was going to hit the road and drive to Red Bank. Pull an all-nighter. I have a place to crash there." It's always better to make them think it's their idea.

"You have a place to crash here," he says. "I'll show you my guitars and amp. You can play them, so you'll have a point of reference when you're ready to buy."

"Are you sure?" I say. "I don't want to put you out."

"Not at all," he says, and just like that, I have a place to sleep tonight. I have someone to talk to. Maybe more.

When we get back across the street to our cars, he offers to drive me to his place. I tell him I'll follow him instead.

"Alright," he says, "be that way." He says it like he's joking, but there's an edge. It kind of throws me off balance, but I'm so tired. My eyes don't want to stay open. I get in my car and follow him. He drives hard. Squeals around corners, blows through stop signs. I have to work to keep his taillights in sight. I start to think that maybe I should just drive the other way, cut my losses and sleep in my car somewhere, but it's one of those rock and hard place situations. Keeping up with him means I haven't been watching the roads. I don't know how to get back to where we started, so I just keep following.

He parks at the dead end of a dirt road. Ranch houses and double wides line the street. He lives in a ranch that looks like a gust of wind could smash it to smithereens. The front steps are decaying. The outside light is busted. The only light in the driveway comes from his neighbor's house.

He's already out of his car and opening the front door when I park. I bring my guitar and my purse with me. I never leave them in my car if I can help it.

"Come on in," he says.

He has four guitars, a futon, a glass-topped coffee table, and a television in his living room. The TV is one of those ancient ones with dials on the front, and it has rabbit ears tipped with aluminum foil.

His house smells like old tires. Just this hint of it at the end of breathing in. I wonder how close we are to the highway. I listen, but I can't hear road noise. I leave my guitar and my purse by the door.

"Okay," he says, "you have to play the Martin first. That's my favorite. That's the one you should get if you have a windfall. I got it in trade a few years ago. Swear it sounds better the more you play it. It'll cost you, but the tone is unreal."

He checks that it's in tune and hands it over to me. It's much heavier than my guitar.

While I'm playing, he dumps a small baggie of coke on the coffee table and cuts it into lines with a guitar pick.

I try to ignore it and just keep playing. It's not like I've never seen people do coke before, it's just that I've never been so close to it. It was something I glanced from the other room at a party, or I saw people come out of the bathroom at a bar with white powder ringing their nostrils. I try to pay attention to my fingers and the way the stiff strings press into my calluses, but it's so close. I feel like the dust will get everywhere. Tiny particles will cover my lips and get in my eyes.

He rolls up a five and snorts one of the lines and then another. It's hollow and loud like his nose is a deep cavern. He shakes his head, blinks his eyes a bunch of times, and snorts again. His face is red.

"Oh, you know," I say when he tries to hand me the rolled-up five, "I'm kind of tired. And I should hit the road early. I'll just crash. I'm good right here." I pat the couch.

"We haven't fucked yet."

"What?"

"Oh, come on. I know what this is."

My whole body shakes. "You don't even know me."

"You're all the same. Aren't you?" he says, straightening his next line with the guitar pick. "You fuck for drugs. You'll be gone in the morning. You'll take the rest of my bag while I'm sleeping. I have to get mine now, so at least it's a fair trade."

I stand up and rest his guitar on the couch.

"I'm gonna go," I say. I start walking to the door. He gets up and grabs my wrist so quickly.

"Don't play games with me, April. You know how this works."

His grip is tight. I twist my wrist to try to find a weak spot, but he squeezes harder and gets so close that I feel like he's taking all the air away.

I back toward the door. He grabs my other arm.

"You look so young." He tries to kiss me. I turn my head away. My back hits the wall. I can see my guitar and my bag by the door. I think it through. Picture it all in my head. It has to be quick.

"This could be so dirty," he says. His breath smells like booze and burnt plastic. "I get the feeling you like it that way, don't you, April?"

"You know what?" I say sweetly to throw him off guard. It's the hardest thing I've ever done. "You're right. I like it dirty." I take a deep breath, like the extra air will make me bigger and stronger, and then I knee him in the groin as hard as I possibly can. My kneecap feels like it could crack in two. He lets go of my wrists and reaches for his crotch. I push him over while he's off balance. Grab my guitar and my bag, open the door, and run as hard and as fast as I can. By the time I'm at my car, I have my keys out of my bag. He's in the doorway. He's hobbling out to me.

"Get away," I scream, hoping neighbors will hear. "Get the fuck away from me!"

I unlock my car, throw my guitar and bag on

the passenger seat, and climb in, closing the door just in time. He smacks my window. His face is right there. His glasses magnify his eyes, big and bulging.

I start the engine. Lean on the horn. Flash my lights. I hope someone will notice, that one of his neighbors will come help me. No one does.

"Bitch!" he screams. "You goddamned bitch!"

He raises his fist like he might try to smash it through the window. I throw the car in reverse. Feel a bump. I hear a crack. He screams, like maybe I ran over his foot. He's doubled over on the ground. I have to keep going. I back down the driveway to the road. My tires screech as I speed away. I don't know which way to go, but it doesn't matter as much as getting distance. I make turns on gut feelings, and eventually I'm out at the highway and I have no problem keeping my eyes open.

I drive until daylight, until I can't stay awake for another second. I sleep in my car in a playground parking lot. There are kids playing and moms waiting with juice boxes and the sounds of all of it make me feel safe enough to close my eyes.

When I wake up, everything feels too bright and too loud. Like another world, totally different from the one I was in last night. I wish this one felt real and that one didn't, but it's the other way around. These moms in the park, their kids, they aren't even close to being a part of my reality. I don't know them. I don't remember anyone ever sitting on a bench with snacks and band-aids in their purse while I played on the swings. I could never be like those women. I wouldn't know how. I sit in my car, watching them all. I feel like an alien.

Scribbling with a broken golf pencil, scraping back the wood with my fingernail when the lead gets too low, I write on the back of one of the flyers from the show. I write it all down. Everything. I always do.

At night, when it's dark, when I'm in a strange motel room or parked at a rest stop, when there's enough light to see by—a streetlight, the TV flicker—I write. When I have a pen and the back of an envelope, a receipt from the gas station, or a motel postcard, I write lyrics, thoughts, flashes of things I could use in a song.

Mostly I write to Carly. I've been doing it for years. Since I left. Vows and proclamations have evolved into confessions. Sometimes you need to feel like you could tell someone everything if you wanted to. That there's someone to tell.

I, April,
have loneliness so large it's like a frostbitten
explorer
I have to drag down the mountain.

298

I, April,
ate an entire plate of chili cheese fries at a diner
on Rt. 9 at three in the morning.
It's the first thing I've eaten in days.
This will not end well.

I, April,
think red maple leaves against grey skies
are some kind of sweet magic.
You should go to Vermont, Carly.
You'd love it.

I never send my confessions. Almost never. After I write one, I keep it in my pocket, thinking when I round up an envelope and a stamp I'll tuck it in the mail. But the next time I do laundry I add the note to the mess of napkins and receipts hidden under the lining of my guitar case. As long as I keep writing to Carly, I get to believe that maybe someday I'll see her again. Maybe I'll really tell her everything. She was my first true friend, and I haven't met anyone like her since. You don't get over someone like that.

This time my confession starts:

I, April,
am so stupid.

Even though it's safe and bright and shiny at the park, it still takes everything I have to open the car door, to not feel like someone will attack me the moment my feet hit the pavement, to not look at my tires and think about bones cracking.

The pay phone has that same rubbery plastic smell from last night. I worry that maybe it's stuck in my nose, that it's the only thing I'll ever smell now.

I call Cole to tell him I can't go to Red Bank this time. I don't tell him why, just that something came up.

"I'll miss you, sweet stuff," he says, his voice carrying the weight of too many cigarettes and late nights.

"Miss you too," I say, and there's a sharp sadness in my chest for the missed chance to walk through Marine Park with Cole after the gig I was supposed to play. He always hums riffs at me like a challenge and I make up words to go along. We watch the sunrise over the Navesink River and then we get breakfast sandwiches from the deli on Broad Street and record songs in his basement until we can't stay awake anymore. It's one of my favorite ways to spend time. I know it's a long shot that Ray will follow me, that he even could, but I feel like I have a target on my back. I told him where I was going. I broke a rule. I broke so many rules.

I make more phone calls and drive to New York City instead.

— Chapter 33 —

I scan the restaurant. He isn't here yet. I try to sneak out before anyone notices me, but the host comes over and hustles me to a table by the window.

Now he'll see me before I see him, unless I stare out the window and try to catch him walking down Bedford Street, but that would look desperate. I rustle through the contents of my bag, wishing I had a day planner or a fancy purse—something classy to play with while I wait. My messy hair and long skirt are starting to look more street urchin than free spirit, and I'm surprised the host put me right up front in the window. I am not what this restaurant is trying to advertise. Everyone else is in a dark suit or done up in an outfit that looks like it came off a mannequin in a department store. Even though I tried to straighten up in the car, I look like I came from the bottom of a laundry hamper. My thrift store peacoat has a hole in the elbow.

Matthew suggested this place. "You'll love it. Fantastic paninis," he'd said on the phone. I wasn't sure which word sounded weirder coming out of his mouth, *fantastic* or *paninis,* but I just needed to hear his voice.

I take a CD out of my bag and decide I'll sign it

for him in advance, but then he walks in wearing a brown leather jacket. Sparkling sunglasses and shiny watch throwing light everywhere. His old life must seem ridiculous to him now. I bet he never goes deer hunting. I bet the things he used to want feel like a bad dream he had once. He's not Matty anymore.

I shove the CD back in my bag and stand. My thigh hits the table. Water spills on crisp paper placemats. Ice and silverware clink.

"God, April, you're a sight for sore eyes," he says, like he's reading a script. His sunglasses are still on, so I can't see how sore his eyes really are. He hangs his jacket over the back of the empty chair and meets me at the side of the table.

"Matthew," I say, showing my acceptance of his new self. I reach up to hug him and hope I don't smell too sweaty. I hope I don't smell like burning rubber.

He wraps his arms around me and they bulge against my ribs. He used to be all skin and bones; now his chest is tight and hard, like hugging a mannequin. A belt buckle digs into my stomach. His thin black sweater is soft and smells new. It's perfectly pressed, without a speck of lint.

"You look great," I say. It sounds pathetic. Too adoring. Needy. Obvious. People are staring at us. Him. People are staring at him. Not me. Now I know why the host sat me in the window. Matty made the reservation.

"You!" Matthew holds me by the arms and looks me over. His jeans are perfectly pressed too. "Wow."

In the reflection of his sunglasses, my hair is more frizzy than curly. I wonder if his *wow* is like saying someone looks like a picture but leaving out what kind of picture they look like. I wanted to feel safe when I saw him. I wanted seeing him to feel like home, in the way normal people feel about home. The safe place you're supposed to be from. But it just makes me nervous, how different he is.

We sit. His chair is in the sun, and I worry he might not ever take his sunglasses off. Then he does, and he's Matty again, eyes so pale they're almost yellow. And looking at him starts to quiet my nerves.

After school, when we'd draw pictures of each other with his little sister's crayons, the one I used to color his eyes was called *raw sienna.*

My bag is on the table. I go to move it, but before I can, he grabs the CD that's poking out.

"Wow, this isn't . . ." He flips it over and touches the picture of my face. "Ape! That's fantastic." He opens the jewel case and stares at the disc. "Can I have it?"

"Of course," I say softly. I look at the table and scratch my fingernail on the placemat, leaving a rippled scar on the wet paper. Three of the songs are about leaving him and I know it won't take him long to figure that out.

He looks at my wrist. I see him notice the finger marks that are starting to bruise. I wait for him to say something, my hand frozen mid-scratch, wet paper stuck under my fingernail.

"You know, I'm friends with the music director," he says, clearing his throat, "on the show."

I pull my sleeve over my hand. It's easier that way. It's not like I want to talk about it.

He closes the jewel case and looks at my picture, the one Cole took on the beach in Asbury Park, then he looks back at me, like he's seeing if it all adds up. "I'll slip this to him and see if we can get it on the show."

I hate the idea of my songs scoring a fight between a woman who has come back from the dead and her lover (who's really the evil twin of the man she thinks he is), but I could use the money.

"Take another one then." I dig through my purse and hand him a second CD. "You should have one too."

The waiter comes around and asks if we're ready. I haven't even opened my menu. "I always get the same thing here," Matty says, smiling, big and crooked, like he used to. He orders a sandwich called The Bowery Basil.

"I'll have that too," I say to keep things simple.

"It's so good to see a real person." He stares at

me with a warm kind of wonder, like the fact that I left him has been forgotten.

"Yeah," I say. "It's good to see you."

His eyes rest on my nose and stay there even after I lower my head, trying to make eye contact again.

"When'd you get this?" He taps my nose with his index finger.

"Right after—" I breathe in through my nostrils and feel the post of the tiny silver stud touch my septum. "Right after I left," I say. My napkin is still wrapped around the utensils. I unroll it, place it in my lap.

I have this picture in my head of Matty coming home from school, sitting on the sagging yellow plaid couch in the living room, re-reading the letter I left on his pillow. I can picture it so clearly even though I wasn't there. Afternoon sunlight through the brown slatted blinds making lines on his face and the wood-paneled walls. He reads it and puts his head in his hands, and in my mind he stays just like that. He never gets up. He never moves. He never moves on. He doesn't get discovered in the mall on a trip to Minnesota to visit his aunt. He doesn't win a Daytime Emmy. He's not one of the most beautiful people. He's just Matty and he keeps his head in his hands, the promise ring he gave me hooked on his little finger. He stays on that couch. Waiting for me to come back for him.

"I'm sorry," I say, looking up at Matthew.

"No." He smiles his benevolent hero smile. I think they've given him new teeth. "You were right. We had to get out of there."

There's a big difference, I think, between leaving by yourself in an old Mercury with a fistful of tip money and being whisked away in first class by a fairy godmother casting director. Before he was discovered, his dreams were only as big as a double wide and a job at the factory, a child bride to make him venison burgers, finally being old enough to buy beer. The waiter comes with our food, saving me before I say something snotty.

There are different colored sauces swirled on the plates, grill marks on the bread, and green beans in some sort of dressing, stacked like pick-up sticks on the side.

Matthew eats the green beans but leaves his sandwich. His movements are mechanical: take a bite, rest fork on plate, chew, wipe mouth, sip water, wipe condensation on napkin, pick up fork, start again. The stack of beans dwindles slowly. I wonder if someone taught him how to eat. I remember him devouring an entire foot-long sub in nanoseconds, eruptions of shredded lettuce spewing all over the couch.

I try to leave my sandwich too, but I'm hungry. I haven't eaten more than a street pretzel since I got into New York, and with the exception of a sandwich at the coffeehouse, my meals lately have mostly consisted of Slim Jims and corn nuts. I pull my sleeve over my wrist under the table every time I put my fork down.

"I went home a few weeks ago," he says between green beans. "I did a signing at the Big M. Crazy. It was mobbed."

"The women of Little River do love their soaps."

"Brandy Baker was there, waiting in line for an autograph."

"Seriously?"

Brandine Baker was head cheerleader and class president, and after being in school with her since kindergarten, she called me June at the homecoming dance when she wanted to borrow my hair spray.

"Man, she peaked in high school." He laughs and holds his arms out from his sides to show me how she's gotten fat.

"It hasn't been that long."

"She's already had two kids."

We would've too, I think, and I'm not sure if that would be good or bad anymore. "I hope nobody thinks I peaked in high school," I say.

"You haven't peaked yet," he says, his yellow eyes squinting in the sunlight.

I know he means it as a compliment, but I think I could find an insult in it if I wanted to.

Two women with lots of shopping bags get very

close to our table on their way out. "It *is* him," one whispers loudly to the other.

Matthew looks up and smiles at them, flashing pearly porcelain teeth.

The women scurry out in a mess of rustling shopping bags and sighs.

Now even the businessmen are staring at us, trying to figure out what the fuss is about.

The last bite of my sandwich is too big. I hate chewing with everyone watching our table. I take a sip of water and try to wash it all down. The bread is dry and scratches my throat.

The waiter takes our plates—mine scraped clean, Matthew's with his untouched sandwich—and asks if he can bring us anything else. It's all I can do not to ask for that sandwich wrapped up to go. The looks I would get are only slightly sharper than the hunger I never seem to chase away.

"Just the check," Matthew says.

I want to ask our waiter to pull up two extra chairs, one for the me I thought I'd be if I married Matty, and one for the me I really could have been if I had.

One is pregnant and sweaty, strands of peroxide blond hair sticking to her flushed face, wearing a smocked maternity dress from Sally Ann's over stretchy stirrup pants. A gold ring jammed on her swelling finger; tiny diamonds in a clump, trying to look like one decent-size one.

The other me is smooth. A glossy brown bob cut to fall in her face so she can push it away. Impossibly white teeth, the snaggly one finally fixed. A big square diamond on a platinum band. Her black dress skims her sculpted figure, without a trace of lint or panty lines. Her underwear comes wrapped in tissue paper, not plastic, and always matches her bra. She wears sky-high heels that cost more than my guitar.

For a moment, I think that I'd happily swap lives with either girl. Either version of me would be easier than this one.

A woman appears at the edge of our table, two decades older than us at least. Hands shaking, the slightest hint of tears in her sharp brown eyes.

"Do you mind?" she asks, handing Matthew a pen and a scrap of paper from her purse.

"Of course," he says, flashing those brilliant teeth.

"To Mary Jo, jay oh." There's a breathless quiver in her voice, like she's just been blessed. "My sister. Oh! She's never going to believe I met you."

I watch him sign like it's just one more autograph and realize that if I'd stayed, neither of those other versions of me would have happened. If I hadn't been the one to go first, Matty would have left me. He'd still be Matthew now, and he wouldn't have brought me along.

The woman leaves. The waiter brings us the check.

"I have bad news," Matthew says, handing the waiter his credit card without looking at the bill. "I can't make it to your show tonight."

It's not my show, just a set at a coffeehouse. It was last minute, hardly even pays, but I don't tell him that. I don't want him to know I'm less than what he thinks I am. That we're even further apart than it seems.

"I'm so sorry," he says. "It's a publicity thing. It's in my contract. I tried."

"It's okay," I say, nodding. "I understand."

"But I was thinking—do you have a place to stay?" He gives me his crooked Matty smile again.

I let myself imagine going home with him. The strawberry birthmark on his thigh and expensive sheets. I let myself think he wants me back.

Then he says, "I don't have a guest room, but the couch is really comfortable." Because really, who wants some bruised up girl who smells like corn nuts in their bed?

"Yeah, I do." I take my napkin off my lap and fold it up next to my plate. "Have a place to stay."

He looks mildly disappointed, but not as much as I wish he did. I'm not what I used to be to him. I never will be again. He will never be my home.

The waiter brings his card and the receipt in a

little black book. Matthew adds the tip, signs it with a squiggle and shuts the book with a slap. "It was great to see you, Ape. Really." He stands and grabs the CDs. "I've got a costume fitting in fifteen, so I got to run."

He kisses me on both cheeks, pulls me in for another hug. "The next time you're in town . . ."

"Of course." My throat tightens. I don't want to let go, but he pulls away. I blink and look up at the ceiling so my eyes don't drip. "Of course." I give him the biggest smile I can.

The whole restaurant is watching. He kisses my forehead, grabs his jacket and dashes out the door.

Before I leave, I go into the bathroom to clean up for my set. I avoid making eye contact with myself in the mirror and concentrate on smoothing my hair. When I come out of the bathroom, no one watches me leave.

I blow town right after I play my set. Don't even stay to sign CDs, just sneak out the back. It was a tough crowd and my music didn't fit. Everyone else's songs were edgy, less melodic. Leaving my car parked in the city costs way more than I'd ever make in CD sales. I know when to cut my losses.

I drive until I hit Scranton and find a motel off 81. I push the dresser against the door and keep the television on all night, scraping words into the backs of motel postcards with a ballpoint pen that's almost out of ink.

> *I, April,*
> *want too much and never get enough.*

Slowly, I twist the words. Twist the power. It turns into a song.

> *I don't want you*
> *To fall back into me*
> *And I don't want to want you,*
> *'Cause it's so easy*
>
> *I want your love*
> *I want you to want me*
> *Make a choice in my direction,*
> *But don't fall into me*

I press my fingers into the strings on my guitar, without strumming, because it's late and I can't risk getting kicked out of the motel. I work chords to the edge of blisters. Hum so softly it may just be in my mind. More words push through.

I don't want to close my eyes, but eventually I can't fight it anymore.

The sliver of light through the motel curtains is already strong by the time I wake up. I call the front desk to ask for late checkout and shower with water so hot I feel like my skin could disintegrate and take the bruises with it.

When I'm done, I sit on the bed in my wet towel and flip channels on the television until I find the right one. There's Matthew. Stuck in a bomb shelter with a woman in a frilly red dress. I guess she's about our age, but she looks so much more mature than I do. I don't watch often, and I haven't seen her before, but clearly she's meant to be Matty's new love interest, even though his character is engaged to Sandra's daughter. I catch them just as he's reaching for a ration can on a storage shelf behind her. It looks like they're about to kiss, but then they cut to a scene where Sandra is reading her sister's will.

I dress and braid my hair and when I look back at the television, there he is with that woman again. He didn't kiss her. Not yet. The one little candle that's been lighting the room so brightly will burn out soon. They can't find another. She's afraid of the dark. "That's because you've never been in the dark with me," he says, and gives her that crooked Matty smile. The one that used to be mine. And it looks so real. Maybe it is and their chemistry goes beyond the camera and the lights and the makeup. Maybe she's why he offered me his couch. Or maybe that smile was never mine to begin with, and I was just as charmed by him as everyone else. He's not my Matty anymore. Maybe he never really was.

I leave my sweater in the motel. My navy blue cotton roll neck. Even though it's sweater weather and I could use more layers, it feels good to let it go, leave it draped on the dingy flowered armchair in the corner of the room. I throw it at the chair a few times, until it falls just so and looks like maybe I forgot it. The right cuff is unraveling from getting caught in my guitar strings. I'll never have to fix it, sneaking yarn from the inside seam to bind the sleeve. Robbing Peter to pay Paul.

I give the sweater a half wave and a sympathetic smile before I close the door.

— Chapter 34 —

No matter how many miles I put in, I can't get myself back to normal. The bruises on my wrist are yellowing, but I can't bury the fear. Can't forget the bump and Ray's scream, the feeling of bones cracking under the car. It's there every time I give it space in my head.

I don't listen to the radio. The people who talk between songs sound too real. It makes me lonely. The tape deck is busted. I drive, listening to the sound of the tires on the pavement. They're too soft. I can hear the way they stick to the road. It reminds me of being a kid, pressing my cheek to an inner tube, the kind that are really from old truck tires. I remember the smell of rubber baking in the sun, and the way it sounded when I tapped my finger on it. *Ping, ping.* A metallic, inflated echo. I loved that sound even more than I loved the way the river felt creeping up the fibers of my bathing suit, making the colors darker, until all of it was wet.

I drive up to Binghamton. There's a dive bar on Main Street that lets me play whenever I roll into town. Arnie has an old PA that's usually collecting dust in the corner, so if I want to set it all up, he's happy to charge a cover and give me a cut. The PA pops and hisses, and it's full of distortion, but the crowd is mostly college kids and they're usually too drunk and horny to care if I don't sound perfect. The drunk kids are pretty good about buying my CDs. And they like to sing along with me if I play a song they know. It's nice, really, to have fans, to see familiar faces in a crowd sometimes. I need that right now, I think.

It's ten a.m. when I get into town. Arnie is behind the bar wiping down bottles and checking inventory. I knock on the window. He yells, "Closed!" but then he sees that it's me and lets me in.

"It's April in March!" he says. "What gives? We never see you in the cold weather."

"I missed you," I tell him. I grab a rag and help him wipe bottles. He pours me a coffee in a pint glass, loading it with milk and sugar until it's light and cloudy like his.

"You're the craziest girl I know," he says. "Who has the freedom to travel anywhere and ends up in the Southern Tier in March?"

"Only the cool kids," I say, snapping my rag at his arm.

"Well, it's good to see you."

"Yeah," I say, "you too."

I like Arnie. He's got salt and pepper hair and a salt and pepper beard. He spends his life dealing with drunk college kids, but he has more laugh lines than frown marks. Wears worn out jeans and threadbare concert T-shirts like a uniform. Today's is a yellow *Wings Over America* shirt with a bunch of little holes across the back like it got chewed by a zipper in the washing machine.

"Good timing," Arnie says as I climb on the back bar to reach the top shelf bottles. "Spring break's next week. We all have cabin fever."

"I always have good timing," I say.

"It's always a good time when you're here," Arnie says.

I needed this. To show up and clean bottles and chat with Arnie like I just saw him last week, like I belong. It's the thing I love about bar people. We have to put on a show all the time for everyone else, and when the crowd isn't around, we don't ask too many questions or expect big answers. It's just good chatter. People like Arnie are the best kind of break.

We clean bottles for an hour or so. I stand on the back bar and call off levels to him. "Tuaca, three-quarters," I say. "Tia Maria, almost empty."

"Tuaca!" He laughs. "That bottle came with the bar. I don't think anyone's ordered it."

"Triple dog dare you," I say, jumping down with the bottle to pour us shots. "Cheers." I slide his shot across the bar.

We clink glasses.

"One, two, three," he calls, and we down them.

"Not as weird as I thought it would be," I say,

breathing hard through my nose to try to figure out the aftertaste.

"You're a bad influence. Got me drinking before noon."

"It's like one thirty," I tell him, laughing, even though I don't really know what time it is.

"Lunch," Arnie says. He gets up and goes into the kitchen. His limp is worse than it was last time I was here. He has bad knees from being on his feet so much. Needs surgery but can't take the downtime. I get the polish from the cabinet under the sink and shine the bar for him.

He comes back with two fat burgers and a big plate of well-done fries. We sit next to each other at the bar, studying the wall of clean bottles while we eat.

"Thanks for the burger," I say.

"You look anemic."

"Sure know how to charm a girl," I say, taking a huge bite of my burger.

"You okay?" he asks. He's looking at my wrist. The bruises.

My sleeve rode up when I held my burger to my mouth. I should be more careful.

"Other guy looks worse," I say, staring at the now-shiny bottle of Tuaca on the top shelf.

Arnie pats me on the back. Just one pat, his hand resting lightly between my shoulders for a split second.

"Thanks," I say.

We finish our burgers and share the plate of fries in silence. It's a nice quiet. It's a good burger. Arnie remembered that I like my fries crispy.

"Need a shower," he says, throwing me his keys when we're done eating. It's a statement, not a question.

"Do I smell?" I ask, sniffing my pits.

"Like roses," he says, gathering up our lunch plates. "But you have twigs in your hair."

"You could have told me that like an hour ago." I comb my fingers through my hair and pull out one leaf. It was probably in my car. But I'll take the hot water and the quiet.

"Wouldn't have been as much fun."

"Butthead." I grin. "I'm totally going to mess with the settings on your beard trimmer while I'm up there."

"Do it," he says, tugging at one of my curls. "I could use a new look."

Arnie's place above the bar is old, cramped, and cleaner than you'd expect from a guy who's always single and works until three in the morning. I've been here before. He lets me shower and use his phone to call ahead and book new gigs. I've crashed on his couch a few times when I rolled into town over summer break or Columbus Day or something. He's never made a pass or even hinted he might want to. He's old enough to be my dad, but that's not always a limiting factor with guys. Some of them seem to like that more. Arnie is just quiet and easy and likes having company that doesn't expect too much from him. There's nothing there, but there's nothing missing.

I shower, making the water as hot as I can stand, scrubbing every inch of my skin with a washcloth lathered with Arnie's bar of Irish Spring. Sun streams through the frosted window in the shower, and I watch how it makes the water sparkle on my skin. I let myself cry. It's safe to cry here. The water will run cold eventually. Arnie will come back upstairs to grab a CD or change his shirt. The sun will set. It will be time to play. It's okay to let go when there's an end in sight. When I'm alone, on the road, it could go on forever.

Chapter 35

The last Friday night before spring break—I don't know why I didn't think of it before. The place is packed. Arnie can charge a cover for me and I get sixty percent. It's not a bad deal. Plus, it's good for my ego. No one here will ask me to play *Margaritaville* or *Free Bird* or one of those awful standard covers old drunk people are prone to suggesting. They want me to play my originals. They know them. These kids are here because they saw the sign Arnie put outside. They came to see me.

Justin cut his hair. I wasn't even looking for him and then there he is. He's leaning against the wall, watching me play, holding a beer bottle by its neck. He smiles when I make eye contact. The last time I saw him, sometime in June, his hair flopped over his eyes and hung down to his shoulders. I remember it was thick and coarse between my fingers. Now it's short and spiky and I almost didn't recognize him in the crowd. He's with a guy who has a mop of ringlets blooming from his head. They come up to the stage after my first set.

"Just-man!" I say as he kisses me on the cheek. "Good to see you."

"You're never here in March!"

"Good surprise?" I ask, wondering if he has someone now.

"Great surprise." He smiles wide.

"I missed you," I say, and while I haven't thought of him much at all since the last time I was in Binghamton, seeing his face makes it feel true.

"I told Sam about you. We were gonna hit the bars on Water Street, but we saw the sign and I told him we had to hang here." He gestures to his curly friend.

"Thanks for coming out, Sam." I use his name while it's easy, so later when I call him *friend* he won't think it's because I don't remember. It's my trick for dealing with too many names and too many faces.

"You were great." Sam offers his hand to shake mine. His palms are warm and sticky, like a gum eraser that's been kneaded a long time.

"Aw, thank you." I've practiced my humble, genuine face in many a motel mirror. It's an awkward thing to take compliments. It's harder than you think.

"Can I get you a beer?" Sam pats his back pocket.

"Thanks, friend. Magic Hat. Tell them it's for me." I wave over to Arnie and point to Sam. Arnie nods. "House covers mine."

Justin pulls on one of my braids. "Got a place to crash?"

I put my hand over his. "Do I?"

"I have a house this year with a few other guys, but everyone else left for break already."

"Imagine that." I smile. I can feel the current. He's stuck in it, paddling like a puppy dog, his tail wagging madly. I know what this is. He does too. It's our arrangement. He's my place to stay. I'm his excitement. We have a history.

Someday, when he's married and middle-aged, he will listen to my CD in his car on the way home to crockpot dinners and tricycles in the driveway. He will pull the jewel case out from the crack between the seat and the console at a traffic light, run his fat fingers over my picture, and remember what it felt like to cup my breasts in his palms while my hair streamed down his arms. There won't ever be an us, but he'll never forget me.

Sam comes back with my beer. I smile and wipe the rim off with my sleeve. "Thanks, friend."

"Anytime." He winks and shoots a finger gun in my direction.

I clink my bottle with Justin's and go up to start my second set. A song from my first CD. Angsty and fierce. *Snakebites and heart attacks. I'll never make you mine, go back.* People sing along. I finally feel like I don't have to think about anything but lyrics and chords and the faces in the crowd. Like things can be simple for a moment.

After my second set, Sam has disappeared. Justin waits for me. He hangs around while Arnie counts out the register to give me my cut.

Arnie slides beers down the bar to us while we wait.

Justin rests his hand on my thigh and drinks his in big gulps. I don't know anything about his real life, what he does when I'm not here. He's grown into his looks, less awkward. He should have a girlfriend, but he always seems to be available when I roll into town. We never talk about it. And the things I do know, I forget. I can't remember what his major is, or where he grew up. I can't remember his last name.

Arnie slides a wad of bills across the bar to me. "You are a little bit of magic, I think," he says. "Good haul tonight." I hop up to sit on the bar so I can give him a hug.

"Thanks, Arnie," I say, kissing his cheek. He blushes a little.

"Don't be a stranger," he says softly, looking me in the eyes, sizing me up. "Okay?" It's his way of taking care of me. "Okay?" He's making sure I'm not falling apart. That my bruises will heal. It's his way of saying something without saying anything specific, and I love him for it.

"Yeah," I say. "Okay."

Justin's new place is two streets over from Main. We're both too drunk to drive, so we leave my car at Arnie's and walk over. Justin carries my guitar for me. There aren't many people left walking around. It's still cold and crisp and the puddles ice over at night. Binghamton won't see the last of the snow for months.

I shower when I get to Justin's. I'm in wash when you can mode. It doesn't matter that I just showered at Arnie's. I smell like bar and smoke and I'm sweaty from playing.

Justin's shower isn't too gross. The house is big and empty. It's just me and him and it's sweet, because of all the people I know, of all my pockets, Justin is my favorite. He's my marker. I count time against him. I've watched him grow up. He's older than me, two years, I think. So, he must be twenty-one now, but it feels like he's a kid and I'm something else.

I tie my hair in a knot and pin it with some bobby pins I keep in my bag. I wrap myself in his towel and walk down the hall to his room.

Justin lit candles while I showered, the globe kind with psychedelic patterns that glow as the wick burns down. The candlelight reflects in the sheen of his *Sports Illustrated* posters. Patchouli clouds the room, but it doesn't mask the fact that he's stoned.

"Wow," he says when he sees me. He already

has condoms out. I can see the shiny wrappers next to a skull candle on the shelf over the bed. Three of them, lined up like a goal he's set.

"What happened to your hair?" I ask, rubbing my hand over his head. The wax he slicked it with makes my palm sticky.

"I cut it."

"I liked it long." I wipe my palm on his comforter when he isn't looking.

"Internship interviews. I'm a junior now." He raises his eyebrows, tilts his chin down and looks up at the ceiling. He's posing for me. *Look how much I've grown.*

"Ah." I nod.

I reach over him and pull the joint out of the ashtray.

"Saved you some," he says.

"Good call." I light up and suck in hard. Hold my breath until I feel my eyeballs bulge, and then I exhale the smoke slowly through the tiny O I form with my lips. Before it's all out, Justin is working his tongue into the O.

He pulls the pins from my hair. Wet strands slap my shoulders as they fall. Drops of water run down my back. Justin licks them up. He cups my chin and holds my head at my shoulder, working his tongue up my neck on the other side. He has learned things since I saw him last year.

We slide until we're lying down. I feel him hard on my thigh. His arms are smooth, muscles firm and round. He loses his cool when he tries to undress and get the condom on. Underwear stuck on ankles.

"Oh, crap," he says. "Close your eyes."

I do. The light goes on for a second.

"Okay," he says. The light goes off. I hear him fumble with the condom. I hope he pinches the tip to leave room. I had to show him how last time.

It's good, but not great. He tries too hard. He's still wearing his socks. He picks me up and carries me over to the wall, but it's cold stucco. The bumps scratch my back.

"Remember last time?" I whisper in his ear. "On your desk?"

"Yeah," he whispers, and carries me to his desk. He keeps holding me while he throws notebooks on the floor. I wrap my arms around his neck even tighter and think about what it would be like to stay with him.

When he sets me down gently on the desk it doesn't take him long to finish.

We make goal by morning.

"Stay another day," he says when we wake up.

I nod and kiss his face. There's barely any stubble.

"No, I mean it. Don't say you will and leave while I'm in the shower. Stay for real this time."

I kiss him hard, running my finger along the

bottom of his lip and the dent above his chin, memorizing the way his lips feel. I wait for the panic I always get when I think about staying in one place for too long, the electric itch in my veins. It doesn't come.

"Short shower. So short. Don't go," he says, rolling over me to get out of bed. He pulls on his boxer shorts and leaves the room.

I look around, taking quick inventory of where my stuff is so I can exit efficiently. I can't stay. Keep moving or get stuck. Those are the only options. If I go for breakfast with Justin, before you know it, I'll be living here, working for Arnie, falling completely and totally short of every fantasy Justin has ever had about me. The whole reason people like me is that I always leave a little too soon.

I hear the whine of the shower starting. I have ten minutes at most. My limbs are leaden, lazy, brain full of fuzz. I can't get up. It's cold and lonely out there. I pinch the inside of my wrist with my other hand, hoping I can snap myself out of it, but my eyelids feel heavy. I don't have any fight left.

And then Justin is back. Body on mine. The wet towel wrapped around him falling to the way-side.

"Where are you headed next?" Justin says after, rolling on his side to look at me.

I shrug. "My plans got pushed around." I was going to book more gigs from Red Bank. It's the first time in a long time with a big span of empty in front of me. I should have called places from Arnie's but it felt nice to just be there.

"So you can go anywhere? Like whenever you want to?"

"Yeah," I say. "Mostly. I mean, I have to fund it, so there's work involved."

"God, you're so lucky. Even on spring break I'm supposed to be home going to interviews for a summer internship I don't even want."

"So why go?"

"My dad's making me. I want to intern in New York or Washington, someplace real, you know? But I have to spend the summer in Rochester. He won't pay for me to live anywhere else. He hates the idea that I might actually have fun at some point in my life."

Justin looks so defeated. It's real hurt that his dad won't pay for him to have fun. I can't imagine his world. He probably can't imagine mine either. But I do understand feeling stuck and misunderstood.

"What would happen if you came with me instead?" I say. It's hypothetical. A gift to him, so he can feel like he has choices. It's safe. He won't take me up on it.

Justin laughs. "My dad would shit himself."

I laugh too and run my finger along his arm.

"See, technically, you could, though. You have more than one narrow path."

"Yeah," he says. "Technically, I could." The gears are turning. He might actually be considering it. I wait for the fear to hit, but it doesn't. Instead, he wraps his arms around me and I can still breathe all the way in and all the way out. I don't know what's wrong with me. I learned not to travel with people. I know better. But this is different. It's Justin. He's the first person I met after I left Ithaca. I've known him for a long time. I run my finger along his forearm from one freckle to the next, like I'm connecting stars.

Over hash browns and coffee at a diner on State Street, we start plotting. We'll go south until it gets warm enough to swim in the ocean. He has a ton of mixtapes. I'll pay for gas. He'll pay for rooms. He has his dad's credit card. For emergencies. "This *is* an emergency," he says, halfway between funny and earnest. "It's my junior year, and I've never even gone anywhere good for spring break. At some point I have to live my life, you know?"

I nod, willing my mind to ignore how far apart we are. I need a break from myself, and this is the closest I'll get to taking one. We pick up my car from the parking lot at Arnie's without stopping in to say hi. I think we both know our getaway plan will fade fast if we lose momentum.

Back at Justin's, he throws things in a duffle bag, quickly, like the house will burn to ashes around us if we don't get out.

And then, we're gone.

— Chapter 36 —

Justin has terrible taste in music. I'm almost offended he likes my songs so much. The broken tape deck in my car wasn't even a problem for him, because he brought his boom box, so we could listen to his ten thousand mixtapes that are a jumble of songs by the same five shitty college radio bands in slightly different order. He can't read a map. He won't pee on the side of the road, and he's an endless pit of hunger. He's the opposite of practical.

Here's what Justin gets at our first gas station stop: pork rinds, a jumbo bag of pizza-flavored Combos, two giant slushies (blue and red, because *why should we have to choose*), couple Cokes for later, Fruit Stripe gum, and a Zagnut bar with a wrapper that's sun-faded and dusty, because he's never seen one before. He swears he's not going to eat it. It's just because the word *Zagnut* is funny.

Here's what I get: thirteen gallons of gas.

Most of what I eat is convenience store food. It's not amusing. It's just convenient. I have a hard time holding my tongue about how he chewed up good daylight laboring over his junk food choices. But then he smiles between bites of fossilized Zagnut—"Want some? It's disgusting!"—and I feel like I have to play along and pretend all of this is novel and fun, the way you don't tell other kids the truth about Santa after you know. It's not fair to ruin the end of the movie for everyone else. But the end of his movie is better than mine. It's not something I have to think about when I leave after one night, but it's sad to see up close. I feel like I've found a new kind of lonely.

"That's okay," I tell him, shrugging off the Zagnut. "I'll let you keep that all to yourself."

"It's so stale!" He laughs, and crumbs of decaying chocolate spray from his mouth. This is an adventure to him, and I will myself to feel the same way. I want to believe there will still be newness in the world for me. That it's not all faded and dusty. A few miles later, I look over, and he's rocking out to some horrible shouty song with a pseudo-Egyptian riff, grinning like a dog who escaped the pound. Knowing I've made him so happy helps tame the churn in my stomach and kills the urge to leave him in the next rest stop bathroom. I like him. I swear, I do. But it's hard to like someone. It's a job that's never quite finished.

"Hey," Justin says, pointing toward an exit sign. "Do you think the water is warm enough in New Jersey?"

I laugh, thinking he's making a joke, but when I look over, his face is serious.

"No," I say carefully. "I don't think that's south enough for swimming in spring."

"Oh."

And then, "Do you think we can stop? For a restroom?"

After we get back in the car, he falls asleep. His mixtape runs to the end and I'm left to my thoughts and the road noise.

I glance at him from time to time. There's something sweet about someone feeling comfortable enough to sleep in front of you. The light from the setting sun makes his eyelashes glow. He doesn't even stir when I hit a pothole. He has so much peace. He believes the life ahead will work out in his favor, and it probably will. In the grossest of thoughts, I wonder if I could go with him. If I could piggyback on his life, the end of his movie would be mine too. I could stay in Binghamton while he finishes school. Arnie could get his knee surgery, and I'd take care of the bar while he recovers. I'd be safe and warm and clean. Maybe, if this trip goes well, Justin would want me there. Or maybe, at least, I could visit him more. I could rest.

The sun goes from a sliver to nothing. Justin snores.

— Chapter 37 —

It's easier, I think, to plunk down in the middle of romance. Or lust, or whatever it is. Justin and I know what roles we're supposed to play, what goes where. There's a script. A way to act. Friendship is so much harder. It needs time and I never have any. I don't ever stay long enough to be a friend. The one time I tried to make a friend on the road, it turned upside down, and I never saw it coming.

I met a girl at a gig about six months after I left Ithaca, and she played guitar too. Her car was having problems and wouldn't it be so much more fun if we traveled together? Wouldn't it? It was easy, right away, which should have been a sign. I mean, Carly didn't walk up to me and say, "Let's be friends." But I was too lonely to be leery, and that girl made me feel important.

She taught me to play barre chords and crack lockbox codes on empty rental houses. How to push back when a bar owner claims the take from the door was lower than it obviously was. How to pick the right guys to go home with, so you don't have to spring for a motel room but you don't have to give more than you want to. I needed her.

She found out, three days in, that I'd never been to the ocean, so she called a guy she knew in Asbury Park and booked us a gig. Two days later we were at the boardwalk. She ran straight into the waves with all her clothes on. I did too, dunking my head under water so she wouldn't notice my tears. I felt like she gave me the ocean. Like all of it was ours.

Half the contacts in my notebook are because she introduced me to someone. Or she introduced me to the someone who introduced me. She was so much fun until she wasn't. Until I caught her trying to take my guitar to a pawnshop because we could both use hers. Because she needed the money for a "thing" she couldn't tell me about yet, and she'd get more cash for mine. The fight we had was brutal, and it got worse from there. I had to leave her. You can't travel with someone you can't trust. I did it the best way I could. Told her I was going. Tucked a bus ticket and some twenties in her bag before I drove away, but somehow I was stuck with gasps of guilt that still take over in the quiet.

Women notice more. They pay attention to tiny details, so it's easier for them to break you apart from the inside. Maybe I should have been willing to share my guitar. Maybe the "thing" was going to be more than a little plastic baggie she'd empty in a day, and I *was* a horrible person for thinking otherwise. Maybe I'm too chipped and cynical and stale, finding the worst because I'm looking for it.

Now I always ask who else is playing before I book a show to make sure we won't cross paths. But she never is. Cole told me that the last time she gigged at The Downtown, she looked like "death on a coke bender," and the songs she played were mostly mine. He said some people live hard and burn out fast and that I should learn not to get too sad about it. I try to not even think her name.

It's late. I'm tired. Justin's been sleeping for most of the trip, so when he stirs and gives me a dopey smile, I suggest he take the night shift, even though I feel funny about him driving my car.

"We'll just stop at a cheap hotel," he says, yawning loud. "We're not in a hurry." He stays awake to watch for lodging signs. The mixtapes start again and I miss the quiet.

Justin has a very different idea of what constitutes a cheap hotel. A good lock on the door and a mattress that doesn't smell like piss is as fancy as I can justify. And even that feels like a splurge. In my notebook I keep a list of the motels that aren't so bad and the ones I will never, ever set foot in again. I assumed we'd look for something on my list, but Justin points out a Holiday Inn sign from the highway and says, "There. That'll work." Hands his dad's credit card across the counter without asking what the rate is. Orders burgers for both of us from room service.

The room just smells like clean and I don't even feel like I have to check the lock.

"I can't believe you don't like live off of room service," Justin says, jamming a stack of steak fries in his mouth. "That's what I would do."

"I don't usually stay in places that have room service. Plus," I say, trying to make it all sound better than it is, "most of the places where I play feed me."

"Where do you live when you're not on the road?" He puts his pickle slices on my plate. He always remembers things about me that I've forgotten he could know.

"Nowhere," I say, trying not to let the word settle into my brain.

"So the traveling never stops?" He looks at me, mouth open, horrified. There are still pieces of french fry stuck to his tongue.

"Not really," I say, forcing a smile. It's hard to see him process how little I have. "I mean, there are a couple of places—friends let me stay for a week or two to catch my breath sometimes."

"What about your parents? Do you ever go home?"

"That's not . . . that's not really an option for me."

He hugs me close. "Add me to the list. You can always catch your breath at my place."

I love the feel of his arms through his soft, clean shirt. He kisses me hard. I can feel the ridges his teeth make through his lips. And then it evolves and he's kissing me everywhere like he's trying to memorize me. We have lazy sex with the TV and all the lights on.

When it's over, that itch I get to escape is so diluted I can barely feel it. I rest my head on his chest. He's watching *Billy Madison*. I like hearing him laugh from the inside. I feel myself fall away without trying to stop it.

I wake up startled. I'm not sure what sets it off. A dream that disappears when my eyes open, or my body rejecting sleep. My cheek is damp against his chest.

"Hey, sleepyhead," he says, and I wonder if his mom says that to him. "You were zonked. And you drooled."

"Sorry," I say, wiping the puddle from his chest, feeling my cheeks burn.

Justin laughs. "Don't be sorry." He smooths my hair and lets me rest on him again, rubbing my back absentmindedly. The movie has switched to something with Jim Carrey that I haven't seen, but I can't keep my eyes open long enough to watch any of it. It's the best sleep I've had in years.

— Chapter 38 —

In the morning, Justin makes coffee in the machine on the dresser. We lay the map across the bed and figure out our route. Florida for sure, but we have to decide which part. Justin wants to go to Weeki Wachee to see the mermaids. It seems kind of ridiculous, but really, why shouldn't we? That's what a vacation is, to the best that I can tell. Driving to see what there is to see without any other purpose.

I'm always careful about my expenses. I have money saved. Two hundred, plus the extra forty I always keep hidden in my guitar case. But when I hesitate on Weeki Wachee because we don't need to go all the way to the left side of Florida to get to warm water, Justin jumps in with "I'll even pay for gas. Don't worry about it." So really, there's no reason not to see the mermaids.

Justin goes downstairs to check out while I brush my teeth and dry my hair. I'm supposed to meet him at the car, but a few minutes later the room phone rings and it's Justin saying, "Can you come down here?" So I leave my stuff in the room and sprint down the stairs to the lobby, because his voice sounds desperate and the elevator is probably slow.

There's a manager at the desk looking stern. Justin is red-faced, hands shaking.

"My dad canceled the card," Justin whispers in my ear. "Declined the charges. Manager says he might arrest me." He looks like he will break into sobs at any moment. He hands me the bill. The movies were pay-per-view, not regular cable. Plus room service. Plus tax. It's a hundred and thirty-seven dollars.

I want to shout at him about calling me into it. I'm terrified they've already sent someone to the room and they'll take my guitar. But Justin gets messier by the moment. He looks young, defeated, and I realize that he is not equipped to handle this.

I put my hand out to shake the manager's. It throws him off, which is the point.

"I'm so sorry for this misunderstanding," I say, using my best waitress voice. "If you could give us a chance to go upstairs and make a phone call, I'm sure—"

"I'm afraid we can't allow—"

"If he calls collect, can he call from the lobby? It's just a misunderstanding." I smile sweetly. There are other people in the lobby. I can tell Justin is embarrassed to have witnesses, but it's our asset. The manager won't want a scene, and as long as I use a calm and reasonable voice, he'll look terrible if he loses his cool.

He allows Justin to use the courtesy phone in

the lobby, next to a mauve couch and a table with a vase of fake flowers. The manager and I stand at the corner of the desk, watching him. Dial, wait, hang up, dial. Justin's dad denies the first three calls but accepts on the fourth. Justin wipes tears from his cheeks as he talks, cupping the phone to his mouth for privacy.

The manager shifts his weight from one foot to the other. His name is Brian. It says so on his name tag. He sighs. I smile at him, cool as a cucumber, and settle into the silence. I'm okay with quiet, but chances are he's not, so again, I have the advantage.

I study his face and make up his life. He was probably kind of cute in high school, when girls could still dream about him being something more. Button nose, brown eyes, reddish-brown hair that's starting to grey at the temples. Freckles. His chin will disappear soon. Divorced, definitely. Long enough that the pale band on his empty ring finger has tanned up again. Ex-wife is pretty in an Ivory soap and water kind of way. Two kids, who would rather not go to his sad apartment on weekends. He'd rather not have them there and wonders what kind of person that makes him. That's why he drinks. Late at night, after he gets home from work, microwaves a Salisbury steak, when the talk shows turn into reruns, he snorts a line or two off the glass coffee table he rents from one of those lease-to-own furniture places. He will never own that coffee table.

He blushes in my gaze. His hand goes to his cheek. Self-conscious about his freckles. That's why I stare at them. I guessed right.

"So where are you from?" he asks after several minutes watching Justin whisper arguments into the phone.

"Western New York," I say brightly, as if I'm thrilled to chat with him. This is not a problem. If I act like it's not a problem, it won't be.

"Staten Island?"

"Outside Buffalo."

He nods. Everyone seems to forget New York is more than a city, that there's a world beyond the boroughs and the people who live there are real. But I don't want to sound snotty and I'm worried maybe I did. I'm about to say more, and then Justin hangs up the phone and waves me over. I smile at Brian. " 'Scuse me for a sec."

Justin tries to whisper in my ear when I sit next to him. "No," I say quietly. "Smile. Talk softly, but smile."

"My dad's pissed that I didn't come home for my internship interviews and he's not going to pay for my *dalliance*." He uses finger quotes. "But he won't press charges."

I feel my hands loosen up. I hadn't noticed I'd clenched them into fists.

"He's not going to take the hold off the card,

though," Justin says. "And if the hotel decides to arrest me, he won't help. There's nothing I can do. I have like ten bucks left." He sobs and buries his head in my shoulder. I want to ask if his dad would pay if I just turned right around and drove him to Rochester, but I don't feel like I can with how hard he's crying. The terms are so completely different, but the disappointment is familiar.

"I'll pay for it," I say. "I have cash. I'll fix it."

His relief is instant and beautiful and being able to give that to someone else feels triumphant. I can do more than just survive. I can do more than take. He kisses me hard.

Brian is still watching. I give him a thumbs up. Cool as a cucumber. But there's a slight scuffle when I tell Brian I have to go up to the room to get money to pay him. He insists on coming with me while Justin stays in the lobby.

"So, Buffalo," Brian says in the elevator, his breath loud in the small space. He stands closer than he needs to and I wonder if his insistence on coming with me is about more than making sure we don't bolt. "Good wings."

"Of course," I say, smiling.

He smiles back. "I like wings."

I get the feeling there's another way to solve this. He's not so awful, just sad and spent. It wouldn't be the worst way to get out of a bad spot.

The elevator doors open. We walk down the hall together and I think about Ray and the crunch of his foot bones under my tire. His black-framed glasses. How he rolled the flyer from my show in his hands and seemed so harmless and earnest. I try not to think about that burnt rubber smell, but then it's like the air won't fill my lungs anymore and the things that are real hide behind my thoughts.

I stop smiling at Brian. I swipe my room key. Rummage through my bag. I pretend I don't notice the way he watches me from the doorway. He holds the door open with his back, and I'm relieved to feel like I could scream and be heard. That he understands the need for that courtesy.

"Here," I say, handing Brian a hundred and forty dollars. "Can you tell Justin I'll meet him in the car?" He looks like he doesn't want to leave me in the room.

"I just want to pack up and use the restroom," I say.

He shifts his weight and the door swings shut. I gasp. I don't mean to. He's shocked. It was an accident. He's scared that he scared me. Worried what I think. He reaches for the door handle.

"Sure," he says. "Give him the change?"

"Keep it." I don't know if I'm supposed to tip. I don't stay in places this nice. If a tip is expected, it's a terrible one.

"Have a nice trip," he says. "I'm sorry about . . . all the confusion."

He shuts the door and the tears come fast. I run into the bathroom and splash cold water, but it feels like drowning. I cough and sputter and cry like there's something inside me trying to escape.

Deep breaths and I sit on the bed and put my head between my knees. In. Out. Dig my thumbnail into the fleshy part of my opposite hand. I get it under control. Choke it down. Banished to the very bottom of my lungs. But still there.

When I get to the car, Justin is sitting on the trunk, with his duffle bag in his lap, swinging his legs. He smiles and waves when he sees me. I expected him to be upset about his dad, but relief has made him perky.

"I can probably get you back to Binghamton on what I have." I'm sure Arnie will let me play again or tend bar or something, so I can pull together what I've lost.

"I don't want to go back," Justin says. "If I do, my dad wins." He's not concerned with my drained reserves. It's paid for. It's over. He's not getting arrested. He wants to win this battle I don't even understand. But I'm not sure I have it in me to tell him I'm done. To stay in the car with his disappointment all the way to Binghamton. And then to be alone again.

If we keep going, I don't know how Justin

will get back. But I don't make an issue of it. He knows how much money I have left. I decide he can make his own decisions, but then he says, "There's always Motel 6," and I realize he doesn't understand.

"I think I know a place where we can stay," I tell him. "On Anna Maria Island."

"Is there a beach?" Justin asks.

"Yup." I've been there before. I know my way around. Stay for free. Pick up a gig or at least play on the beach. Bradenton is half the miles it would take to get to Binghamton and I'm still tired. I'd rather push the crisis to the end of the week.

"That works," he says, smiling. He hops off the trunk and gets in the passenger seat.

— Chapter 39 —

It's past midnight when we get to the house. No cars in the driveway and the lawn is long. They send someone to cut the grass when they're expecting guests.

Justin slams the car door too loud. My heart thuds like a bass line as we walk the path to the front door of the cottage. I'm surprised Justin can't hear it.

If they've changed the code, I'll have to make up a story. I know numbers for a house a few blocks over. I used to bounce between the two last year. But the other house looks totally different from this one. I can't say I got confused. I don't know what my story would be. We could sleep on the beach. It's warm, at least.

I hold my breath. Squeeze my keychain flashlight so I can see. Press the buttons for 2-3-5-6 on the lockbox and then it opens and we have the key.

"Whose place is this?" he asks as I unlock the door and push it open.

"My uncle's," I say. My father had a brother, but he died in Vietnam. It's easier if Justin doesn't know that last summer I spent a few hours after dark with my flashlight, trying out combos until I got the right one. It wasn't hard. Six of the ten buttons were worn and finger-grubby, so the code had only been changed maybe two or three times over years and years of use. The order doesn't matter on punch code boxes. Just that you pick the right numbers.

Justin turns the lights on in the living room and I resist the urge to turn them off. Old wicker furniture with palm tree prints on the cushions. The air is stale and damp. There's dust on the coffee table. Odds are with us for a night or two at least, but we'll have to be careful and I don't know how to tell Justin to be careful without explaining.

It's probably okay. I know people who squat as if they're legit, taking long showers, leaving the lights on. People around here don't keep track. Most of them are only on vacation anyway, renting the house next door for a week or two. They don't know who belongs where, or which houses are supposed to be vacant. Maybe I call more attention to myself when I try to go under the radar. Maybe Justin and I are safer being conspicuous.

We bring our clothes in. I leave my guitar in the car when I stay in houses like this. I never do it otherwise, but Justin doesn't know me well enough to think it's strange. It makes for a cleaner getaway if a getaway becomes necessary.

"Let's walk over to the beach," Justin says after we've thrown our stuff in the bedroom.

"It's late. I've been driving all day."

"That's why you need to walk," he says. "Come on!"

The only reasons for not going are ones I can't tell him, so we go.

He holds my hand as we walk down the road in the dark and cross to the beach. The moon is the slimmest sliver, hidden behind clouds. It's disorienting. The blackness of the horizon. My hair flying in the wind. I can hear the power of the waves, even though I can't see them clearly. It's dark music they make. I could walk right into the water and become part of the movement, but I'm tethered to Justin, fingers hooked. Our feet sink in the sand. The air is thick and smells alive.

"We made it," he says, laughing.

"We did."

"Fuck you, Dad!" he yells to the waves. His voice is tired, ragged, young. "Now you." He squeezes my hand. "Your turn."

"Fuck you, Dad!" I yell. Because the waves are too loud for anyone else to hear us. I can barely hear myself.

"Yeah!" Justin yells, and then he lifts me up and kisses me. His face is wet. I wipe his cheeks.

"Fuck 'em both," I say.

He stumbles and we fall, landing soft in the sand. I wish the world would always catch me this way. Justin holds on to me still, tucks his head into my neck. "Thank you," he says. "I need to be myself sometimes, you know?" His breath is warm. I find his lips with mine. The waves are loud and the night is dark, and no one will see us.

We sleep late, even though the mattress is old and sagging. Musty pillows. Sand in the sheets. Justin takes forever to open his eyes. Even after I extract myself from his grasp and get out of bed, he lies there, breathing in slow rhythm. It's better if we leave. This is not a place to linger.

"Gypsy rules!" I say, shoving the pile of clothes Justin left on the floor into his duffle.

"What?" He sits up fast. Looks around, trying to make sense of where we are.

"We're on an adventure. We could end up anywhere. We may as well put our stuff back in the trunk. So if we decide to drive to Mexico next, we don't even have to come back here."

"Mexico is kind of far," Justin says. "If we go to Mexico, I won't be back at school in time."

"Proverbial Mexico," I say.

"But we're just walking over to the beach, right?"

"Manatee Beach is way better," I tell him, eager to get him in the car, "and it's kind of a hike. It makes sense to drive." It's not that far, but I'll wind through a few neighborhoods and make it seem further than it is, so he isn't tempted to run back to get something. It's best for us to stay away from the house all day in case someone shows up. People usually check in before dark. There's still a risk at night, but if someone wasn't here Sunday night, it's not likely they're coming now. Friday it gets dangerous again. But I like this house because it's kind of run down, so I don't think they rent it out much. It's not what I would pick if I were paying. "My uncle always drives over to Manatee instead of walking."

It's funny, even when it's bright and sunny and warm, when I close my eyes, branches and frozen rain are what I expect to see the next time I open them. All I have to do is blink and the shiny palm trees and bright yellow sun are suddenly shocking.

Justin runs into the water until it's up to his waist, then dives in, pulling his arms back to hurl himself forward. Strong strokes he probably took lessons to learn, in a clean blue pool with floating ropes to mark out the lanes.

My mother taught me how to swim in the river in late summer when the water was low and calm. She'd hold me with both arms under my belly. She'd say, "Kick your legs, baby," and I'd get mad at her for calling me baby when I was a big girl.

The next summer, when we went, she sat on the rocks on the shore, humming to herself, twisting her hair with her index finger and watching it uncurl. I swam alone, under the water, pretending

352

I was a mermaid, testing my lungs to see how far I could get on one breath. I wonder if she ever panicked when I disappeared into the yellow-brown water. Or maybe she wished I'd never come back up.

The summer after that, she was gone.

I don't follow Justin out to the big, rolling distant waves. Swimming like a mermaid is silly in the face of his perfect, metered strokes. I never learned to really swim, with my head above the surface. I shed my skirt, walk in shoulder-deep, and float on my back until the waves push me to shore.

"Shit," Justin says, tilting his head to shake water from his ear. "We didn't grab towels from the house."

"Here," I say, handing him my skirt. He looks at me funny but uses it to wipe his face. He's not used to making the most of what's in front of him.

"We'll dry fast in the sun," I say.

He hands the skirt back to me and I spread it on the sand so we can sit down.

"Don't you want to put it back on?" he asks, eyeing my tank top and underwear. He seems embarrassed, but they're black. It's not like they're see-through. Everything's covered. Bathing suits are expensive.

"I'm good," I say, but I hate watching him take

in the frayed strap of my tank top and the outline of my nipples in wet cotton. I hate the way he looks around to see if anyone is watching us. I try to ignore the twinge of shame creeping up from my chest, like when all the other kids in my class had big packs of pristine crayons in September and I had the same old sandwich bag of broken ones from a rummage sale.

Once he's sure no one is paying any particular attention to us, he sits on my skirt next to me.

"Not a big swimmer?" he asks.

"Nah," I say, "not really." But I do love the water. It makes me feel better. If Justin weren't here, I'd have stayed in, swimming under waves until my fingers pruned up and salt burned my nose. We're all small at the ocean; none of us have control. I like being reminded of that.

We stare out at the waves. We're waterlogged and sun-touched. It makes us quiet.

Once we're mostly dry, we get hot dogs at a snack bar across the street from the beach. I hate hot dogs, but they're cheap. Justin orders three and a soda. He has no understanding of money, or the fact that everything always costs so much more than it seems like it will. I try not to be the kind of person who's always running calculations, but I can't shut my brain off. We won't get back to Binghamton on what I have left.

I grab a free tourist newspaper from a plastic stand by the register. We shoo seagulls off the only empty table. Justin eats his first hot dog in two bites and is on to the second before I even start mine. I thumb through the paper to the "Happenings!" page and check the music listings while I eat. Ollie's—the bar where I play when I'm here—has shows listed for the rest of the week. A cover band, some girl I've never heard of, a reggae band, and this guy who plays Beatles covers on the ukulele. I saw the ukulele guy play the last time I was here. He's awful. But he's booked. If they didn't have anyone, I'm sure I could play. They're always nice to me. But there's no point in asking now. I wouldn't want to make anyone uncomfortable and ruin a chance in the future.

"Was your hot dog bad?" Justin says when he finishes his third. He crumples his paper plate and tosses it into the garbage can.

"It was fine," I say, forcing a smile.

"You had a look on your face like—" Justin exaggerates a pout.

"Just thinking," I say, shaking my head. "We need funds. I'm going to have to play."

"Oh, cool," he says, smile full of hot dog bits. He reaches across the table to squeeze my hand. "I like hearing you play." And it's nice, the way he likes me. It is nice.

"I thought you meant like at a bar or something," Justin says when I stop to get my guitar from the car on the way back to the beach.

"Getting a gig takes time," I say. "The places I know here are booked. You can't just walk in someplace and play."

"You do at Arnie's."

"But that's Arnie. I don't have that here."

"Is it legal?" he asks. He looks truly worried. I wonder if he's imagining a phone call to his dad from jail.

"I'm not killing anyone."

"I mean, do you need a permit or something?"

"Not unless someone complains."

"But what if they do?"

"They're not going to arrest us. At worst, someone will ask us to leave."

He looks at me like I'm suggesting we knock off a liquor store or throw water balloons at babies.

"It's fine," I say. "We don't have other options."

I claim a patch of sand near the path everyone takes to get from the parking lot to the beach, sit cross-legged with my guitar, and throw a few crumpled ones in my open case so people will know what to do.

Justin stands awkwardly next to me, shifting his weight from one foot to the other while I tune my guitar.

"Sit down, at least," I say. "You're going to make people nervous."

"We're not even totally out of money," he says, kneeling next to me.

And the way he says *we* makes me angry.

"How are you going to get home, then?" I say, maybe a little bit snotty. It's not like future account managers can set up on the beach and *manage* for loose change. I'm the only one who can get us back to Binghamton.

Justin rakes his fingers through the sand and doesn't look at me. Maybe he's embarrassed for his situation, not just embarrassed by me. I don't want to feel like he's a liability. I don't want to treat him like he is. I'm scared I'm not made for other people and I wonder if this is how my mom felt inside too. If maybe she works best wandering out in the world alone—if the way Justin feels like an anvil tied to my leg is how she felt about me.

"Go swimming," I tell him. "I think I'll do better on my own."

There's relief on his face, but he walks down to the water slowly, looking back a few times. To make sure I'm okay. Or maybe to try and figure out if I'm angry.

I play *Buckets of Rain*. I can always count on Dylan.

Justin dives into the waves. A big family walks by—four little kids in varying sizes and stages of undress, and a mom, dad, and teenager armored by beach chairs, firm grips on their umbrellas, like they're about to do battle with the sea. The smallest of the children, a little girl with big red curls, wearing only a diaper, walks right over to me, fat little feet sinking in the sand. She touches my guitar while I'm playing.

"Imogene!" the mom yells.

"It's fine," I say, smiling. I switch to playing *If You're Happy and You Know It*. Imogene squeals and claps and stamps her feet. She slips to her knees, sitting in front of me. The other kids sit next to her.

They're like a magnet. Everyone else who uses the trail to get to the beach stops, for at least a moment, to see what's going on. I don't know that many kids' songs, so I mix in ones that their parents will know. Even *Maggie's Farm* sounds like a children's song if you brighten up the chords and sing it too fast for the kids to understand the words.

Ten songs in, Justin comes back, red-shouldered, dripping, sand stuck to his ankles like sugar on a cider donut. There are at least a dozen kids seated in a semicircle around me, parents lingering to watch them. Justin stands back with the adults and gives me a wink when I make eye contact, like maybe he's impressed.

I play for two more hours, to a revolving group of little ones. Cycling through the same songs when the crowd changes over. My fingers are blistered and my throat is dry, but there's a growing mound of bills in my case.

Justin takes off for a while and comes back with a paper liquor store sack and three Chinese food cartons. It's dinnertime and the crowd has thinned to two kids and a frazzled nanny, who takes the hint and ushers the kids away when she sees Justin.

"Hungry?" he asks, and puts the food down next to me.

"Very," I say. He pulls two sets of chopsticks from his pocket. Opens cartons of egg rolls, chicken fried rice, and vanilla ice cream.

"It was a special," he tells me. "The woman insisted."

"I'm not complaining," I say.

We eat the ice cream first, since it's melting, scooping at it with our chopsticks held together tightly.

The wine has a screw top and tastes like old vinegar, but it was a sweet touch. He only had ten dollars left. I'm not going to be mad that he spent it on nonessentials. It's nice that he wanted to help, that I'm not eating dinner alone, and I have someone to talk to about my day.

We eat slowly, watching the sun creep to the horizon. I dig my toes into the sand.

A little kid runs over, his mom chasing behind. I saw him in the crowd of kids earlier. He's five or six, big ears and a bucket hat like Gilligan.

"Do you know that song about the dragon?" he asks me, the *S* in *song* revealing his lisp. He holds his hands up, fingers curled like dragon claws.

"Cory!" his mother yells, catching up. "Don't bother the nice lady." She bends to grab his arm. He pulls it away.

"But . . ." They exchange a look. He cups his hand to her ear and whisper-shouts, "I was asking nicely."

Justin nods in the kid's direction, grinning at me. It's all adorable.

"Don't worry about it," I say to Cory's mom. "I do know that song."

I pick up my guitar and play *Puff the Magic Dragon*. His mom sits in the sand. He sits in her lap. Justin doesn't even look awkward about it. I think I catch him mouthing the words to the chorus. I play two more songs for Cory, and his mom gives him ten dollars to put in my guitar case before they leave.

"Thanks, buddy," I say to Cory. "It was fun to sing for you."

"Yeah, dragons are good," he says, his *S* failing him again. I smile and wrinkle my nose. He wrinkles his nose back at me. He's so damn cute.

Justin and I watch Cory and his mom trudge across the sand to collect their beach chairs. The sun disappears, leaving a line of fading orange light just above the waves.

I drive us home with one hand on the wheel and the other holding Justin's.

The mattress springs squeak so loudly. Justin tries hard to keep his game face on. Serious sex. Very serious. But then the single squeak turns to double. Flex, release. The bed sounds like an old hoarse donkey, and I laugh out loud. Justin breaks into a smile and falls on me, giggling. We shake together. And kiss and laugh more. I roll over, so I'm on top, and make the bed squeak again. His smile is beautiful. I could love this if I tried. Unlatch the door and let him in. It wouldn't be the worst thing.

— Chapter 40 —

Justin is dead to the world when I wake up, making that funny click in his throat that happens when he sleeps on his back. He doesn't even move when I get out of bed to pee. But I worry if I try to climb back into bed, I'll wake him. I stand in the doorway of the bedroom and watch him for signs of stirring. There are none. One of his hands is resting on his chest. He'll wake up with pins and needles in his fingers. I think about trying to move his hand, but I'm sure it would startle him. I leave to avoid the temptation.

I decide to shower so we can clear out faster once he does wake up. It takes forever for the water to get warm, which seems so strange to me, since it doesn't start from cold pipes like it does up north. Once the water is warm, I'm lazy about it, humming to myself, taking the time to shave my legs with soap and everything, instead of a few swipes of dry razor on wet skin. In for a penny, in for a pound, as Margo would say. Justin's been using water and electricity like nobody's business, so it doesn't even make sense for me to scrimp. I use the Paul Mitchell stuff on the side of the tub to shampoo twice and I let the conditioner sit in my hair for two minutes like the bottle says, counting a hundred and twenty Mississippis to time it.

When I get out of the shower, Justin is awake, sitting on the bed. He hangs up the phone.

"You used the phone?" I say.

"Yeah." His voice is gruff. He's not making eye contact.

"Who did you call?" I'm hoping it was just to get the surf report or find out movie times. Nondescript. Local.

"My dad," he says.

"Oh." I try to play it cool while my heart flops like a fresh-caught fish. It'll show up on the phone bill. It'll raise suspicion *and* give them a place to start looking.

"This isn't your uncle's house," he says. It's not a question. He's sure.

He points to a picture on the dresser. I hadn't noticed it before. *We* hadn't noticed it before. A family on the beach. Mother, father, daughter, son, like a perfect dollhouse set. Their brown skin is warm and beautiful against the sand. They look nothing like me.

I could invent family connections to make it right. There's no saying I couldn't be their cousin. But I feel so suddenly tired. I am out of story to spin. "No," I say, "it isn't."

"How did you know the code to get in?" he says. Dull eyes; he's done.

I shake my head. If I talk, I'll cry.

"My dad is buying me a ticket," he says. He clenches his jaw. I can see the muscles move.

I don't try to convince him to stay. I don't want to hear all his reasons for leaving. I see them on his face. It's more than just the house.

"I have to get to the airport," he says.

I don't point out how his kind of broke is not the same as mine. How he can get off this ride with a phone call. Our words don't mean the same things. He doesn't care anyway. I've fallen apart for him. The same way he's fallen apart for me. But it hurts worse because I tried so hard to keep him together.

He goes to the bathroom to brush his teeth. I want to leave. Let him find his own way to the airport, see at least a little bit of struggle. But I don't. I sit on the bed next to his bag. It smells like him. That mix of boy and college. The zipper isn't closed all the way. I take one of his shirts. A long-sleeve blue one with NOFX written on the front the right way and backward on the back, like you can see through the person wearing it all the way to the underside of the letters. I take it out just to smell it, but then I hear him flush the toilet, wash his hands. Instead of putting it back in his bag, I shove it in mine. I don't even know why I want it. He's expensive and loud and he listens to awful music and can't make do with what we have. It's stupid to want him around anyway.

— Chapter 41 —

The airport is all the way in Tampa. About sixty miles. I measure on the map with a strand of my hair before we leave. He gets in the car while I put the key back in the lockbox. He doesn't look at me when I get in the driver's seat. He doesn't play his mixtapes. Road noise, breathing. He pretends to read the owner's manual for my car, flipping pages faster than the words could register. Then he just looks out the window, and that's worse. Head turned away from me like he's trying to pretend I don't exist.

Finally, finally, he says, "It's this exit coming up. Thirty-nine."

I nod and change lanes. "What time is your flight?" I ask.

"Five fifteen."

It's a quarter to noon.

"Do you want to stop? Get something to eat?"

"No," he says. And nothing more.

"It's a long time to wait," I say when the silence starts to get to me.

"I just want to go." He heaves a disgusted sigh.

I feel wrong. Dirty. Less than. Angry. "How is staying at that house so different from stealing your dad's credit card?"

"I didn't steal it!" he yells. "He gave it to me.

365

He's my *dad*. You broke into someone's house. You made me a thief and I didn't even know it."

"We didn't take anything," I say. "We just used—"

"Whatever you have to tell yourself to sleep at night."

I follow the signs to the airport. The things I want to explain are thin and wispy. Too delicate for words. His life is so simple and mine is full of knots. He'll fly home and forget me. Pretend this didn't happen. Maybe pull it out as a drinking story when he wants someone to think he has a wild side. One time he took a trip without a plan. One time he broke into a house with a crazy girl. But I don't think he'll let himself believe it was the time he followed his heart. He won't let me matter that much.

I stop at the curb for departing flights.

"Bye," he mumbles, getting out of the car without looking at me.

The door slams. I drive. I cry. There's no end in sight. No gigs to get to in time. No one waiting for me. Nobody missing me. Nothing. I could disappear completely and no one would even notice.

It gets harder and harder to follow the road. My ribs ache from fighting sobs. My eyes can't stand the sun.

I stop at a pay phone and dump all the change

from the bottom of my bag into the slot. It's been way too long since I called. A year. Maybe more. I probably have no business calling at all.

Four rings, and I'm about to hang up when I hear: "Margo's Diner! The special today is beef goulash," but it's some girl. A voice I don't recognize. I choke tears away and ask for Margo. When the girl puts down the phone to get her, I can hear the faint chatter and clink clank of dishes, The Weather Channel too loud on the TV above the receiver. I can hear my old life going on without me and it's horrible. By the time Margo comes to the phone and says, "This is Margo," the recorded voice is already telling me I need to add money. I only have pennies. I sob harder.

"Why don't I matter to anyone?" I'm not even sure my words sound like words, but she knows it's me. I hear her say, "Oh, girlie," before the phone goes dead, and I imagine she says, *You matter to me.* Because I have to. I have to matter to someone.

I don't go back to the house. It's far and there's no point. I'm done with wanting what can't be mine. I drive until I can't stay awake and sleep in my car at a truck stop, parked next to one of the parking lot lights to feel just a little bit safer.

Chapter 42

I wake up when the truck engines start, hours before sunrise. Before I leave, I buy a postcard and a stamp at the rest stop store. It's a picture of two beach chairs at the edge of a lake, sharing the shade from one big umbrella.

This one I send. I don't write anything but her address. I drop it in the blue mailbox outside and pretend Carly is right where I left her and will understand everything when she gets the card. I pretend that I meant as much to her as she did to me. That when she looks at those two chairs, she'll picture us sitting together, me with my guitar, her with a blue pack of American Spirits balanced on the arm of her chair. She'll blow smoke out to the water while she tells me all the things I've missed.

I pump five bucks' worth of gas into my car and hit the road.

Right before sunrise, when the sky changes to brighter blue, I see a sign for Asheville, North Carolina, and decide to go, because everyone says Asheville is like Ithaca but bigger. Because of all the places I've been, Ithaca is my favorite and I can't go back.

• • •

I get to Asheville on fumes and busk in a tiny park in the middle of the city. It's sunny and breezy and the people who stop are friendly. I keep my guitar case open and start it off with the ten from Cory's mom. I decide it will bring me luck, and it does. There's a steady stream of foot traffic. Children step up to my case with quarters from their parents, staring cautiously as they chuck them in, like I might stop playing to reach out and grab their arm. College kids throw pennies and pocket lint. Older people, professors and the like, hover with folded ones in their fingers, waiting for me to make eye contact before they drop them in. I play for three hours and make thirty-three bucks and a bunch of change I don't bother to count.

As I'm packing it in, a man comes up and introduces himself. His name is Ethan. He's wearing a rumpled white shirt and loose, faded khakis. Bright blue eyes, small nests of lines that frame them when he smiles. My best guess is he's pushing forty, because I think he's one of those people who look younger than they are.

"I've been listening all afternoon," he says, pointing to a bench a few feet away. He's soft spoken, but his voice has a melody that makes me think of the low bars on a xylophone.

"Thanks," I say, wishing I'd left my guitar case open a little bit longer. If he listened all afternoon, he should pay me something, but I hate taking money from a stranger's hand. I hadn't noticed him or the bench, which makes me feel a little sideways. I'm usually good at keeping track of what's around me, but my mind keeps drifting away, trying to avoid thoughts about Justin.

"Hey, can I buy you dinner?" he asks, and he's not nervous or awkward about it, but he seems intently hopeful that I will say yes and we will eat food and it will bring something to his life he didn't have before. It doesn't feel like he's hitting on me. His eyes are sad in a way I recognize.

"I know a place that makes great gazpacho," he says. "I think this is the first batch of the season."

I probably look kind of rank. The offers to feed me come more frequently then. Although it's usually a bagged lunch left in my case, not the commitment to sit across from me in public eating cold soup.

"Thanks," I say, "but I need to hit the road." My stomach is hollow and aching, but I have to be done falling for people just because they seem fine. I pick up my guitar case.

"It's a short walk," he says. "You have to eat anyway, right?" He does this little shrug of his shoulders.

I study his face, lines in places that tell me he's smiled a bunch, but worried more. I try to picture him grabbing my wrist, slamming me against a wall. I can't. It's a ridiculous thought.

He cares too much. Wears it on his sleeve. He put his feelings into asking me to dinner, trusting I'd be careful not to hurt them. I wonder if my eyes look familiar to him too, if that's why he liked my music so much. Takes one to know.

"I could eat," I say. Stupid, but hungry. Stupid, but lonely.

"Can I carry that for you?" Ethan points to my guitar. "It looks heavy." His teeth are big and straight. He's thin, but he has chipmunk cheeks.

"It's okay. You have to hold it just so or the handle comes off." I'm lying, but we lose something if he thinks I don't trust him.

He's my height and there's a coziness to it, like we're old chums. His eyes are right there when I turn my head.

He's a painter at heart, he tells me, but he's not poor because he teaches at the university, does freelance design work on the side.

"I'm too into creature comforts to starve for my art," he says, flashing teeth.

I wonder if he's trying to convert me.

The restaurant he takes me to wants to be bohemian, but it's too clean and calculated. Each wall is alternately mustard and rust colored. Light fixtures wrapped in copper mesh. Everything on the menu has goat cheese or pine nuts.

Ethan orders two bowls of gazpacho as soon as we sit down, nodding for my approval after the fact. I nod back, smile sweetly. When the waiter comes with our soups, I order the same entrée Ethan does.

"I told you it was good," he says, a chunk of green stuck in his teeth. He doesn't notice that I haven't tasted my soup yet.

"Mmmm," I say. "Thank you. This was a good idea."

He's beaming. I understand now. I've seen this before. He's clinging to that part of himself that would like to be me and have the guts or the stupidity to just go for it. Live in your car. Eatsleepbreathe for your art. As long as we're together, he's a painter who has the courage to let go of all the creature comforts, to feel like he's living the dream without the bruises.

"I like your lyrics," Ethan says. "You have an interesting way of saying big things with simple words."

I wonder if he's giving me credit for Dylan songs. I only played a handful of my own. "Thanks," I say.

"How did you learn to play?"

"Taught myself."

"That's how I started painting. Funny what we're drawn to, isn't it? What it fixes. I knew as soon as I started to paint it was mine. Did you feel like that with the guitar?"

I smile, because I did, but no one else has ever described that feeling to me. I think I knew even before I started—watching my dad play—that this music was something I needed. "Yeah. I did."

"It's so uncomfortable until you find the right way to get that part of yourself out, isn't it?"

As soon as we finish our last spoonfuls of soup, a tall man with perfect posture and thick brown hair pulled in a stubby ponytail brings us two heaping plates of greens. "Ethan, how goes it?" he says, switching our bowls for the entrées. The sleeves of his faded denim shirt are rolled to the middle of his muscled forearms. "Greg said you were here."

Ethan stands. They shake hands and lean into a hug with back slaps that sound hollow, like their bodies are just skin stretched over drum frames.

"Robert, this is April."

"Nice to meet you, April." He reaches for my hand.

I'm the only one sitting, so I bunch my napkin next to my plate and stand up. "Nice to meet you."

Now we're all standing and it's awkward. The smell of food makes my stomach rumble, even though it looks like some sort of meat substitute on a bed of fancy lettuce. I imagine thick strips of rare roast beef oozing rosy juice all over the plate.

"Robert, join us," Ethan says, sitting down.

I wonder why he's Robert and not Rob or Bob. I think maybe they're both gay, but Robert pushes my chair in for me, and our eyes lock. His are light green, and they can't break away. He's stuck.

I smile and watch his lips mimic mine. I look away. I'm not going to get caught up again. There's no point.

Robert pulls a chair from another table and sits on it backward like a high school kid.

"This seitan looks delicious," Ethan says, spearing a chunk of fake meat.

My first forkful of greens flops against my lips, spraying dressing across my cheeks. I wipe my face with the napkin and focus on trying to fold the leaves with my fork. This food is not going to fill the depths of my hunger. I should be busking or driving or calling around for gigs, not hanging out with strange men in exchange for free lawn clippings.

"April plays guitar." Ethan gestures to my case. It's wedged between my chair and the table so I can keep one foot touching it to make sure it's still there.

"Are you my new talent scout?" Robert nudges Ethan's arm with his knuckles.

"You should be so lucky." Ethan grins. Leaning across the table toward me, he whispers, "I have impeccable taste," like it's a secret.

"I'm flattered." I smile and crinkle my nose, trying extra hard to be charming even though my neck is stiff and my eyes hurt. It is always in my best interest to have people remember me fondly.

"You should be flattered." Ethan turns back to Robert. "She's amazing. I'm not even joking."

"Are you actually looking for a job?" Robert asks, hugging the chair back. He seems amused by Ethan's exuberance.

"I usually spend the summer playing in Florida. Might head down early," I say, like I haven't just been there. Like I'm not running away.

"Who summers in Florida?" Ethan says. "April, no! Stay here."

Robert laughs. "He met you, what, ten minutes ago?"

"Fifteen," I say. "We walked over from the park."

"He's right," Robert says, "I do need someone. Band for tomorrow canceled again." He rubs his palms on the top of the chair. "No pressure, but I own the bar across the street too. If it works out, we could get you a regular dinner gig. And I need someone to run open mic. So maybe it could be worth it for you to stick around? See how tomorrow goes?" He smiles.

"You don't even know me." I smile back, keep his gaze too long. It's dumb. I like them both more than I should.

"You don't even know me, so we're even." There's a little bit of South in his words. Not much, but it's there. "I need someone. Ethan says you're good, and he's really picky. Play tomorrow. If you suck, or you hate it, we'll go our separate ways. If it works, we'll talk. How's that?"

He's a good salesman. He makes this all sound very practical. But I broke my rules with Ray. I broke my rules with Justin. I know better.

"Thanks, but there's a room waiting for me in Florida," I say. It's close to truth. I could go back to bouncing between rentals. Get on the schedule at Ollie's and play for kids on Manatee Beach. That broke down house will only feel haunted if I let it.

"You can stay with me," Ethan says. "I have an extra room."

I absolutely cannot picture Ethan snorting coke and attacking me. It's an impossible thought. He wants me to like him too badly. But maybe my instincts are shit. Maybe that's the thing I've learned about myself.

"You guys are really nice. I just can't put anyone out that much." I take another messy bite of salad. I need to shovel it in and get gone before they melt me.

"You'd be doing him a favor, I think," Robert says. He grabs Ethan's shoulder and gives it a squeeze.

"My boyfriend moved out last week." Ethan sighs. "*Ex*-boyfriend. It's possible that I'm not so great at living alone."

Robert laughs. "That's an understatement. This man is lonely."

"Hey," Ethan says. "I bring ice cream."

"And stay on my couch watching sad movies all night."

"See, April," Ethan says, "you'd be doing Robert a really big favor."

My head aches like someone is tightening a band across my temples. It's more than ten hours back to Anna Maria Island. I can't spare motel money on the way. It's not a route I know well enough to have notes on campgrounds and truck stops recorded in my notebook. And I'm lonely too.

"I can't pay room and board right now," I say.

"I don't need a roommate," Ethan tells me. His eyes have pinwheels of grey mixed in the blue. "I need the house to feel less empty."

"I do take up space," I say, and the tightness in my shoulders starts to give a little. Just for tonight. It's only bending the rules, not breaking them. I will leave in the morning, before Ethan wakes up, with a full night's sleep and maybe some aspirin.

"Do you cook?" Ethan asks, like I've agreed to a long-term arrangement.

"No."

"Neither do I. Ivan was an excellent cook."

Robert clears his throat.

"Not as good as you," Ethan says, "but you never cook for me."

"What do you call this?"

"I mean at home." Ethan pats my arm. "Robert lives next door."

"If I stay, you better come over and cook for us," I say. It's a reflex. Pretend we're already good friends, in the middle of things. It's the way I get what I need.

"He will," Ethan says, beaming, and I decide I may as well play through.

— Chapter 43 —

Ethan's house is small and old and adorable. The floors are slightly crooked—just enough to throw me off balance, like it could be me, not the house, that's askew. Every window has a glass ball, wind chime, or dreamcatcher hanging in it. The curtains are yellow linen and the air smells like sandalwood and aftershave.

"It's all yours," Ethan says, opening the door to a tiny room with a white metal daybed and a patchwork quilt. There are paint stains on the floor and a big roll of white canvas in the corner. "Sorry it's not cleaned up. It was Ivan's studio. Mine's on the sun porch."

"Better than my car."

"You really sleep in your car?" He looks like he's worried for me. Touches his hand to his mouth and sighs.

"Sometimes," I say.

"Our little bag lady has a bed."

I can tell he likes the idea that he's rescued me. It's okay to let him believe he has. People can do so many horrible things to make themselves feel important, so if he feels important from being kind, he's better than most. "Thanks, Ethan," I say. "This is nice."

"Do you think you'll stay for a while?" He

grabs the top of the doorframe and hangs on with both hands over his head.

"I don't know," I say. I'm still not sure what I'm doing. I'm too tired to keep mucking around on my own forever, but this is ridiculous. You don't just move in with a guy you met on the street.

"I come off as needy, don't I?" He swings on his arm and smiles.

"Sort of," I say, smiling back, because the way he asked felt like when someone wants to know if they have spinach in their teeth.

"I guess I am needy. Ivan just left and I'm pulling girls off the street to keep me company. I'll get better. It'll get better." There's something fragile about him that breaks my heart—he can't cover it up—he's broken and leaking and he knows that about himself, and here he is trying anyway.

"Better than picking up girls in bars," I say.

Ethan snorts when he laughs and it makes me laugh too. He leaves me to get settled. I lean my guitar case against the wall and plop down on the bed. The quilt is soft and worn and smells like finger paint.

I wake up and it's dark. I don't remember where I am. I'm in a bed, on top of the covers, but there's an afghan tucked over my arms, all the way to my chin.

Someone stood over me, touched me while I was sleeping, and I didn't wake up. I try to retrace my steps to here, but my thoughts are crowded out by the feeling of Ray's fingers digging into my wrist. It's not real. I know it's not real, but that memory is too bright, too loud to let other thoughts through, like there wasn't anything before it, or after.

I feel around on the floor until I hear the jangle of keys and dig through my bag for my buck knife.

Streetlights leave tree-branch shadows on the floor. I see the paint stains and remember where I am.

I wake up and it's bright. I see the glow of sunlight through my eyelids and try to remember what room I'm in before I peek. Paint stains. Ethan in the doorway. He was nice. I remember he was nice. I open my eyes. My buck knife is on the pillow next to me. The afghan is knitted in clown colors. A crystal in the window casts rainbows on the floor.

I hear a sizzle. Plates clink. A spatula scrapes on a pan. I slept too long to sneak away, but those are friendly noises. And also, I'm hungry.

I clip my buck knife to the waistband of my skirt, knife on the inside. Pull my shirt over the clip. I can make an excuse, leave after breakfast. I'm still only bending the rules.

I follow the noise to the kitchen, expecting to find Ethan, but Robert is standing in front of the stove wearing flip-flops and bleachy blue pajama pants. He doesn't have a shirt on. It's a nice view. He's thin, but he's all muscle. His hair hangs almost to his shoulders and it's shiny and smooth like I wish mine was.

"Morning!" he says with an easy smile that doesn't leave me room to feel awkward.

"Did you sleep over?" I ask. I was so sure he was straight.

"I live next door." He breaks an egg over a big skillet. "The man has nothing but paint and canvas here," he says, shaking his head. "I had to bring my own pan."

Robert sits me down at the kitchen table with a cup of coffee that smells like spices. I watch him flip eggs and butter toast. We don't talk, but I don't feel like we have to.

The kitchen is a mishmash of bright colored things and well-tended houseplants. The curtains are embroidered with tulips, the fridge plastered with tourist trap magnets. By the back door there's a concrete statue of a woman carrying a jug on her head, a spider plant spilling its off-spring like a veil over her face. A chain of ivy starts in a jar on a shelf over the sink and travels along the wall on hooks for half the room. The salt and pepper shakers on the table are dachshunds wearing hot dog buns.

When Ethan wakes up he pads into the kitchen barefoot, wearing paint-stained scrub pants, a faded R.E.M. tee, and wire-rimmed glasses that take up half his face. He pats my shoulder and says, "A half-naked man cooking breakfast. We could get used to this, April, huh?" I think maybe he's using my trick, jumping into the middle of our friendship so we all feel like we belong together.

Robert hands him a mug of coffee. Ethan takes a sip and sighs. "Oh, cinnamon. Robert, you make better coffee than Ivan." He looks at me. "I don't need Ivan one bit, right?" The way he says it, it's like he's hoping I'll actually have the answer.

"Right," I say firmly, as if I know all there is to know about the situation. The buck knife is digging into my side. I feel ridiculous for carrying it.

"Good coffee," Ethan says. "Good people. What else do I need anyway?" I have the overwhelming urge to hug him and tell him everything will be okay. I don't. But I want to.

"How do you like your eggs, April?" Robert asks.

"Over easy," I say. I've never liked eggs, but people at the diner always ordered them that way, and mostly they came out looking less gross.

"I like mine scrambled," Ethan says.

"Eggs or men?" Robert asks.

"Both, apparently," Ethan says, flashing me a grin.

Robert has to go to the restaurant so he can start working on lunch. He leaves me and Ethan with topped-off mugs of coffee and bellies full of eggs and potatoes.

"See you later, Alliga-tor-idae!" Ethan yells after Robert. He leans in and says, "He makes me watch PBS."

"In a while, Crocodylidae," Robert calls back, laughing. They sound like little boys who can't wait to meet up later and play trucks in the dirt.

Ethan gets up and puts his plate in the sink. "So, what do you need to do to get ready for your performance tonight?"

"Tune my guitar," I say, shrugging. "But not until I get there." I may as well stay for the gig at this point. Sneak out tomorrow morning instead. Maybe I can busk downtown again before the gig to grab some extra cash. Leave here caught up on sleep and food and money.

Ethan looks disappointed. "No pre-gig ritual? Smudges of sage? Herbal tea and complete silence to channel your muse?" He takes my plate for me.

"My muse?" I laugh. "I just get up and play. When I'm done I have a beer or something. That's about it."

"No fanfare?" He pours me more coffee and empties the pot filling up his own cup.

"On a good week, I play three to five gigs and I drive the rest of the time. There's no room for fanfare." I could tell him about my dad's guitar pick. I bet he'd like to hear it. But I don't think I've ever said those words out loud.

Ethan smacks the table. "I'll give you fanfare! Come on." He downs the rest of his coffee. His eyes tear a little. "Bring your guitar."

"Where are we going?"

"Up, up! You'll see when we get there!"

We walk across town. I like the way our footsteps sound. Half a beat apart. It's sunny and so much warmer than New York. It seems strange to me that people choose to live with winter when they could see the sun in March.

Ethan points out things while we walk. The one perfect cloud in the sky, crocus buds peeking through the damp spring soil, a tails-up penny he flips over so the next person who sees it gets some luck.

We make our way through campus to a big brick building, stopping at a grey metal door. It's a back entrance. No signs or windows. Ethan pulls keys from his jacket pocket.

"Close your eyes," he says, grabbing my free hand and squeezing.

And I do it. So stupid, but I do it. I squeeze his hand back.

I hear him unlock the door. He leads me inside. The door closes behind us with a slam that makes my heart jump. He keeps walking. I take baby steps, trying not to stumble over my own feet, not sure what I might bump into. Both my hands are spoken for, guitar in one, Ethan's cold, dry palm in the other. I open one eye, trying to figure out where we are and what we're doing. Everything is black. The eggs and buttered toast sit heavy in my stomach. I'm locked in the dark with a man I don't know.

I open both my eyes. It is darker than the woods behind the motorhome at the new moon. Something's hanging from the ceiling, brushing my arm as I walk past. Ropes maybe.

Shit. Shit. Shit.

I wonder if Ethan can feel my crazy pulse. I will my eyes to adjust faster. They don't.

Shit. I let my guard down, like an idiot. I know better. I know better. I've walked into the exact kind of scene Margo used to warn me about.

Ethan's grip is tight on my hand. I try to keep my breath calm and plan escape moves in my head. We haven't turned. The door is straight behind me, a few feet away. My knife is in my bag somewhere, not ready at my hip. If I drop my guitar, I'll still have to search for the knife.

My palm sweats against Ethan's. Or is his palm sweating too?

He lets go of my hand. "Stay there."

I inch backward, fumble in my bag with my free hand. I feel my wallet. Flashlight. A tampon. Chapstick. I can't find my knife.

I hear the patter of Ethan's feet walking away and tighten my grip on the handle of my guitar case, ready to swing if I need to. It's probably fine. I try to picture his face. Kind eyes, sweet smile. He's not going to hang me from the ceiling and hack me to pieces. He's not. It's probably fine. But I really don't know how I'm ever supposed to trust myself.

"Okay," Ethan says. "Open."

I hear the click of a switch and I'm surrounded by light so bright that I still can't see anything.

And then my eyes adjust.

The light makes blue and purple puddles around us. We're on a stage, behind a curtain. A swooping staircase climbs to nowhere. A chandelier hangs low, near a giant crescent covered in silver glitter. The ropes make sense, at least. I can see the door. I could escape before Ethan could get to me. My heart starts to steady.

"What is all this?" I ask, wiping my palm on my skirt.

"We're doing *Mame*." Ethan gestures to the crescent like a goofy game show host, big sweet smile, and I feel ridiculous for having any fear of him. I'm like frayed wires, sparking at all the wrong times.

"For Drama Club?" I ask. My heartbeat is almost normal again.

Ethan laughs. "For the drama *department*."

"So, what exactly does that mean?" I ask, using a phrase Margo employs whenever she doesn't want to let on how much she doesn't know.

"Our students study acting, stage management, set design, or dramaturgy," Ethan says in an announcer voice like he's narrating an info-mercial, "with the goal of working in professional theatre." He kicks at a rope coiled on the floor. "I teach technical theatre and design."

"That's a thing people go to school for?" I set my guitar case on the floor and run my hand along the banister of the stairs. It looks like brass but feels like wood.

"Yup," Ethan says.

"And you did this?"

"Well, my students did this," he says, climbing into the crescent. He reaches for my hand to help me step into it too. There's scaffolding and a seat hidden just behind the glitter. "I have a student who wants to do rig work, so we're going all out for *Man in the Moon*, lowering Vera from the heavens." He points to the metal walkways above us.

"You get paid to help students build things like this?" I shake my head, amazed.

"April," Ethan says, "you get paid to travel around and sing songs to people."

"It's a way to get by."

"Your way of getting by is a lot of people's dream."

"People dream of being rock stars. They don't dream about living in their car."

Ethan gives me his worried look again. "Maybe not, but they do dream of flying." He points to the seat. "Sit."

I do. I think I know where this is going and maybe you're not supposed to climb in a moon with a guy you met on the street, but I survived the darkness just fine.

"Okay, legs over the front of the moon," he says. "Can you reach the footholds?" He guides my feet to small metal platforms, then straps a harness around my waist. He smells like woodsy cologne. He is calm and patient and sure of himself as he works the buckles. From some angles he looks a little like Elvis, if Elvis had gotten older without getting fat: sleepy eyes, pillowy lips, a slight cleft in his chin.

"It's safe?" I ask.

"Completely. I let my students use me as the crash test dummy." Ethan jumps from the moon, opens my case, and takes my guitar out like he's carrying a newborn. He gathers my hair to one shoulder, looping the strap over the other, adjusting it just so.

It reminds me of Carly. Of getting ready to go see Cat Skin. The way she took care of me. I don't let myself think that Asheville could be the Ithaca where I get to stay. Or that Ethan could be my friend like Carly, and Robert could be someone too. The best way to keep your heart from getting broken is not to get your hopes up in the first place.

Ethan ties down the tail of the waist strap. "Voilà! Fanfare," he says. "You can sing from the moon." He runs off stage.

The lights dim. I brace myself, clutching my guitar like it will somehow keep me safe.

The ride up is so smooth it feels like the floor is falling away from me. I glance past my feet and watch the distance grow. My stomach wobbles.

"Locked in!" Ethan yells. And then the curtain opens to a sea of empty red velvet seats. "Wait! Wait." He runs to the shadows at the back of the theater.

A loud click and I'm in the spotlight, glitter shining.

"Sing, *bellissima*! Sing!" Ethan calls from the audience.

"Okay," I say softly, and I'm stunned by the way my voice travels.

It feels silly, playing just for Ethan, but I desperately want to know what it's like to sing in a theater like this and hear my voice echo back to me.

I start with the song I never play at gigs. I love it the most, so it feels like too much to share. But Ethan doesn't have to know how much it means to me.

I've been north, I've been south
Traveled here and there.
I shed the lives I've left
Without a single care

I've been up, I've been down
I'm forever free to roam
But never in my life,
Have I ever made it home

I sing the whole thing with my eyes closed so I can hear the way the sound surrounds me. When I strum, the moon swings and I really do feel like I'm flying. I imagine looking out over a packed house. I imagine what the applause would feel like in my chest.

After I've finished, Ethan stands and claps for me. He shouts, "Woo-Whoo!" and his voice fills the room.

"You have the cutest little waist," Ethan says, unbuckling the straps once I'm safely on the ground. He shouted encore until I had no songs left. "What's your secret?"

"Corn nuts and Diet Coke?" I say, not sure if

I'm supposed to have a secret. My body is the way it is, and I haven't thought about it much one way or another. I feel exposed in a way I don't when I play shows to more than one person. There's no reason to run away and I kind of want to anyway. Flee to the wings, wrap myself in those thick velvet curtains, and hide from the world.

"Corn nuts and Diet Coke!" Ethan says, laughing. "You must have good genes. There are girls here who would kill to have your figure." He unbuckles the last strap. "I mean that literally."

"I'd kill to go here," I say, handing him my guitar so I can jump down. I'm surprised by the fact that it's true. School was crappy math quizzes and notes scribbled on folded loose-leaf, passed to every girl except me. But this kind of school, where kids get up on stage and sing and it counts, where maybe I wouldn't be so different— if I had known college could be like this, I might have finished high school to get here. Of course, it's not like my dad saved money for me to go to college, or there are Rotary scholarships to send that weird kid from the motorless motorhome to drama school.

"You are amazing, Angel," Ethan says, handing my guitar back to me.

"April," I say, feeling awkward that he doesn't remember my name.

"I know." Ethan smiles. "It was a term of endearment."

"You barely know me."

"Then it's a testament to how endearing you are." Ethan studies my face. I feel like he knows a lot about me, even though I've hardly told him anything.

The university is on spring break, so Ethan doesn't have class. He buys us corned beef sandwiches from a deli and we take them back to his house. I eat all of mine and half of his and he seems strangely satisfied by watching me eat.

After lunch, he says he's going out to the sun porch to paint and I'm welcome to read anything on his bookshelves if I want. I know I should go downtown to busk, but I choose a book called *The Bean Trees* and sit in the sun on the squeaky porch swing while Ethan paints blue streaks on a fresh white canvas. He hums to himself, a song my dad used to sing: *The water is wide, I cannot cross o'er.* I don't even know exactly when I start to hum along with him, but I catch my voice twisting around his notes, and it makes me smile. His back is to me, but I hope maybe he's smiling too.

Later, we walk to Robert's restaurant for my gig. This time, when Ethan offers, I let him carry my guitar case. When we pass a streetlight I see the shine from a stray piece of moon glitter on my cheek.

— Chapter 44 —

The restaurant is warm and humid and smells like garlic and fresh bread. It's been at least two years since I've gotten nervous about a gig, but I feel butterflies. I know better than to want things, and then here I am all wound up because I liked spending the afternoon with Ethan, and let myself think what it might be like to be warm, fed, clean, and rested as a matter of habit.

The tables are pushed away from the far corner of the restaurant to make a stage. There's a wooden stool and two mics. Next to the stool is a side table with a fresh white towel and a glass of water garnished with a sprig of mint and slice of lime.

"Look at you, Angel, with your performance space waiting," Ethan says, carrying my guitar case across the room for me.

Robert walks out from the kitchen. Greets me with a kiss on the cheek and says, "Thanks for saving my ass. I'm hoping we'll get a good crowd."

"I'm sure we will," Ethan says. "You should have seen the mass of people who stopped to watch her play in the park yesterday."

Ethan is so certain, but I know these things don't translate. I caught those people at the right time on a nice day. They didn't know my name, so it's not like any of them could see it on the board outside and know they should come in to hear more of me.

I do my sound check. I always make sure I blow in the mic so I can hear if it will crackle. I hate when I hit a note so it's light and airy and it sounds like a wind tunnel coming through the PA. I tune up and get the guitar mic positioned in the right place.

This is nothing, I tell myself. I've played in bigger places. I've played on the street and gotten crowds to gather. This is just a little restaurant in a little city and the stakes aren't high. I'm not really going to stay. Even if Robert wants me to, even if Ethan does, I'll probably still go back to Florida. I'm singing for my supper. I'm leaving in the morning. That's all.

But when the clock over the door says it's six fifty-seven and I'm supposed to start playing at seven and there are only two tables of people, and one of them has just paid their bill and is getting up to leave, I have to breathe really deep a few times to get my hands to stop shaking.

I start with a cover of *Wild World*. Because as much as I'd prefer to play my own stuff all the time, people like covers. They like to know the songs you're singing. I always change something—sing it at a different tempo or do a new arrangement—but hold on to the heart of the song so it's just familiar enough. The audience listens harder then, like it's a quiz. Can they figure out the song before I sing the chorus? And then they're invested, so I can slip in a few of my own songs too. I can only get away with playing a solid set of originals at places like Arnie's where the crowd knows me. Even then, I'll throw in a couple of covers, just to fuck with them. Something silly we can all sing together, like *Girls Just Want to Have Fun* or the theme song to *Mannequin*, because we're all drunk and in it together at that point.

Here, I'll stick to classics. The couple who stay are boomers: the man wears a really big shiny watch, and his wife has her hair cut into a sleek silvery bob. So I play the stuff they would have heard on the radio when they were in college. When they wore daisies in their hair and made vees with their fingers.

They don't applaud after *Wild World*, but when I play the opening chords of *Like a Rolling Stone*, the man nods his balding head in approval. And by the time I play *You're So Vain*, they're singing along. They don't leave, even after they finish eating. They order more coffee and turn their chairs to watch me play. But no one else is coming in, and there's nothing I can do about it.

Ethan sits at a table in the corner by himself and orders a bowl of soup and a glass of wine. The waitress and the busboy stop to watch me.

There's not much else for them to do. At the end of my songs they clap almost as loudly as Ethan does and it keeps the applause from sounding painfully thin.

Finally, another couple comes in. Mid-twenties. Awkward with each other, like it's a first date. He keeps watching me instead of paying attention to what she's saying. I want to stop and tell him that the poor girl got all dressed up to impress him and he better damn well pay attention to her.

I play *I Can't Make You Love Me* by Bonnie Raitt and then *Alone* by Heart. The girl even turns around to clap when I'm done. Ethan stands and whistles.

Robert comes over to see me. "That was fantastic! Want to take a break and eat dinner?" His face is shiny. It must be hot in the kitchen. His T-shirt sticks to his back.

"I'm okay," I say. "I'm not big on eating between sets."

"Alright," he says. "But let me get you some tea or something."

Before I can say anything else, he goes into the kitchen and comes back with a tall glass of iced tea and a plate of toasted bread with some kind of tomatoey stuff on top. "Just in case you're a little hungry," he says as he hands it to me.

Robert goes back to the kitchen, and Ethan comes over to sit with me at the table closest to the makeshift stage.

"You're amazing," he says, putting his hand over mine and giving it a squeeze. "I'm so proud of you."

It's a weird thing to say. Pride for someone else always seemed to me like it had to come from seeing the journey. You knew how hard it was for them to get there and you felt invested in their success. But Ethan says it with assurance. Maybe it's enough to understand that there's been a journey. Maybe he's tricked himself into actually believing we're already in the middle of our friendship. I don't think I mind. It's nice to have someone rooting for me.

I eat two of the toast things. The tomato bits explode in my mouth, kind of like that gum that has a liquid center. Only this is a pure, clean taste that makes me remember the little tomato plants Margo always tried to grow on her fire escape in the summer. I could eat forever. But I stop so I don't get that dull, thick feeling in my stomach when I try to play my next set.

Ethan eats the rest. He stays at the table nearest to me, clapping loud when I pick up my guitar again.

The sounds of getting started—the click of the strap buckle against the guitar, pop of the mic as I switch it on, the way the strings of the guitar vibrate ever so slightly when I rest it on my leg—those are my favorite sounds. I used to notice them every single time I played, but this is the first time in a long time that I've even heard them.

The couple who was already done with dinner is about to leave, but they sit down again and order another bottle of wine when I start to play. The date couple orders dessert. He gives her a bite of his lemon meringue pie, holding the fork across the table, hand under it, ready to catch pieces of the crumbling crust. I do a little cheer for her in my mind and play *Something in the Way She Moves*. James Taylor. Not Beatles. Because it's the sweetest song I know. Because maybe it will help. Because I still want to believe that people can fall in love and stay there, the way I desperately wished the unicorn Margo took me to see at the Renaissance Fair wasn't just a white goat with one horn sawed off.

I hope for a bigger crowd, but it never happens. A guy comes in and sits by himself in the corner. He orders coffee and pie and reads a book the whole time like I'm not even there. No one runs in from the street, moved by the music leaking out to the sidewalk. Robert won't ask me back. This wasn't enough.

While I pack up my guitar, I make a mental note of the things I need to gather from Ethan's so I can head for Florida first thing in the morning before he wakes up. So there's no need for awkward breakfast talk. It's easier to leave when you aren't burdened with goodbyes and loose promises about keeping in touch. Just go if you're going to go.

Robert comes out of the kitchen and says, "Thank you, April." He's formal when he says it, looks at an order pad in his hand, and I feel like it's the way you would dismiss someone if you were of the high and mighty variety. *Thank you, April. That's enough of you.*

But he flips the page on his pad and says, "Can you play at the bar tomorrow, and then back here on Saturday?"

"Yeah," I say slowly. "I can do that, possibly." You have to adjust quickly. You can't be too eager. Eager people get screwed. But I want to cry from the relief of it.

Robert says, "Oh, that's great!" and claps his hand to the side of my arm excitedly. "That couple"—he points to their now empty table— "ordered two very expensive bottles of wine. One more than they would have if you hadn't been here. And them"—he points to the table where the daters had been—"they never would have ordered dessert if it weren't for you. Thursdays are always a little slow over here, but you turned it into a good one for us."

"It's what I do," I say, smiling as he pulls a small wad of bills from his back pocket and hands it to me. When you have happy accidents, it's best to own them. They don't happen often enough.

— Chapter 45 —

The bar the next night is fine. Nothing to write home about. But on Saturday night at the restaurant, the wine couple is back. They've brought friends and the bottles of wine come and go more often than I can keep track.

The following week when I play at the restaurant, there's a huge crowd. People stand and listen while they wait for tables. Robert rushes around. Every time he catches my eye he smiles. Ethan sits at a double by himself, holding a cup of coffee in both hands, mouthing all the words along with me. He's been listening to me practice.

Monday morning, I wake up and there's light streaming in through the lacy curtains in my room at Ethan's house and I know I've slept in way longer than I ever let myself.

"Hey, sunshine," Ethan says when I stumble into the kitchen. He has a mess of papers and pamphlets all over the table.

"What are you doing?"

"Filling out applications," he says, handing me one of the pamphlets. "Help me!"

It's for Emerson College in Boston.

"Are you going back to school?"

"Looking for a new job." Ethan points to the

coffeepot. I pour a cup for myself and give him a warm-up.

I sit at the table and spread out his pamphlets so I can see them.

"Looks like I'll be moving to cold weather," he says. "All the good theatre schools seem to be up north."

"It's not so bad," I tell him, holding up a Middlebury brochure. "I did a gig at a bar near Middlebury last year. It's nice."

"You like it?"

"Yeah. Gorgeous hills. Snowed like a motherfucker and I didn't have snow tires, so I got stuck there for a whole week longer than I meant to, but you know . . . if you don't need to get anywhere because you live there to begin with, it's probably nice. Stay in. Eat waffles. The maple syrup's real."

Ethan buries his head in his hands.

"Or get snow tires," I say. "Trade in your Saab for a Jeep?"

"Thin blood," Ethan says into his hands and shakes his head from side to side. "I have thin southern blood. I'm going to freeze to death." He hugs his arms around his chest and chatters his teeth. "I'm cold just thinking about it."

There's a reason he works in theatre. I wonder why he's a behind the scenes person instead of an on the stage one.

"Why aren't you staying here?" I ask, trying

to keep my disappointment hidden. It's not like I thought I could live in Asheville forever, with a regular gig, and a comfy bed, and Ethan refusing to let me pay rent, but I'm not ready for it to end either.

"Oh, you know," he says. "Bad breakup. Time for a change. Tomorrow was supposed to be our anniversary. You waste three years of your life on someone, it seems like a good idea to get out of town when you wake up."

I drink my coffee and push pamphlets around the table. So many weird names I don't recognize. Carnegie Mellon. Brandeis. Sarah Lawrence. And then there's one I do: Ithaca College.

"Here." I tap the Ithaca brochure with my finger. "Go here."

"Ithaca?" Ethan says. "That's a great program. Cold, but good."

"It's warmer than where I grew up," I say. "And snow feels nicer in Ithaca. I don't know why. Everything is nicer there."

"Do you play in Ithaca a lot?" Ethan asks.

"I lived there for a bit." The air catches in my throat. "It's a hard place to leave." I stare into my coffee cup and will my eyes to stay dry. "And," I say, taking a deep breath, pulling myself back together, "it's a super gay place. You'd love it."

"Super gay?" Ethan says. "Would I have to get a cape?"

"No," I tell him. "But tights aren't frowned on."

— Chapter 46 —

I decide to make Ethan an anti-anniversary dinner to celebrate that we got all of his applications in the mail. I check my wallet so many times before I get up to the checkout. My heart thuds in my throat until I make it out of the store, like groceries are the beginning of the end, even though I know they aren't. Some things get written into your body and your mind can't reason them away.

I walk home with my bag full of food. Pasta and sauce from a jar. Some onions and peppers to dress it up. It's the most I really know how to cook, but it's something. I'm hoping the thought counts more than the end result.

There are tulips blooming in front yard flower-beds and the air smells full and mossy. It's not quite dark when I get home. The door to the sun porch is open wide and the door to the living room isn't closed all the way. I hear Ethan say, "That wasn't what I meant," and his voice is full of tears.

I stand on the sun porch and peek through the open door. There's a man in the living room holding Ethan against the wall. Ethan's nose is bleeding down his neck. I hold my breath and push the living room door open slowly.

The guy screams, "You're the one who should be sorry. You're the one who had such a big problem with it!" He's screaming so loud he doesn't hear me come in.

When Ethan sees me, he turns his face away. The guy slaps Ethan's cheek, and then the other. "Look at me when I talk to you!"

My body feels like it might never move again, but Ethan is crying and the guy doesn't look like he's going to stop. I'm still holding the groceries, so I grab the jar of sauce and throw it at the guy. It hits with a thump between his shoulders and falls to the floor, exploding, sending sauce and glass everywhere. "Stop!" I scream. "Stop!"

He drops his hold on Ethan and turns. His face is bloated, cheeks trembling. Red eyes. Raw knuckles. He looks like he's going to come after me instead. I chuck a pepper and catch him on the side of his head and then an onion that hits him right in the eye and I scream and scream and throw everything from the bag. I pretend I'm bigger than him and bigger than everyone and if I look at him hard enough, he might just burn up and die. He might turn into nothing. He gets in my face. His breath smells so sour. I can see in his eyes he's deciding if he's going to hit me too. I'm all out of groceries. There's nothing else to throw. He grabs my hair, all of it, in his fist and pulls me out of his way. Away from the door and I don't know what he's going to do. He pulls so hard. I stumble. Hit the floor, hip first. All I can think about is the bruise it will leave. Dark purple. I can feel my blood pooling.

"You like little girls now?" he says to Ethan.

"Go!" Ethan screams. "Ivan! Leave!" His face is wet, nose pouring snot and blood, all the color drained right out of him.

Ivan kicks my leg, hard. And then he finally walks out the door, slamming it behind him. I scramble to latch the lock. Push a chair against the door, and then I run to Ethan. He's holding his face, sobbing so hard. I think maybe it will hurt if I hug him but worry it might be worse if I don't.

"I'll call the police," I say.

"You don't really think the cops are going to want in on a fight between a couple of queers, do you?" Ethan says, sniffing and wiping his face with the back of his hand. Blood smears across his cheek.

"Hospital?"

"I don't want anyone to see me like this. I don't want to go out there. I don't want—" His face wrinkles. It hurts him to cry and that makes him cry harder. You can see it—how it hurts.

"Okay. It's okay," I say over and over because I have no other words. I run to the bathroom and get a washcloth. Soak it under the faucet and bring it to him. He's crying so hard his whole body trembles.

I clean his face. Wash the blood from his hair the best I can. And then we sit on the floor in the middle of all the smashed groceries and I hold him and tell him everything will be okay, because that's what I always wished someone would tell me whenever I got hurt.

"I shouldn't have tried," Ethan says. "I knew better. But he was here when I got home. He still had the key, and I missed him. I didn't realize he was drunk. I let myself hope."

When he's stopped crying, I slide the refrigerator against the back door in the kitchen. My hip aches when I push. I pile more furniture in front of the front door and check every window latch. We sleep in Ethan's room, with my arms around him, the TV on like a night light, my buck knife hidden under the mattress, just in case.

The next morning, I get up before Ethan does to clean the tomato sauce and blood and broken glass off the carpet the best I can. I call Robert and ask him to help me change the locks.

Ethan cries when he wakes up. We hear him all the way downstairs. I bring him a wet washcloth. His nose is swollen and bruised. The cut on his cheekbone is thick and crusted over. It's hard to tell where one bruise stops and the next one starts. He holds his stomach. Tries to stop crying. He can't. I kiss his forehead and clean his face. When I change the bloodied pillowcase, Robert sits on the bed and lets Ethan rest his head in his lap.

Robert has some Percocet left over from a back injury last year, so we give that to Ethan and I get him more ice for his nose and hold his hand. When he falls asleep, we go down to the kitchen and pull together something for him to eat. Scrambled eggs, yogurt, and canned peaches, because it will be easy on his jaw. We wake him up. He looks at us and chews when we tell him to, but he's not really there. I'm sure it's easier not to be.

"I wish you'd met Rodney," Robert says while we're cleaning up the breakfast dishes. He's wiping the juice tumblers with a bright blue sponge that squeaks against the glass. "Ethan and Rodney were like the romance you always dreamed you could have, you know?" He stacks the glasses gently in the drying rack. "They were so happy. It made everyone around them feel better to know there was love like that in the world." When he scrubs the frying pan, dried yellow flakes of egg fall into the sink like leaves.

"Why did they break up?" I ask, swigging the rest of my coffee, handing my mug to Robert to wash.

He puts the mug down and it clanks against the porcelain sink. "I don't know why I thought you'd know about that."

"I just got here. I'm basically a stranger."

"This," Robert says, waving his hand toward the living room, where the blood on the rug will never come out all the way, "this makes us not strangers."

He picks up the mug and wipes it down with the soapy sponge. I'm convinced he's not going to tell me what happened, and then he says, "Rodney died in a car accident about four years ago."

I think about how Ethan's eyes look older than the rest of him, and the weary way he carries himself to bed at the end of the day.

"They were going to adopt a kid," Robert says. His eyes are red. He doesn't try to hide it. "This little girl from Mexico. She was beautiful. They got pictures in the mail. They were planning their trip to pick her up. And then, Rodney was on his way home from work. A tractor-trailer . . ."

I cover my mouth with my palm. Robert rests the mug in the sink and wipes his eyes with the back of his hand.

"Ethan saw the accident on his way home from work. He saw the car. Followed the ambulance to the hospital, but they wouldn't let him in to see Rodney because he wasn't *immediate family*." Robert's hair is falling in his eyes. He pushes it away. "So, Rodney died alone while Ethan was sitting in the waiting room. They wouldn't let him in. Ethan fell apart and he couldn't adopt his little girl so he lost both of them all at once."

"I'm so sorry," I say, which seems like the wrong thing, but I can't think of anything right.

"After that, Ethan seemed frantic to replace what he lost. Or maybe he knew he never could, so he was ready to settle. Whatever it was, Ivan took advantage."

Robert yanks the rubber band from his ponytail and lets his hair fall around his face before he pulls it up and twists the band around again. "It was hard to watch. But you can't make a friend break up with someone. If you tell them they should and they don't, you lose them. I didn't want to risk it."

"You can't blame yourself for this," I say, because he looks like he does. His eyes are so sad.

"I never thought Ivan was this out of control. I didn't like him, but Ethan kept telling me how great he was, and I thought—I mean, Rodney was my friend. I thought maybe I didn't want to accept Ivan because it meant Rodney was really gone. If I'd known Ivan was this bad, I would have done something."

Robert gives up on the dishes. We sit at the bottom of the stairs together so we can hear Ethan if he wakes up. So we can be right there if he needs us. We don't say much. We just sit there, knees touching. When Robert starts to cry, I hold his hand.

— Chapter 47 —

Ethan spends a few days in bed. Robert and I take turns with him so he's never alone. Robert gets a substitute chef when I play at the restaurant and I stay with Ethan when I'm not playing.

We lie in bed and watch soap operas. Matty is in a coma. If he wakes up, his fiancée is going to tell him the baby isn't his. She has conversations about it with her new lover in his hospital room.

"He's lying right there!" I yell, twisting the edge of Ethan's quilt in my hands. "She's such a bitch."

"I wouldn't have guessed you for a soap fan," Ethan says. He smiles as much as he can manage. The bruises around his nose and jaw are dark purple.

"I know him," I say, pointing at the TV. "Jake Jacobson. I know him."

Ethan gives me a blank look. "You understand this show isn't real, right?"

"The actor who plays Jake Jacobson. Matty— Matthew Spencer. I know him. I used to."

"Like know him, or *know* him?"

"Second one."

"Do you miss him?"

"If someone changes so much that they're

411

barely the same person, who are you even missing?"

"I miss him, you know," Ethan says. I think he's telling me about Rodney, but then he says, "I'm sure no one wants to hear it. But it's not like I didn't love Ivan. It's not like every bit of him and me was a fight. It didn't start out that way."

He looks at me. The bruises and the sadness in his eyes are almost too much to bear. I grab his hand under the blankets and squeeze it tight.

"I still miss him and it hurts and I wish he would come back and be okay and love me and not hurt me again," Ethan says, all in one breath, like it's a relief to say the words. "There were good parts. There were tiny little parts of a good person and I miss having hope that those parts would take over."

He starts to cry. He tucks his head into my shoulder and I rub his back.

When he falls asleep, I go into the bathroom and hang a towel over the mirror so he doesn't have look at his bruises until they're better.

— Chapter 48 —

Robert's Friday night band at the bar cancels. It's not my scene. It's not Ethan's either, so he stays home to paint. It's the first time we've left him alone since Ivan showed up. His bruises have faded from purple to green. They look like shadows. He promises he's fine. Says the alone time will be good for him. I check the locks on the doors before we leave.

The crowd was expecting a Blue Öyster Cult cover band. I sprayed my hair so there are curls in every direction and lined my eyes with black shadow. There's big hair and acid-washed jeans everywhere. I think about playing *Don't Fear the Reaper*, but it might be twisting the knife, and the guitar part is too complicated for me anyway. I stick to my angrier stuff, hit my strings as hard as I can. I keep scraping my knuckle. Sometimes the crowd listens; mostly they drink. After I've played a few songs, half the bar clears out. The ones who stay seem to like me. At the very least, they buy a lot of beer.

Robert tends bar. The liquor shelf lights change from blue to purple and back to blue, chiseling his face into sharp lines as he moves from one side of the bar to the other. A woman with big boobs corralled in a leather vest leans over as she orders, showing off her wares. He gives her enough attention to keep her buying drinks and leaving wadded bills on the bar.

He brings me a beer. I tuck it under my stool and take it with me to the bathroom on the break. I don't want to be rude, but after Ivan and his breath in my face, the smell of alcohol makes me sick. I pour my beer down the sink and leave the empty on the end of the bar.

When everyone's left and Robert is slopping out the spill mats, I slip behind the bar to help him.

"Whatcha doing, cowgirl?" Robert kicks my boots lightly with his toe.

"Helping."

It's weird to be with him out in the world. We've spent so many nights at Ethan's together. He's different here. He has his hair down, tucked behind his ears. He's beautiful.

"Thank you," he says. "April." And the way he says my name is like he also knows something is different.

"Robert," I say back. I feel my face flush. I take the rag that's hanging from his back pocket and spray club soda on it.

I wipe down the bar. He refills the napkin holders.

"Why aren't you Rob?"

"I don't know," he says, honestly, like it's

just occurred to him that he could be Rob if he wanted to be.

"Well, think about it and get back to me," I say, smiling. Just to say something. I'm not sure if it's okay to feel the way I'm feeling. We've been through something together. I don't know where that leaves us.

After I'm done wiping down the bar I hop up on it, swinging my legs over the edge while Robert finishes counting out the drawer. His eyebrows furrow, lips moving ever so slightly as he stacks bills on top of each other.

When he's done, he pours himself a drink and climbs on the bar with me. "Thanks for helping," he says. He leans in and kisses me, and it goes from being a friendly kind of kiss to a ravenous one, like every moment spent sitting together on Ethan's staircase or brushing past each other in the kitchen has added up to this.

Some drunks bang on the window. They can see us because the neon beer signs are still lit up. "Hold on," Robert says. He runs around pulling the chains on the signs to turn them off so no one else will know what we're about to do. He climbs back on the bar.

Chapter 49

On the nights I don't play, Ethan and I curl up on the couch with popcorn and ice cream watching old black and white movies. Tonight, it's *Top Hat* and too much mint chocolate chip. When it's over, Ethan hits the remote on the stereo, drags me to my feet, and tries to twirl me around like Ginger Rogers.

"You're too stiff," he says, shaking my arm to loosen me up.

"Trying to dance like Fred Astaire to R.E.M.," I say, shaking his arm back, "is your first problem. Second is that I'm a terrible dancer. Terrible." I head back to the couch to sit down.

"It's just what was in there," Ethan says. He's smiling, and it's good to see him smile. His bruises are yellowed ghosts. You can only see them from certain angles. "Come on. Try. I'll find something that fits better."

He thumbs through his CDs, puts on Ella Fitzgerald, and offers his hand to me. I take it. He tries to teach me the foxtrot and I step all over his toes. He lets me stand on his feet until I get the steps, singing *Cheek to Cheek* in his best Fred Astaire voice, even though Ella is singing something completely different. He spins me out and back in and my feet start doing the right things.

"Look at you, Ginger." He presses his cheek to mine. "You, here, makes my whole life better."

I cry. Big fat tears rolling down my face, splashing on Ethan's cheek. "Jerk," I say, sniffing and laughing and wiping my face. "Why did you have to say that?"

"Because"—he sops tears from my cheeks with his sleeve—"it's true. And I get the feeling not enough people have told you how much you matter. How amazing you are."

"You're the only one crazy enough to think it."

"Possibly," he says, but shakes his head.

"You know what?" I tell him, taking the lead, twirling him around. "Being here makes my whole life better."

"Look at us lucky ducks," he says.

We dance and talk and get more ice cream from the freezer. He tells me about Rodney and the little girl who never got to be theirs. I don't tell him I already know. I'm not sure if Robert would want me to. He shows me pictures from the adoption agency. She had the sweetest apple cheeks. Her name is Luz, and Ethan says that means light. The agency promised him they found her a good home. He says it's amazing how much you can miss someone you've never even met.

I tell him about me and Little River and Margo and my dad. I tell him about squatting in vacation homes in Florida, and Ray, Justin, and how

Matty doesn't love me anymore. I tell him about Adam and Carly and pancake-shaped pancakes, Rosemary and why I had to leave Ithaca. I say that it's amazing how much you can miss people you only got to be with for one tiny little perfect bit of time; how a place where you barely got to live can be the closest thing you've ever had to home. Ethan listens to all of it and he still likes me when I'm done talking. He's the only person I've ever told everything to.

Chapter 50

S o, just because you and Robert are all lovey dovey and whatnot doesn't mean you can't be my date for the Pride costume ball, right?" Ethan says.

He's standing in the doorway of the bathroom while I get ready for a shift waiting tables at the restaurant. Robert is short-staffed for lunch and I promised I'd fill in.

"Of course not," I say, leaning into the mirror to put mascara on. I didn't realize he knew about me and Robert. It's not that I specifically wanted to hide it from Ethan, it's just that no one wants to feel like the odd man out, and he's still sad about Ivan. He puts on this brave face and thinks I don't notice, but he's working on a new painting and it's all dark mean blues and crashes of red. Even though it's abstract, I know what it's about. Plus, I have no idea if Robert feels the same way I do.

"Of course not, you can't be my date?" Ethan asks. "Or of course it *doesn't* mean you can't be my date?"

This, I know from experience, could go on forever. It's a game we play, talking ourselves in circles. Normally I love to twist words with him, but I'm in a hurry. I fell back to sleep with wet hair after my shower this morning and now it's sticking out in weird directions. I stop the game by saying, "Ethan Turner, my dearest darling, there is nothing in the world I would love more than to be your date. In fact, being your date would make me the happiest girl in the whole wide world."

"Good," he says. "Me too."

"You're the happiest girl in the whole wide world?" I say, grinning.

"Yes," Ethan says. "It's a date."

"Deal. But only if you buy me a corsage." I quit trying to make my hair look right and just pull it all up in a ponytail. "Hey, who says Robert and I are all lovey dovey?"

"Robert," Ethan says, smiling big.

My face flushes and I know Ethan can see me turning red.

"Yeah," he says, tugging my ponytail. "He's got it bad for you."

When I get home from my shift, there's a blond wig and a silver beaded dress with tags from the vintage store artfully arranged on my bed, even though the ball is still two weeks away. I try the dress on. It hangs tight at my waist; the skirt swishes and twirls. It's the prettiest thing I've ever worn. It fits perfectly.

— Chapter 51 —

Robert makes me dinner at his place. I think Ethan is a little miffed he's not invited, but he's trying hard not to let it show. He says it's good that I'm going to Robert's, because he can use the time to paint. He likes to work on his canvases at different times of day so he can get all the layers just right. I think he burned the blue and red one. I came home one day and there were ashes in the fireplace and the house stunk of burnt plastic. He didn't say anything about it, so I didn't ask, in case it was something he needed to keep private.

The new painting he's working on is abstract too. Full of brown curves and squiggles. It doesn't really look like anything, so I don't get how he'll know when he's done. I don't ask, because I don't want to hurt his feelings. I like it, even if I don't understand what it's supposed to be. Something about it is soft and sweet.

When I get to Robert's, he opens the door before I even knock, hands me a plate loaded with lasagna, and says, "Do me a favor. Run this to Ethan. He never remembers to stop painting to feed himself." I bring the plate back to Ethan and we swoon over Robert and how kind he is.

Ethan plasters a kiss on my cheek. "Go on

your date already, silly girl! I won't wait up." He sits down with his plate of lasagna to study his painting while he eats.

Robert has a stillness to him. Even when he's moving around the kitchen, chopping cucumbers for the salad, or pouring wine in my glass, there's nothing frantic about it. Everything is purposeful, like what he's doing at that moment is the only thing he could possibly want to be doing.

I feel like I can tell Ethan every little bit of myself. Every inch of my brain, even the stupid stuff, and he always wants to hear it and he always understands. But with Robert, I don't talk much. My words feel heavy when I do. Gestures have more meaning. His fingertips grazing the back of my hand. A look. It's calming. It leaves me with room for my own quiet.

When Robert sits at the table with me, he smiles, and I smile back, and it's comfortable and exciting at the same time. The lasagna is gooey, with layers of mushrooms and smoked sausage.

"So," I say softly, "I heard this rumor that you like me."

"Do you think it's true?" he asks. I like the way his eyes crinkle when he smiles.

"Yeah," I say. I kick at his boot under the table. He grabs my ankle with both his legs. We eat dinner with our feet entwined.

We eat until our plates are clean, soaking up

sauce with big chunks of rosemary bread Robert made from scratch. I don't drink my wine. It stays on the table, mocking me. Ethan doesn't drink anymore either. We can't.

"Is the wine too dry?" Robert asks when he pours himself a second glass.

"No," I say, "it's perfect. I just—I was nursing a headache today."

"You know what the best cure for a headache is?"

I expect him to say sex, because I've heard that line before. Too many times. I feel disappointed about it, that he's actually the kind of guy to use a line like that. But then he says, "This," and stands behind me. He rubs my shoulders with his strong, strong hands, which, of course, leads to sex, on the kitchen floor, on the stairs, in his bed, but nothing about it is disappointing in the least.

I sleep at Robert's house. All night. I don't leave before he wakes up. Sex is one thing—just putting parts together. It's another thing entirely to exist together. Robert is someone I want to exist with.

— Chapter 52 —

Ethan is so excited about the dance that he's been in his top hat and tails since before I even got home from waiting tables.

He helps me get ready. We twist small sections of my hair and pin them as flat as we can against my scalp.

"You know," Ethan says when we finally get the wig on my head, "I like you as a blond."

"Personally," I tell him, "I think you should wear a top hat all the time."

I get the makeup perfect, copying a picture Ethan found for me: big red lips, eyeliner only on the top lash line.

When I go to my room to put my dress on, the zipper won't pull up. It was fine before, but now, once I get it past my hips it starts to stick.

"Almost ready?" Ethan calls from the hall-way.

"Almost," I yell. I empty out every last little bit of air I have in my lungs and suck my stomach in as far as I can. I pull on the zipper hard and it finally slides all the way up. I have this fleeting thought that makes my heart stop and my insides flip-flop around, but I push it to the far corners of my mind. I've been eating three meals a day like a normal person since I got here. It's catching up to me. The seams are straining, but I'm in the dress and I'm hoping that with all the beads and shine no one will notice it's too tight. I bought a lacy shawl at a thrift store last week. I wrap it around myself before I go out in the hallway so Ethan won't notice. He desperately wants everything about tonight to be perfect. I'll just try to keep my shawl on as much as possible.

"Smashing, my darling. Positively smashing," Ethan says when I meet him in the living room. He's holding a plastic clamshell box with a huge wrist corsage of pale pink roses and sprigs of rosemary. It's the first time anyone has given me roses. Matty never brought me flowers when he took me to homecoming.

Ethan opens the box and slips the corsage on my wrist. "As promised."

We stop in to see Robert at the bar to show him our costumes and bring him a microwave lasagna.

Robert laughs. "You guys do realize we serve food here."

"It's what we do, right?" I say. "Bring lasagna to the person who doesn't have a date?"

"We didn't want you to feel left out," Ethan says.

Robert kisses me and ends up with a mouth full of red lipstick.

. . .

Ethan takes me to a club on Grove Street that's decked out like an old-time dance hall. Punch in big bowls. Streamers hanging from the ceiling. We dance like Fred and Ginger all night long, even though the music is wrong and everyone else is swing dancing. We almost win the best costume contest, until someone realizes I'm not a drag queen.

"Next year, I'll be Ginger. Then we'll win," Ethan says, laughing so hard at the whole misunderstanding that he looks like he might wet his pants.

On the way home, we dance down the sidewalk in front of his house. Ethan sings *Top Hat, White Tie and Tails* at the top of his lungs while he twirls me around. When he tries to dip me, we stumble to the ground. We lie on the sidewalk laughing, and stare at the stars. It feels like a movie. I didn't get to go to my prom, but I'm sure this is so much better.

"See that one?" Ethan says, pointing at a strip of stars that may or may not be a constellation. "That's Cassiopeia, and that one is Orion, and that one's Steve."

I giggle, and it eggs Ethan on.

"That one is Phyllis, and there's Charlie. Over there, Esmerelda."

"And that one . . ." I point up, tracing my finger in the shape of a top hat, even though there aren't necessarily stars to back it up. "That one is Ethan."

Ethan tips his head to the side and looks at me. "Oh, I love you, Angel. This is the best night I've had in such a long time."

"I love you, E.T.," I say. "This is the best night I've ever had."

He grabs my hand. "Well, sure," he says, smiling. "One up me."

— Chapter 53 —

Robert is cooking breakfast again. It's a Thursday morning. I just played the restaurant last night and the bar over the weekend. Robert can't find reliable bands. I draw crowds. I sell CDs. So it's not like I'm complaining, but I'm tired. Every morning when I wake up, I feel like a bag of bones.

Ethan is drinking coffee and pushing scrambled eggs around his plate. "Why don't you ever make pancakes?" he says.

"April doesn't like pancakes. Hey, honey." Robert kisses my cheek when I walk in the room. "I need a favor. That Celtic band canceled."

Tightness creeps up from my belly and into my throat. I burst into tears and run to the bathroom.

I hear Robert talk, but I can't hear what he says. Ethan's response is clear. "She's pregnant, you dope." I don't know how he knows. It wasn't even something I let myself think.

Robert opens the bathroom door without knocking. He sits on the side of the tub next to me. His eyes are full and shiny. He hugs me, kisses my head. "She's going to be beautiful," he says.

Chapter 54

Ethan has job offers to teach at Oberlin, DePaul, and Ithaca, but he swears he's right where he wants to be. He loves the baby too much. He loves me too much and I need him, so he can't possibly go. He says he needs to be needed. It's this heartbreaking thing, because we all know it would be best for him to take one of those jobs, and then the thought of being here without him is too hard to even think about. It's so selfish for me to need him the way I do, but I can't help it.

Ethan ran into Ivan last week. At the grocery store. He hid in the stock room and they thought he was shoplifting. Even though he didn't have anything on him, they couldn't get creative and think of any other reason a person would ever be hiding in a stock room all sweaty and shaking. It's not like he had a grapefruit shoved down his pants. Robert had to go get him from the store security office and vouch for him, whatever that means.

If anyone ever deserved a fresh start, it's Ethan. I wish we could all go with him. Me, Robert, and the baby. But Robert can't leave the bar and restaurant and I can't leave Robert, and Ethan doesn't want to break up our weird, wonderful little family. If I were a better person and a better friend, I would tell him to go. I think about how I would do it. Plan it out in my head. I would sit him down and make him coffee and have cookies from that place he likes on Biltmore and tell him we'd call and visit and write and send so many pictures. I would tell him there will be new people for him to love. But I can't. I know it's wrong that I want to keep him. But I do.

Chapter 55

Robert books a doctor's appointment for me. There's talk of a wedding. Of health insurance. Of things that leave me gasping for air if I think about them too much. But this first appointment he's just paying for. We want to hear the heartbeat without having to wait for all the paperwork.

I heard once that before you drown, you get euphoric. That's what this feels like. Happy drowning. I have a family now. I have a home. I am terrified.

Robert waits outside the exam room while I undress and put on that paper gown and drape like the nurse told me to. It's funny how there's sex-naked and doctor's-office-naked and they're not at all the same thing.

When Robert comes back in, it's awkward. He holds my hand and makes a very concentrated effort to look at my face and not at the paper I'm wrapped in like a cut of beef from the meat market.

"So," Dr. Katim says, looking at her clipboard when she walks into the room, "April and Robert. Looks like we're having a baby!"

She's young. Like medical student young. She has perfect straight hair and black-framed glasses that I think maybe she's only wearing to make her look smart. Women like her are too perfect for glasses.

I don't like the way she says *we*. *We're having a baby.* There are already enough people on this baby's team. And it's not like she'll be changing diapers.

"Have you confirmed that you're pregnant?" she asks, flipping through my forms.

"Yeah," I say, and Robert smiles. Ethan bought every kind of pee stick the drugstore had. He and Robert stood outside the bathroom cheering every time I slipped another positive one through the huge gap under the door. They were all positive.

She pulls my gown up and the drape down. "So, how far along are we?"

"About a month?" I say.

She grabs a calendar off the desk and shows it to us. Robert points to the day. The bar. Our first time. "I think it had to be then," he says.

"When was your last period?" she asks, and I turn beet red.

I never keep track. "I don't know," I say, and feel like an idiot. I look far off and pretend I'm counting out days, but I can't remember anything. I shake my head.

"Okay," she says, "well, we'll take a look and see what your baby can tell us today." She grabs a bottle that looks like the kind you put ketchup or mustard in, but it's white, not red or yellow.

She holds it over my belly, smacks the bottom of it, and squirts cold blue jelly all over. It's gross. I don't like the way that being pregnant seems to make everything about you fair game—your pee, your belly, your period.

"It might be too early for a heartbeat. Don't worry if we don't hear one," she says.

She holds this flat wand thing against my stomach. It doesn't hurt, but when she presses harder and pushes it around, it makes me queasy.

Then we hear it. The heartbeat. Loud, thumping static. Alien communications. Like our baby is saying hello to us. And then I'm crying. Robert is too. Like that thumping is the most beautiful sound we've ever heard.

We look at the screen, where she's pointing, "See, that's your baby!" she says, but it looks like TV reception in a snowstorm. So we focus on the sound. Robert's hand squeezes mine ever so slightly in time with the beat. I don't even think he knows he's doing it. I don't want it to stop, but then Dr. Katim takes the wand off my stomach and says, "Alright, Daddy, I'm going to have you step out to the waiting room now, while Mom and I do some girl stuff."

Robert looks panicked. And it takes me longer than it should to realize that I'm the mom. I don't want him to leave, but Dr. Katim says, "Nothing to worry about." She grabs a tissue and wipes my belly. She doesn't get all the goo. There's a clump of it right by my belly button that she can't seem to see. She pushes some buttons on the machine. "Just a few simple tests, but it's all a little unflattering. We'll try to keep some sense of mystery in your relationship, right?"

She looks down at her clipboard and makes notes while Robert gets up and kisses me goodbye. He walks slow and rubs his forehead as he leaves, like he can't quite believe the static he saw. I wipe my belly with the palm of my hand and wipe my hand on the corner of my paper gown.

As soon as the door closes, Dr. Katim looks up from her clipboard, like she was only pretending to read it. "April," she says, and kicks her legs to wheel her chair closer to me, "I wanted us to have some privacy, because I don't know what the situation between you and Robert is."

"He's the father," I say. "He's my—" I can't think of the right word, because he's more than my boyfriend the way Matty was my boyfriend, but we're not married. I get a sinking feeling that's just drowning without the happy. "Is my baby okay?" I ask, even though I think I know what she's going to tell me.

"Your baby looks perfectly healthy, has a strong heartbeat, and has to be at least eight weeks old."

She grabs a printout from the machine and shows it to me. It's a photo of the static, but when

I look closer, I can see shapes. I think maybe even a face.

"See here," she says, using her pen to point to a spot in the snow. "That's one of your baby's elbows. I can see feet and hands and even the beginnings of fingers." Thin streaks of blue ink from a glob on the point of her pen drag across the photo as she points to different parts of my baby. "These are levels of development we can't see until eight weeks. So we're a bit off from Robert's estimate."

She gives me the picture. My hands shake.

"I didn't put the fetal age on the picture," she says, "because I want to let you have that discussion on your own terms." She reaches out and puts her hand over my hand. "If there's a discussion to be had."

"Are you okay?" Robert asks when I get to the waiting room. "Is the baby okay?"

"Yeah," I say. "It's just overwhelming, you know? It's just—it's a lot." The picture is folded up in my pocket. I don't show him. He'd want to show Ethan and Ethan's been reading about babies too much. He'd see the elbow. He'd know.

Robert holds my hand as we walk to the parking lot. His fingers are still tapping out the heartbeat.

— Chapter 56 —

I buy a book. One that tells you everything you're supposed to know about having a baby. I sit at the kitchen table and read the whole thing while Ethan is at a meeting. I hope to find some kind of wisdom that will put everything right in my brain, but each chapter makes me feel worse. There's all this stuff about what you should eat and what you shouldn't and pain management and tearing in places you wouldn't even think could tear. Then there's the section on how to take care of the baby when it's actually here. None of it tells me what I most need to know.

I don't want to be growing a person in my body. Even if the baby was Robert's, I think I would still feel like I am trapped inside myself and my skin is too small and I can't breathe enough air into the deepest parts of my lungs. I press my forehead to the cold enamel tabletop, panting like a puppy on an August afternoon.

"What are you doing, Angel?" Ethan asks when he walks through the door. "Are you okay? Is the baby—"

"Ethan—" I try to catch my breath. "Ethan—" and for a moment I think I will tell him everything. Ask what I should do. But if he knows, this family we have won't work the way we have it. Ethan could tell Robert. Or he could not tell Robert, and I don't know which is worse. I don't want him to have to carry my secret or exist in the middle. He was Robert's friend first. "Ethan, there are bones in my stomach," I say.

"Huh?"

"There are bones. Like actual baby bones growing in my stomach."

"That's kind of the point, right?" Ethan says, putting his bag down. "Babies are supposed to have bones. It's a problem if they don't." He kisses the top of my head and gives my shoulders a squeeze. "What are you worried about, sweetheart?"

So I say the other things I'm thinking instead. "What if I can't do it, Ethan? What if I can't stay in the same place? If I'm like my mom and I just can't handle it?" It's not hard to push aside the Robert problem when these fears are also true. I can remember watching my mother pack a duffle bag with clothes. And I can so clearly imagine myself in her place, saying, *It's just for a day or two. To clear my head, baby. I'll be back by the weekend.* It's not that far a leap.

"You aren't going to wimp out on your kid," Ethan says. "You're the toughest person I know." He fills two highball glasses with ice, pours us some sweet tea, and hands me a glass. Sits across from me, hands folded on the table, like we're having a meeting and I have his full attention.

"I do feel it," I confess, swirling my tea to hear the ice cubes clink. "That thing I think she felt. The only way I know to fix that kind of restless itch is to put miles between me and wherever I was."

"You're self-medicating with survival," Ethan says, studying my face as if he knows there's something there to find. "You're addicted to drama."

"Sure," I say, pretending I know exactly what he means so maybe he'll drop it. I worry whatever thread he's tugging will lead to what I'm trying to hide.

"If you're in survival mode you can keep problems buried, because the way you grew up, that wasn't okay. When you upend your life, you don't have to sit with how unfair it was. And whatever drama you come up with won't be worse than the anger and hurt you're carrying around, because that was the original hurt. That's the deepest cut."

He might be right about the part he understands. When I close my eyes, I always see it: pine needles, my mother's diamond ring, and my broken guitar, Irene's Christmas tree, and the stars on Matty's ceiling, like every moment of my life gets loaded in that motorhome. Everywhere I go, I'm dragging it with me, collecting more hurt and loss and sad sweet memories that I don't want to hold. But this time I think the drama could be the worse kind of pain. If I tell Ethan and Robert the truth, I could lose everything that's good, and if I don't, I'm ruining the good thing anyway.

"I could be your drama sponsor," Ethan says. "We'll have meetings, and when you're about to grab your keys and hit the road you can call me and we'll stage an intervention. I'll bring donuts."

"I don't think that's how it works." I wish he could fix everything the way he thinks he can.

"Don't say no to donuts," Ethan says, grinning.

I wish I could go back to what it felt like when Ethan knew everything about me.

— Chapter 57 —

July 1997
Asheville, NC

The baby is four and a half months for real, but three and a half to Ethan and Robert. It gets harder every day to remember that their timeline isn't the real one. Late at night when Robert is working and I don't have to play, Ethan is asleep, and I'm alone, I have to remind myself. When it's just me and the baby, I put my hands on my stomach and remember what's true.

Robert rubs my belly all the time. "You're carrying precious cargo," he says.

I feel like a steamer trunk.

On the fridge in his kitchen, he keeps a list of all the dad things he wants to do. Every time I'm over, he's added something new. Fishing and riding bikes and seeing a Rolling Stones concert, camping in the Great Smoky Mountains, sailing on Lake Julian, Frisbee at the park, building a tree house, catching fireflies in a jar.

"I was raised by my stepdad," Robert tells me one night while we're lying on the couch after dinner. He runs his fingers through my hair, coaxing out the tangles. "I always felt like a guest. I can't wait to have someone who's mine."

His fingers snag a knot in my hair, and he thinks that's why my eyes start tearing. "I'm so sorry," he says.

The baby kicks for Ethan, but not for Robert. He keeps trying.

Ethan calls the baby "our little overachiever" for kicking so early. Every time he says it, I feel like it really means *April is a big fat liar.* I feel like they should just know. They should have figured it out. Sometimes I even hate them for not knowing, but I love them too much to tell the truth.

Since Robert works late, I stay at Ethan's mostly. They don't want me to be alone, just in case. They're overprotective.

Robert buys an old dresser for my room at Ethan's. He strips it down in the garage and paints it white to match the daybed. "We'll move it into the baby's room next door, after," he says, like it's already decided where I'll live. I like having two houses. I like living with Ethan. I don't tell Robert that one house would make me feel caged. I don't tell him that sometimes even two houses doesn't feel like enough space.

On the nights I stay at Ethan's, I think about calling Justin. I listen to Ethan brushing his teeth in the bathroom. I hear him spit, swish, spit again. Pee, flush, walk into the hallway. I've memorized his patterns like a song. Two steps, creak. One step, creak. Five steps, big creak.

"Night, Angel," he yells.

"Night, E.T.," I yell back. "Bite the bedbugs." I hear his bare feet on the stairs, and then I hear the bedroom door close and pop open and close harder. I imagine little white paint chips falling to the floor.

I think about leaving and driving to Binghamton to tell Justin. I remember running my finger along the dent in his chin and the spikes of his new haircut.

Justin's shirt doesn't smell like him anymore. It smells like a rabbit cage from the funny little cedar cubes Ethan puts everywhere.

Ethan thinks the baby is a girl. He says I'm "carrying high." I'm sure it's a boy. I don't know why. I just am. I want to name him Max. Robert likes Rierden. It was his mother's maiden name. Ethan likes Ethan. We never discuss what his last name will be. I'm going to give him Justin's shirt someday. Maybe when he leaves for college. It will be cool and retro by then, like bellbottoms or a Stones T-shirt. I won't tell him where it came from.

Chapter 58

I go to Dr. Katim in secret, alone. Twenty-dollar bills counted out in my purse ahead of time. I still don't have insurance. Robert keeps saying we need to fix that. I worry about the paper trail. Somewhere on something it will say how old the baby really is.

"Does Robert know?" she asks.

"I can't," I say. I cover my face with my hands and sob. Dr. Katim hugs me, awkwardly, around my arms. She smells like Listerine.

It is a boy, just like I knew. She gives me another picture. When I get home, I peel back the lining of my guitar case and hide it with the first one.

The next morning, Ethan leaves early, before breakfast. Robert cooks eggs over easy. There are flowers on the table. He doesn't talk while we eat. I don't talk either. I'm afraid of what I might say. I drop my fork by accident, or maybe just to hear a noise, to have something happen. He goes to pick it up and then he's kneeling. There's a ring in a box and he's shaking. "I should have asked you a long time ago," he says. "I just—I was scared. Don't say no. Please don't say no. I want us to be a family."

Of course, I say yes. I can't say anything else.

The ring was his grandmother's. He wants to go to city hall. He wants to be married before the baby comes.

He holds me. My heart could shatter like river ice all over the kitchen floor.

— Chapter 59 —

I leave almost everything. I take my guitar, a few skirts, and the shirts that still cover my belly all the way. I leave my Ginger dress and Robert's grandmother's ring. I leave a note for Ethan. I tell him everything. I think it's better that way. That Robert doesn't have to read it. That it's coming from a friend. I know it isn't fair to Ethan, but what I've done is already unfair. Nothing will make it less wrong in the end. At least they'll have answers and Ethan won't feel like he has to stay here for me.

I leave the note on Ethan's sun porch. I leave him my buck knife. Prop the knife and the note up next to his canvas, the brown painting with the squiggles and curves. He's been working on it for so long now, so many layers of color and light. I see it all of a sudden. It's me. It's my hair falling over the body of my guitar. It's brown and gold and soft and beautiful. It's me and it's what Ethan thinks of me and it's almost enough to make it impossible to leave. It's almost enough to keep lying, but I can't. I love them too much. I can't make them responsible for this part of me they had nothing to do with.

— *Part Three* —

— Chapter 60 —

November 1997
Bradenton Beach, FL

It's twelve hundred and sixty miles from Anna Maria Island to Little River. I know, because I measured out the map key with a strand of my hair. My car has developed a wheeze, I'm two islands away from the mainland, and it's a fucking Sunday afternoon—so I'm stuck in bumper to bumper traffic with all the tourists clearing the island to get back to their real lives, where they don't wear Hawaiian shirts that smell like mothballs and ask the poor pregnant house singer at Ollie's to play *Margaritaville* every single goddamn night.

I'd rather stay on the island, but if I have to go, I'd like to speed. I'm eight months now. Max spends all his time doing tap routines on my bladder, like maybe he learned from Ethan and me and all the Fred Astaire movies when he was just starting to be. I'm going to have to stop so many times that it will take me eons to get there.

I'd rather stay as far away from Little River as humanly possible. I'd rather eat rusty nails and slurp down dirty shoelaces like noodles. But what

449

kind of person doesn't go see her dying father? What kind of person doesn't even go back for that?

I'd gone to the pay phone outside the library to call Margo at two o'clock because that's our schedule. Every Sunday. We started up again when I got to Florida. She'd update me on Ida Winton's latest food aversion and Gary's new twenty-five-year-old whore of a girlfriend, and I would promise her I was fine.

Mostly I talked about the tides and oranges and confirmed what The Weather Channel told her about Florida that day. I never said anything about the baby. I didn't know how. I didn't want her to tell me to come home.

Today when I called, the phone didn't even ring. Margo grabbed the receiver on the first microscopic blip of sound.

"Hey, honey," she said softly.

"Hey, Margs, what's up?"

She took a breath I could hear.

"What is it?"

"Sweetie, your dad's dying," she said, and burst into tears.

I'd never heard her cry before. I didn't know what to say. It was too much at once to even feel anything.

"Lung cancer. It's bad. I don't think he has much longer."

"Why didn't you tell me?" I asked. "Last Sunday? The week before that?"

"Girlie, your dad is the only one who knew. Not even Irene." She let out a big sob. "He didn't want treatment. Said he didn't want to lose his hair. Likes smoking better than he likes living."

"How long?" I touched my fingers to each of the phone buttons without pressing them in.

"Maybe a week, maybe a few days."

"How did Irene not know? How did she let it get so bad?" I spelled out my name with the phone buttons—two-seven-seven-four-five.

"You know how he gets in his own way. Him and Irene haven't been getting along for a while. He's been living in the motorhome for the past few months. Hiding from her. She's with him now. That woman is some kind of saint, I tell you. It's not her fault she didn't know."

"I got to go," I said, because I wasn't in the mood to hear Margo talking about Irene like a goddess. "Ollie needs me to help prep for dinner shift, you know?"

"Look, girlie. I'm not saying you've got to be here. Lord knows you got to have buckets and buckets of feelings about this. I'm just saying that if you want to be here, or you think someday maybe it'll be hard that you weren't here, then you should come."

"Love you," I said, and hung up the phone before she could say anything back.

I walked out to the beach and thought about staying. Jumping in the ocean and floating on my back, watching my belly bob in the waves, forgetting I ever even had a father. But instead I got in my car.

— Chapter 61 —

I usually like the drive north from Florida. I call ahead, book gigs at places I've played before, take three or four weeks to wind my way up the coast. I like to drive the scenic roads and watch the palm trees disappear into hills and fall colors. I visit all the pockets of people I know and find some new pockets to replace the ones that disappear. If my friend Slim has work for me, I head to Nashville and record backup tracks for a few days. Otherwise I'll drive straight to Savannah and spend a couple nights singing with the house band at a bar on Bay Street. Camp a few nights on Cape May, then make my way to Red Bank to play at The Downtown and stay with Cole while I book my next leg of gigs. It's the way I pass time. A system that works for me. It's not a bad life. I get to be nothing but wonderful to people I love and move on before it goes stale. But on this trip there's no time for gigs or visits or seeing old friends or following the coast.

My plan was to stay south this year. All summer, when I wasn't playing gigs, I waited tables for Ollie. Took every shift my swollen feet would allow. I found a house on Bimini Bay with a roof partly covered with tarps, like the money for construction ran out. Plumbing still worked just fine and no one ever came around. Crashing there and living on shift meals let me save up money to rent a real apartment for a few months after the baby comes. Maria, one of the other waitresses at Ollie's, has a toddler and said maybe we could trade off babysitting and shifts. I tamped down my panic about settling down with the idea that when Max is a little older, we'll get to hit the road again. I want his world to be big, not just an island. I want him to know the ocean, but I want him to see seasons and meet all the people in my pockets too.

Somehow, I am sure he'll be a traveling baby, happy in his car seat, letting the sound of the road lull him to sleep. Once we reach the mainland, Max gets quiet in my belly while I drive, so maybe he's already in love with the road. I'm happy to have him with me. To feel like I'm not completely alone. I don't like the middle of Florida—cows and farmland and I feel like alligators and giant snakes must be lurking in every body of water. I drive straight through to the Georgia border. I don't drink anything so I won't have to stop to pee.

Once, when I was in Boston, my friend Slim called the bar where I was playing to say he was recording a single for some country singer and my exact voice was what he needed to fill out the sound. I drove all the way from Boston to Nashville after my gig. Right on through. I couldn't see straight by the time I got there, but Slim pumped me full of coffee and tuned my guitar and I was fine. The song didn't really take off, but every once in a while, if I leave a country station on long enough, I'll hear it on the radio and I can pick out my voice singing *oohs* and *awahoos* through the static. That road trip was killer. This one is worse—I don't even want to get where I'm going—but I make it over a thousand miles with only four stops and a quick nap, pregnancy bladder and back pain and everything.

Fifth stop is when I call Margo just after I cross the Pennsylvania border to tell her I'm four or five hours away.

"Oh, girlie," she says. "He's already gone."

And here I am, some dirty, stinky, hungry, pregnant girl, crying into a truck stop pay phone like a damn country song.

"I drove too slow," I whisper, two dimes later when I can finally talk again.

"You know that old saying about procrastination on your part doesn't equal an emergency on mine?" Margo says. "Your father made this an emergency, not you. He had three years to make things better. He had three years to come looking for you."

She listens to me sob on the phone and there's something about knowing she's listening that makes my tears seem less futile. She's my witness. She always has been.

She asks me to come for the funeral.

"I can't do it," I tell her. "I can't come back. I don't want to see Irene and the boy and I don't want to see that baby. I don't want to. He's already dead. It's not like he cares if I'm there."

"Funerals are for the living," she says. "To hold up the people who get left behind."

"I don't want to hold Irene up. She wouldn't want me to."

"I could hold *you* up," Margo says.

I feel like I need her.

Chapter 62

I haven't thrown up since about five months in. But when I get off I-90 and I'm on back roads and everything is familiar, I feel it building. Starts low and gets bigger. I sweat. No matter how hard I grip the steering wheel, I can't stop shaking, and finally, I have to pull off the road and puke in a drainage ditch. I don't even feel better after. Just spent and sour. I swish my mouth out with some flat warm Sprite left in the bottom of a bottle that's been in my car for who knows how long. It's all I have left.

Margo's Diner looks the same, only smaller than I remembered it. Everything about Little River seems smaller than it used to be.

Margo must have been watching out the window, because the second my car pulls into a spot up front, she runs out the door, waving her hands like I might miss her. She looks smaller too. Her hair is washed out and less bubbly than it used to be. Her face is pale and bony. The breakup with Gary was messy. She's still wearing one of her itty-bitty skirts, but even her killer gams look like they need a bit more oomph.

She tries to open my car door before I've even unlocked it. I think about driving away. I'm scared about what she'll say. What she'll think of me. But her face in my window and her big, bright smile make me remember that she's never ever said anything mean to me on purpose. No reason she'd start now.

"Girlie," she says when I open the door, "you are a sight for— Oh my god!" She sees my belly and looks like you could just about knock her over with a chicken feather.

My legs wobble when I stand up. "This is Max," I say, resting my hand on top of my bump.

She's quiet for a sec, staring at me in the glow of the diner lights. I hold my breath.

She reaches out to touch my face like maybe I'm a hallucination. "Now, I know you don't tell me everything, but how did you go all this time"—she arcs her hand outward from her own belly—"without saying a word about it?"

"I guess I didn't want to worry you," I say.

"Didn't want to worry me? My well of worry for you goes all the way to the core of the Earth, girlie."

She laughs, but I see how I've been a weight she's carried and I think she sees that I understand that now.

She kisses my forehead.

"If I didn't love you *and* this baby so much, I'd strangle you." She pats my belly and says, "You just wait until Grandma Margo tells you all her stories about your mom." Then she looks at me, eyes full of tears, like she's hoping I won't object to Max having her for a grandma.

I hug her the best I can with my belly in between us.

The diner is empty. It's just before closing time. Margo feeds me a burger and fries and a milkshake for calcium and a big plate of spinach because she says I need extra iron. She drowns the spinach in butter because she knows it's the only way I'll get it down. We sit in a booth, since I'm way too huge to try and balance on a stool at the counter like we used to.

She stares at my belly a lot. I wonder if she's trying to picture Max, all curled up and napping in there. Maybe sucking his thumb. Babies do that sometimes, before they're even born. I try to picture him all the time. I wonder if he'll be familiar when I get to meet him.

Margo doesn't ask about his father, about where I'm planning to live with him, or even when he's due. Over the years, she's gotten used to the idea that I'll only tell her what I want her to know. But I wish she'd ask, because it's hard to just say things sometimes. I wish I could talk to her about Robert and ask if she thinks I did the right thing, but I don't know how to start. I only tell her about Ethan, that I stayed at his house for a while and we dressed like Fred and Ginger, and he made a painting that looked like lines and curves but it was really me.

"I'm glad you have solid friends in the world," she says, because she doesn't know about how I always end up leaving them all.

We see Mrs. Spencer walking slow past the diner like it's normal for her to take a late-night stroll through town. She stares at us through the window, but when Margo waves, she looks away like she didn't see us at all. I wonder how much she talks to Matty. If she knows I saw him about nine months ago and she's worried Max is somehow his. I wonder who saw me and called her, if the whole town already knows I'm here and pregnant. Probably it took ten minutes for everyone to find out.

"That woman," Margo says, "thinks she's pretty high and mighty these days. Her big star of a son bought her a Cadillac, which she believes gives her perpetual right of way." She rolls her eyes. "Like Cathy Spencer needed an excuse to be a bigger bitch."

It's funny to think of Mrs. Spencer as a bitch. I always just thought of her as a grown-up.

"I saw him," I tell Margo, "Matty. This spring. I think they did his teeth."

"Like they aren't real?"

"Exactly. They don't look like they used to."

"Amazing." Margo shakes her head. "What will they think of next? They nip things that don't need tucking. Give fake teeth to someone with perfectly decent ones. That boy had fine teeth to begin with. He never had any problems chewing."

I yawn. I can't help myself.

"Well," Margo says. "What's say we close up here and turn in for the night. You must be exhausted."

I think of the motorhome, the way it used to smell like mildew and rust. I think about driving down the dirt road to get there. I worry I'll end up puking on the side of the road again. "I don't think I can do it, Margo. Go to the motorhome. I don't think—"

"Don't be silly. I have my couch all pulled out and made up for me to sleep on so you can have my bed."

"You do?"

"Of course," she says. "Your father can't very well yell at me for overstepping my bounds now, can he?" She claps her hand over her mouth. Her face goes pale. "I'm sorry. I just—I always felt bad taking you back to that motorhome. I didn't mean to . . ."

I'm ready to cry, to know that Margo might have actually wanted me. To know that she really would have taken me home with her if she could. But I think if I cry she will and if she cries I'll cry harder and between us, we might have too many tears to ever stop. So instead, I say, "I can sleep on the couch. Really, it's okay," because I can't let any of it sink in. I could drown, so easily, I could drown.

"April," she says, grabbing my arm and shaking it, "use that delicate condition to your advantage. Take the bed."

Margo's apartment looks pretty much the same as it always has, except she has a cat now. "I'm one of those ladies," she tells me when a dark blur darts across the living room as we kick our shoes off. "That's Stuart." She points to the chair he's taken refuge under. Yellow eyes stare back at us.

Later, when we're gabbing in her kitchen over a piece of chocolate cake I just know will give me indigestion, Stuart emerges and rubs his skinny little body against my leg. I can feel his ribs ripple along my calf. He's inky black except for a white muzzle and three out of four white feet. He has too many toes on each paw and a cauliflower ear. He's not pretty.

"I didn't take you for a cat person."

"I'm not," she says, reaching down and swishing her fingers together. He runs to her and rubs his face into the side of her hand. "I'm getting lonely in my old age, I guess." She smiles this sad, tired smile.

And something about all of it just makes me fall apart—Margo being so lonely that she has to get an ugly little cat, and my father dying, and the fact that all I can picture is some bones on a hospital bed in the shape of him, hooked up to machines like the ones that flashed and beeped while Matty was in a coma on *All My Days*. Something about the whole thing makes me so sad that I can't even stand it. "What kind of a person am I that I wasn't even here?" I say. "I should have driven faster."

"Sweetie," Margo says, handing me a napkin, "you know I've done my best to never say a bad thing about your father. You search back and think on what I've said and you'll be hard-pressed to find many ill-meaning words." She sighs. "I did that for you and I thought I was doing the best I could. But not now when you're beating yourself up. He made this choice. He chose not to get treatment and push everyone away. He made the choice to not go after you when you left."

"Gary told him not to," I say. "I begged you, so you got Gary to tell him to let me go. It was *me*. He was just doing what I wanted."

Margo takes a deep breath and presses her lips together, like she's holding back her words until they get in line. "When Gary went to talk to him that time, it wasn't so he'd give you the car. It was to make him come get you. Gary told him that no man lets a little girl go out on her own like that. No man lets his responsibilities pass him by. That's what really happened."

I feel the same drop in my stomach and flush in my veins that I get when I'm driving away and realize I've left something behind. Margo pulls another napkin from the holder on the table and gives it to me. Mine is soaked already.

"I'm sorry," she says. "I thought I was protecting you. I tricked myself into thinking you wouldn't notice what a bad father he was if I didn't point it out too much. I thought it was better for you to think he was letting you go because he thought it was best than for you to know that he wasn't even thinking. Don't you go feeling responsible for his failings. They aren't yours, April."

"When both parents crap out on you—I'm the common denominator, you know."

Margo grabs my hand and squeezes. "You're the gift that came from two broken people. They were weak, and hurt, and cowardly, and somehow managed to make this miracle girl who is so full of piss and vinegar that she survived it all. Maybe you need to mourn who they weren't. Maybe that's what you're here for now."

"You're too good to me, Margo," I say, wiping my face with the napkin.

"I don't think I've been good enough," she says, and I realize she's crying too.

Chapter 63

M argo is gone before I wake up. She told me last night she was headed out early to make egg casseroles and crumb cake for anyone who stops by the diner after the funeral. Said she didn't want "that poor Irene" to feel like she had to feed people on top of everything else.

I call to her anyway, wishing for an answer, hearing only the rattle of the heater. I have a crying hangover. Puffy face. My nose feels like it's filled with cement. It's strange to be in Margo's apartment alone. When I walk into the living room her cat jumps off the coffee table to hide under the couch.

In the kitchen there's a note, a strawberry Danish, and a glass of orange juice on the counter. The kitchen smells like coffee, but she didn't leave me any. I'm sure it was on purpose. There's a navy blue maternity dress hanging over the back of one of the kitchen chairs. The note says: *Thought you might need this. Love, M.* I wonder if it was one of Irene's maternity dresses. It has a drop waist, a pleated skirt, and a square flappy collar with white trim like a sailor's uniform. You know, because of all the pregnant ladies in the Navy.

I think about cutting the collar off and trying to

make it something else, the way Carly would, but my father never cared what I looked like when he was alive I don't think it'll start to matter now. My long skirt with the stretchy waist is good enough.

On the back of the note she's written the calling hours and the funeral time. There's a viewing this morning. Like I'm supposed to go down to the church and have people stare at me while I look at his dead body so they can spend the next three years talking about how I didn't react the right way. So they can pretend they know more about me than they really do.

I take the note with me so I'll remember what time the service is. I know enough to know it won't feel good to see the motorhome, but I can't stop myself.

— Chapter 64 —

Mrs. Varnick's place is abandoned now. Margo says they had to put her in a home last year. Her son wanted her to live with them, but after years of Mrs. Varnick calling her daughter-in-law "the fat cow," she was what Margo called "persona not gratas."

Weeds grow up fast. There are sumac saplings where Mrs. Varnick used to park her car. Virginia creeper curling into a broken window.

And then, at the end of the road, there's the motorhome. It's not a clubhouse. It's a closet. A tomb. It's where he left me so he could forget I existed, the way Margo sends her fake Christmas tree to storage after New Year's.

The white metal sides have rusty stains at every bolt, and one of the windows is broken. I feel like I should go in and search for some kind of understanding. Or maybe to clean everything, because whatever mess is in there shouldn't be all that's left of someone. But I can't make my feet take me to the door. I don't want to see what he left behind. I don't want to remember what it felt like to live there. The whole motorhome leans like it might tip over, and I'm not exactly light on my feet.

The thing of it is, the motorhome doesn't look

much worse than it did when I lived in it. It hasn't changed enough. I feel like if I look hard, I could still find splinters from my guitar in the dirt. I can almost feel the sting of my father's hand on my cheek.

I walk out to the flooded house foundation. It's so overgrown that I have to step around roots and bushwhack my way through. Something thorny scratches me and leaves a thin line of blood across the back of my hand. I sit on the edge of the foundation and rest my feet on the first step of what would have been the stairs to our basement. The water comes up to the step below, a film of leaves across the surface. It smells like rot.

It's November again. Everything is dead or sleeping. I feel like it's always November here. There's never enough warmth or light or any of the things a person really needs. I poke at the leaves with a stick and think about who my parents weren't until the cold seeps in through my skirt and I start to worry it might not be good for Max. My jacket won't close over my belly anymore. I wonder if he can get cold in there.

— Chapter 65 —

I get to the church early. It's this stone building with stained-glass windows and steps that look like they were designed just for wedding pictures. It's probably the fanciest building in Little River. I've never been inside the chapel, just the basement for rummage sales. It's weird to think about my dad walking through that arched doorway with Irene on Sundays. He didn't even believe in God until she made him. And it's not the kind of church that's like, *Jesus was nice so you should be too* and feeds homeless people and all that stuff. It's more like *Here's a bunch of ways you can judge people and feel better about yourself for it*—the kind of church that would tell Ethan he was going to hell.

I sit in my car. I'm waiting to sneak in right before the service starts, so I can sit at the back without having to deal with all the people walking past me. But while I'm sitting there watching everyone go in, I start getting mad. The whole town shows up: Mrs. Hunter, Ida Winton, Molly Walker, Gary and his whore of a girlfriend, the Spencers. None of these people even liked my father. And all of them knew about me. They knew where I lived. They knew that he left me. They left me too. Instead of thinking

469

that maybe a kid who lives in a motorhome in the woods might want to come over for cookies and milk after school, they told their kids not to play with me. They looked at me like I should be ashamed for existing, because my parents were divorced and my shoes were ratty and my hair was stringy and I always had dirt under my fingernails. I was something they could catch if they got too close, like my shame would rub off on them. They were happy to forget me, same as my dad. And now they're all here in their Sunday best like they're going to get God points for showing up to mourn a man who wasn't even worth it.

I don't go in.

The crowd from the parking lot slows to a trickle. Someone closes the doors and there's nothing to see. I watch anyway. Like maybe my dad will sneak out the back. Like maybe it was all a big sick joke.

Twenty minutes later, I'm still sitting in my car. The silence is making me crazy, but I don't want to play the radio and drain the battery. I've already turned the car on twice to heat it up. I pull out my map, study the roads that look like worms tangled across the states and think about where I want to go next.

There's a knock on the passenger window.

"What are you doing in my car?"

It's Mrs. Ivory. She's got a kid with her. A

little girl with pigtails in a pink dress is twirling around on the sidewalk, watching her skirt spin out. One of Mrs. Ivory's grandchildren. She has about fifty of them.

The passenger window doesn't like to roll back up once I've rolled it down, so I haul myself out of the car and walk around to the sidewalk to talk to her.

"Mrs. Ivory," I say. The girl is small and hides behind Mrs. Ivory's skirt when I get close.

"Oh, Autumn!" Mrs. Ivory says, putting her hand over her heart. Her fingers are so thin that her old ruby ring hangs between her first and second knuckles. "It's only you! I thought I was being carjacked."

I don't even know what to say. I don't think it will help to explain things. She was barely on this side of sensible when I left. What do I care if she thinks I'm my mother? What does it matter anyway? I'll be gone again momentarily.

"You have some nerve showing your face around here!" Mrs. Ivory says, her eyes scrunched up and mean.

"What—"

"Leaving your husband and this one." She pulls the little girl's hand.

The little girl looks like a picture I saw of me when I was that age, when I still had a mother to put me in pigtails and clean dresses.

"You broke his heart," Mrs. Ivory says.

"He broke mine," I tell her.

"Well, I don't want to get into it," Mrs. Ivory says. "You'll have your day of reckoning."

The little girl doesn't even have a jacket on. I'm worried she's cold.

"What are you doing out here?" I ask Mrs. Ivory.

"Well, this one needs a snack," she says, pointing to the girl. "So I'm going to drive her to my house."

The girl hangs on to two of Mrs. Ivory's fingers and uses the toe of her patent leather shoe to poke at a crack in the sidewalk. She's going to get scuff marks. I'm sure her mother will be mad.

"Do you have my keys?" Mrs. Ivory says. She shakes off the girl's grip on her hand and walks around to the driver's side.

"Mrs. Ivory, you can't drive."

"Nonsense," she says. "What do you know?"

"I'm here to drive you," I say, changing tactics, praying it works. "I'll take you home."

I open the passenger door for her and she gets in without much more argument.

The little girl watches me. She has icy blue eyes like my father, the same hard stare, and it feels like seeing a ghost. I open the door to the back seat. She shakes her head no.

"Yeah," I say. "Mrs. Ivory is watching you. I'm taking you to her house. For cookies."

That gets her and she climbs on the back seat. I have to help her up, but it's hard to with my belly in the way. Buckling her in is also a challenge. She wiggles around and I can barely fit myself back there. I'm pretty sure she should be in a booster seat or something. She's so little.

On the drive to Mrs. Ivory's house, the little girl busies herself sticking her hand down the crack between the seats. I hope there's nothing gross in there, nothing sharp that could hurt her.

"My son John-John won first place in the science fair. Did you hear?" Mrs. Ivory says. "He trained a field mouse to run through a maze. They gave him a big blue ribbon."

John-John has got to be at least forty now. Maybe fifty.

"What's her name?" I ask, pointing to the back seat. Margo told me when Irene had the baby, but I said I didn't want to know anything about it. Maybe the baby was a boy. Maybe I'm only making ghosts in my head.

"Oh," Mrs. Ivory says, giving me a blank look. "Oh, that's my daughter Mary Beth. Don't you remember?"

I know I can't leave this kid alone with Mrs. Ivory. But it's not even a problem, because when we get to her place, Mrs. Ivory gets out of the car and walks into the house, without so much as saying goodbye to me or the kid.

"What's your name?" I ask the girl. I turn

and look at her, trying not to notice the way the flyaway hairs around her temples curl just like mine.

"Ju-ly," she says.

"Julie?"

"No! July!" She giggles and bobs her head back and forth, rolling her eyes. "Aprilmayjunejuly!" she shouts in her singsongy little voice. "August! September! Ah-tober! Ah-tober!"

What kind of idiot names their kid July? April is bad enough, but at least it's a real name. Thank goodness she wasn't born in December or on Independence Day or Halloween.

"What's *your* name?" she asks, pointing at me, like I won't know who she's talking to otherwise.

"April."

"That's my sister's name!" July says, kicking her feet against the seat and pulling on her seat belt. It sags around her. I'm afraid she's going to slip through the belt and fall on the floor. I wish I had a car seat for her. And a jacket and a snack. I wish she had a better father.

"I know," I say, taking a deep, slow breath. "I think I'm your sister." I back out of Mrs. Ivory's driveway so I can return July to the church.

July laughs like I told her a joke. "Why you have a big fat belly?" she asks.

"That's your nephew."

July laughs again. I watch her in the rearview mirror. She's beautiful.

"You're going to be an aunt," I say, just so I can hear her talk more. She's really smart, I think. I don't know very much about these things yet, but for a kid so little it seems like she has a lot of words and she says them pretty well. "What do you think about being an aunt?"

"Ewww!" She wrinkles up her nose. "An ant bited my finger in the sandbox." She holds up her hand to show me which one. It's her middle finger and it's really funny, this pretty little girl in her frilly dress, sitting on the back seat giving me the finger. I try hard not to laugh. I don't want her to learn bad things. "I squished it," she shrieks, pinching her fingers together to show me how.

When we get to the church, Irene is standing in the street. The church doors are still closed and no one else is around. It's just Irene, right in the middle of the road, red faced, crying.

I park in the same spot, get out, and open the door to help July with her seat belt.

"Oh my god!" Irene says, running over, crouching to hug July, lifting her out of the car. "Oh my god! April!" She looks up at me. Her eyes are so puffy. I almost feel bad for her.

"What is wrong with you?" I say. "Leaving her alone with Mrs. Ivory! She doesn't even know who anyone is anymore."

"I didn't!" Irene says, sobbing and hugging July to her chest. "She was with my cousin at the back of the church and then she wasn't anymore and I don't— I—" She stops talking and just falls apart. Grabs at July like she's making sure all her parts are still there. All four limbs, every finger, both ears.

July is shell-shocked. She reaches for her mom's barrette and tries to pull it out of her hair. Irene just lets her.

"Thank you for bringing her back," Irene says.

"Yeah," I say. I turn around to get in my car. I don't need to talk to Irene. I don't need to have this conversation.

"I named her after you," she says. "I mean, sort of. You know, like names that go together."

"You left me there," I say.

"I'm sorry, April," she says. "I'm so sorry."

"Well, that's good. That just fixes everything."

"I had these blinders on," Irene says. "I wanted a dad for David. I kept thinking that somehow your dad would turn into the man I needed him to be."

I watch her for a minute, watch tears rolling down her cheeks. "He was really good at not being who anyone needed him to be," I say.

The doors to the church open and everyone starts the reverse trickle to the parking lot. I don't want to be their entertainment.

"Take care of July," I say, and wave to my

sister. She waves back with her perfect little hand.

I cross the street to my car and don't look back. I'll call Margo from the road to say goodbye. It's easier that way.

— Chapter 66 —

It's after midnight when I finally make it to Binghamton. I took every back road and lingered at rest stops, steeling my nerves and searching for words. The walk from my car to Justin's door feels longer than the whole entire drive. The baby kicks. I have to knock for a long time before anyone answers. I worry he doesn't even live there anymore, that I won't be able to find him at all. But I have to try.

Through the window, I see some guy with messy hair and sleepy eyes turn on the porch light. He opens the door and says, "What?" his face freezing when he sees my belly. "I don't know you," he says, loud and fast, like he's reassuring himself, and I realize that I am every college boy's worst nightmare. That I'm about to be Justin's.

"Justin," I say, and it's all I can say before the guy runs from the door and yells for him. I hear bare feet on the wood floor, harsh whispers. Someone says, "What the fuck?" And then there's Justin, in his boxer shorts and nothing else. He closes the door behind him and stands out on the porch with me, even though it's freezing. Even though a few minutes ago he was sleeping soundly with no idea that his child had the hiccups and was kicking my ribcage.

"It's not mine," he says in a sharp whisper. "You have to leave."

"I'm sorry," I say. "I should have told you sooner."

"It's not mine."

"It is."

"I don't know what you're trying to pull. I have a girlfriend." The way he tips his head when he says *girlfriend* makes me think that she's upstairs. Maybe that's why he's being so quiet. Why he won't let me in. I step closer to the house, so if she's looking out the window she can't see me. I don't want to make things any harder on him than they already are. I don't want to hurt him. I just want him to know. I just want him to help.

"I'm graduating," he says. "I have a job lined up. I won't let you ruin it. We used a condom. I always used a condom with you. It's not mine." His chest is getting red and splotchy from the cold.

"There wasn't anyone else," I say. "There wasn't anyone it could have been."

"Bullshit," he says. "You drive around and sleep in other people's houses and fuck anyone who looks at you the right way. You think I don't know that?"

"You're the only one it could be." I don't know why I thought Justin would somehow be thrilled that I'm telling him the truth. Like I expected a fucking parade for being honest.

"No," he says, "I'm the one with a future to kill. With something you can steal."

"Justin—"

"Don't think I never noticed how you always took something. Money missing. Other stuff. I don't owe you more."

"That wasn't what it was. I always—I always liked you."

"You're basically a prostitute," he says, opening the door to the house, "and you need to leave."

"It's a boy," I tell him. "Your baby."

He shuts the door behind him and turns the porch light off.

I sit in my car across the street digging my fingernails into my palm. I can't bring myself to drive away, just in case Justin will suddenly come running out and invite me in and put his hands on my belly and he'll feel Max kick and everything will change for him. Everything will change for us. I would give up the road. I would give up my guitar. I would give up everything in a second if I could have a good home for me and Max. A real place with a floor that isn't on wheels, where there aren't any lies left to catch up with me. I fall asleep waiting and by the time I wake up, the cars in the driveway are gone and no one answers when I knock on the door.

— Chapter 67 —

Driving will fix things. Changing direction. Gaining distance, getting to the kind of numb where miles fill in for feelings. I like the way the road sounds. I like the rhythms that come from the tires and the windshield wipers, rain and the rush of wind, and how the sounds change when I raise or lower the window. My dad used to say that good folk music is etched with the rhythm of the road. I always listen for it in songs and I find it in the best ones. So when I'm driving, I pay attention to all the noise; I take in the smells and everything I see and everything I am and I start my song. It begins like a story in my head and then somewhere in the middle it isn't about me anymore—my love songs aren't about Adam or Robert, that song about leaving home isn't about Ithaca or Little River, *Missing You* is about a made-up girl missing a made-up friend. It's not about Carly.

I can make a better song when it's less about the truth of what happened and more about making everything fit together in the most perfect way. Then when I sing my songs in front of an audience, it's safer. I'm not giving everything I have, laid out for them like a flawless map of my insides. I'm singing songs about a parallel me, in some other voice, in code they don't even know. And when I'm driving and the words are all coming together, I feel the most like myself and like someone else entirely at the very same time.

I drive to Ithaca. It's my magnet. Every time I'm near, it pulls. It's the place I'd stay if I could ever stay someplace. It's the place I wish I'd never left. I'm tired of fighting it. I just need to go.

Carly is gone, I'm sure. Rosemary probably is too. So I walk through The Commons. It's one of those weird days when it's way warmer than it should be. It's even sunny. Like the weather is trying to fool us into thinking it isn't November and winter won't be long and cold and cloudy.

I walk past Decadence. It's called Juna's now. It's still a coffee place, but it's not dark and moody and perfect anymore. It's all yellow tile and big windows.

I get a cup of tea from the bakery across the way, from the little lady with the long white braids. She doesn't recognize me. She sees kids come and go over and over. I'm just another face.

I sit outside on a bench and watch people, looking for faces I recognize. I see all the same types, but not the same people. It's the next crop of college kids. The faces who fill in for the ones who have left. I know it's ridiculous to look for who I'm looking for, but I have a flash of a perfect happy ending in my head. Of Adam and me raising Max together, making pancakes for him in the morning. And then the more I think of it, the less it feels like our ending. That's not the life I want for Max, those lies I'd still have to tell.

Adam was my port in the storm and maybe I was his. It's easy to fall in love with someone when you need them, but that doesn't make it real or right. I don't think how we were in our time together is how we'd always be. There's a way you hold yourself in when love and need get tangled. It's hard to know what would last and what would wear too thin to keep.

I hope the thing Adam remembers about me isn't the part where I left. I hope what he remembers is that for a moment we shared a bright little corner of life. That's how I will choose to remember him. But I want to believe that love can exist on its own. I want Max to believe that too.

I stop looking for Adam and I just look. Watch the wind scrape dry leaves across the concrete and the way the light comes through the bare tree branches. I watch this guy with a wiry red beard, sitting at a table by the window at Juna's, reading a battered paperback, chewing on his bottom lip. And then I see Carly, through the window. Her hair is long now, black and past her shoulder blades. She's wearing a blue dress and she has a big green tattoo winding its way up her arm into her sleeve. I can't tell what it is. A snake, maybe. A vine. She looks like a mermaid or a superhero or a warrior. She looks beautiful. She pours coffee for the paperback guy. He says something to her. She throws her head back and laughs a real laugh. The kind you can't fake. And I love that she looks so happy, so different and new. Like maybe she doesn't hurt the way she used to. Maybe I don't have to either.

I walk back toward my car. On the way, I stop in Woolworth's and buy a big envelope, the yellow kind with the metal clip to close it.

When I get in my car, I carefully strip the lining of my guitar case and shove all my letters in the envelope. The thin metal clip scrapes at the calluses on the tips of my fingers as I press it closed.

I scribble *Carly* in bumpy letters on the top with an old marker so spent I have to lick the felt to get it to write anything. I lock up my car and walk back to The Commons. There's a crack in the bottom of one of my boots. A click when I step with my right foot. I'm not sure if I can hear it or I'm just feeling it, the way the broken rubber sticks to itself and breaks apart every time my foot flexes.

I sit on the bench again and watch Carly ring up customers at the register until she walks away and I can't see her through the window anymore.

484

I get up and walk closer and I still can't see her. She must be in back. Hopefully it's a smoke break and I have time. I want to run, make it quick, but I figure it's better to walk in. Not call attention to myself. I don't think I can run anyway.

The bell on the door may as well be a siren. Part of me wants her to catch me. The rest of me doesn't want to hurt anyone anymore. I don't want to impose on the life she has now. I just want her to know that even though I left, I never stopped thinking about her. I just want her to know what happened.

I place the envelope on the counter near the register and walk away before anyone comes out of the kitchen to try to take my order. I walk out the door and the bell rings again. It's all there. I've left it. Everything. The paperback guy watches me, still chewing at his bottom lip as I walk past the window.

— Chapter 68 —

The campground is closed for the season. I park my car off the road down the street and drag a blanket and my guitar around the gate. I can barely walk. It's more of a waddle and all the muscles in my back ache. But I make it to the right place and build a fire with twigs and left-behind wood. I play Dylan songs to the lake, even though my belly makes me hold the guitar funny and my singing is breathy because my lungs don't have enough room anymore. One song after another. My fingers throb and my throat is raw. *Don't Think Twice, It's All Right* bleeds to *All Along the Watchtower* and runs into *Tangled Up in Blue*.

I play until I run out of songs I know all the words to, and then I make up my own words and fudge the chords. It's my funeral for my father. It's my funeral for all the things I've wanted.

I play until what Margo said finally makes sense. It wasn't about Irene and the boy, or my mom leaving. It wasn't about me at all. He did what was easy. He didn't have it in him to do any better.

Just because my father was a coward doesn't mean I have to be. I won't leave my child. I will do what it takes to give him a real home and a real bed and a real parent. I will do what it takes to be a person Max can be proud of.

Somehow these things make sense to me as I play, and I can't stop playing because I want to figure it all out. A song I never finished comes back to me. *Where you gonna stay, where you gonna stay, whereyougonnastay,* and I sing it again and again, playing with the chords until the rest of the words come out.

Where you gonna stay
When flesh turns into bone
Where you gonna stay
Now that you're not alone

When the sun shines past the treetops
The light's no longer dim
Where you gonna stay, stay, stay . . .
Stay with him.

I wake up on the bare rocks with my guitar still in my hands, not even in my makeshift tent. The fire is only embers and smoke. The sun is just breaking the horizon. My back throbs and my fingers are stiff like claws, but I don't feel wrong. I feel like that place in me where all the wrong lived doesn't exist anymore, like how I used to think there were monsters under my bed and there never ever were.

Before I leave, I bury my father's cracked

guitar pick under the rocks by the shore, because it feels like the best way to say goodbye to the person I wanted him to be.

It feels like the best way to start over.

I wad up my blanket. My legs are shaky and the pain in my back is getting so much worse, but I'm ready to go. To call Margo and tell her I need help. Face Little River and figure out what's next. I might even be ready to sit down and have a talk with Irene.

I reach for my guitar case and all of a sudden there's a flood of wet and warm and pain like I might break in half. I try to get up, to get to my car, but I trip and fall. I hear the crack of bone against rock. I taste dirt and blood.

— Chapter 69 —

I hear a voice calling to me, but there's buzzing around the words, like someone turned up the drive on an amplifier.

"April. Come on! April! April!"

I want to answer, but I feel far away. My eyelids are heavy. Or maybe it's dark. Maybe it's dark. I forgot to tie a lifeline.

"Come on, April!"

There's static behind my eyelids and the pressure churning through my body is so great that my ribs might shatter and my hips could explode. The pain goes beyond what I thought was possible until it gets so big I can't feel anything at all. There's a moment of peace and nothing. The static goes to black, and then the pain crashes through me again. I see blue sky and splintered wood and then my own static.

"Let's get you up, April," that voice calls through the feedback.

I think about an octopus with bright blue limbs.

"Let's get you up." It's such a nice voice.

Arms hook under my armpits, pulling me to my feet. I try to make my legs work. They don't want to, but I try. The ground blurs into the trees. Everything that isn't my body feels far away.

"I got you," she says.

It's Carly. It's a dream.

I can see the lake, so blue.

I'm in a car.

"Max," I say, or maybe I just think it. I don't hear the sound at all. *Max, Max, Max.*

I rest my cheek against the cold window. I can't tell what's static and what's pavement whizzing by. There are so many bumps in the road. That pain crashes through my body again and the static turns to stars.

Chapter 70

There's a hand holding mine. I can't get my eyes to open.

There's humming, off-key, I think it's Dylan. I can't find the song in my head, but I know the voice.

"Margo," I say before I even open my eyes. It comes out like a long lazy string of sound.

"Girlie, you're going to give me a heart attack one of these days." She squeezes my hand hard.

When I open my eyes, everything is blurry. I blink until my vision clears. Margo is sitting in a chair next to the bed holding my baby. He's a little bundle tucked safely in the crook of her other arm, wrapped in a white and yellow blanket, wearing a tiny blue hat. An entire person, outside my body, and all I want to do is hold him.

"It's your mommy," Margo whispers like they're already good friends and she's telling him a secret.

She sits on the edge of the bed so I can see Max. His eyes are tiny slits, mouth pressed in a frown like he's thinking hard about something impor- tant. I feel like I know him already. Like I've always known him. I cry. Margo puts her arm around my shoulder and we hold Max between us, because I'm still too shaky to take him on my own.

I touch his chubby cheek. I have never met anyone so beautiful.

"I love you," I say, as soon as words will take shape in my mouth. Max yawns and makes a squeaking sound like a kitten. My tongue feels thick and my head is fuzzy and I worry none of this is real. I don't understand how it's possible for love to feel like the entire ocean churning in my chest.

Max stretches his arm in the air. I touch his hand and he wraps his fingers around my pinky. I don't know for sure, but I think he's very strong for a baby.

"He's okay?" I ask.

"He's absolutely perfect," Margo says. "Nurse confirmed."

She pushes hair from my face, and my forehead feels funny. I reach up and touch a bandage taped across my head.

"You're okay too," Margo says. "You knocked your noggin pretty good, and you had a C-section, so you've got stitches in both places. Nothing that won't heal, but your head might feel swimmy for a few days."

I think I can feel the pull of stitches in my stomach, but everything is numb. I try to wiggle my toes and I'm not sure if any of them move.

I don't remember going to the hospital. I was at the lake. I remember the lake.

"How did you find me?" I ask.

"Carly called." Margo gestures to the chair in the corner and there's Carly, curled up, fast asleep. Her tall black boots are splayed out on the floor and my guitar case is leaning against the wall beside her. I didn't look any further than Max. I didn't realize there was anyone else here. But there she is. So close and she's not a dream. I remember her calling my name now. It wasn't a dream. I want to wake her up, but her sleep looks necessary.

"That girl hasn't left this room. I told her I would stay and you were fine and she could go home and sleep, but she wouldn't leave you," Margo says, smiling, her eyes welling up.

"How did she find you?" I ask. The thread from Carly to Margo doesn't make sense. They're from different pockets.

"My number is in your notebook."

"How did she find *me?*"

"I'm not sure," Margo says. "She called and told me she brought you here and you were going into surgery. I got in my car so fast I didn't stop to put on real shoes." Margo points to her feet. She's wearing fuzzy pink slippers. "I didn't guess you were going to Ithaca, sweets. I thought maybe you were headed back to Florida." She sniffles.

"I was going to call you," I say. "I didn't mean to—"

"You don't get to disappear anymore. You can't go running off into the woods like a wounded deer. You lean on me when it hurts. That's what we're here for—to lean on each other." Margo nods like we've made a pact.

I nod too.

It is so warm, the three of us, huddled on the bed. The room smells like summer. There are flowers. Lots of them. On the nightstand, on the windowsill.

"Did you go crazy in the gift shop?" I ask.

"Carly and I called all your friends in your notebook to tell them you had the baby. I thought they'd want to know. And then these started showing up."

There are daisies from Arnie and roses from Cole. All the girls on staff at Ollie's in Florida sent lilies. Slim sent a basket of violets. And there's a big vase of sunflowers. I wonder where anyone gets sunflowers like that in November. Margo tells me they're from Irene and David and July. She says July wants to meet her nephew and they're all coming to visit me tomorrow. For once, the idea of seeing Irene doesn't seem like the worst thing in the world.

— Chapter 71 —

Margo is out getting us lunch because she says no one ever enjoyed a hospital meal before and she doesn't expect it to happen now. She left me her slippers and wore my boots. She looked hysterical.

Carly is still asleep, and I don't know how she's comfortable all wound around the arms of the chair, her hand hanging over the side and I know her fingers will have pins and needles.

The sound of Max's breath and then Carly's then Max's makes me feel like all the air I'm breathing is coming from their lungs. I imagine it making me strong, healing the ache in my guts. It seems like some kind of miracle that a doctor could excavate Max from the depths of me and introduce him to the world—that I am still here to see him after being taken apart and stitched back together.

Max was stuck, Margo said, turned upside down. They were worried about the cord, and my head was bleeding pretty bad and the doctors couldn't wait on any of it.

I don't know what I remember and what I'm imagining, but there's so much in my mind that feels new, like a movie I watched when I was fighting to stay awake. One scene jumps into the middle of the next.

There's Carly driving us up to the hospital doors, screaming for help, and so many hands on my body. There's the way it hurt to be lifted, how everything inside me was shifting, and I could feel Max, all elbows and feet, fighting to free himself like a raccoon in a pillowcase. Someone cut away my clothes and there were too many people touching too many parts of me.

He's breech! someone said.

Get scrubs for her partner! someone said.

Count backwards. Count backwards. No, backwards, someone said, so I started at *Z* and Carly laughed even though she was crying.

A woman with a baby blue mask on her face stretched my arms out on a big white cross and the room was cold like the walk-in fridge at Ollie's, but Carly's fingers were sweaty between mine. Just as clearly, I remember the surgeon was a grizzly bear in a white coat and the room we were in was full of laughing salmon hanging from the ceiling on meat hooks. So how am I supposed to know if any of my memories are real?

I stare at Max through the clear plastic sides of his bassinette and hope with all my heart that I'm not stuck in some kind of dream. He's already my favorite thing that ever happened to me. He reminds me of Justin in the shape of his nose, and his dark eyelashes, and I think that's okay because Justin was someone I used to love to see. He was smart and sometimes he could be very sweet and maybe I can teach Max to be sweet even more of the time. I'll always look at Max and think about shouting into the waves at night and how the sand was still warm from soaking up the heat from the day and it felt like the world was a wild beast who allowed us to walk on her back. That was a good moment, and it's where Max came from, so it's even better as a memory than what I knew at the time. I wonder if maybe when Max meets the sea, he will understand how it's his oldest friend. He'll think, *Oh, I know you,* and he'll feel like he belongs. I'm going to take him soon, I think. As soon as I can. Maybe Margo will come with us, maybe even Carly, and I'll sing songs for my own baby on the beach.

Max fusses and I don't know what to do. My stomach is full of stitches. It hurts to move. I'm scared I'll drop him.

I catch Carly stirring out of the corner of my eye. "Oh," she says, sitting up and looking around the room like she's trying to figure out where she is. "April."

"I can't pick him up," I say, in a panic. His cries make me sure we're not in a dream, but they also make me want to cry.

"Can I?" Carly asks.

"Please."

She nestles Max in her arms like she knows

what she's doing. "Hey, hey, little man," she says. "It is all okay. Everything is okay." She jiggles him and he starts to settle.

"You're a natural," I tell her. I wonder what she thinks of me. I can't believe she's here.

"I was the first one to hold him," she says, tears spilling down her cheeks like they belong to those words.

"You were there?"

Carly nods. "One of your nurses demanded they let me in. I didn't want to leave you. They said they had to put you under. I didn't want him to be alone. Max, right? You said in your letters."

"Max," I say.

"He looks like you." She sits on the bed next to me so I can see Max and smell his head and touch his cheek and he can get used to being near me. "He has that serious thing going on right here." She points to her brow with her free hand. "And he's beautiful. He was beautiful right away. He cried before they even got him all the way out and then he peed on the doctor."

I laugh and it hurts, and Carly can see it on my face. She winces too.

"I saw your insides," she says. "They told me not to look over the curtain they put up, but I heard all these noises and then Max was crying, and I thought, 'Oh no! He's hurt!' instead of remembering babies are supposed to cry when they're born. So, I looked over like he might need help and I could be the one to help him. They were still pulling his legs from you. Your blood is very red. And Max looked blue until he cried enough oxygen into himself. I had to sit down before I held him, because my knees were wobbling."

"I'm sorry," I say.

Carly shrugs. "Don't be sorry. Everyone has insides. I'm glad I got to be there with both of you."

We watch Max close his eyes and open them again, like he knows there's so much to see even though he's still exhausted.

When Max finally falls back to sleep Carly says, "I remembered Margo's name—I remembered you talking about her. I hope she was the right person to call."

"She was the perfect person. Thank you."

"I can't believe you didn't tell me why you were leaving."

"I didn't want anyone to get hurt."

"So you hurt yourself instead?"

"It was my fault," I say. "All of it."

"You were a kid." She rests her head on my shoulder. "You were a scared kid. You weren't in it to hurt anyone. I could have found a way to help you." She has that same perfume on. The one I remember. Like flowers pressed in an old book. "Rosemary was so full of herself. I'm sure

I had some kind of leverage. You could have stayed."

"How did you find me?" I ask, changing the subject. I don't want to think about all the things that would be different if I'd stayed. It's too hard to pick apart what I might have gained from what I would have lost.

"After I found the envelope, I figured you were already gone. But I was reading your letters last night. You wrote about how you could always see the lake in your mind, and then I knew I'd find you at our campsite."

Max screws up his face in another kitten yawn and we both get really quiet until he settles back in.

"You talked to me, when I found you, remember?" Carly says.

"No." I try to search my brain to see what I can recall about being at the campground. It's not much.

"You kept saying, 'Carly, don't leave me here,' even after I already had you in my car."

"Thank you," I say.

"That's what friends do."

The ocean in my chest feels like it will spill out around us. After all this time, she's still my friend.

"How is Adam?" I ask.

"He moved to Boston last year. He got a job there. He's seeing someone. I think he's good."

Carly says it carefully, like it might be hard for me to hear, but it's a relief to know that I didn't break him. "He was so sad when you left, but I think, overall, you fixed him a little."

"He fixed me a lot," I say softly. So softly I'm not even sure if Carly can hear it.

Carly readjusts Max in the crook of her arm. It's gorgeous, the way he's soft and pink against the green inked vine twisting up her forearm. By her wrist the vine branches out into a white flower with a yellow center and rainbow colors all around it. It's the tattoo Bodie drew for me. The one I didn't get.

I touch it with my index finger.

"I missed you," she says.

"I missed you too."

"It's a mayflower," she tells me. "It's the good stuff that comes after too many storms."

— Chapter 72 —

Where's my favorite baby?" Margo asks when she comes back with an armload of grease-spotted takeout bags and a tray of milkshakes.

"He's in the nursery," Carly tells her. "They had to weigh and measure him."

It actually hurt when the nurse took Max. When I started to cry, Carly didn't act like it was silly. She let me rest my head on her shoulder and promised over and over that he'd be back soon. He's only been gone for five minutes but being away from him is painful in every inch of my body. It's a good hurt. I'm not afraid of myself anymore. I know that I will never ever leave him. I couldn't. He's mine and I'm his and it's just that simple.

"I miss him already," Margo says.

"Me too," Carly says. "Those tiny, tiny feet! I wish I could be here when he gets back." She gets up and my arm feels cold where her body was warming it.

"You can't stay to eat?" Margo asks, giving Carly the same worried look she's given me so many times.

"My shift starts soon." Carly pulls her jacket on and steps into her boots.

"You need to eat," Margo says, handing Carly a takeout bag and one of the milkshakes. She gives Carly a big hug and a kiss on the cheek. "Thank you for finding our girl."

I expect Carly to bristle at the affection, but she hugs back and says, "Of course."

They've been through something together now. They already matter to each other.

Carly slips the bag of food in her backpack. She picks up my guitar case with her free hand.

"Wait," I say. "What—"

"Don't worry about it," Margo says.

"It has a little crack," Carly tells me. "From when you fell. Nothing to worry about."

There were splinters in the dirt. Was that now, or was it then? I try to remember, but my thoughts feel like wadded up fishing line. "It's broken?"

"Oh, sweets. It'll be alright," Margo says, trying to coax me from panic. "We called the guitar store. They fix these things all the time."

Carly nods. "I'm taking it over now."

I look around the room for my bag. "My wallet—I can give you—"

"Shush." Margo shakes her head. "It's taken care of."

"We got you, Pilgrim. I promise." Carly looks me in the eyes to show me she means it. "I'll see you all tonight."

"Thank you," I whisper, trying not to cry.

Carly is careful to keep from banging my guitar case on the doorframe as she leaves. We hear her boots clomping down the hallway, then she shouts, "Hey, half-caff, double espresso!"

Another voice says, "Hey, tattooed coffee girl!" And then he walks into my room wearing a striped knit hat with earflaps and fingerless gloves like the ones I used to have. He looks ridiculous. He looks good. He looks really, really good.

"Angel," he says. "Oh my god!"

I don't know how I thought I'd make it through the rest of my life without hearing him call me *Angel* again. His voice is a vital need; like blood or air or water when there hasn't been enough.

Carly pokes her head back in the room, wrinkling her forehead. "Wait! How do you guys know each other?"

"Ethan," I say, through tears. "It's Ethan."

And she's read my letters. She understands.

"I'm Carly."

Ethan claps his hand to his mouth. "Oh my god! You are, aren't you? All this time, all that coffee . . . I had no idea. It's so good to know you."

"This is wild! How did you end up here?" Carly asks.

"April convinced me I belonged in Ithaca," Ethan says. "I'm teaching at the college."

"No way! I love this! I'm so glad you're you!"

Carly says. "I'm late for work, but I'm bringing dinner tonight. You'll stay?"

"Not going anywhere," he tells her, and I like the sound of that so much.

"Later!" Carly yells as she leaves again.

Ethan sits on the bed and hugs me so hard I think my stitches will burst.

"How are you here?" I ask. I never even let myself believe I'd see him again.

"How could I not be?" he says, taking off his gloves. He grabs Margo's hand and gives it a squeeze. She must have tracked him down.

"I'm going to check on the baby," Margo says. I know she's giving us time to talk.

"I lied," I say to Ethan. "And I left you."

"And I love you anyway," Ethan says.

"You shouldn't." I cry and it shakes my scar and makes me cry harder.

"You don't get to decide that," he says.

"I don't deserve you."

"When . . ." Ethan sobs. It takes him a minute to get his voice back. "When are you going to get it through your thick little head that there is nothing you could do to make me stop loving you?" He wipes his face with the back of his hand. "Stop trying already, okay? I *know* you." He hugs me and talks into my shoulder, muffled and warm. "Everything else is noise and words. I know your heart. Always, okay?"

"Always," I say. The collar of my hospital

gown is soaked. I want to ask him about Robert. I want to know what happened after I left. If he's mad. If he hates me. If maybe he'll still want to meet Max someday. "I didn't know how to make it right. I couldn't—"

"I know," Ethan says. "Robert knows. Once you escape this hospital we can give him a call. We'll figure it out."

"I am so sorry," I say.

"I am so happy to see you again." He pulls the hat from his head and the static electricity turns his hair into a halo.

I laugh.

"I'm not used to all this bundling up," he says, smiling back.

"I can't believe you live here now."

"You were right. Ithaca is freezing! But it *is* where I belong. I bought a big old house near Fall Creek."

"You did?" I smooth his hair, wipe a tear from his cheek. He has stubble on his face. He never used to let it grow.

"With plenty of room for you and Max," he says.

I hold Ethan's face with both hands. He's real and he's here and he knows everything about me. "You want us to live with you?"

"It's empty without you," Ethan says. "I need you there. We'll paint wild things on the walls in Max's room."

Margo comes back with a nurse and Max, and Ethan gets to hold him. "I've been waiting so long to meet you, kiddo," he says, and Max opens his eyes and gurgles and I think that maybe he remembers Ethan. All that time Ethan spent talking to my belly counted for something. Ethan being here, holding him now, counts for everything.

Carly returns with eggplant pizza from The Nines and her girlfriend, Erin, who has a mass of crazy yellow curls and round wind-burned cheeks. Carly blushes when she introduces her. And Erin gives me a hug that makes me feel like we're already good old friends.

We all camp out on my hospital bed and everyone takes turns holding Max so someone else can eat. I'm sleepy, but I can't let my eyes close. I can't stop watching. They already love him. It's the most beautiful thing I can think of. Even if I had all the things I could ever need, I would still love these people. I would have chosen them anyway.

Carly dances around the room with Max, singing Cat Skin songs to him, using *fudge* and *shush* and *mothertruckers* instead of the real words. Erin sits next to me and tells me about how it took her five espressos to get up the nerve to ask Carly out. The way she looks at Carly when she says it is the way Carly deserves to be adored.

Margo tells Ethan how I started working for her at the diner when I was a kid.

"Oh, she was so cute," Margo says. "Marching up to people and writing orders in her school notebook. 'Hi, I'm April, may I take your delicious order today?' I don't know where she got that from." Margo smiles at me. "You're something else, you."

Ethan laughs and gives my foot a squeeze.

"She was just so serious about it," Margo says, laughing too. "In the beginning, she wrote all of her orders out in full sentences! 'Ida Winton would like french fries with melted cheese and some gravy, not too much, but enough, on a plate, please.'" She wipes her eyes. "April just figured it all out on her own. I've never seen a kid with her kind of determination."

"Sounds about right," Ethan says.

"That first apron went all the way to the tops of her sneakers."

"Do you have pictures?" Ethan asks with his mouth full of pizza.

"Sure do," Margo tells him. "I'll bring them with me next weekend."

She hugs me. "Girlie, get ready to see a lot of this face. Now that I know where you are, you and Max are gonna get sick of me!"

"Never," I say, fighting tears.

• • •

Later, when the nurse brings paperwork for Max's birth certificate, I write Ethan's name on the line for who his father is.

Someday I'll look for Justin again and give him another chance to be a good person to Max. But Max already has a family—the kind that counts the most. Me and Ethan and Carly and Margo. We have people we get to keep, who won't ever let us go. And that's the most important part.

That's what's true.

Acknowledgments

After turning in the final draft of this book, I went digging through my files for the first glimpse of April and found my original short story about April and Ethan. It was dated September 22, 2006. By the time this book is published, my relationship with April will be about a year shy of April's age in part one. Thinking her thoughts and loving her people has been my favorite pastime for so long that the characters in this book exist in my mind like old friends who are just a phone call away—like if only I could find the right phone number scribbled on a napkin buried in the pile of papers on my desk, we'd have a good long chat. So although there's a part of me that knows this is a bit silly, my first thank you is to April Sawicki, who popped into my head while I was writing something else and gave me a parallel universe where I could paint new stories with every feeling I've ever had. And then, of course, I have to thank Ethan, and Carly, and Margo, because getting to keep them in my heart for this long has made my whole life better.

There is a vast list of real people who have

offered solace and advice, read drafts, and talked through timelines, titles, and all things mid-nineties. I know there's no way to write these acknowledgments without leaving someone out. I want you to know I am keenly aware that this book would not have been possible without everything I've learned and felt through the twists and turns my life has taken. I am grateful to everyone I've had the privilege of knowing along the way. If I've forgotten a mention, please understand it's a failure of my cluttered mind, not my heart.

Hannah Braaten, oh, how I adore you. You are exactly the editor this book needed, and I am endlessly thankful for the ways you nudged this story into shape and loved it into being. It's a great privilege to work with you. Thank you for giving this book a home at Gallery.

Thank you also to Jen Bergstrom and Aimée Bell for seeing the heart of this story. And everyone at Gallery who has worked to usher this book into the world in such a gorgeous package—including Jen Long, Caroline Pallotta, Sally Marvin, Lauren Truskowski, Bianca Salvant, Allison Green, Iris Chen, John Paul Jones, Laura Cherkas, Jaime Putorti, Daniel Taverner, John Vairo, and Lisa Litwack. And, of course, Andrew Nguyễn, who has kindly, patiently guided me through all the little details.

Deborah Schneider, I spent so long hoping to

find an agent like you, and getting to work with you is even better than I'd hoped. Thank you for seeing me. Thank you for understanding April, and always honoring how much this work means to me. Cathy Gleason, I appreciate your kindness and all of the guidance and wisdom you've shared with me. Thank you also to Penelope Burns and everyone at Gelfman/Schneider ICM. I'd also like to thank Joe Veltre, Katy McCaffrey, Davina Hefflin, Tori Eskue, and Kaitlyn Berry at The Gersh Agency. Thank you to Eric S. Brown at Franklin, Weinrib, Rudell & Vassallo for being so careful and so lovely.

Thank you, Ingrid Serban for bringing your music to my words, and your sweet brilliant spirit to my life. Now I know that love at first sight works for friendship too.

Caroline Angell, you relit the pilot light on my creative spirit so many times in my journey with this book. Thank you for believing in me and my work. I don't know what I'd do without you and your fierce, gorgeous heart.

Cassandra Dunn, one of the best parts of my life is knowing that whenever I'm stuck in my writing or anything else, I get to hike it all out with you. I am always astounded by the depth and breadth of your perspective and compassion. Thank you for putting in all those miles with me.

Thank you, Ann Mah, for the many, many ways

you've helped me get here and for the joy of being your friend.

Regina Marler and Renee Swindle, I am dreaming of the long breakfast we will have in the future, and so thankful for all of the kindness, understanding, and confidence you've given me over our breakfasts in days past.

Bruce Holsinger, your belief in this book changed me on a cellular level, and I am so grateful.

Michele Larkin, thank you for all the times you've picked me up, bolstered my courage, and understood where I'm coming from. It's such wonderful luck to be in your family.

Thank you to everyone who read drafts and shared your hearts with me, including Therese Walsh, Brenda Kirkwood, Julia Whelan, Brantley Aufill, Rainbow Rowell, Michelle Rubinstein, Cullen Douglas, Dash Hegeman, Melanie Krebs, Sarah Playtis, Neil Gordon, Ben Jackson, Julie Smith, Erica Curtis, Liz Valentine, Evan Dawson, Keith Pedzich, Jennifer Deville Catalano, Julia Claiborne Johnson, and Brunonia Barry. And, of course, Joan Pedzich, who understood the power of kind words to an orphaned soul and talked with me about April as if she were a dear girl we both knew.

Special thanks to Therese Fowler, Jan O'Hara, Sarah Callendar, Jeanne Kisacky, Barbara O'Neal, and Greer McAllister for those beautiful

Ithaca moments. Thank you to Jack Hrkach and all the teachers and friends who made Ithaca the place where I started.

Katherine Frances Billingsley, my darling Evergreen! What a joy it was to grow up being weirdly creative with you and to still be *yes and*-ing our friendship after all these years.

Thank you to Julie Buxbaum, Amy Franklin-Willis, Ann Marie Nieves, Matthew Andreoli, Savannah Butler, Emmett Tucker, Elizabeth Roberts, and Nikki DeLoach. Whether you know it or not, you've come along with the right words of encouragement exactly when I needed them. I appreciate your kindness and perspective so much. Thank you, Ania Szado, for saving me with research! Thank you to Angela Terry, Carrie Medders, and Patrice Hall for helping me feel like I belong by this bay.

Thank you again and always to Linda and Roger Bryant, and the wonderful folks of the Titles Over Tea book group, who have taught me so much about what it means to be a reader. Thank you to the members of The Fiction Writers Coop, WOMBA, and my friends at Untitled, for sharing all the textures of what it means to be a writer.

Thank you to John Cuk, Marty Heresniak, Jan Callner, Joseph Ilardo, Jonathan Klein, Brian Maillard, and Daniel Holabaugh for bringing music into my life. And a huge thank you to

Ken Wilcox for being the best darn guitar teacher.

To my Facebook, Twitter, and Instagram friends, and all the readers who have reached out to me, it is one of the greatest honors of my life to be understood by you and to know we have such kindred spirits. Thank you for chiming in with answers to my weirdo research questions and letting me know you were hoping for another book.

In 1997, I saw Peter Mulvey play at Ithaca College, and since then, most of the music I listen to is in some way related to his beautiful slice of the folk world. Steadily and with great empathy, he carries on the tradition of being a folksinger, and by following his work and the way he navigates the world, I've learned a great deal about the kind of creative person I want to be. I have also been greatly inspired by Chris Pureka, who writes the most wise and beautiful songs I've ever heard, and whose lyrics helped me navigate my intentions for this work.

The soundtrack to this book and this phase of my life has been full of Mark Erelli, Kris Delmhorst, Jeffrey Foucault, David Goodrich, Tracy Chapman, Dar Williams, The Waterboys, R.E.M., Counting Crows, Indigo Girls, Steve Earle, Glen Phillips, Meg Hutchinson, Gordon Lightfoot, Arlo Guthrie, Carole King, James Taylor, Yusef Islam, and (of course) Bob Dylan. I am so grateful for their brilliant work.

It is very hard to write this part because I don't know that my dear old friend Stella will still be here when this book comes out, but she has been with me while I wrote it, snoring at my feet for twelve years of this journey. Everyone should have such a steadfast friend. I have loved every moment of her.

Jeremy Larkin, I freaking love you. You've lived with this book as long as I have and believed in me in times when I forgot to. Thank you for loving me. Thank you for making me laugh. Thank you for dancing. What a great adventure we've been on this far. I'm so glad to be home with you.

Books are produced in the United States using U.S.-based materials

Books are printed using a revolutionary new process called THINKtech™ that lowers energy usage by 70% and increases overall quality

Books are durable and flexible because of Smyth-sewing

Paper is sourced using environmentally responsible foresting methods and the paper is acid-free

Center Point Large Print
600 Brooks Road / PO Box 1
Thorndike, ME 04986-0001 USA

(207) 568-3717

US & Canada:
1 800 929-9108
www.centerpointlargeprint.com